# Also by Julia Brannan

### HISTORICAL FICTION

**The Jacobite Chronicles**
Book One: Mask of Duplicity
Book Two: The Mask Revealed
Book Three: The Gathering Storm
Book Four: The Storm Breaks
Book Six: Tides of Fortune (Early 2018)

### CONTEMPORARY FICTION

A Seventy-Five Percent Solution
The Bigger Picture (Autumn 2017)

# Pursuit of Princes

The Jacobite Chronicles,
Book Five

Julia Brannan

Copyright© 2017 by Julia Brannan

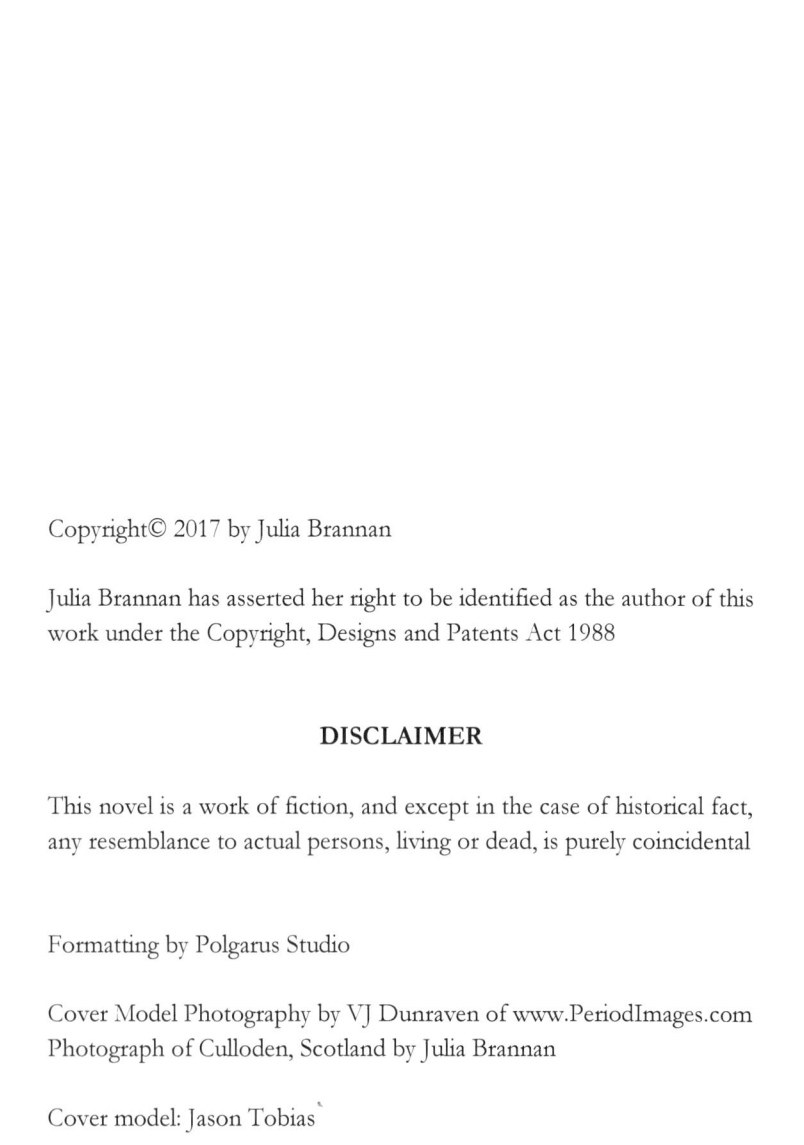

Julia Brannan has asserted her right to be identified as the author of this work under the Copyright, Designs and Patents Act 1988

**DISCLAIMER**

This novel is a work of fiction, and except in the case of historical fact, any resemblance to actual persons, living or dead, is purely coincidental

Formatting by Polgarus Studio

Cover Model Photography by VJ Dunraven of www.PeriodImages.com
Photograph of Culloden, Scotland by Julia Brannan

Cover model: Jason Tobias

Cover design by najlaqamberdesigns.com

To Bob Macchione and Dolores Lowe
For believing in me.
Thank you.

# ACKNOWLEDGEMENTS

First of all, as ever, I'd like to thank Jason Gardiner and Alyson Cairns, my soulmates and best friends, who put up with me on a day-to-day basis, and who understand my need for solitude, but are always there for me. They've both supported me through every stage of my writing, and, indeed, in all my other endeavours, both sensible and madcap!

Thanks to the long-suffering Mary Brady, friend and first critic, who reads the chapters as I write them, critiques them for me and reassures me that I can actually write stuff people will want to read.

Thanks also go to Mandy Condon, who sends me useful articles, has already determined the cast list for the film of my books, and who has been a wonderful and supportive friend for over twenty years. Long may that continue!

Thank you to Kym Grosso and Victoria Danann, both successful and talented authors, who have been extremely supportive and have generously given me the benefit of their invaluable advice, gained through experience. They have both saved me a lot of time, money and tears, and I value their friendship enormously.

And thanks also go to Jason and Marina for doing an excellent job of formatting my book, to the talented and very patient Najla Qamber, who does all my covers, puts up with my lack of artistic ability, and still manages to somehow understand exactly what I want my cover to look like! Thanks too to Jason Tobias the cover model for Pursuit of Princes – you make a perfect Alex!

Finally, but VERY importantly, to all my wonderful readers, who not only buy my books, but take the time and effort to give me feedback, and to review them on Amazon and Goodreads – thank you so much. You keep me going on those dark days when I'd rather do anything than stare at a blank screen for hours while my brain turns to mush…you are amazing!

# HISTORICAL BACKGROUND NOTE

Although this series starts in 1742 and deals with the Jacobite Rebellion of 1745, the events that culminated in this uprising started a long time before, in 1685, in fact. This was when King Charles II died without leaving an heir, and the throne passed to his Roman Catholic younger brother James, who then became James II of England and Wales, and VII of Scotland. His attempts to promote toleration of Roman Catholics and Presbyterians did not meet with approval from the Anglican establishment, but he was generally tolerated because he was in his fifties, and his daughters, who would succeed him, were committed Protestants. But in 1688 James' second wife gave birth to a son, also named James, who was christened Roman Catholic. It now seemed certain that Catholics would return to the throne long-term, which was anathema to Protestants.

Consequently James' daughter Mary and her husband William of Orange were invited to jointly rule in James' place, and James was deposed, finally leaving for France in 1689. However, many Catholics, Episcopalians and Tory royalists still considered James to be the legitimate monarch.

The first Jacobite rebellion, led by Viscount Dundee in April 1689, routed King William's force at the Battle of Killiecrankie, but unfortunately Dundee himself was killed, leaving the Jacobite forces leaderless, and in May 1690 they suffered a heavy defeat. King William offered all the Highland clans a pardon if they would take an oath of allegiance in front of a magistrate before 1st January 1692. Due to the weather and a general reluctance, some clans failed to make it to the places appointed for the oath to be taken, resulting in the infamous Glencoe Massacre of Clan MacDonald in February 1692. By spring all the clans had taken the oath, and it seemed that the Stuart cause was dead.

However, a series of economic and political disasters by William and his government left many people dissatisfied with his reign, and a number of these flocked to the Jacobite cause. In

1707, the Act of Union between Scotland and England, one of the intentions of which was to put an end to hopes of a Stuart restoration to the throne, was deeply unpopular with most Scots, as it delivered no benefits to the majority of the Scottish population.

Following the deaths of William and Mary, Mary's sister Anne became Queen, dying without leaving an heir in 1714, after which George, Elector of Hanover took the throne, as George I. This raised the question of the succession again, and in 1715 a number of Scottish nobles and Tories took up arms against the Hanoverian monarch.

The rebellion was led by the Earl of Mar, but he was not a great military leader and the Jacobite army suffered a series of defeats, finally disbanding completely when six thousand Dutch troops landed in support of Hanover. Following this, the Highlands of Scotland were garrisoned and hundreds of miles of new roads were built, in an attempt to thwart any further risings in favour of the Stuarts.

By the early 1740s, this operation was scaled back when it seemed unlikely that the aging James Stuart, 'the Old Pretender,' would spearhead another attempt to take the throne. However, the hopes of those who wanted to dissolve the Union and return the Stuarts to their rightful place were centring not on James, but on his young, handsome and charismatic son Charles Edward Stuart, as yet something of an unknown quantity.

**I would strongly recommend that you read the first four books in the series, Mask Of Duplicity, The Mask Revealed, The Gathering Storm and The Storm Breaks before starting this one! However, if you are determined not to, here's a summary of the first four to help you enjoy Book Five…**

# The Story So Far

### Book One – Mask of Duplicity

Following the death of their father, Elizabeth (Beth) Cunningham and her older half-brother Richard, a dragoon sergeant, are reunited after a thirteen year separation, when he comes home to Manchester to claim his inheritance. He soon discovers that while their father's will left her a large dowry, the investments which he has inherited will not be sufficient for him to further his military ambitions. He decides therefore to persuade his sister to renew the acquaintance with her aristocratic cousins, in the hope that her looks and dowry will attract a wealthy husband willing to purchase him a commission in the army. Beth refuses, partly because she is happy living an unrestricted lifestyle, and partly because the family rejected her father following his second marriage to her mother, a Scottish seamstress.

Richard, who has few scruples, then embarks on an increasingly vicious campaign to get her to comply with his wishes, threatening her beloved servants and herself. Finally, following a particularly brutal attack, she agrees to comply with his wishes, on the condition that once she is married, he will remove himself from her life entirely.

Her cousin, the pompous Lord Edward and his downtrodden sisters accept Richard and Beth back into the family, where she meets the interesting and gossipy, but very foppish Sir Anthony Peters. After a few weeks of living their monotonous lifestyle, Beth becomes extremely bored and sneaks off to town for a day, where she is followed by a footpad. Taking refuge in a disused room, she inadvertently comes upon a gang of Jacobite plotters, one of whom takes great pains to hide his face, although she notices a scar on his hand. They are impressed by her bravery and instead of killing her, escort her home. A secret Jacobite herself, she doesn't tell her Hanoverian family what has happened, and soon repairs with them to London for the season.

Once there, she meets many new people and attracts a great number of suitors, but is not interested in any of them until she falls in love with Daniel, the Earl of Highbury's son. The relationship progresses until she discovers that his main motivation for marrying her is to use her dowry to clear his gambling debts. She rejects him, but becomes increasingly depressed.

In the meantime, the Jacobite gang, the chief members of whom are Alex MacGregor (the scarred man) and his brothers Angus and Duncan, are operating in the London area, smuggling weapons, collecting information, visiting brothels etc.

Sir Anthony, now a regular visitor to the house, becomes a friend of sorts, and introduces her to his wide circle of acquaintance, including the King, the Duke of Cumberland and Edwin Harlow MP and his wife Caroline. Beth does not trust the painted Sir Anthony and thinks him physically repulsive, but finds him amusing. Following an ultimatum from her brother that if she keeps rejecting suitors he will find her a husband himself, she accepts a marriage proposal from Sir Anthony, partly because he seems kind, but chiefly because he has discovered a rosary belonging to her, and she is afraid he will denounce her as a Catholic, which would result in her rejection from society and her brother's vengeance.

The night before her wedding, Beth is abducted by Daniel, who, in a desperate attempt to avoid being imprisoned for debt, attempts to marry her by force. Beth's maid, Sarah, alerts the Cunninghams and Sir Anthony to Beth's plight, and she is rescued by her fiancé. He then gives her the option to call off the wedding, but thinking that being married to him is the best of the limited options she has available to her, she agrees to go ahead as planned.

## Book Two – The Mask Revealed

Sir Anthony and Beth marry. The following evening at a function, he has to remove his glove and she sees his hand and its scar for the first time, and remembers where she has seen it before. Having removed his furious wife by force from the company before she can give him away, Sir Anthony admits that he is a Jacobite spy, and that he is really Alex MacGregor. He explains the odd circumstances that led him to follow such a strange double life, and admits that he married her mainly for love, intends to make her dowry over to her and effect a separation, thereby giving her her freedom. She, being of a very adventurous spirit, refuses, stating that she intends to stay with him. He tries to persuade her against this, as his lifestyle is a dangerous one, but eventually he agrees, and they go on honeymoon to Europe together, as Sir Anthony and wife.

He explains that he will be visiting Prince Charles Stuart, son of the exiled King James, as a few weeks ago the Duke of Newcastle, not knowing him to be a Jacobite spy, recruited him on behalf of the Hanoverians, to become acquainted with the prince and report back any useful information.

On the way to Rome, Angus (who has accompanied them as a servant) overhears a private conversation between two French courtiers, in which it is revealed that King Louis of France is secretly planning to invade England, and that one of the men (Henri), intends to give the plans to the British. Alex now decides he must do something to prevent this, but must first carry on to meet Charles and convey the news of the prospective invasion to him. He does, and Beth and Alex are married again in Rome under their real names.

After giving a misleading report of his meeting with Charles to Sir Horace Mann who is the Hanoverian envoy in Florence, Alex, Beth and Angus travel to France, where, at Versailles, Beth becomes acquainted with, and starts to like, the man Henri. Alex, as Sir Anthony, pretends jealousy and challenges Henri to a duel, during which he kills him, as though by accident.

Beth, having not been entrusted with his plans, and also having been kept in the dark about some other things, is very hurt and leaves suddenly, travelling back first to London and then

Manchester, on her own, where she settles in with her ex-servants.

Alex's return is delayed as he is held in prison for duelling. He sends Angus to Rome to stop Prince Charles riding to Paris to join the invasion and thereby raising British suspicion and Louis' anger. Alex then returns home to London, where he is expecting Beth to be waiting for him. When he discovers she has left, he follows her to Manchester, where they are reconciled.

## Book Three – The Gathering Storm

Following their reconciliation, Beth and Alex return to London, where Beth engineers a marriage between Anne Maynard and Lord Redburn. The prospective French invasion of England is unsuccessful and shortly afterwards the MacGregors journey to Scotland, where Beth meets the rest of her clan and is initiated into the Highland way of life, which she adapts to very quickly. She also meets her MacDonald relatives, including her grandmother, now a very old lady. During a short stop in Edinburgh, Beth, accompanied by Duncan, unexpectedly encounters Lord Daniel, and after an acrimonious and almost violent exchange, Beth realises he is now her sworn enemy.

On their reluctant return to London, Beth is confronted by her brother Richard, requesting funds from Sir Anthony. Incensed by this, Beth ejects him from her home, whereupon he secretly courts and marries Anne, who is now the wealthy widow of Lord Redburn. Beth is concerned about the safety of Anne, and Lord Redburn's unborn child, whom Anne carries.

Prince Charles lands prematurely in Scotland, and the clans start to rally to him. Alex sends Duncan and Angus to raise the clan but he, as Sir Anthony, feels that he will be of more use gathering information if he remains with his wife in London. He consoles himself with the knowledge that this will be a temporary measure, and he will soon be able to take his rightful place as chieftain of his clan in Scotland and fight for the Stuart cause.

Whilst attending a social evening at the house of the Prince of Wales, Sir Anthony is challenged to a duel by Lord Daniel, which he declines to accept. The prince sides with the Peters and Daniel vows revenge. He begins secretly investigating Sir Anthony's background.

Shortly after this encounter Alex receives a message from Prince Charles, asking him to stay in London gathering information about troop movements, until the invasion is over, and James III and VIII is crowned in London. Alex is distraught, but cannot refuse a direct request from his prince, so reluctantly accepts that he must remain Sir Anthony for the foreseeable future.

## Book Four – The Storm Breaks

Alex discovers that he is about to be betrayed and he and Beth flee and join the rebels at Edinburgh, where the Jacobites are victorious in the battle of Prestonpans. The Jacobite army then begins its progress southwards, arriving in Manchester, with more people rallying to their call. At Derby, much against the wishes of Alex and many other members of the clans, it is decided that the army should not march on London, but retreat to Scotland to await French reinforcements.

On reaching Manchester, Beth discovers the child Ann, daughter of her servant Martha who was dismissed by Richard on his first arrival home. The child has suffered badly at the hands of her mother's killer, who Beth suspects is Richard. Alex doubts her suspicions, and Beth is driven to tell him of her brother's attack on her. Alex is enraged that she has not trusted him and this leads to an estrangement between them. The army continues northward and Beth, convinced that their marriage is over, attempts to leave Alex. She is attacked and in rescuing her, Alex realises what he has nearly lost, and they are reconciled.

They continue northwards, where the Jacobite army eventually meets with Cumberland and the government forces at Culloden, while the women, led by Beth, shelter in a barn. The battle is lost, Duncan is killed and Alex badly wounded. Angus, after getting his brother to safety, goes in search of the women.

Their hideout has been discovered by a group of rampaging soldiers. The sergeant stabs Maggie, Beth kills him and whilst running away is recognised by the Duke of Cumberland, who gives the command not to shoot her, but too late. The remaining women are raped and killed and their bodies burnt with the barn.

When Angus arrives he finds Maggie who tells him of Beth's death, before dying herself. Angus searches for but cannot find Beth's body, and assumes it has been burnt along with the others.

He returns to Ruthven, where the surviving Jacobites have gathered, determined to fight on. He tells Iain and Alex the bad news. The MacGregors resolve to continue the rebellion and avenge the death of Maggie and Beth.

# STUART/HANOVER FAMILY TREE

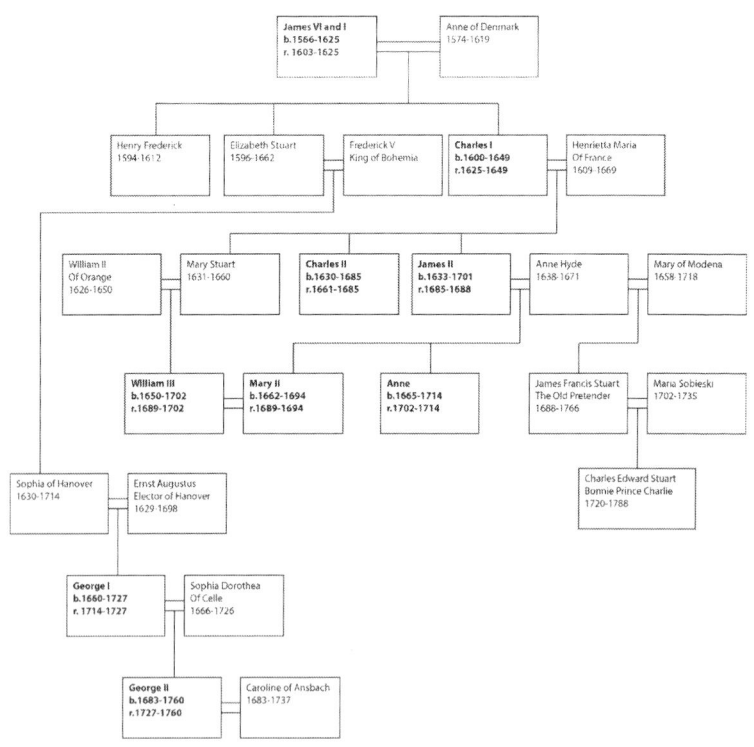

# LIST OF CHARACTERS

Alexander MacGregor, Highland Chieftain
Angus MacGregor, brother to Alex
Morag MacGregor, fiancée to Angus

Iain Gordon, liegeman to Alex
Alasdair MacGregor, clansman to Alex
Peigi MacGregor, wife to Alasdair
Kenneth MacGregor, clansman to Alex
Janet MacGregor, clanswoman to Alex
Dougal MacGregor, clansman to Alex
Hamish MacGregor, brother of Dougal
Lachlan MacGregor, a child

Alexander MacDonald (MacIain) Chief of the Glencoe MacDonalds
Ealasaid MacDonald, grandmother-in-law to Alex
Allan MacDonald, great-nephew to Ealasaid
Robert MacDonald, brother of Allan
Meg MacDonald, sister of Allan and Robert
Fergus MacDonald

Prince Charles Edward Stuart, eldest son of James Stuart (the Pretender), exiled King of Great Britain
Donald Cameron of Lochiel, Chief of Clan Cameron
John Murray of Broughton, former secretary to Prince Charles


Prince Frederick, Prince of Wales, eldest son of King George II of Great Britain
Prince Edward, youngest son to Prince Frederick
Prince William Augustus, Duke of Cumberland, second son of King George II

Thomas Pelham-Holles, Duke of Newcastle
Benjamin, his secretary
William Anne Keppel, Earl of Albemarle

Lord Edward Cunningham
Isabella Cunningham, eldest sister to Edward
Clarissa Cunningham, middle sister to Edward
Captain Richard Cunningham, cousin to Edward
Anne Cunningham, wife to Richard
George Cunningham, Anne's son

William, Earl of Highbury
Lord Daniel Barrington, his son

Thomas Fortesque, MP
Lydia Fortesque, his daughter

Lord Bartholomew Winter, great uncle to Anne Cunningham
Lady Wilhelmina Winter, his wife

Edwin Harlow, MP
Caroline Harlow, wife to Edwin
Freddie Harlow, their son
Toby, their manservant
Lady Harriet, Marchioness of Hereford, aunt to Caroline
Lady Philippa Ashleigh, cousin to Caroline
Oliver, Earl of Drayton, husband to Philippa

Graeme Elliot, Jacobite soldier
Thomas Fletcher, former steward to Beth MacGregor
Jane Fletcher, his wife
Ann, their adopted daughter.
Sarah Browne, a businesswoman
Mary Browne, her infant niece
John Betts, Jacobite soldier

Edward Cox, a solicitor

Colonel Mark Hutchinson, a dragoon

Captain Matthew Sewell, a British soldier
Sergeant Williams, a British soldier
Sergeant Applewhite, a British soldier
Private Thomas, a British soldier
Private Ned Miller, a British soldier
Thomas Miller, brother to Ned

Mr Carlton, Yeoman Warder
Kate, a maidservant

Richard Jones, Keeper of Newgate Prison
Downes Twyford, a turnkey

Catriona, Fiona, Annie, Màiri, Isobel, Jacobite prisoners

Mr Platt, surgeon to Prince Frederick

# PROLOGUE

**Inverness, late April 1746**

Prince William Augustus, Duke of Cumberland, was sitting in his quarters enjoying a rare moment of solitude. Reluctant to disturb his peace even to call for a servant, he poured himself a glass of brandy, unbuttoned his coat, and sat his considerable bulk down by the fire to enjoy the warmth. He took a deep draught of the amber liquor and sighed with satisfaction, sitting back in the chair and stretching his legs out toward the hearth.

There was something deeply satisfying about staying in the rooms previously occupied by your enemy, drinking their brandy, eating their food. It was all the sweeter when you knew that enemy was now probably sleeping in a smoky primitive hut or hiding in a cave, and living off whatever meagre provisions his fugitive cohorts could come by.

As if on cue the rain pattered against the window and the sky darkened in preparation for the deluge soon to come. The duke smiled. Yes, very sweet indeed. He would have to call someone to close the shutters and light the candles soon, but for now he was happy to sit by the light of the fire and contemplate the two glorious weeks since his overwhelming victory over the rebels on Culloden Moor.

The last days had been busy to say the least, and the following weeks would also be filled with activity; but the worst was over. The rebels were defeated and scattered, and by God he would do his utmost to make sure they never rose again. He had made a good start; around fifteen hundred of the vermin had died on the battlefield itself, and many more, most of them wounded, had been hunted down and killed by his soldiers in the following days as they hid in the woods and huts around the area.

It had been a good idea to set guards around the moor for a couple of nights after the battle; it had stopped the women and surviving rebels from collecting their wounded, and had in the main saved the soldiers from having to wade through the dead finishing off the injured rebels, as a good many of them had happily perished of their wounds. He'd heard that one or two of the sentries had been upset by the cries and moans of the dying men as they'd guarded the field, but he had no time for such sentimentality. He had not begun this affair, but he fully intended to end it, once and for all, and every rebel that died on the field was one less to hunt down later.

Of course a good many had escaped; too many. He would not be able to kill them all, but he would make their lives hell in whatever way he could. To that end even now four more battalions were riding north from England to join him, and he had dispatched bodies of soldiers all over the Highlands to scour the country for rebels. The men had been ordered to leave no stone unturned, and to destroy all means of livelihood of the rebels as they went.

In fact his intention was to pacify the Highlands as a whole. It was ridiculous that in an otherwise civilised country with a sophisticated legal system and a just government, there were still vast swathes of the north inhabited by barbarian savages dressed in rags which barely covered their private parts, speaking gibberish, attacking each other and anyone else they took against on a whim, and paying heed only to their chiefs, in defiance of the laws of the land, the monarch and even God Himself. It was insufferable and could not be tolerated any more. The whole of Scotland was steeped in rebellion to the bone, and must be brought to heel.

He had not disclosed his intention to break the power of the chiefs and bring the Highlanders to accept the civilised ways of the south to his men, of course; there were too many Highlanders in his own army for that to be wise at the moment. To give them their due, his Highland regiments had fought well, although he was uncertain whether that was because they were loyal to their rightful monarch or because it gave them the opportunity to settle old scores with rival clans. Whatever their motives, he needed them for now. But that did not mean he had to trust them. Any of them.

Now the fighting was over he'd had to start taking prisoners, although they cost money to keep and were damned inconvenient; but he had already received word from London of murmurings as to why so few of those wounded in the battle had been taken prisoner.

Damn them for mealy-mouthed old women! They would not be quibbling about mercy if they had had to spend a winter as he and his men had, in this Godforsaken gloomy hellhole with its horrendous weather, treacherous bogs and dark looming mountains, continuously threatened by bands of filthy bare-arsed heathens.

He had responded to the murmurs by reporting that before the battle Charles had ordered the rebels to give no quarter to the government troops. A signed order to that effect had been conveniently discovered on one of the dead rebels. Cumberland was pretty sure it was a forgery, but it had silenced his detractors, and for that he was grateful. And he could also argue that his men had finished off the injured while their blood was up directly after the battle; that was understandable, and would explain the miniscule number of wounded prisoners.

Anyway now, if the reports recently arrived from London were to be believed, the country was singing the praises of the conquering hero in every newspaper, bells were ringing day and night and a multitude of balls were being held in his honour. In the people's eyes he had delivered the country from a papist king, had ensured the continuation of the Hanoverian monarchy, and had restored peace to Great Britain. It was a wonderful feeling, and he would like nothing more than to head straight to the Capital and bask in the glory of his victory.

He smiled to himself, drained his glass, then got up and poured himself another.

He must not let the adulation go to his head. It was not over yet. In order to justify the adoration of the population, he had to ensure that there would not be another rising. There were still thousands of rebels at large, no doubt plotting another campaign. Many of them had gone back to their hovels, presumably thinking they would be allowed to continue their lives as they or their fathers had done after the '15, hiding their weapons in the heather thatch of their squalid little huts and waiting for the next call to arms.

Not this time. His men had their orders; and he would ensure they were obeyed. The rebels would come to heel or they would die, and Cumberland didn't care much which option his commanders chose to adopt. Every dead Scot was one less to rise again.

Some of the chiefs had been killed at Culloden, which was helpful, and the first reports had put Lochiel, the bastard who had effectively started the rising, among them. But he had now heard that the Cameron chief, though wounded, had been carried from the field by his men and was hiding out somewhere. Well, a large body of men was now on its way to lay the Cameron lands waste. They would burn the whole damn place to the ground, and as many Camerons as they could with it. It would be good to take Lochiel alive if possible, but dead would be fine, too.

His third cousin Charles was another matter. He had also escaped the field, and it was imperative that he be caught before he could find a ship to carry him to France to cause more trouble. All that was known of his whereabouts was that he had spent the night of the battle with Lord Lovat, the wily old Fraser chief, and had then headed west, towards the coast.

A number of search parties had been sent out to apprehend the Young Pretender, and the duke was confident they would succeed. They had been instructed to take him alive, although secretly Cumberland hoped that he would be killed. The thirty thousand pound reward for his capture did not specify that he had to be alive, and it would be a good deal more convenient if his troublesome cousin did not survive to come to trial. Should he die, then all chance of the Stuarts ever regaining the throne would die with him. The Old Pretender James was too old and dispirited and his second son Henry had neither the personality nor the reputation to raise an army.

But Charles had proved that he not only had the physical ability to lead a rebellion, but also the will and determination.

And, Cumberland grudgingly admitted, his cousin also had what King George would never have; the charisma to win people to his cause, and the ability to enchant commoner and noble alike.

He shuddered at the thought of Charles bringing all that intelligence and personality to his trial with the eyes of the world on him, and what a monumental problem that would create for the House of Hanover. Like it or not, he was of the blood royal, and by right of heredity heir to the throne, and executing a member of the royal family, no matter how troublesome, had never been an easy matter. No, far better if he were to be regrettably killed while resisting capture.

There was another rebel though, that the Duke of Cumberland most definitely *did* want taken alive. Officially he was third on the list of wanted men, after the Young Pretender and the Cameron chief; but secretly, if he could only capture one of the three, he would, without a moment's hesitation, choose the traitor known only as Sir Anthony Peters. What he wouldn't give to have that simpering, painted bastard rotting in the filthiest darkest dungeon he could find.

Charles had been brought up to believe his father was the rightful king of Great Britain, and that it was his mission in life to regain the throne for him; that he had attempted it was fully understandable. Similarly the Camerons had never pretended to be anything other than Jacobites; Lochiel's grandfather had fought at Killiecrankie with Viscount Dundee in 1689, and his father had fought in the '15; and the current chief was respected by friend and foe alike and said to be a man of honour, if such a thing was to be found in the Highlands.

But Sir Anthony Peters, whoever the hell he really was, was the most dangerous of all; intelligent, charismatic, and a consummate actor, he had deceived everyone. No one, not even the arch-spymaster Newcastle had suspected him for a moment of being anything other than an incompetent, bumbling molly. And all the time he had been collecting intelligence and passing it on to France and to the Stuarts. The royal coffers had even financed the bastard to go to Rome and entertain Charles!

The duke shuddered as he thought of the times his father had entertained Sir Anthony in his private chambers. As a personal friend of the king he had never been searched; had he wished to, he could have assassinated the monarch at any moment. It did not bear thinking about.

He had made a fool of them all, and Cumberland hated him more than he had ever hated anybody in his life. It had been impossible to even attempt to apprehend this chief of traitors; no one knew what he looked like, what his real name was, or even his nationality.

Until now.

Now the duke had a prisoner, someone who knew exactly what Sir Anthony looked like, and most probably his true identity, too. A prisoner who had also been thoroughly deceived by the man, and in the worst way possible. A prisoner who would no doubt be happy to divulge all, once recovered from the life-threatening injury. He had already sent his captive to London in utmost secrecy accompanied by one of his most accomplished surgeons, who had been told to ensure the survival of his patient at all costs. The surgeon had protested; to move the injured person could, in itself, be fatal.

But Cumberland had felt he had no choice; whilst it was possible that Sir Anthony lay dead on the battlefield or was amongst the corpses that had strewn the road all the way to Inverness, he could not be certain. And if the traitor found out about the duke's secret ace, he would no doubt attempt a rescue, or more likely a murder. With his skills, he could no doubt infiltrate the barracks at Inverness and sweet talk any jailor into allowing him in to see the prisoner.

No. The only way to discover the identity of Sir Anthony Peters, and to bring him to justice, if he was still alive, was to remove the prisoner from any danger of rescue, regardless of the cost.

Now he awaited news from London of their safe arrival. Once he had that, he could relax a little. His surgeon would do his utmost to restore the prisoner to health, and then, when he returned to England, he would undertake the interrogation himself. He felt himself to be in a unique position to do so. After all, the prisoner had professed a deep fondness for him, back in those happy days before circumstances had torn them apart.

Now things were different, very different, and the duke was confident that this time there would be nothing to stop him achieving his heart's desire and capturing his nemesis, all in one fell swoop. It was a cheerful thought, and one that would lighten the dark days to come while he brought this foul country to heel.

The young prince smiled, and wrapping his podgy fingers round the glass, raised it to his lips in a silent toast to providence, who was, indeed, smiling on him.

Life was good. Very good indeed.

# CHAPTER ONE

**London, April 25th 1746**

"God, do we really have to do this?" said Edwin gloomily as the carriage, having managed to travel the prodigious distance of twenty yards down the road, lurched to a standstill yet again. He pulled the leather curtain to one side to ascertain the reason for the delay, although he already knew what it was; the whole of London was ablaze with bonfires, lit in celebration of the Duke of Cumberland's great victory over the rebels at Culloden, and the streets were thronged with people in various states of inebriation. The news had arrived in the Capital two days ago, and since then, between the noise of people singing and shouting and the incessant ringing of bells, Edwin had had no sleep at all. "Now I know what the great fire must have looked like," he grumbled, letting the curtain fall back into place.

"Yes we do," his wife replied briskly, answering his question rather than his observation. "You can't spend the whole of your life working. You have to have *some* leisure time."

"I don't call attending a party I don't want to go to, full of people I don't want to speak to, leisure time," he protested. "I was hoping for a quiet evening in front of the fire with you and Freddie."

Caroline looked across at her husband, and softened. He was not a grumpy man by nature, but the last weeks had taken their toll on him. Even in the dim orange glow of the fires she could see the shadows under his eyes. He had lost weight too. Hopefully now the rebels had been soundly defeated he would be able to spend more time at home.

Not tonight, however.

"We have to attend at least one party, Edwin," she reasoned gently. "We must be seen to be celebrating William's victory, and this one is as good as any. At least we know everyone, and there will be no contentious people there."

"That's true. But there will be no interesting people there either."

"Thomas will be there."

"I see Thomas every day in parliament," Edwin contested, determined not to be consoled.

Caroline sighed.

"Alright," she said. "Let's get this over with, and then tomorrow we can spend the whole day together, just the three of us. We'll give the servants the afternoon off and stay in our dressing-gowns all day. Or do you have to be in parliament?"

"No, I do not have to be in parliament, and yes, that sounds like heaven," said Edwin, finally brightening. The carriage moved again, travelled another few yards and came to a halt. "At this rate by the time we get there the whole thing will be over." He looked out of the window again. "We're not far away now. We could walk from here."

"*You* could walk from here," Caroline said. "I, however, could not." She gestured down to her dress, the voluminous skirts of which took up the whole of the bench seat, and at her matching delicate silk slippers. "I would rather arrive late than covered in filth."

In spite of setting off half an hour early, they were nearly an hour late, and when they arrived at Grosvenor Square the party was in full swing and most of the guests were already there. In view of the short notice, Lord and Lady Winter had decided against a formal dinner; instead a line of tables, positively groaning with food, had been set up at one end of the great hall, with small circular tables and chairs dotted around the edges of the room, at which guests could sit to eat. The centre of the room had been cleared for dancing, but at the moment it was thronged with groups of people chatting animatedly.

The hall was ablaze with light from two enormous crystal chandeliers which hung from the ceiling of the room, and due to the mildness of the evening the windows had all been opened to allow the heat from over a hundred candles to dissipate. Through them the sound of bells could clearly be heard even over the cacophony of the musicians tuning their instruments in preparation for the dancing, and the chatter of the multitude.

Glancing around the room Caroline had to admit that she was impressed; to arrange such a vast quantity of food at such short notice, including a marchpane subtlety of the battlefield complete with soldiers, horses and cannon, was a feat in itself; the cooks must be on their knees with fatigue. But how Lady Winter had managed to come by an ensemble of musicians, when absolutely *everyone* was throwing a party tonight, was beyond Caroline.

One thing was certain, though; this was a clear demonstration of the influence and power of the host and hostess, which, after all, was the overriding purpose of the evening, and far more important than the stated reason for the party - patriotism and relief at the defeat of the Jacobite army.

Caroline deftly lifted two glasses of wine from the tray carried by a passing footman, and handing one to Edwin, braced herself to be greeted by her hosts, who were bearing down on the late arrivals, Anne Cunningham trailing in their wake.

"Mr and Mrs Harlow!" cried Lady Winter, beaming at them. "We had given up on you arriving at all!"

"Our apologies," said Edwin, bowing. "We set off early, anticipating that the roads would be difficult to negotiate, but we underestimated just how crowded they would be. It seems that the whole city is celebrating."

Lord Winter sniffed.

"It is quite ridiculous," he stated. "One cannot set foot outside the door without being accosted by the drunken rabble. The gutters are littered with them, lying in their own vomit and filth. The militia should be called out to deal with them."

His wife winced at this unconventional greeting, and patted his hand, as one might a petulant child.

"Really, Bartholomew, I am sure our guests do not wish to hear about the common people. We are here to celebrate the glorious victory of our dear prince in a proper manner, with dancing and music."

"I think it is commendable that the population wish to celebrate the victory," Anne put in tentatively. "After all, they stood to lose the most, had the rebels entered London."

Caroline looked at her and smiled encouragingly. It was the first time she had heard Anne volunteer an opinion at all, let alone in public.

"They hardly stood to lose more than the king, madam!" Lord Winter retorted. Anne blushed patchily and subsided immediately, mortified. Her eyes filled with tears.

Caroline tried to think of something encouraging to say, but was forestalled by Lady Winter, who took hold of Caroline's hands and held her at arm's length, examining her dress.

"I must say that your dress is utterly exquisite!" she exclaimed, eyeing Caroline's chiné silk gown with admiration. It *was* beautiful; heavy cream silk, woven with a pattern of red flowers and green foliage. The outlines of the flowers were blurred, giving a watercolour effect. "Where on earth did you come by such material? I have never seen anything like it!"

Edwin looked at his wife properly, noticing for the first time that evening not just how beautiful the dress was, but how flawlessly beautiful she was, too.

*I have neglected her these last months*, he thought. *I must remedy that, now the worst is over.*

Lady Winter was turning her round now, exclaiming over the workmanship of the seamstress and the apparent lack of any seam in the skirts. The pattern looked familiar to Edwin, but he couldn't remember where he had seen it before. *But that's not really surprising,* he told himself. *I'm so exhausted it's a miracle I can remember my own name.* He suppressed a yawn, and tried to concentrate on the conversation, reminding himself that tomorrow he would stay in bed all morning, and spend the whole afternoon with his wife and son.

"I believe it came from Paris," Caroline was saying. "It was a gift from a dear friend."

"Would that we all had such dear friends," Lady Winter enthused.

Edwin remembered where he had seen the material before.

"And you are wearing your own hair!" Lady Winter continued. Before Caroline could ascertain whether that was a compliment or an insult, her hostess continued, "that style is so becoming! You must tell me who dressed it for you."

Caroline eyed the older woman suspiciously. She hated wigs,

and always wore her own hair. And whilst her maid had taken some pains to dress it well, it was nothing out of the ordinary. Wilhelmina was laying it on thick tonight.

"My maid," Caroline replied. "She is a little out of practice, as Miss Browne normally dresses my hair, but I think she made a tolerable job of it."

"Indeed she has!" exclaimed Lady Winter. "Really, it is most inconsiderate of Miss Browne to depart the city at such a crucial moment, when I am desperately in need of her skills. There are so many balls to attend, and Lord Winter and I intended to visit St James's this week, you know, to offer our personal congratulations to His Majesty."

"This is what comes of depending upon the lower classes, Wilhelmina," Lord Winter interposed. "They are fickle and unreliable at the best of times."

"I am sure that Miss Browne would not have left the city at such a time, were her errand not urgent," Caroline commented. "After all, she is a businesswoman, and a most astute one. She stood to make a fortune from her talents this week, especially since she now makes house calls for a small consideration."

Sarah Browne in fact made house calls to Caroline for no consideration whatsoever, but she was not about to reveal that to the biggest gossipmonger in London.

"Sarah is visiting her family," Anne said. Everyone turned to look at her and she looked down at her hands, and with a conscious effort stopped wringing them together.

"That is hardly urgent, surely?" Lady Winter said.

"Her sister is about to give birth, and their parents will give no assistance. I believe they are very religious, and the child will be fatherless," Anne explained, blushing furiously.

Lord Winter sniffed and looked down his nose at Caroline.

"Well, there you have it," he said disdainfully. "Your *astute businesswoman* has abandoned her clients to attend someone who is clearly no better than she should be, and who has brought disgrace upon her family. No doubt the chit's father has thrown her out, and quite rightly so. And this is the woman whom you allow into your houses." He made a sweeping gesture which took in half the room. "Why, it's a miracle we have any silver left at all. One cannot –"

"I think it is commendable of Sarah to abandon everything to take care of her poor sister, who must be distraught. It is the Christian thing to do," Anne interrupted, to the amazement of all, including herself.

Lord Winter stared at his former charge with utter astonishment, in the same way he would had he petted a small fluffy kitten which had then promptly proceeded to shred his hand with her claws.

Caroline smiled. Anne's friendship with Harriet and Philippa was doing her a world of good; she was far more confident now than she had been six months ago. Nevertheless, having asserted herself twice in the space of a few minutes, Anne looked about to faint. As amusing as it was to watch Bartholomew's mouth hanging open in shock, Caroline decided to intervene before he could come to his senses and say something which would destroy his great-niece completely.

"I must ask you, Wilhelmina, before you are swept away by your other guests," she said, "where you came by that beautiful chandelier. I am searching for one for the salon at Summer Hill, and such a one as that would be just the thing."

Lady Winter beamed.

"Well, it is unique, Bohemian crystal, you know," she said. "Each piece was hand cut by a craftsman, which is why it reflects the light so beautifully."

It did. The candlelight enriched the mellow gold of the wall mouldings, and the faceted crystals cast a myriad of tiny rainbows round the room.

"It is a fitting accessory to your delightful house, my dear Lady Winter," came a male voice from behind Caroline, making her jump. She turned and curtseyed. The gentleman bowed, then taking her hand he politely kissed the back of it before relinquishing it.

"William!" she said, smiling with genuine warmth. She liked Highbury, always had. It was a shame he had such a wastrel for a son. "What a pleasure to see you. I thought you to be at your house in Sussex."

"I returned to London as soon as I heard the good news," the earl said. "I would not have missed the celebrations for the world. And how is your country house coming along, Caroline?"

"Very well," she replied. "The building work is almost finished, and soon I will be looking to decorate and furnish it. I am thinking to commission William Kent to design the garden, if Henry can be persuaded to part with him."

Edwin would never get used to his wife addressing the highest nobles in the land so familiarly. He could never imagine calling the Earl of Highbury 'William', any more than he would think to address the Prime Minister as 'Henry'. Not yet, anyway.

"Oh, I am sure he will!" Lady Winter enthused. "After all, it is most important for those in power to have a country home in which to entertain distinguished guests! And the garden is such a crucial part, a setting in which the jewel of the house is displayed to perfection."

The party, discussing interior design and landscaping, moved further into the room, where they were soon joined by Edwin's friend Thomas Fortesque, and by Anne's cousins-in-law, Lord Edward, Isabella and Clarissa. Pleasantries were exchanged. Charlotte, it seemed, was indisposed and had regretfully been unable to attend the party.

Lord Edward seemed also to be somewhat indisposed, Caroline noted with wry amusement. By the way he looked at her it was clear he had not forgotten that at their last meeting she had called him the cousin of a traitor. She was surprised that he had joined them at all. She had expected him to steer well clear of her and Edwin tonight.

She smiled sweetly at him and curtseyed, forcing him to bow politely to her. As she rose, Edwin placed his arm around her waist and squeezed it gently. She heeded the warning, although in truth she was not in the mood for conflict tonight. She just wanted to get through the evening, go home, and spend some precious time with her husband, of whom she had seen far too little since the Pretender's son had landed in Scotland last July.

Now that there were a number of men in the group, the talk inevitably turned to the ostensible reason for the party.

"So, Edwin, Thomas," said Highbury, "has there been any further news from Scotland?"

"Dispatches are coming in all the time, my lord, but at the moment we know only that the Young Pretender's forces are scattered, and that he is on the run. We presume that he will attempt to return to France along with many of the prominent rebels," Thomas said.

"Although of course there is always the chance that he will try to rally his forces and attempt another rising, perhaps a summer campaign," Edwin added.

"Preposterous!" Lord Winter stated. "Are not the majority of his forces killed?"

"Indeed, a large number, perhaps as many as two thousand were killed in the battle – the numbers are still uncertain - but many more escaped. And don't forget some three thousand or more were not at the battle at all, being on expeditions around the country. Of course a number of those who escaped were wounded and may have died since, but even so, we must allow that there are still enough rebels at large to cause us a great deal of trouble, should they be allowed to organise again."

"Then it must be of primary importance to ascertain the whereabouts of the Pretender's son and arrest him," said Highbury. "I think that would be the best way to prevent another rising. After that, I am sure the common men will return to their homes and abandon the idea of a Stuart restoration."

"That may be true," mused Thomas. "But I believe the duke intends to teach the rebels a lesson. It has always been his view that they were treated far too leniently after the '15."

"Quite right too," put in Lord Edward. "Hang the lot of 'em, Charles included. That'll put a stop to them, once and for all."

"We have to catch him first," Highbury pointed out. "Is there any news of his whereabouts?"

"It is known that he spent the night after the battle with Lord Lovat – the Chief of Clan Fraser," Thomas added for the benefit of the ladies present. "Nine hundred men have been dispatched to attack all the rebels they may find on the Fraser lands. But I doubt that Charles would have remained there. I am sure he will keep moving for now, in the hope of taking ship or of organising a rendezvous with his men."

"Is there not a thirty thousand pound reward out for information leading to his capture?" asked Caroline.

"There is indeed," affirmed Highbury. "But that reward was offered last August, and no one has come forward to claim it yet."

"Is that not incredible? Thirty thousand pounds is an

enormous sum even for someone of means, but many of the Jacobites are just common men, are they not, living in extreme poverty, if the newspapers are to be believed."

"The Highlanders have a strange notion of honour, though," Highbury said. "They hold their honour higher than anything."

"Honour?!" spluttered Lord Winter. "How can you even mention the word 'honour' where these traitorous savages are concerned? There is no honour in rising against your anointed king!"

Caroline opened her mouth, and then closed it again. She was determined to say nothing controversial tonight.

"But they do not consider George to be their anointed king," Highbury replied. "They believe James to be the rightful king and Charles the rightful heir. And misguided though they are, they are willing to lose everything to fight for what they believe in. I am not sure such men would betray their prince, not even for thirty thousand pounds. And there is something admirable in that, I think."

There was a shocked silence whilst everybody absorbed the fact that the Earl of Highbury found something admirable about traitors. Caroline was amused. Had she said such a thing the whole company would have challenged her, dismissed her in fact as an ignorant woman. But nobody wanted to make an enemy of the vastly powerful Earl of Highbury. And he could get away with such remarkable observations, as his allegiance to the Hanoverian regime was indisputable.

As was hers, but like Highbury, she *did* find it admirable that no one had yet given the Pretender's son up for such a sum.

"Perhaps once they realise their cause is dead, they will be more willing to take the money," Edwin said. "Because by all accounts, Cumberland intends to take immediate steps to pacify Scotland, whilst the rebels are disorganised. And we must do our utmost to ensure that the ringleaders do not succeed in escaping to France to cause more trouble for us."

"Do you think Sir Anthony will escape to France?" Lydia asked. Thomas frowned at his daughter. By unspoken agreement the name of Sir Anthony Peters was not mentioned when in company with people who had been completely taken in by him. As that number of people was very considerable, the name of Sir

Anthony Peters was not mentioned at all in public.

"I am sure he will try, if he is not there already, Lydia," Thomas replied, hoping that would put an end to the subject.

"Or if he was not killed in battle," Highbury added.

Lord Winter sniffed loudly.

"I cannot imagine such a person venturing within fifty miles of a battlefield," he said scornfully. "Why the man used to have hysterics if he got the tiniest spot of mud on his ridiculous clothes. No doubt he is already in France with his whore, prancing about Louis' Court, and attending mass. I never trusted Elizabeth; she was far too forward for my liking. I remember how entranced they were by the papist Court when we met them at Versailles. Why they even attended a mass there! The French King and his whole Court were in attendance. It was an appalling experience." He sniffed again to signify his disgust for Louis' Court, and France in general.

"Did you attend the mass yourself, then, Bartholomew?" Highbury asked innocently.

Caroline gave a most unladylike snort of laughter, which she quickly attempted to turn into a cough, covering her face with her handkerchief.

"Are you unwell, my lady? Should I fetch a glass of punch for you?" a familiar voice asked her. She turned to see Lord Daniel standing to her right, feigning concern. *There will be no contentious people there,* she had told Edwin. *Wrong.* She was grateful that her handkerchief covered the instinctive look of distaste that crossed her features. Much as she liked the Earl of Highbury she couldn't stand his son, and found it very difficult to hide her dislike.

"No, I am quite well," she replied curtly before turning pointedly away from him.

"Have you heard from Richard, Anne?" Isabella asked, clearly anxious to divert the topic of conversation away from her cousin, but thereby earning a look of gratitude from Lord Winter.

"No, not as yet," replied Anne.

"Well, I am sure he is very busy at the moment, and will write as soon as he has time," Isabella reassured her cousin-in-law.

"Unless he was killed in battle," Edward said tactlessly. "He was at Culloden, was he not?"

Isabella winced.

"I am not too worried on that score, my lord," Anne said coolly. "I have heard the casualties amongst the dragoons were very light, not above twenty in total. And his name is not mentioned in the list of dead published in the newspapers."

*Yes*, thought Caroline approvingly. *You have changed a great deal. Well done Harriet, and Philippa.* Richard was in for a shock when he returned home. If he returned home. She wondered whether Anne was hoping Richard was among the twenty dragoon casualties. She knew she was.

The dancing was announced, and the conversational groups moved from the centre of the floor to its edges, Caroline taking the opportunity to get away from Lord Daniel by accepting his father's offer to dance.

"You seem to have recovered well from your coughing fit, Caroline," the earl remarked as they took their places on the floor. Caroline glanced across at him. His expression was solicitous, but his eyes were merry.

"Thank you, yes. It was merely a temporary affliction." She smiled. The music began, and the couples stepped forward, pliéd and turned to greet each other.

"You seemed upset by Bartholomew's comment," he said. "I thought to divert him from uttering any further remarks on the subject. You were close to Elizabeth, were you not?"

"I was," Caroline said.

They moved apart, looped around, and did not meet again until the end of the dance.

"Have you heard anything from Elizabeth?" the earl asked casually as he led her from the floor.

Shocked, Caroline stopped and turned to look at him, but his face was unreadable.

"If I had, William, do you not think I would have informed the authorities immediately?" she said.

"I beg your pardon, Caroline," he responded at once. "I did not mean to offend you. After all Elizabeth is thought by most to have been duped by Anthony, as were we all. In view of that I thought perhaps your sense of loyalty to a friend might have overridden your sense of duty. She was very lovely. I would like to know if she was safe."

"Have you heard from Anthony?" Caroline asked. "You were close to him, were you not?"

The earl smiled. "Touché, my lady," he said. "No, I have not heard from Anthony. I do not think he would correspond with me."

"In view of your son's actions?" Caroline asked.

"Ah, Daniel," Highbury said tiredly. "No. In view of the fact that he would not wish to compromise his friends."

"Did he not compromise all of us by his actions?" Caroline retorted.

"Indeed he did, from the king downward. And in doing so, he compromised none of us after all, did he? Thank you for the dance, Caroline. It was a pleasure." He bowed and moved away.

Caroline contemplated joining another group but wanted a moment alone to digest what Highbury had said. If anyone else had said what he had, she would have thought them to be accusing her of withholding crucial information, but his tone had been anything but accusatory.

*And he was right,* she thought uncomfortably. *My loyalty to Elizabeth* did *override my duty to King George.* She was not in the mood for further conversation at the moment, and decided to get some food instead. She made her way over to the table, choosing from amongst the many delicacies on offer.

"I would recommend the pheasant," Lord Daniel said from beside her. "And the quails' eggs in aspic are delightful."

Caroline closed her eyes and took a deep breath.

"Thank you, my lord," she replied. "But I have already made my choice."

"Would you care for some marchpane then? It is really exquisite."

Why was he persisting in talking to her? She disliked him, and he knew it. She looked up at him just in time to see him bite the head off a kilted almond-paste rebel, chewing with relish.

"No thank you. Too much sweetness nauseates me."

"A glass of champagne, perhaps?"

She put her plate down on the table and turned to him.

"If you are looking to oil your way into a political position, it is Edwin you must try to win over, not myself. I assure you, I am a lost cause in that respect," she stated bluntly, hoping he would now go away and leave her alone. In the distance she saw Edwin look up from his conversation with his political cronies and start to make his excuses, clearly noting by her posture that she would appreciate his presence.

"Really, Mrs Harlow, I am surprised that you are so hostile to me. After all, the king himself has thanked me for my services to the crown, and these are delicate times. Anyone suspected of Jacobite sympathies is certain to be treated harshly by the authorities." He smiled smugly down at her.

She had picked up her plate intending to meet Edwin halfway across the room, but at Daniel's words she slammed it down on the table again, hard enough to make the serving-man jump.

"You forget who you are, sir," she stated icily, every inch the aristocrat now. "May I remind you that my family was fighting for a constitutional monarchy when your ancestor was being created the first Earl of Highbury by the Stuart King Charles, when he was in exile, as I remember. How dare you speak to me of loyalty, you insolent brat!"

"If you are referring to Sir Anthony, my lord," Edwin added, who had abandoned politeness on seeing his wife smash her plate down and had joined her in time to hear her final sentence, "then I can assure you that either of us would have given him over to the authorities without a moment's hesitation, had we suspected what he was."

"And yet your wife seems to have taken a dislike to me, sir," Daniel retorted. "Perhaps she resents me for giving Anthony up after all."

"You are mistaken," Caroline interjected before Edwin could come to her defence. "I have not *taken* a dislike to you, I have *never* liked you. But yes, I do resent your reasons for giving Anthony up, because they were not motivated by loyalty to the crown but by petty spite against Beth, who quite sensibly rejected your marriage proposal, and who was the clear victor in your impromptu duel at Prince Frederick's."

The protagonists had been oblivious to the fact that half the company were by now listening to this heated exchange with interest, but on hearing Caroline's final sentence several of them laughed and one gentleman in blue velvet actually applauded.

Daniel flushed scarlet and looked at the company, suddenly aware of how many people had observed the argument, and how few of them were on his side. He turned abruptly and left the room.

Caroline picked up her plate once again, retrieving a slice of pork pie which had leapt off it when she had crashed it down earlier. She turned to her husband.

"Would you get me a glass of punch, Edwin?" she asked calmly, as though nothing untoward had happened.

He moved to do her bidding, and the onlookers, realising that nothing else of interest was going to happen, resumed their conversations.

\* \* \*

"How do you do it?" he asked once they were safely in their carriage and making their way home.

"How do I do what?" Caroline asked, sitting back on the seat. She flexed her toes carefully, and winced. Her shoes were a little tight.

"Wipe the floor with somebody, and then proceed to spend the next three hours as though nothing whatsoever had happened?"

"Nothing whatsoever had happened. I have thought him an insolent jumped-up puppy for a long time. It was a relief to tell him so, and even more of a relief to be applauded for it. If we are ever unfortunate enough to attend the same party again, I expect he will keep a good distance away from me. Which is also a relief. Would you have done it?"

"Called him an insolent brat?"

"No. Given Anthony up without a moment's notice."

"Of course I would, had I known. Any one of us would have done," Edwin responded immediately. "But I am glad I did not have to," he added quietly after a pause.

She leaned forward in her seat and kissed him.

"What was that for?" he asked, smiling broadly.

"Am I not allowed to kiss my husband without a reason?" his wife retorted. She sat back again, spreading her skirts across the bench. Edwin eyed the gown appreciatively.

"A very dear friend," he commented.

"You remember, then." She laughed.

"I didn't at first, but Anthony's favourite term of endearment was 'my dear', so when you used it, it reminded me of him. That dress could be used in evidence against him, you know."

"Evidence of what?"

"Smuggling. I remember you enthusing over the fact that there was enough material to make a dress without a seam, and that the only way he could have come by that was through associating with smugglers."

"If he is caught, Edwin, I think being accused of smuggling will be the least of his worries," Caroline replied. "But enough of that. What on earth was wrong with Wilhelmina tonight?"

"Nothing, as far as I know. She looked in the peak of health."

"No, I mean all the overblown compliments. The dress I can understand, because it is quite unique, but my hair is nothing special, yet she commented extensively on it. And then Edward, who's avoided me since he tried to tell me who I could associate with, actually approached me voluntarily. Even Daniel was trying to win me over at first, asking me if I wanted champagne!"

"Ah, they will have heard the rumours, then," Edwin replied enigmatically.

"What rumours?"

"There are rumours floating around the commons that King George is about to bestow titles on a number of politicians to whom he's particularly grateful."

"Really? And are you among them?"

"I don't know, but presumably Wilhelmina, Edward and Daniel think so, from what you say."

"This is remarkable news, Edwin! Why didn't you tell me?" Caroline asked.

Edwin looked at her with some surprise.

"Firstly, because they are only rumours. Parliament is rife with them, and most of them are unfounded. And secondly, because you couldn't give a damn about titles and nobility. Unless you're using them to put down an insolent puppy."

Caroline laughed.

"True. But even so, it's a great honour to be awarded a peerage. And I have a lot more respect for a title that's actually been earned. My family's titles date back so far that most of them can't remember what the hell our distant ancestor did to get his earldom in the first place. Which means that idiots like Great-Uncle Francis prance around lording it over everyone when they wouldn't know what true nobility was if it hit them with a cricket bat."

"So you'd be honoured to be the wife of a lord, then, in the unlikely event that I become one?" Edwin ventured.

"I'm honoured to be your wife anyway, Edwin. You're worth a hundred of most of the peers I know," she said. "But I'd be very happy if you were rewarded by George for all the work you've done over the past months to keep the country in Whig hands."

They travelled in happy silence for a while, rejoicing in the fact that the bells had finally, after two days, stopped ringing. Edwin closed his eyes. He couldn't wait to get home, and to bed. The thought of being able to get a really good night's sleep and then wake up in the morning with plenty of time to make love to his wife delighted him. He smiled in drowsy anticipation of tomorrow.

"Speaking of nobles, though, William said a strange thing tonight," the object of his fantasy suddenly inserted into the silence. Edwin opened his eyes and realised that he had slumped sideways in the seat. He sat up and wiped his face with his hands in an attempt to stay awake until they arrived home.

"What was that?"

"He asked me if I'd heard from Elizabeth."

"Did you tell him you hadn't?"

"No."

Edwin was suddenly very wide awake.

"My God, Caro, you didn't tell him you had, did you?"

"Of course I didn't!" she exclaimed. "I insinuated that if I had I would have gone to the authorities."

"Do you think he was trying to trap you into admitting something?" Edwin asked, his mind racing now. Who else knew about the letter Beth had sent? Sarah. Anne. Would they have said anything? Surely not. Sarah was fanatically loyal to Beth, and the letter and Caroline's response to it had effectively saved her life, and Anne's child's life, too.

"That's what I thought at first, too," Caroline mused. "But no, I think he genuinely wanted to know how she was. But that's not the strange thing."

If that wasn't the strange thing, then Edwin wasn't sure he wanted to know what was.

"What was it then?" he asked after a pause in which it was clear Caroline was too busy musing on it to volunteer the information.

"I asked him if he'd heard from Anthony, and he said no, he didn't think that Anthony would wish to compromise his friends. I pointed out that he'd already done that. Then William said something like, he had compromised all his friends, from the king down, and by doing so he hadn't compromised anyone."

Edwin digested this in silence for a while.

"I've never thought of it like that before," he said finally.

"Neither have I," agreed Caroline.

"Do you think Anthony realised that?"

She thought about the baronet's final farewell to her, the rib-cracking hug, the profession of love.

"Yes I do," she said. "The man's a genius. And I do believe he cared for us, in his way. They both did. I think he knew all along that we would not suffer unduly were he to be discovered, and I think his refusal to act as Freddie's godfather was nothing to do with superstition. I think it was because he didn't want our son to bear the name of a traitor. William is right. And that makes me feel a lot better."

"About what?"

"About the fact that I'm praying that wherever he is, he's alive and well, and that Beth is too. Because however much he deceived us, I don't believe he deceived her, not once they were married, anyway. And I believe he loved her from the moment he met her, and risked everything to have her. A love like that is very rare. And although we'll never know, I'd like to think they are still together and as happy as they can be, given the circumstances. And I would not admit that to anyone else, even under torture," she finished.

He reached forward and took her hands in his.

"I have loved you from the moment I met you too, Caro. I can't imagine what my life would have been like without you. You know that, don't you?"

"I know that," she said. "I feel the same way. And that I *would* admit, to anyone who cared to ask."

# CHAPTER TWO

**Scotland, Early May 1746.**

*"Bas mallaichte!"* Alex cried in frustration. He fell back onto the bed, his face contorted with pain and frustration, his chest heaving.

He lay there for a few minutes, staring at the ceiling of the cottage until his breathing returned to normal, and then he sat up again, bracing himself on the edge of the bedframe.

He had waited all morning for the right time to attempt to stand for the first time since his leg had been broken at Culloden, and this was it. His men were all away, either hunting or searching for news, and Peigi had dropped by an hour ago with some food, and had lit a fire. The weather was atrocious; the wind howled down the chimney and the rain battered at the windows. Everyone would be indoors, he thought.

He was unlikely to be disturbed for several hours; his persistent dour mood had discouraged even the most garrulous clansmen from making social calls. No one wanted to have their head bitten off by the foul-tempered chieftain, so his men had taken to steering well clear of him, unless they had important news to relate which he needed to hear.

He didn't blame them for that. In fact he wanted to be left alone, most of the time. His favourite occupation was to just lie there and indulge in memories, to relive again all the precious moments he'd had with Beth, moments that all too often he'd taken for granted at the time, but which were now priceless.

And breathtakingly painful.

After recovering consciousness and learning of his wife's death, he'd spent the best part of a week lying with his face to the wall, alternating between numbness and a heartache so unbearable that he prayed he'd die from it. People had come, lighting fires and bringing him food and drink, then taking the untouched platters away again later. One or two had asked how he was feeling, but he'd ignored them, and they had not persisted.

For the first few days Angus had called on him regularly, asking him questions about everyday clan affairs, but Alex had ignored him too, knowing that he could make such trivial decisions as when the cattle should go to pasture and the oats should be planted, without his help. Angus had persisted for a while, but getting no response had finally taken the hint and had not called in for several days.

And then, two days ago, just when it had seemed to Alex that his life had settled into a routine that he could cope with for the next few weeks until he died of starvation - sleep for twelve hours, wake up, drink a little water and a lot of whisky, daydream about Beth, drown the physical and emotional pain with a lot more whisky, and repeat - Iain had called to see him, had brought him food, and had not gone away.

Instead he had pulled a chair up in front of the fire and had sat in silence for a while. Alex had ignored him, sure that after a short time he would get up and leave, as everyone else did. Some considerable time had passed, during which the sun moved across the sky and Iain stayed where he was. Alex tried to pretend he wasn't there. He had grown accomplished at pretending people weren't there for several minutes at a time, but not for several hours.

He tried to think about Beth, about the way she had looked and felt the last time they had made love, but the fact that someone was sitting in the room silently distracted him, and the memory wouldn't come.

*What the hell does he want?*

"What the hell d'ye want?" he said when he could bear it no more. He had intended to sound impatient, authoritative, but his voice came out as no more than a croak, ruining the effect.

"She wouldna want this, ye ken," Iain said conversationally. "Neither of them would."

"Fuck off," Alex replied. He closed his eyes. Now Iain would get up and leave him in peace.

"She'd be disgusted an she saw ye lying in bed, wasting away, when there's work to be done."

Alex turned to face the room, wincing at the pain the movement caused him. Iain was staring into the peat fire, which gave off a dull red glow.

"Iain," Alex began.

"Ye're wanting to die, so ye can be with her again," Iain interrupted quietly. "I can understand that. It's what I'm wanting myself. But what do ye think she'll say, if ye die in such a way as this? She didna give in. The last thing she did was kill the redcoat bastard who stabbed Maggie. That's a fine way to die, if ye have to. If ye lie in your own filth till ye starve yourself to death, and go to her reeking o' self-pity and sweat, d'ye think she'll still want ye?"

With a strength born of pure instantaneous rage, Alex had launched himself from the bed, forgetting everything except the need to kill this bastard who sat there so calmly, daring to tell him what Beth would think! Iain had no idea, no idea at all, what he was going through!

He had stood, his hand reaching for the dirk on the small table at the side of his bed, had taken one step forward and screamed in agony as his injured leg took all his weight and collapsed under him, bringing him first to his knees, and then to the ground.

For a moment he had lost consciousness, and when he'd come round, Iain had been standing over him. He picked up the dirk and replaced it gently on the table.

"Aye," he'd said, nodding. "Ye can still feel, then. That's something. I'll fetch Peigi."

He'd walked out, leaving Alex lying helpless on his stomach on the dirt floor of the cottage, gritting his teeth and moaning as the pain tore up his leg, obliterating everything else, even Beth, from his mind.

A few minutes later the door had opened, bringing with it sunlight, a fresh breeze and Peigi, her arms full of bedding, followed by Kenneth. She put the bedding down on the table, deftly stripped the bed of its filthy, sweat-soaked linen and, wrinkling her nose in disgust, threw it out of the door, followed by the mattress and pillow.

"I'll be back shortly," she said, and disappeared out into the sunlight.

Kenneth knelt down by his chief, and very slowly and gently turned him over onto his back. Sweat poured down Alex's face, which was white and contorted with pain. The muscles on his neck bulged as he fought the agony, and tears trickled down his cheeks.

"*Isd,*" Kenneth said softly, although Alex hadn't spoken. "Lie still a minute, while I look at ye." His fingers moved gently over the injured leg, feeling for any sign that the bone had rebroken, and then he sat back on his haunches. "Ye'll be fine," he said reassuringly.

Alex took a deep breath and tried to sit up, but Kenneth pressed him back down.

"No' yet," he said. "Bide a while, and Peigi'll change the bed."

As if on cue, Peigi had bustled back in with a fresh mattress.

"I've emptied the other one," she said, "but the cover'll need washing. Several times," she added. "So ye can have mine for now." She shook the heather-filled mattress out and laid it on the bed, then started to make it up.

Alex had lain there waiting for the pain to subside, not daring to open his mouth to speak, fearful that he would burst into tears if he did. The pain was terrible, but the emotions swirling round in his mind were worse; rage, humiliation, grief. Better to remain silent.

"There," Peigi said, patting the bed in satisfaction. "Ye can put him back now," she told Kenneth. "I'll away and get a bannock and some broth."

Kenneth very carefully scooped Alex up as though he were a small child, and laid him gently back on the bed, pulling the blanket over him.

"I'll away and get some whisky to go wi' the bannock and broth," he said, winking.

Alex had waited until they were gone, and then had tried to pull himself up into a sitting position, his arms trembling with the effort of merely levering his body up. How could he have lost so much of his strength in so short a time? He sat there and thought.

In due course the broth and the bannock had arrived, and for the first time in over ten days Alex had attempted to eat, managing around half of the bowl of soup and a bite of the bannock before giving up. Then he sat there and thought some more, until Kenneth came back with the whisky. He put it down without a word and started to leave, but Alex reached out and grabbed his sleeve.

"Will ye help me take my shirt off?" he asked. "There's a clean one in the press."

Kenneth helped him to pull it over his head.

"Shall I get ye some water to wash wi' afore ye put on the clean shirt?" Kenneth offered.

"Aye, that'd be good."

Kenneth rolled the dirty shirt up into a ball and turned to go.

"One more thing," his chieftain said.

"Aye."

"Fetch Iain, will ye?"

Kenneth hesitated.

"Alex," he said, "Iain's grieving. He didna mean-"

"Aye, I ken," Alex interrupted. "I'm no' angry, man. I want to speak wi' him, that's all."

Kenneth nodded, and turned to go.

"Thank you," Alex said. "For the whisky, and…" He pointed to the floor where he had so recently lain helpless.

Kenneth smiled, and left.

Ten minutes later, Iain had returned. His face was closed, his mouth compressed in a tight line.

"Sit down," Alex said.

Iain brought the chair from the fireside and sat stiffly down near the bed, but out of arm's reach.

"Did Kenneth tell you I'm no' angry with ye?" Alex asked.

Iain nodded.

"I'm sorry ye fell, but I'm no' sorry for what I said," he stated. "It needed saying, and I'd say it again. I spoke the truth as I see it."

"I wanted to kill you for it," Alex said. "I lay there like a wee bairn on the floor, and all I wanted to do was find a way to kill you."

"I'll leave the morrow."

"And then I thought about it," Alex had continued as though

Iain hadn't spoken, "and I realised that ye're right. I think ye're the only man in the clan who could make me see it. Because ye're the only other man in the clan who's grieving the way I am."

Iain closed his eyes and swallowed.

"I thought about what Beth would say, if she were to walk in now and see me lying here wi' my muscles wasting, while the others go out to find out who's willing to fight on, and Angus does his best to act as chieftain, though he's sore afraid to. And I was ashamed of myself."

He'd paused, and there was silence. In the distance he'd heard a child laugh and the sound of women talking. Life was going on, and he had to find a way to go on, too.

"I'm no' going to pretend I want to live without her," he'd continued. "But ye're right. When I die, whenever that is, and we meet again, as I'm sure we will, I want her to be proud of me. And between now and then, that's what I intend to do – to make her proud of me. She died well and bravely, and so did Maggie. And I canna tell ye how sorry I am to be the cause of it. I dinna expect ye to forgive me, for I canna forgive myself."

Iain's eyes shot open.

"What the hell are ye on about?" he said rudely. "Ye didna kill them!"

"I'm your chieftain," Alex said. "I should have made them go home, the pair of them. I should never have let them come wi' us. If I'd sent them home with Angus and the others after Prestonpans, they'd be alive now."

To Alex's surprise, Iain had burst out laughing.

"Made them go home?" he'd said. "Have ye forgotten them entirely, in such a short time? God Himself couldna have made them go home! If ye'd tied them to their horses and ordered Angus and the others to take them, they'd have ridden straight back again the moment they were left, and ye ken it well, man. If ye're wanting to blame someone, blame Cumberland and the redcoat bastards that killed them and thousands of others. And then get out of that bed as soon as ye're able, and do something about it. It's a powerful incentive to live; it's what's keeping me going. And then when we die, we can look Beth and Maggie in the face wi' pride, for we'll have died doing as they'd have expected us to."

Alex stared at his adopted clansman, astonished. And ashamed. This was the rallying call to arms of a true chieftain to his men, and he should be saying the words, not listening to them.

"Christ, Iain," he said softly, after a moment. "What have I come to?"

Iain stood, and leaning over the bed, took Alex's hands in an uncharacteristic display of affection.

"Ye've come to your knees wi' grief," he said. "We all understand that, and no one blames ye for it. She was your life, as Maggie was mine. But now it's time to come to your feet, and fight back. Because it's what the MacGregors do, and we do it well, and we all want to. But we need you to lead us. Angus canna do it, not yet. Will ye do it?"

He let go of Alex's hands abruptly, and swiped the tears away from his eyes.

"Aye, well," he said, trying to regain his composure and turning away without waiting for an answer to his question, "I'll away to my bed. It's been a tiring day."

"Before ye go to bed, will ye do something for me?"

Iain waited.

"Will ye ask Kenneth if he can fashion a crutch of some sort for me until Angus gets back frae the hunting and can make me a proper one?"

Iain grinned. He had his answer.

"Aye," he said. "I'll tell him."

So it was that now, two days later, Alex was trying, and failing, to stand, even on his good leg, for long enough to get the crutch into place. Without the rage to fuel him he didn't have the strength in his muscles to support himself.

*This is ridiculous*, he told himself. *Three weeks ago I marched all night on a biscuit, and fought the next day, too. I should be able to stand up. I can stand up.*

He pulled himself to the edge of the bed again, picked up the makeshift crutch Kenneth had made for him until Angus could fashion a more comfortable one, and hanging on to it for dear life, managed to stand on his good leg. Very carefully he tucked the top of the crutch into his right armpit and leaned his weight on it. So far, so good. Balancing on his good left leg, he moved the crutch forward a few inches, then putting all his weight on it, tried to hop forward. His leg was already trembling just from the effort of taking his weight, and shards of white-hot pain were knifing up his injured leg. Try as he might, he couldn't move. He would have to sit down again.

With the crutch still under his right arm he reached back with his left, feeling for the bedpost and realising that it was too far away for him to grasp without leaning for it.

"Shit," he said, softly, but with great feeling.

He couldn't move. He would have to stand here until someone came in, and that could be hours, because he had deliberately waited until no one would be around to see his pathetic efforts to walk.

The door opened, and Janet walked in.

Alex jumped in surprise, and the crutch slid out from under his arm. He started to lose his balance, felt himself falling, and then Janet dropped the basket of food she was carrying and leapt across the room, managing by a Herculean effort to grab his right arm and support him as he sank gracelessly back onto the bed.

They both sat there for a moment while they got their breath back, his arm still wrapped round her shoulder, and her hands gripping his wrist for dear life. Then she released him and standing, retrieved the basket and its contents from the floor.

"I made oatcakes, and thought ye might like some," she said. "I waited till the rain let up, and brought them for ye."

"Thank you. Ye came at the right moment," Alex admitted.

"Hmmph," she replied. "Ye shouldna be trying to walk yet. Ye need to build your strength first."

"I canna do that lying in my bed," Alex pointed out, frustrated.

Janet thought for a moment.

"Wait there," she said tactlessly, and walked out of the cottage.

Alex waited there. The pain in his right leg was easing a bit now. If he shuffled up to the end of the bed he could try standing again, bracing himself on the bedpost.

Janet returned, carrying a large stone in her arms.

"Here ye are," she said, dropping it on the bed next to him. "Before you can walk, ye need to let your leg heal. If ye fall ye could break it again, and if ye do, ye might lose it this time."

He'd been so intent on getting well enough to fight, he hadn't thought about the possibility of breaking his leg again, or that if he did he could damage it beyond repair.

*The blow to my head must have addled my brains*, he thought. It wasn't just his body that needed building up. He needed to start thinking properly again. He'd be no use to the clan if he couldn't think strategically and plan ahead.

"And while ye're waiting for your leg to heal, ye can build your arms and suchlike. This was the best I could find for now, but I'm sure Angus'll be able to find something that's the right weight for ye, when he gets back."

Alex smiled, and reaching, lifted the rock, surprised by how heavy it was. True, Janet had staggered a little under its weight as she'd carried it in, but even so, in his full strength he'd have been able to lift it effortlessly with one hand.

"Thank you," he said. "This will be fine for now. And ye're right."

"Of course I am," she replied. "If ye dinna need anything else, I'll get back to the bairns."

"How are ye doing, Janet?" Alex asked.

"I'm doing well," she replied. "Of course it's no' so easy wi' Simon away, but I'll manage well enough until he comes home."

"Janet," he said softly. "Simon's no' coming home, *a graidh*. Ye ken that, d'ye no'?"

"Ye didna see him killed, did ye?" she retorted.

"No, but-"

"And ye didna see him taken prisoner, did ye?"

"The redcoats didna take prisoners," he said.

"Well, then. If he isna dead, and he wasna taken prisoner, then he'll come home," she affirmed.

"Janet, it's been over three weeks. If he was coming home, do ye no' think he'd be here by now?"

"He isna dead, Alex. If he was dead I'd feel it, here." She put her hand to her chest. "And I dinna feel it. He's alive, and he'll come back to me. Now, I've the bairns to see to."

After she'd gone, Alex cradled the rock in his arms, and sighed.

In truth, he didn't feel in his heart that Beth was dead, either. But he knew she was, because Maggie had seen her die. Wanting her to be alive couldn't make it so.

How long would it be before Janet accepted that Simon was

dead? Dougal had told them how the redcoats had behaved, when he came back. True, he had been rescued by one, but that was a miracle. The vast majority of the soldiers had revelled in their victory, had roamed around the battlefield finishing off the wounded, laughing and splashing each other with their enemies' blood as though it was a game.

If Simon had not died immediately, if he had managed somehow to crawl away and lie low, then he had surely died of his wounds. Otherwise he would have been back by now.

*We all deal with grief in our own way,* Alex thought. *Iain lives for vengeance. I wanted to kill myself.* Iain had saved him, given him a reason to fight on.

Janet was in denial, but she would see the truth, eventually. And when she did, her children would save her. She had them to live for. She would survive.

\* \* \*

And so it was that when the men returned four days later, and Angus walked into the chieftain's cottage full of dread, with a headful of news he knew Alex would ignore completely, he was confronted to his utter delight by the sight of his brother sitting on the edge of the bed, one splinted leg stuck out straight in front of him, the other bent at a right angle, dipping up and down to work his arms. Beside him on the bed were four stones of varying sizes.

"*A fichead 's a h-ochd, a fichead 's a naoi, a fichead 's a deich,*" Alex grunted, then sat back on the bed. His hair had been washed, he'd shaved, and the room no longer stank of sickness, Angus noticed. Clearly something momentous had happened while he was away. Whatever it was, he sent a silent prayer of thanks up to God for it.

"Thirty," Angus said. "Not bad."

Alex shot him a withering look.

"I did a hundred earlier. I only stopped now because ye came in. How was the hunting?"

Angus grinned hugely.

"One," he said cryptically.

Alex stared blankly at him for a moment, then understanding dawned.

"Christ, Angus, ye didna…"

Angus held up a hand.

"Relax, *mo bhràthair*," he said. "I was a good thirty miles away frae here, and it was an accident. The puir wee redcoat was unfortunately burnt tae death in a house he was firing."

Alex looked at his brother sceptically.

"Aye, well, he may have had my dirk between his shoulders a few moments before that, but there was no one else nearby and the smoke from the burning thatch hid me from view anyway."

"I thought ye said the redcoats were riding out in large groups and sticking together, and that it wasna a good idea to attack them yet because the risk of capture's too great."

"Ye *were* listening then," Angus observed. "Aye, they are, and we did agree, but I was watching them from the side of the hill, and this one broke away frae the others to fire a cottage at the edge of the settlement, so I took my chance while I could. In, out, and gone."

Alex shook his head.

"Ye havena changed, have ye?"

"Aye, I've changed," Angus replied earnestly. Then he grinned again, and the moment passed. "You have, too. Ye've wasted away. I can see your ribs."

Alex glanced down. It was true, he had lost a lot of weight. But then they all had, before Culloden. It was just that the others had put it back on again since, and he hadn't.

"I'll catch up soon enough," he said. "I've been working my arms and shoulders while I wait for my leg to heal a bit more. I need another crutch as well, I think. It'll be easier to walk wi' two, and I'm wanting to be out in the fresh air."

"I'll find a branch later and make ye one, nae problem," Angus said. He picked up a chair and pulled it over to the bed and sat down. "But I'm glad to see ye back with us, because I've news for ye. Two ships frae France came in to Loch nan Uamh last week, and they were carrying money, arms and brandy. There's enough tae keep us fighting all summer. The captain didna ken about Culloden, for he'd been at sea for a month. Anyway, once he found out, he didna want to let us have the goods, but then a few days ago three navy ships came in, so they unloaded fast, and then after a wee stramash they set off for France wi' some o' the chiefs that wanted tae go."

"Did they take Charles? Murray? Lochiel?" Alex said, on full alert now.

"No," Angus replied. "Charles was already on the Long Island. They were trying to persuade the captain to go and find him and bring him back to Arisaig for a summer campaign, but then after the fight wi' the other ships, they went straight back to France. They took the Duke of Perth and Lord Elcho, and a few others, and they asked Lochiel, but he wouldna go. Neither would Broughton. But the chiefs are rallying at Loch Arkaig to mount a campaign anyway."

Alex sat silently for a few minutes digesting this, while his younger brother fizzed with excitement, clearly wanting to charge straight into action. Alex understood now why Angus had taken a risk and killed the redcoat; he was desperate to continue the fight, to start to fulfil his blood oath to Maggie. No doubt the others were too. But he needed to know more. How many would rise? Would Charles agree to lead them again? Where was Lord George Murray?

"Will we join them, Alex?" Angus asked finally.

"We need to find out more," Alex replied. "I'll no' drag you all into another rising unless enough come to make it possible."

"But we're going to fight on anyway!" Angus argued.

"Aye, we are. But there's a big difference between another rising, and raiding from our own country, where we ken the land and can attack then melt back into the hills. We've been doing that for hundreds of years. If we rise again properly, Cumberland will come after us, and we need to be able to beat him this time. Call the men in. I need tae speak wi' all of ye."

Angus shot off like a cannonball, while Alex put his shirt on and arranged his plaid as best he could without standing up, and prepared for his first meeting with his clan as their chieftain since the morning of Culloden, over three weeks ago.

\* \* \*

"No, ye canna," objected Kenneth, when he heard what Alex was proposing. There were general murmurs of agreement from the others.

When the men had all assembled, Alex had asked Kenneth to carry him outside, because the cottage was far too small to accommodate them all, especially as many of the women had come too. He was sitting on a bench outside his front door, his clan sitting or kneeling on the ground around him.

"Aye, I can," Alex countered.

"But ye canna even walk two steps yet," Peigi put in. "How do ye expect to march halfway up the country to Arkaig?"

"I dinna intend tae march. I'll ride," he said. He held up a hand to counter the dissenting murmurs from the others. "If Lochiel can ride wi' two broken legs, then I can ride wi' one. I'll go slowly. Angus and Alasdair can walk by the side of me in case I have any problems."

"And if the redcoats come?" Angus said. "Ye canna exactly run away, can ye?"

"The redcoats'll no' come this far south yet," Alex said. "Inversnaid is in ruins, and the nearest barracks after that is Fort William. That's why we're safe here, for now. Once we get closer to Lochaber, we'll cut across country. Aye, if I have tae gallop, the jolting will pain me, but no' any more than it pained Lochiel, I'll be bound. And he's in more danger than I am. There's a price on his head."

"There's a price on your head," Alasdair pointed out.

Alex grinned.

"No, there's a price on Sir Anthony Peter's head," he said. "Alex MacGregor is in no more danger than any other member of the clan." He looked around at the sea of doubtful faces, and remembered that just five days ago he'd lain in bed wasting away, waiting to die, and they all knew it. "I'm back," he said to them. "I'm no' at full strength yet, but I will be, and soon. And in the meantime I've got ye to help me if I need it. Or do ye no' want to continue the fight? Because an ye dinna, tell me now. I'll no' force ye to it."

The roar of the clansmen allayed his fears.

"Well, then," he said. "Angus, away and find me another crutch. I can get a wee bit o' practice in tonight. We leave tomorrow."

\* \* \*

In truth Alex fared better than he'd expected to. When he'd told the others he'd be at full strength again soon, he'd been stating a hope rather than a fact, but it was amazing what determination, fresh air and the support of your men could do for you. He was more grateful to Iain than he could say; without his intervention, Alex realised now that he probably would have given up and died.

The pain of losing Beth had not diminished; he didn't believe it would ever diminish. But he was young, and strong, or could be, and he had something to live for, even if it was not what he'd dreamed of. And that would have to be enough.

He had managed to walk or rather hop a few steps, with two crutches, and was confident that he'd soon manage more. His broken leg was heavily splinted to protect it from breaking again should he have another fall, but the wound where the bone had poked through his shin was healing well, and apart from a constant dull headache he seemed to be suffering no lasting effects from the kick to his head.

Even so, he was very glad to be arriving at Glencoe, three days after they'd set out. He had sent a scout ahead to make sure the way was clear and that he'd find a welcome there, and he felt a huge relief that tonight at least, he'd get to sleep in a bed of sorts. He was looking forward to that.

He was not, however, looking forward to telling Ealasaid about the fate of her granddaughter.

As they neared the MacDonald settlement nestled in the mountains, to his surprise Graeme rode forward from the back of the line to join him. He'd only seen the Englishman a couple of times since he'd woken from his injury, and had thought the man to be keeping his distance.

Graeme reined in alongside him, and slowed his horse to match Alex's slow but steady pace.

"How are you faring?" he asked, nodding at the splinted leg, which stuck out from the horse's flank.

"Better than I thought. It's paining me, but it's bearable," Alex said. "You?"

Graeme grinned.

"I'm fine. I won't be making the ladies swoon any more, but I'm getting used to it now."

Alex looked at the older man's injury. One of the women had made him an eye patch which covered the worst of the sword cut, but even so, the wound extended for a few inches down his cheek, a raised angry welt.

"Did ye wash it wi' whisky?" Alex asked.

"Yes, I did, and I've never known pain like it. I've a fearful respect for your brother now. How he didn't kill Beth after she did that to him, I'll never know."

Alex started involuntarily. Apart from Iain, since Alex had been told of her death no one had mentioned Beth to him at all. There seemed to be an unspoken agreement in the clan not to mention either her or Duncan to him. He knew why; they were waiting for him to bring up the topic, which they'd then take as tacit permission to speak of them.

*But Graeme isna of the clan,* he reminded himself, *and he loved Beth as much as I did, although in a different way. He must be grieving something fierce, too.*

He looked across at Graeme, to find the older man scrutinising him with one shrewd grey eye.

"I miss her too, every minute," Graeme said. "But not speaking of her won't make us forget her." He nodded down the track to where the first of the MacDonald houses were coming into view. "And you might as well make a start now, because you'll have to tell her family soon, won't you?"

Alex looked ahead and shuddered again. He was dreading telling them, Ealasaid especially. They would certainly blame him, he thought, as he still blamed himself, in spite of Iain's words.

"Aye," he answered simply.

"Do you want me with you when you do?" Graeme asked unexpectedly.

Alex's first instinct was to say no, but then he realised that that was exactly what he wanted. He didn't want to do this alone, and who better to face it with than someone who'd loved Beth since she was born?

First, though, he had to meet with MacIain, and tell him the news. He was hopeful that the MacDonalds would join them, but after five minutes with the chief, he realised this was not to be.

"We've no weapons," the MacDonald chief said after listening to Alex's news and proposal.

Alex raised a sceptical eyebrow at that, and MacIain looked away.

"Aye, well, none to speak of," he amended. "I surrendered, Alex. We handed most of our weapons over to General Campbell. So did the Appin men."

"Campbell?" said Alex, stunned. "Ye surrendered tae a Campbell?"

"Aye," said Glencoe. "They're no' all the same. General Campbell is a fair man. I didna want to, but we're too few to hold out, Alex, and we live within a morning's march of Fort William, which is bristling wi' redcoats. Cumberland's already burnt Lovat's house to the ground and ravaged the Fraser lands, and his soldiers are pillaging far and wide. Charles just wants to go back to France. Cluny's hiding out, but the MacPhersons are surrendering. It's over, man. Ye can stay here the night, and I'll no hinder ye, but I canna come wi' ye. I'm sorry. It's over for me."

There was no point in arguing. The chief had made up his mind, and Alex couldn't blame him. They were a small clan, and they had lands and a chance to get through this relatively unscathed if they kept their heads down. It was different for the MacGregors; they had neither legal lands nor a name, and when you had nothing, then there was nothing to lose by fighting for more.

After eating dinner with MacIain he met up with Graeme, and, using his crutches, hobbled over to Ealasaid's cottage, where she lived with her great-nieces and nephews.

They were all waiting in the cottage, sitting on various stools round the central fire. Several candles had been lit in honour of their guest, and as a consequence when Graeme walked in the first thing he saw was a sea of white-blonde heads.

"Jesus Christ," he said in a choked voice.

Alex turned to him in time to see him wipe a tear from his good eye.

"I'm sorry, man," he said. "I should have warned ye, but I didna ken they'd all be here together."

In the corner of the room a bed had been made up for Alex, and he sank down gratefully onto it. His leg was throbbing.

Ealasaid was sitting on the one good chair, her hands resting in her lap. She looked at Alex, and nodded.

"So, she's gone then," she said quietly.

To his utter horror, Alex burst into tears. He hadn't cried since he'd been told of her death, not even in private, and he had expected to tell her family then to somehow console her distraught grandmother. The last thing he had expected was for her to tell him.

She was gone. It was the bleakness, the finality of the word that undid him. Because in that moment it hit him that Beth was, indeed, gone. He would never see her again, never touch her, never hear her voice, never smell her unique feminine scent. She was gone, and no matter how long he lived, he would never be able to tell her how much he loved her, how sorry he was that she'd died and he'd survived. Gone.

It was beyond bearing, and he knew that even if they were to rise again, and win, and James Stuart take the throne; if the MacGregors were to get their name back, and their lands, still he would never be whole again. Because she was gone.

To their credit they left him to cry, until finally, with a huge shuddering sob, he gained control of himself again and looked up at them through tear-drenched eyes.

Graeme was still standing by the door where he'd stopped on seeing the sea of silver-gilt, but now he came in and bowed to Ealasaid.

"*Feasgar math*," he said in heavily accented Gaelic. "*Tha mi toilichte ur coinneachadh.*"

"*Mo creach, tha Gàidhlig agad!*" she exclaimed.

"I don't remember much of it," Graeme continued in English. "Beth's mother taught me a little."

Ealasaid stared at the stranger, her eyes wide with shock.

"I'm sorry, *mo sheanmhair,*" Alex apologised. "This is Graeme. He was a friend of Beth's."

"I was her gardener," Graeme elaborated. "I was with the family when the master married Ann."

"You must stay," Ealasaid said immediately.

"No, I have a place with Alasdair and –" Graeme started.

"You must stay," she repeated. "Robert, ye'll sleep wi' your uncle the night." She turned back to the Englishman. "We have much to talk about, I think." She looked over at Alex. "If you can bear to do so, laddie."

Alex glanced at Graeme, who nodded imperceptibly.

"Aye, I can bear to do so," Alex said.

## CHAPTER THREE

Strangely, although the previous evening had been almost unbearably poignant, and he had found himself weeping again during the course of it, when they rode out the following morning Alex felt lighter, as though some of the weight of Beth's death had been lifted from his shoulders.

Not only had Ealasaid not blamed Alex for her granddaughter's death, she told him he'd done the right thing by allowing her to be with him.

"For she'd have followed ye anyway, and if it had been you to die instead of her, she'd no' have regretted being with ye until the last second, would she?"

"No," Alex agreed. "She tellt me that herself."

"Well then, why should you regret her doing as she wished? Better ye were together for as long as ye could be. At least ye had that. Never regret what ye canna change, laddie. I learnt that lesson the hard way. Now ye must carry on, as she'd wish ye to."

He had lain awake last night, thinking about it. The old woman was right. Iain was right too. He had to stop blaming himself. Beth would not want it so. And so he would stop. Somehow he would stop.

The MacGregors reached the huts sheltered by the forest on Loch Arkaig on the fourteenth of May, to find a number of chiefs still present, including Lord Lovat the Fraser chief, who due to age and infirmity had been carried there by his clansmen, the Cameron chief Lochiel, Gordon of Glenbucket and numerous others who had either survived Culloden or had not managed to get there in time. Murray of Broughton, former secretary to Prince

Charles was also there, still looking very pale and wasted from the illness which had kept him away from Culloden.

He had written out a plan of action, which Alex now read. Certainly if all the clans mentioned in the plan did indeed rise and join together, with the supplies they now had they could mount a summer campaign that would keep Cumberland and his troops too occupied to ravage the Highlands as they were now doing. In that case it was feasible that the clans which had previously been loyal to the Hanoverians, but which were nevertheless suffering Cumberland's reprisals, would join the Jacobites. And if Prince Charles had escaped to France as was rumoured, news that the clans were still fighting and that support for the Stuarts was growing, coupled with Charles' charismatic entreaties, might well persuade King Louis to send the much-needed troops and arms to mount a more successful campaign.

That was a lot of 'ifs', but there seemed no other option but to continue fighting. The duke had made it very clear that the clans were not going to be allowed to go home and continue with their normal lives, and he showed no signs of keeping his word about allowing those who surrendered to go free. No, to fight on was not only the honourable choice, but the only possible one for him. And if you were going to fight, you had to take a positive view.

Although Alex was happy to see so many chiefs willing to continue the rebellion, he distrusted the Fraser chief profoundly and made his misgivings clear to Lochiel once they were alone.

"How can ye trust him, Donald?" he asked. The others had retired for the night, but Broughton, the Cameron chief and Alex, sharing a hut, had slept fitfully due to the pain of their injuries and illness, and so at 3am, all of them having lain awake for a time, Alex lit a candle and retrieved a bottle of brandy from the corner press, which they shared between them while waiting for the dawn to break.

"I'd trust the serpent in Eden before I'd trust Lovat," Broughton said unequivocally. "I canna stand the man."

"His house and lands are burnt," Donald Cameron replied. "He has nothing left to lose now."

"He sat on the fence for the whole of the campaign," Alex reminded him. "He wouldna put anything in writing. He didna raise the clan until last December, and only then because he thought we were going to win. And even then he sent his son out and stayed at home himself, so that if it all went awry, he could say he hadna agreed to send the clan out at all!"

"Aye, well, it was to no avail," Lochiel pointed out. "He's with us now, and we need everyone we can get if we're to continue the fight. The Frasers are a powerful clan."

Alex couldn't argue with this, so stayed silent. So did Broughton, although the expression on his face spoke volumes.

"The Elector's son sent me a message, offering me very favourable terms if I were to surrender," Lochiel suddenly inserted into the pause.

Alex, in the act of refilling his glass, almost dropped the bottle.

"What?" he cried. "What terms?"

Lochiel made a dismissive gesture with his hand.

"It doesna signify," he said. "I rejected them, of course. Even if I trusted him to hold to them, which I dinna, I would never surrender. The French have already sent us enough money and provisions to keep us fighting till the autumn, and I believe that if we make a spirited defence, they'll send us more. But even if it came down to me alone against the whole of Cumberland's army, I would still go down fighting. How could I do otherwise, and hold my head up?"

"Aye," said Alex. "It shows how little William kens of honour, if he could believe ye'd surrender to him."

"It wasna just me," Lochiel added. "Glencarnaig was offered terms too. I thought ye'd have known that, ye being of the MacGregors yourself."

"I've been…ailing," Alex said, not wanting to discuss his emotional issues with the Cameron chief. "What did he offer Glencarnaig, then?"

"He offered to raise the proscription on the MacGregors."

Alex was stunned. This was what they had been fighting for for over a hundred years. The right to use their own name openly, to have recourse to the law, to own property…the list was endless. It was a powerful temptation.

"What did Glencarnaig reply?"

"He said, 'we choose rather to risk our lives and fortunes, and die with the characters of honest men, than live in infamy and hand down disgrace to our posterity'."

Alex let out a breath that he hadn't realised he'd been holding, and took a huge gulp of brandy straight out of the bottle.

"Would ye have answered differently?" Lochiel asked softly.

"Christ, no!" Alex responded immediately. "Glencarnaig had the right of it. There's nae purpose to having the right to use a traitor's name."

Lochiel smiled.

"It warms my heart to see ye, Donald," Alex said. "For a while we thought you were dead."

"Aye, I canna tell ye how it felt to be lying on the field helpless, watching my clansmen cut to pieces around me, and me unable to do anything. I wanted to die myself at that moment. But I didna, and neither did you, and now we live to fight on.

"So, then," he continued, "ye've read John's plan, and it's a fair one. We've to gather those we can, and we march to my house at Achnacarry in a week. We meet Lochgarry's men there. They're out now keeping a watch on Fort Augustus to see what Cumberland's forces are doing. Then we'll cross the Lochy and join wi' Keppoch, then on to Badenoch to meet the Frasers, MacIntoshes and MacPhersons. I've sent a despatch to the rest of the MacGregors to march to Rannoch and join others there. And so we rise again!"

They clinked glasses in a toast to King James. Better to die fighting to the end than surrender and die of shame.

* * *

## London, mid May

After standing uncertainly in the doorway of the shop for a few minutes, Anne Cunningham finally entered.

"I wondered if you had any perfume," she ventured. "I am going to a soiree this evening, and would like something fresh and summery to complement my new outfit."

Sarah finished pinning a curl in place on Mrs Warren's head and then gestured to a table in the corner of the room on which resided a number of porcelain bottles.

"There is a selection of the perfumed waters that I have, Mrs Cunningham," Sarah said. "Rose, lilac, jasmine, orange blossom and violet among others. I also have the same fragrances in a solid version, if you wish to wear it in a pendant or pomade. Would you like to try some? I have almost finished Mrs Warren's hair, and then I can give you my exclusive attention."

Anne moved over to the table, desultorily picking up bottles, taking out the stoppers and sniffing them before putting them down again. Sarah watched her out of the corner of her eye as she liberally sprinkled powder over her client's hair.

"There!" Sarah said. "Perfect!" She held a hand mirror up so Mrs Warren could see the finished confection.

"Thank you! Miss Browne, you really are a wonder! I cannot tell you how much you were missed while you were away. We feared you would never return," her delighted customer enthused.

"My home is here," Sarah reassured her. "I had to visit my family on a matter of urgency, but now I am back I do not envisage leaving again.

"Now, Mrs Cunningham," she continued, as she helped Mrs Warren on with her cloak, "I can see that the scents I have on display do not please you. But I do have another that you may like. I do not put it on display, as I must warn you it is very expensive. But it will certainly turn heads. You will be the talk of the company if you wear it, I assure you. If you would just care to take a seat, I will fetch it for you."

Anne took a seat while Sarah said goodbye to her client.

"What's wrong, Anne?" she said in quite a different voice the moment the door was closed.

Anne, surprised by the sudden change in demeanour, jumped. "Nothing!" she said.

"You haven't come here for perfume though, have you?" Sarah said. "You have something to tell me. Is Richard back?"

"No!" Anne cried, leaping from the chair. "No. I really do want some perfume, but I…" She paused.

Sarah waited for Anne to pluck up her courage.

"Can I see her?" she asked finally. "Would you mind terribly?"

Sarah smiled. "Why would I mind? She's asleep right now, but of course you can see her if you want to. And you can try the perfume too."

She took Anne into her small but cosy living room. A cheerful fire burned in the hearth, on either side of which were comfortable padded chairs. She motioned Anne to sit in one and handed her a small flower-painted porcelain bottle, inviting her to take the stopper out and smell the contents.

She bustled around setting out tea things. She took a tea-caddy out of a small dresser and ladled two spoons of the expensive leaves into a teapot. Then she lifted the kettle, which was suspended from a hook over the fire, and poured the water onto the leaves.

"There," she said. "It won't be long." It was quite nice to have someone round for tea. Since Beth had left, Sarah rarely had visitors. She kept to herself, and told herself she preferred it that way. After a long day on her feet exchanging small talk with customers, and, now having established a reputation for discretion, often listening as they unburdened themselves to her too, most of the time she did want to be alone in the evening. But not always. And in her lonely times, of which she'd had quite a few lately, she missed Beth terribly.

Anne Cunningham was no substitute for Beth, of course, but she was Beth's relation by marriage; they had Richard in common, although that was not a positive thing. But it had brought them together in a strange kind of sisterhood.

Anne unstoppered the bottle and inhaled delicately. Then deeper.

"Oh!" she exclaimed. "This is exquisite! I have never smelt anything like it before!"

"No, I'm sure you haven't," Sarah said. "It's very expensive. That's why I don't keep it in the shop. Most of my clients can't afford it."

"Oh," Anne replied, disappointed. "I'm sure I won't be able to afford it either, then. My allowance from Richard is very small. What is its name?"

"Aqua Melis," Sarah answered. "It contains a lot of expensive spices and flower oils and waters, and it takes a long time to combine all the ingredients exactly."

"Did you make it yourself?" Anne asked admiringly.

"No." Sarah laughed. "I make a lot of my own paints and pomades, but the art of making perfume is a skill all of its own, and takes years to learn. No, I bought it." *From a free trader.* She didn't add that, knowing Anne would be shocked even to be handling illicit goods. She was changing, but was still easily upset.

"If you pour the tea, I'll fetch her," she said, disappearing through a doorway into her small bedroom. She returned a moment later with a tiny, neatly wrapped bundle, which she handed to Anne.

All that could be seen of the sleeping infant was her head, which was crowned with a fuzz of dark hair. She had tiny, perfectly shaped eyebrows, and enormously long lashes, which fluttered against her cheek as she slept. Anne stared in awe at the precious bundle for a long moment, then tenderly caressed the petal-soft cheek with one finger. The tiny rosebud mouth puckered for an instant, and then the baby sighed and relaxed back into sleep.

"Oh, but she is beautiful," Anne whispered reverently. "What is her name?"

"Mary," Sarah said.

"I am so sorry about your sister," Anne said softly, so as not to disturb the child. "Does Mary resemble her?"

"It's a little soon to tell," Sarah replied, "but no, I think she takes after her father."

"What a rogue he must be, to disown such a beautiful child," Anne said, before blushing furiously. "Oh! I did not mean to offend."

"No, you haven't offended me," Sarah said. "He hasn't disowned her. He doesn't know about her. My sister told me that their relationship was very brief, and he was called away on business before she even knew she was with child. She has not…had not heard from him since."

"Oh, you poor creature!" Anne cried.

Sarah had her back to Anne, as she'd gone to the dresser to get some sugar, and had thought her to be addressing Mary, but when she turned back Anne was looking at her, her eyes full of tears.

"I am fine," Sarah said.

"No, you are not," Anne said. "Your terrible loss has clearly taken a toll on you. You have lost weight, and you look very tired. And now you have to work all day, and take care of your niece. And you have not had time to grieve for the death of your dear sister. I will make you a tonic and send it over tomorrow. Or you can come and stay with me if you wish, until you have recovered your strength."

"You're very kind, but I would rather keep busy. And Mary is a very placid baby. She rarely wakes me during the night. Once we knew my sister wasn't going to live, I promised her I would take care of the child. It's a great comfort to fulfil her dying wish."

"Indeed, she was very lucky to have you, especially as you say your father is so rigid in his beliefs," Anne said.

Sarah's mouth twisted.

"Yes. We will not be seeing him ever again," she said with feeling. "He's dead to me."

Anne blushed, aware from the bitter expression on Sarah's face that she was not helping. She looked down at the child again.

"She will grow to be a beautiful child, I am sure," she said. "When she is a little older, I will bring Georgie to see her. Maybe they will be married when they grow up!"

"I hardly think Lord Winter will agree to his noble godson marrying the bastard child of a shopkeeper's sister," Sarah pointed out. "I'm sorry," she added, seeing the distraught look on Anne's face. She had not been trying to offend. *She is so innocent in the ways of the world*, Sarah thought. *God help her when Richard comes home*.

"Richard has written," Anne said, as if reading Sarah's mind. Then she blushed again, clearly realising that she had just committed another faux pas.

"Here," Sarah said. "Let me put her back to bed. You're welcome to visit us any time you wish." She whisked the child away and went into the bedroom, giving both herself and Anne a moment to compose themselves.

Her first urge when she came back into the living room was to change the subject, but she needed to know what Richard had written.

She poured more tea for them.

"So, are you living back in London now, or are you visiting from Lady Harriet's?" Sarah asked.

"I could not impose on Harriet any longer," Anne said. "Particularly now George is trying to walk. She is not over fond of children and I fear that once he begins to run around she will find him quite tiresome. I came home two weeks ago. Philippa and Oliver are staying though, so I am not lonely," she added.

"Was the letter waiting for you when you got home?" Sarah asked.

"The letter? Oh! No, it arrived two days ago, from North Britain," she said, clearly surprised that Sarah had brought the subject up again.

Sarah waited until it became clear Anne was not going to volunteer any more information without being prompted.

"What did he have to say?" she asked finally.

"It was only a short note," Anne replied. "He wrote that he will be in Scotland for some time yet, as he is engaged in the pacification of the Highlands on behalf of His Royal Highness. But as soon as he can, he will return to England. He said that he is anxious to talk about our future," she finished in a very small voice.

Sarah nodded, half to herself. So he would not be back very soon, at least. She could relax for a little longer.

"And do you intend to be here when he comes back to 'talk' about your future?" Sarah asked.

To her surprise, Anne began to weep.

"Oh! Oh, I am so sorry," she cried. She fumbled in her reticule and produced a scrap of lace with which she attempted to stem the flow of tears. "Truly, I do not know what I am going to do," she said miserably once she had brought her sobs under control. "Harriet and Philippa say I should leave him, but if I did it would cause a terrible scandal. I cannot imagine what Uncle Bartholomew and Aunt Wilhelmina would say."

"Does it matter what they say?" Sarah asked.

Anne looked up in shock.

"Yes, of course it does! I will be ostracised from society. It is a terrible thing to leave one's husband. I am sure no one will ever speak to me again if I do!"

"Caroline will speak to you," Sarah pointed out. "And Lady Harriet and Philippa will, as well. And they are friendly with the Prince of Wales. From what Beth told me about him, he would not shun you for leaving a vicious brute. And Prince Frederick will be King one day."

Anne dried her eyes, blew her nose delicately, and considered this.

"You are right," she said. "I had not thought of it in that way.

How clever you are. But, you know, Richard is my husband, and maybe he has had time to think while he has been away, to regret what he has done. I feel I should give him a chance to apologise and to make amends." She looked up apprehensively at Sarah.

*If he comes here to 'apologise' to me, it'll be the last thing he ever does*, Sarah thought. True to her promise, Caroline had taught her how to use a pistol, and she kept it, primed and ready to fire, behind her counter. If he ever threatened her again she would blow his brains all over her shop.

"You are disappointed in me," Anne said sadly, interrupting Sarah's dark thoughts. Really, she was such a sweet, innocent woman. She deserved a gentle, caring husband, not a vicious evil bastard who enjoyed inflicting pain. Very few society women would care if they offended someone of Sarah's social standing. Yes, they confided in her when she was making them beautiful, but as a person she was of no more significance to them than the night-soil men or the link boys. Beth had been different, but she was rare.

And this plain, red-eyed unhappy woman who had married so disastrously into the Cunningham family was another. Sarah was suddenly filled with a fierce protectiveness towards her. On impulse she reached forward and grasped Anne's hands.

"Anne," she said urgently. "Richard will not change. There is something wrong with him, and there always has been. Beth told me that he was cruel even as a child. I do not think he wishes to apologise, to you or me. You should leave him, and to hell with your aunt and uncle!"

Anne's eyes widened in shock.

"I'm sorry," Sarah amended. "I'm speaking out of turn because I'm afraid for you. But if you insist on seeing him, I beg you, do not see him alone, no matter what he wants. And on no account let him near George William. And I would ask a favour of you."

"Of course," Anne said.

"As soon as you know when he will arrive in London, will you send a message to me straight away?"

"Yes, if you wish, of course."

"Thank you. Then at least I'll be prepared, if he visits me again." She squeezed Anne's hands, then released them and sat down.

*And in the meantime, let us hope he tries to pacify the wrong Highlander*, she thought, *and gets himself cut to pieces.*

\* \* \*

## Scotland, 20th May, 1746

By the time Lochiel had assembled his clansmen, now greatly diminished since Culloden and numbering some four hundred men, it was noon and the sun, although hidden behind thick cloud cover, was high in the sky when they began their march east along the shores of Loch Arkaig towards Achnacarry Castle, built by Lochiel's grandfather ninety years earlier.

Alex MacGregor and Donald Cameron both rode, men walking beside their horses in case they should need assistance due to their injuries. Alex had spent the intervening week learning to walk on crutches and building his upper body muscles with the aid of numerous stones of different shapes and sizes. Now he sat erect and proud on his horse, glad to be doing something worthwhile again, although his leg was still paining him and he knew he was not ready to fight yet.

Lochiel's agony was written on his face; he was deathly pale, and his mouth was compressed in a tight line. Alex wondered how the Cameron chief was managing to keep his seat at all with both legs broken, and wanted to suggest that he might be more comfortable if he was carried by his men, as Lord Lovat, now on his way back home to raise the Frasers had been, but he didn't want to offend him so he kept silent. It was but a short distance from the loch to Achnacarry, although it took them longer than normal because the ground was waterlogged due to weeks of heavy rain.

Once arrived, they settled in to wait for Lochgarry's men to join them. Lochiel's house, large and constructed entirely of fir planks, was impressive, masculine and homely, if a little sparsely furnished. The clansmen set up camp. Due to the frequent and heavy rain showers, as many as possible were accommodated in the house and outbuildings, while the unfortunate ones bivouacked in the landscaped gardens among the numerous fruit trees. Alex did not hide his appreciation for either the house, the gardens or the comfort of the sofa he lay on whilst accepting a glass of fine claret.

"It's no' normally as bare as this," Lochiel explained apologetically, indicating the bare walls and floors. "We feared reprisals, so most of our more portable furnishings have been moved to a safer place."

"Will any place in the Highlands be safe, if Cumberland gets his way?" Alex asked.

"No. That's why we have to fight on. If nothing else, we can keep him busy while Prince Charlie makes his escape, and until the French come."

"Do ye really think the French will come now?" Alex asked. He massaged his leg gingerly. It was improving. He could not put weight on it yet, but it was itching something fierce, which was a good sign.

"I have to believe that," Lochiel replied. "For without them we canna win this fight. What choice do we have now? I'm much heartened by the provisions they sent us. We can hold out until help arrives, if everyone who's pledged to fight on does. Lochgarry should be here by now," he added, a frown crossing his handsome features.

"Do ye think he's surrendered?" Alex asked.

"Christ, I hope not. His men are watching the troop movements from Fort Augustus so we'll be warned if they move against us. I've no doubt they know we're moving. I canna understand why anyone would voluntarily surrender, though, after what happened to the Grants."

This was a good point. After Culloden, eighty-one men of Clan Grant had surrendered to Cumberland on the advice of their chief, expecting to give up their arms and be allowed to return to their homes in Glenmoriston and Glen Urquhart. Instead they had been taken prisoner and marched down to the quay at Inverness, where they were now being kept in horrific conditions on board one of the transport ships.

"In a way, Cumberland did us a favour by that, though," Lochiel added. "A lot of men who were thinking to surrender changed their minds after that."

Even so, Lochgarry did not appear either that evening or the next day, with the result that as Lochiel, Alex, John Murray of Broughton and numerous other officers sat down to dinner, Cameron men were sent out to watch the hills and the military road, in case of troop movements.

It was as they were finishing dinner that a visitor was announced, a young lieutenant by the name of Iain MacDonell, who brought money and dispatches for Murray, and the unwelcome news that on the way he had met his cousin Barrisdale, who had told him that both he and Lochgarry were getting their men together in preparation to see what terms of surrender they could obtain from Cumberland.

Lochiel received the young man with the utmost courtesy, offering him a meal and a bed for the night which he gratefully accepted, but once the lieutenant had left, he exploded with rage.

"The bastard!" he roared. "He would surrender without even sending word to me, leaving us open to attack from Fort William! The fool, does he really think that the Elector's son will treat him kindly? We see every day what he thinks of Highlanders! Well," he continued, "he has chosen his path, God help him, and I have chosen mine. Tomorrow we cross the Lochy and join with Keppoch, and then on to Badenoch. Let us retire, gentlemen, and get what sleep we may. It may be long before we enjoy such comfortable quarters again."

\* \* \*

## Fort Augustus, May 1746

Colonel Mark Hutchinson stood smartly to attention in front of his Commander-in-Chief, waiting for him to finish perusing the intelligence report he had just delivered from Lord Loudoun, who had been sent to Loch Lochy to reconnoitre and send back news of the rumoured rebel insurgency in the area.

Some minutes passed, during which the Duke of Cumberland read and reread the missive, then sat staring out of the tiny window of his accommodations against which the rain drove unceasingly, clearly deep in thought. Near one corner of the room a peat fire gave out a little heat and a large amount of smoke which drifted lazily upward to the roof space.

Colonel Hutchinson spent those minutes heartily wishing he had chosen to stand to attention a few inches further to the left of where he now was, where he would have avoided the steady trickle of icy water that was dripping from a leak in the roof to land with unerring accuracy on the back of his neck. He resisted the natural urge to step to the side, which would be an unforgivable breach of military etiquette, and occupied his time wishing all Scots, including both the rebels who did not know when they were beaten and the loyal soldiers who had built this ridiculous hut for the duke to live in, in the deepest regions of hell.

After three miserable days of riding round this godforsaken country in the pouring rain, he had finally returned to Fort Augustus, had divested himself of his sodden uniform, briskly dried himself off, and with a sigh of bliss had donned dry clothes before delivering his missive to the duke. If he had to stand here much longer, however, this uniform would be as wet as the one still lying on the floor of his quarters. He only possessed two uniforms.

Finally the duke finished contemplating and glanced across at the colonel, then up at the roof.

"At ease, Colonel," he said. Colonel Hutchinson relaxed his shoulders and moved slightly to the left, allowing the rain to drip onto the dirt floor. Cumberland glanced up at the roof of his office again and sighed.

"Get someone to put a bucket or some such thing under that when you leave, will you? The floor will be awash otherwise."

Colonel Hutchinson examined the roof with some interest. From the outside the duke's 'apartment' resembled nothing more than a huge heap of haphazardly-piled turf and branches, at the bottom of which could be seen a low turf wall, in which was set a small window and a low door, through which the colonel, although not a tall man, had had to duck to enter the premises. From inside though, he could see that the roof had been constructed with some skill, considering the materials to hand. The branches had been placed at regular intervals, and had been interlaced to make a sturdy base on top of which sods of turf and heather had been placed to seal the roof.

To almost seal the roof. He supposed that given more time and variety of materials, the Highland regiment would have been able to construct a completely weatherproof house, but as it was they had only been informed two days before that the duke was moving to Fort Augustus, which had been burnt down by the rebels two months previously. Of course the officers had commandeered the least damaged areas of the fort, while the common soldiers had shifted for themselves and had cobbled together temporary shelters in the ruined barracks, but the loyalist Highlanders had pulled out all the stops to construct a traditional Highland dwelling for their victorious prince.

Colonel Hutchinson shivered and glanced back at his commander, who looked as though he was chilled to the bone as well. His nose was red, and in spite of his podginess, his face had a pinched look to it.

"I am sure that more…er…comfortable accommodations could be found for you, Your Highness," the colonel ventured. Indeed his own accommodations, though somewhat cramped, were warm and dry at least. "Would you like me to enquire for you?"

"God, no, man," the duke barked. "The men went to an enormous effort to collect together all the materials and build this for me, and all in this horrendous weather. It was a sign of the esteem they hold me in, and I would not insult them by rejecting their kind gesture. I am deeply touched by it. And, being practical, we need to keep the good opinion of the loyal Highlanders, Colonel. God knows, they are few enough."

"Yet the majority of the Highlanders did not come out for the Young Pretender, Your Highness," Hutchinson commented.

"True. But those who did not come out for Charles did not come out for my father either," reasoned Cumberland, "which is why Cope lost at Prestonpans. If all those who had declared themselves loyal to the crown had risen for us then, the rebellion would never have got off the ground. I don't trust the Highlanders, loyal or not. They'll change their allegiance on a sixpence, and I won't risk that at the moment, even if I catch pneumonia in the process. They know the territory, and we need that knowledge to nip this new rising in the bud. Damn Lochiel and that snake Lovat!"

"The Fraser lands have been burnt, and Lovat's house razed to the ground," Hutchinson said. He refrained from saying that that was probably the reason that the Fraser chief had finally committed unequivocally to the Stuart cause, although most of his clan had come out for Charles last December, under Lovat's son.

"Yes, and I intend to do the same and more to the Camerons. They started this whole thing, but by God I will finish it, and now. I will not give them the chance to rise again! I was told there were three thousand of them at Achnacarry, but Loudoun seems to think there are only about six hundred, which is heartening. But the MacPhersons are ready to rise again, I've been told, and most of the Frasers, and no doubt the damned MacGregors will come out too. We must strike before they can and see if we can take Lochiel in the process. That would be a mighty blow against the Jacobite scum. Is Charles with them?"

"No, Your Highness. It is believed that he may have sailed to France on the ships that anchored in Loch nan Uamh to drop supplies for the rebels. But we have no certain news of that as yet."

"Very well, then. Sit down, Colonel. You can scribe for me. This is what we shall do."

The colonel pulled up a chair and prepared his writing materials, while the duke poured them both a brandy and located a map of the area, which he unrolled on the table, placing the decanter on one end to stop it rolling up again.

"Now, as you know, Loudoun is here, waiting at the head of Loch Oich with two thousand men for my orders." He indicated with a fat finger a spot on the map a little to the north of where the Camerons were currently massed. "Munro and Howard have another six hundred men heading along Loch Lochy. On Saturday morning they will ford the river near Moy and attack the rebels from the south, while at the same time Loudoun will come down here," he pointed to a gap between Loch Arkaig and Loch Lochy, "from the north to take Achnacarry and cut off any retreat. In this way, we will be able to capture Lochiel, who is severely wounded and therefore unable to travel at speed."

"It is rumoured that many of the Camerons would surrender their arms if Lochiel was captured," Colonel Hutchinson supplied.

"I have heard that rumour, although I think the only way to ensure the Camerons do not rise again is to wipe them out, as far as is possible. They have been staunchly for the Stuarts since '89. They may submit now and hand in some rusty old swords when we give them no alternative, but I have no doubt they'll be causing trouble again the minute my back is turned. Every damn one of them is false, and has more than one set of arms, of that I have no doubt." The duke sat back in his chair and took a sip of his brandy. "I have no wish to spend any more time than is absolutely necessary in this savage place. I must return to Flanders as soon as possible, and have no time to wait around for these traitors to see reason in their own time. I intend to hit hard, and make an example of this clan. There is no surer way to show the Jacobites that any further insurrection will be dealt with immediately and efficiently."

"You mean to kill all six hundred rebels, if possible?"

"Of course."

"And what of the common people, Your Highness?"

"In my view there *are* no common people. They are all rebels, to a man. You will take back my instructions that all their houses are to be destroyed and their cattle brought to the fort."

The colonel glanced out of the window. It had been raining for days, and the nights were bitterly cold.

"What of the women and children, Your Highness? They will die without food and shelter."

Cumberland looked at him askance, and the colonel wished he had thought before speaking his mind.

"The men should have thought about that before they left their families to fight for a usurper. And in any case, the women are as bad as the men. Look at Jenny Cameron and Lady Mackintosh, who brought their clans out while their husbands were fighting for us! We cannot be soft when dealing with these people, Colonel. They have no notion of mercy and honour. They see it only as weakness. Soon they will be too busy trying to feed themselves to think of rebelling again. And then we can leave this place and get back to civilisation. I am sure you want that, sir, and your men too."

Colonel Hutchinson agreed that that was indeed what he wanted and set to work to write out the duke's orders.

An hour later he was back in his room. A cosy fire burned in the hearth, and his wet uniform had been hung up to dry to one side of it. His sergeant had procured a bottle of wine and had cooked some mutton chops for him. The duke had honoured him by confiding his opinions to him and by entrusting him not only to write them out, but deliver them to Lord Loudoun as well. Colonel Hutchinson was aware that he should be feeling very happy right now.

Colonel Hutchinson was not feeling very happy right now.

It was true that once he had eaten his mutton chops and drunk his bottle of wine he would have to go out in the abysmal weather to deliver the Duke of Cumberland's orders to Lord Loudoun, although he now had the use of an oilcloth coat to help keep the rain out. But it was not this that was making him unhappy.

The truth was that he was far from happy to have the job of delivering orders sanctioning the murder of innocent people, especially of women and children, even if they *were* on behalf of a royal prince. In fact if anyone *but* the prince had asked him to deliver such a message, he would have done his utmost to avoid the task. The colonel had hoped that Prince William would heed the advice of Lord Culloden, who, as well as being unfailingly loyal to the Hanoverians, knew the Highland mentality better than anyone, and who had strongly counselled against draconian measures being adopted against the ordinary people, saying that rather than subduing their spirit, they were likely to be inspired to rise again for the Stuarts, in the spirit of revenge.

The Highlanders were a vengeful people, everyone knew that. And they could hold a grudge for centuries.

However, the duke thought he knew better, and it was not for the likes of Colonel Hutchinson to question his orders, only to obey them.

He sighed. He had not joined the army to murder innocent peasants and watch as their homes were burnt and their wives and children stripped and left to die of cold or hunger. He had joined the army to fight for his country, and to him that meant fighting enemy soldiers on a battlefield. It was true that soldiers sometimes committed indiscretions during and directly after a battle, when their blood was up. While regrettable and to be discouraged, the colonel was a realist, and understood that you could not expect a man fired up to a killing rage to just switch it off at a moment's notice.

But what he was witnessing now was something else; it was the cold-blooded murder of unarmed men, of the old and feeble;

it was the rape of innocent women and girls, and of leaving them to almost certain death by starvation. This was not a task for him. This was a task for arrogant bullies like General Henry Hawley, and Captains John Fergusson, Caroline Scott and Richard Cunningham, who enjoyed brutalising women and children.

For the first time since he had joined the army thirty years before at the age of sixteen, he considered resigning his commission. It might be pleasant to settle down, marry, maybe have a few children. Perhaps he would, soon.

But not yet. He had a job to do. He had thought that job was to put down a rebellion, but now he realised that it was to curb the excesses of the more inhuman of his men. He could do nothing about Hawley, Fergusson or Scott, none of whom were under his command. But he could, and fully intended, to keep an eye on Cunningham, who was enjoying himself immensely in the current punitive environment. He had already heard several unsavoury rumours about the man's treatment of the local women in particular, but nothing substantial enough for him to address. Cunningham's men were mortally afraid of him, which did not help matters. In any case, in view of the orders he was now preparing to deliver, he doubted that he would be able to bring a case against Cunningham for rape and torture, even were he to have firm evidence.

All he could do for now was watch and ensure as little brutality as possible took place on his watch. But the moment an opportunity presented itself for him to be rid of Captain Cunningham, he intended to take full advantage of it.

\* \* \*

## Achnacarry, Saturday 22nd May

Roused from a deep slumber by the sound of an urgent knocking on the door, Alex at first had no idea where he was. This was so unusual for him that he felt an unaccustomed panic clutch at his chest. He sat up, heart banging, then felt the pain start up in his leg, and suddenly his mind cleared and he knew he was at Lochiel's, that he had just had his first deep sleep since regaining consciousness after Culloden, and that it was still dark, so must be very early in the morning.

"Come in," Lochiel's voice sounded in the darkness. There was the sound of steel on flint, and then a flare of light as he lit a candle from the tinder. The flame flickered as the door opened, casting wild shadows round the room, then a Cameron clansman entered, holding a candle of his own. His kilt and shirt were sodden, and his blue bonnet, heavy with water, drooped over one eye. The man put his candle down on the table, pulled his bonnet off impatiently, wrung it out without regard for the polished wooden flooring, and put it back on. This lack of regard for his chief's property told both Lochiel and Alex that the news was certainly worth waking them up for.

"I'm sorry to wake you, my lord," the clansman said, "but there's a large body of troops moving along Loch Lochy in this direction. I thought ye'd want to know straight away."

Lochiel pulled himself further up in the bed. Alex swung his good leg out of bed and used his hands to move his splinted leg across to join the other one. Then he reached for his shirt.

"Which side of the loch are they on?" Lochiel asked.

"The south. We lost sight of them just before Letterfinlay due to the fog and rain, but they're doing a deal of complaining about the weather and the state of the ground even though they're on the road."

"D'ye think they're heading for Fort William?"

"Aye, it's possible, although ye'd no' expect them to be moving at dead of night in this rain," the man replied.

"What time is it?" Alex asked. He was struggling to don his plaid, and wishing he hadn't taken it off the night before. He hadn't expected to have to dress hurriedly this morning.

"About four," said the Highlander.

Lochiel thought for a minute.

"It's verra likely that they're making for Fort William to join wi' Argyll's Campbells," he said. "I dinna want to wake the men for a false alarm. How many others are out there watching, Jamie?"

"About ten or so. I'll head back out myself," Jamie offered.

"No, away and dry yourself a bit and get something tae eat. Come and tell me immediately when there's more news of their route."

The man nodded, picked up his candle and left the room,

leaving a trail of rainwater behind him.

"Are ye going to try to sleep some more, Donald?" Alex asked. He was wide awake now. He'd use the time to do a few exercises.

Lochiel rubbed his hand across his face and yawned.

"No," he said. "It'll take me a while to dress. I'll at least try to do what I can for myself. I hate that I have to be carried everywhere like a wee bairn."

Alex smiled in empathy.

"Aye, well, it'll no' be for long, if we're careful. Are ye healing well? No redness or fever?"

Lochiel shook his head.

"No, the wounds are closing well, and the pain is more tolerable. But it drains the spirit, ye ken?"

"Aye," Alex said simply, feeling honoured to be the recipient of such a confidence, aware that the Cameron chief would have died rather than admit that to anyone else, and was only telling him because he was also injured and would understand, and because he trusted Alex not to speak of it outside this room.

With the aid of his crutches Alex managed to make his way to the hearth and get a fire going, then they both finished dressing and waited for others to awaken.

By the time the second scout returned with the news that the troops were most definitely not heading to Fort William but had left the military road and clearly intended to cross the River Lochy, the sun had risen and a lot of the men were up and breakfasting.

Those who weren't were rudely awakened by the pipers playing *Cogadh no sìth,* or War or Peace, which alerted everyone to the fact that an attack was imminent. Within minutes they were battle-ready and assembled in the grounds of Achnacarry, awaiting instructions.

Lochiel, Alex and Broughton had already conferred, and Lochiel instructed the men to head for the River Lochy as quickly as they could and see if they could stop the redcoats crossing, then watched as the clansmen, fired up to do battle, ran off, both chiefs feeling frustrated and ashamed that they could not charge at the head of their men as they wanted to.

They sat by the window and listened until the skirl of the pipes faded away in the distance, then sat a little longer in silence as the rain slowly eased to a thin drizzle and then stopped, although the clouds were still dark and heavy with the promise of more rain to come.

"I understand now," Alex murmured to himself, only realising he'd spoken the words aloud when Lochiel asked him what he understood.

"When we were leaving to fight Cope at Prestonpans, it was the first battle where Beth had been with me, and she asked me how to cope wi' waiting for the men to come home. She was always one for action, hated waiting for anything. I said I hadna a clue. I was impatient tae fight, and didna think overmuch about what she was going through.

"We've been here maybe an hour now, and I feel I'm losing my mind waiting for news. She and the other women had to wait four days to find out if we'd won. I ken now how she felt."

"Ye miss her verra much," Lochiel said softly.

"Aye," Alex said. "Aye, I do. At times it hurts more than the pain of my leg, just in a different way."

"It'll get easier wi' time," Lochiel replied.

"So they tell me," he said. But the grief showed no sign of abating; it was just that he was learning how to live with it now, instead of giving in to it.

He *did* understand Beth's impatience now. He also truly understood for the first time Duncan's grief at the loss of Màiri, Kenneth's grief at the betrayal of Jeannie, and Iain's for the death of Maggie. And he understood now that if you truly found your soulmate, the pain of their loss never went away; it became a part of you, which you carried with you to the grave. He did not believe the burden became lighter with time. You just learned how to bear the weight of it.

A short while later Angus returned, streaking across the grounds like lightning. He crashed through the door then stopped when he saw them, his chest heaving as he fought for breath.

"It isna any good," he gasped. "There's too many o' them. And no' just redcoats. Munro of Culcairn's clansmen are there too. We havena a hope against so many. We started to retreat, but they sent me ahead to tell ye, to find out what ye want us to do." He was looking at Alex as he spoke, but as the vast majority of the men were Camerons, Alex waited for Lochiel to speak.

"We've lost enough good men already fighting a battle we couldna win," he said after a moment. "We must retreat, I think. We'll go to Loch Arkaig, where we can get a good view of the country and see what they intend. Better to save our men now, until we can join with Keppoch and the MacPhersons, and then we can give them a proper fight."

Angus listened, then glanced to Alex, who nodded his head; and then he was off again, running across the grounds at full speed to take the news back to the clansmen. Both men watched him with envy.

"We'll be back to full strength soon enough," Alex said.

"You will be," Lochiel said. "I'm no' so sure about myself. I've twenty years on you."

"You will, man. Ye're in fine health otherwise. I've seen men of sixty injured and recover. And ye're needed, as am I." Alex smiled. "Ye've no choice in the matter."

Lochiel laughed.

They were not laughing a few hours later as they congregated at the foot of Loch Arkaig. Being unable to ride at any speed above a slow walk, Lochiel had been carried by two of his clansmen while Alex had submitted to being thrown over Kenneth's shoulder like a child. It was humiliating but practical, and this was not the time to stand on his dignity.

Now they stopped and watched in horror as the enemy swarmed across the Cameron lands and billowing smoke started to rise from the villages as the houses were set on fire. They were too far away to see what was happening to the people, but they had heard enough of the reprisals being visited on other parts of the Highlands to know that any men found would be killed out of hand, and the women stripped and turned out of their homes with their children if they were lucky, raped and possibly murdered if they were not.

"How are they setting the fires?" one of the younger Camerons asked. "The thatch is soaking."

"From the inside where it's dry," said Alex. "The heat dries the outer layer. That's why there's so much smoke. Let's hope they're allowing the people to leave wi' their belongings before they fire their houses."

"The Munros are Highlanders too. Surely they'll not treat fellow Highlanders too badly?" Angus said hopefully.

Lochiel's mouth twisted in a parody of a smile.

"It was Camerons who killed Sir Robert and Dr Duncan Munro at Falkirk," he said. "I doubt Culcairn will have forgiven or forgotten that we killed his brothers. Even if it was in battle."

Alex could feel the change in the mood of the clansmen as they watched the smoke from the burning houses thicken, and was just about to suggest that they move on before the men charged into a fight they could not win regardless of the consequences, when another scout, covered in mud, approached, stumbling with fatigue and momentarily relieved that he did not have to run another few miles to Achnacarry.

"There are redcoats coming from the north," he said. "We think about two thousand or so of them. A lot. They're making heavy weather of it, up to their arses in mud and water, but they're maybe an hour away, if that."

There was no more time to lose watching their houses burn. They continued their retreat, down the track which ran along the north of Loch Arkaig to its head. It was clear now that this had been a highly organised attack, intended to wipe out the Camerons altogether. Had they disputed the passage of the River Lochy, they would have been trapped by the troops sweeping down from the north and massacred. Instead, once at the head of the loch, they had a short discussion, after which Lochiel ordered his men to disperse into the hills for now, and await further orders.

Then he turned to Alex.

"Will ye come with us?" he said.

"Where will you go?" Alex asked.

"We'll head over toward Loch Shiel," Lochiel said. "The redcoats'll no' find us easily there, and I can get messages out to Cluny and his neighbours tae tell them what's happened here and to advise them to separate and wait for news from the French, who will surely help us."

"D'ye truly think they'll send help now?" Alex asked.

"I have to think that. Charles will be on his way there now. He'll talk the king round. Ye ken how good he is at persuading others to do his will. And we must keep ourselves in readiness."

"I hope you've the right of it, Donald," Alex said, the doubt apparent in his voice. "But if it's all the same to you, I'll head home. The redcoats'll no' venture so far south as Loch Lomond yet, because they've no fort to live in and get supplies from unless they can rebuild Inversnaid. We can hide out more easily there and still be ready if ye send us news that the French have landed."

"It's no' finished yet," Lochiel said with conviction.

With that sentiment Alex could most certainly agree. It was by no means finished yet.

"What are ye intending now?" Iain asked after they'd said their farewells to the Camerons and were headed south, making a wide detour around the Cameron lands, which were now shrouded in a thick pall of black smoke. Alex was still being carried by Kenneth in case they should need to make a sudden run into the mountains. Angus walked to one side of him carrying Alex's crutches, Iain to the other.

"I'm intending to go home, as I said, and get myself walking again as soon as possible. And then I'm intending to make a start on fulfilling my oath. As I told Donald, the redcoats'll no' come as far as Loch Lomond yet. And they dinna ken the land at all. Put me down a minute, Kenneth."

They had come to a small clearing, and Kenneth carefully lowered Alex onto a fallen log. His men gathered round.

"I ken well that ye all agreed to join wi' the Camerons to try to continue the fight. Ye've seen how that's worked out. For now all we can do is keep ourselves fit and ready to fight, and wait to see if Louis will send troops to help us rise again."

"D'ye think he will?" Alasdair asked.

"I dinna ken. I've no great hopes of it myself," Alex said candidly. "But he did send us supplies for a summer campaign, so maybe I'm wrong. But it seems to me we've a number of choices. We can surrender, give up our arms and hope that Geordie will be merciful."

"Geordie merciful? Tae MacGregors?!" Kenneth said incredulously.

The outburst of laughter that followed this proposal and Kenneth's retort gave Alex his answer.

"Or we can go home, carry on living as we did before, or as

best we can, anyway, and hope Cumberland'll be satisfied wi' burning the lands he can reach from Fort Augustus and Fort William, and will leave us alone."

"D'ye think that likely?" Angus asked. Alex pondered for a minute.

"I'd no' say likely, but it's possible, aye. I think William's hitting hard at the clans he can reach because he wants to bring us to heel so he can go back to Flanders as quick as possible. It's likely that, once he thinks we're cowed he'll leave someone else in charge and head back to England with as many men as he can spare."

"So we can all go back to our families and carry on as before?" Alasdair said.

"Aye. Here's what I think. Those of you with wives and bairns should go back to them and start the spring planting, which is already late, although with the weather we're having, that's no bad thing. The women can go up to the shielings wi' the cattle, but their menfolk'll need to keep an eye on them in case the soldiers come. We canna in fairness go reiving our neighbours' cattle, for they'll be suffering as much as we are."

"Even the Campbells?" someone asked.

"We may make an exception there," Alex conceded, to general approval.

"And those of us without wives and bairns?" Iain asked. Alex glanced at him, and caught the sparkle of tears in Iain's eyes before he ducked his head and looked away.

"That's for each of you to decide for yourselves," Alex said. "For myself, as I said to Iain a minute ago, I intend to get fit and walking, as fast as I can. Then I've a blood oath to fulfil. I'm thinking that right now the redcoats are staying together in large groups for the most part. They're being careful. Even so, Angus has already killed one o' the bastards. Give them another few weeks and they'll start to get over-confident, and careless. And then we can start taking them out, a couple here, a couple there, and be gone almost before they know they're dead. That's what I intend to do."

"And me," said Angus immediately. Iain nodded his head. Alex smiled grimly. It would be just the three of them, as was right; they were the only ones honour-bound to fight by the blood oath of vengeance they'd taken.

"I'll come too," said Alasdair to a general chorus of agreement from the other men with families.

Alex held up his hand and they fell silent.

"No, Alasdair. Ye've no' taken the oath. And ye've a family," he said. "I want the men wi' families to go home to them. The women and bairns have suffered more than enough, waiting for ye all to come back. Before ye object," he continued on seeing the reluctant expressions all around him, "we need the MacGregors to continue, and to do that we need children, and to do that we need…well, if ye dinna ken that, I'm no' telling ye." He fell silent for a minute and they all laughed. "But those of us still fighting will also need feeding, for if we're to get our two hundred redcoats before we all die of old age, we'll no' have the time to raise cattle and oats too. And we'll need scouts to keep an eye on the land and tell us if soldiers are coming.

"The sort of fighting we'll be doing now is verra different to what we've done for the last year, as ye ken well. Sneak attacks in the night, lying out in the rain for hours waiting for an opportunity to hit, and without the support of an army round us. Sometimes we'll just need a fireside to sit round and tell stories, wi' people who are living properly, to keep us human," he added with disarming candour. "And for that we need you to be wi' your wives and bairns, so we've something normal to come home to. If the French do land and Charles comes back to lead us again, then we'll decide together what to do."

There was general agreement, and after a short rest they set off again at a brisk walk, all of them eager to be home now they knew what they would be doing once they got there. Alex was glad that they'd agreed so readily to his proposal; he was tired, in body and mind, and not in the mood for an argument. Once they got back Angus and Iain would move into his house and would make it their base of operations, from where they would plan how to start fulfilling their oath.

"I'm coming with ye too," Kenneth said suddenly.

"Aye, well, I hope so, because there isna another man who can carry me home alone, and it'd take me an awfu' long time to hobble back."

"I dinna mean that, as ye ken well," Kenneth said. "I'll join you in your blood oath. Jeannie was a vain wee lassie, but I loved her well, and if it hadna been for a redcoat bastard turning her head wi' his flattery and false promises, I'd still have her wi' me now. I need to do this, Alex," he finished, as though Alex had already forbidden him to.

Alex was struck dumb for a moment. Since the day he'd killed his wife, Kenneth had never spoken a word about her, and all of the MacGregors had come to believe he never would. That he had now broken his silence spoke volumes about how desperately he wanted revenge. Alex could not deny him that. It was his right as a Highlander.

"Aye," he said.

"And me too," an English voice came from a short way behind. Alex braced his hands on Kenneth's back and raised his head to meet Graeme's grey gaze.

"I thought ye'd want to go home, now it's over," Alex said.

"We're not sure it *is* over yet. I'm not ready to go back to growing carrots and cabbages," Graeme replied. "I'm not sure I could stand Thomas and Jane saying 'I told you so'. And it's a long way back to Manchester. I'd just as soon get a bit more sword practice in before I go. And," he continued in a softer voice, "I wouldn't be averse to killing a few more of the bastards myself. I've known Beth since she was born. She's…she was precious to me."

"Aye," Kenneth said. "We'll make a Highlander of ye yet."

"Not if I've got to wear that stupid petticoat you're all so attached to, with nothing underneath," Graeme retorted. "My balls still ache just thinking about it."

They all laughed, and the serious moment passed. Then they continued in silence, each occupied with his own thoughts, but all of them looking forward to arriving home, if for different reasons.

**Fort Augustus, May 23rd.**

"What, all of them?" the Duke of Cumberland said incredulously.

"We did take five of them prisoner, Your Highness, one of them an officer," Colonel Hutchinson said nervously.

"How the hell did six hundred men manage to escape nearly three thousand coming at them from all sides?" Cumberland said, making it clear that he didn't consider five prisoners to be even worth mentioning.

"Er…it was not an easy march," Hutchinson said. "Colonel Howard said it was the most fatiguing march he'd ever made, and Lord Loudoun's troops were held up by the treacherous conditions coming over the mountains at Glengarry. The weather has been truly awful," he finished.

"I know what the weather's like!" Cumberland said hotly. "I've marched all over this bloody country for months. And so has Loudoun. And what of Lochiel?"

"He got away, Your Highness."

Cumberland closed his eyes and took a deep breath.

"So a man who's been shot in both legs and is a complete cripple can run all the way along the loch and disappear into the mountains, while Loudoun's men, all able-bodied, are incapable of catching up with him?"

Colonel Hutchinson opened his mouth.

"I don't expect an answer to that, Colonel," Cumberland said wearily. "So, they all got away. Is there any good news?"

As far as the colonel was concerned, no, there was not much in the way of good news. But he was not here to give an opinion, as he well knew.

"Colonel Howard is going to dinner in Lochiel's house, Your Highness. He awaits your orders as to what to do with the house, but he has demolished all the dwellings he came across on his way there, and the men are rounding up the cattle to drive here to be sold. And Lord Loudoun says that some of the Camerons have sent to say they will surrender their arms tomorrow."

"How many is 'some of'?" the duke asked.

"We believe about a hundred, Your Highness," Hutchinson said.

"Well, that's better than nothing, I suppose," Cumberland conceded. "Tell Howard to burn Lochiel's house and all its outbuildings to the ground. All of it. I want there to be no sign that there ever was a house at Achnacarry. The Camerons as a clan are finished, and I want them to be very clear that I mean that."

After the colonel had left to snatch a hasty meal before riding off yet again to deliver his commander's orders, Prince William

Augustus sat back and sighed. Some people just had the luck of the devil. It seemed that Charles had escaped to France, although that had not yet been confirmed. But he had been sure that this time Lochiel would have been dragged before him as his prisoner. How he had managed to escape was beyond him.

It was this bloody country. Dull and gloomy, with black brooding mountains and never-ending rain, it was enough to sap the spirit of the most cheerful of men. No wonder morale was low. After all, many of the men had been here for months. They needed a distraction, a little fun. He would organise some games for them, horse riding contests and suchlike, to lift the spirits.

He had no idea why the Highlanders not only endured living here, but apparently had a great attachment to the place. It would be understandable if they had seen nothing else, but most of them had marched as far south as Derby, had seen the beauty and fertility of the English countryside, and how superior it was to the bogs and crags of Scotland. How could they still cling to their little hovels and have such blind allegiance to their petty tyrant chiefs, once they had seen an alternative? It was incomprehensible.

Damn the Camerons, and their chief! It was not over yet. He might have lost Charles, but he would not give up the hunt for Lochiel, and would see the traitor's head on a spike at the Tower of London yet, next to Lord Lovat's.

And speaking of the Tower of London…Cumberland smiled. It had been five weeks since Culloden. Surely his prisoner would be well enough by now to be questioned, gently? He had hoped to do it himself on his return to London, but he realised now that he would have to stay another few weeks at least, to ensure that Scotland realised he meant business. And he would never forgive himself if the man he wanted most of all were to escape to France because he insisted on conducting the interrogation himself.

He would write to the Duke of Newcastle tonight, and see if the prisoner was willing to volunteer the identity and whereabouts of Sir Anthony Peters to him without any persuasion at all. It was highly likely, he thought.

He reached for the bell to call a clerk, and then changed his mind. He could not risk the secret being exposed to anyone, not while he had no idea who Sir Anthony was. He would write the letter himself and send it by the most secure route possible.

He pulled out paper and ink, and taking out his knife, sharpened a quill, whilst pondering how to word his letter to his friend Thomas.

He would salvage something from this otherwise disappointing day after all.

# CHAPTER FOUR

**London, June 1746.**

The young woman sat in an armchair and gazed blankly out of the window of her well-appointed second-storey living room at the expanse of grass below. She sat there for many hours every day, and every day the view was the same. To the right she could see the huge brooding edifice of the White Tower and the wall of the inner ward. To the left she could see the buildings of the Royal Mint.

Occasionally a uniformed yeoman warder or his wife would cross the grass, and sometimes some of their children would play there, throwing a ball to each other or spinning crazily until they became dizzy and fell over. It was strange to see children playing so happily on the green which had seen so much death; Lady Jane Grey, Anne Boleyn, Catherine Howard, to name but a few, all of them for treason. The young woman wondered idly and disinterestedly if she would one day join the list, and if she, along with so many other traitors, would be buried in the Chapel Royal of St Peter ad Vincula, which could be seen on the other side of the green. She doubted it. More likely her body would be buried in an unmarked grave somewhere, and she would be forgotten.

The chair she was sitting on had a comfortable padded seat and was covered in expensive blue silk brocade, as was the cushion she had placed at her back. The frame and legs of the chair were elaborately carved with acanthus leaves, which were covered in gold leaf.

The chair was one of a matching pair, its partner being situated around a beautiful walnut tea-table, the legs of which were decorated in a similar pattern to that of the chairs and the three-seater sofa which flanked one side of the table, ideal if the young woman were to entertain friends.

The young woman had no friends to entertain, and if she had, they would not have been allowed to visit her in any case.

A large and exquisitely patterned Aubusson rug covered most of the floor, and two ornately carved tables stood at either end of the sofa. On each a candelabra was placed, each one holding five expensive beeswax candles which in the evening would be lit and would enhance the cosiness and luxury of the room, the walls of which were decorated in shades of cream, with gilded mouldings. The fireplace was of marble, and a fire burned merrily in the hearth. Above the fireplace was a space where at one time a mirror had hung, but this had been removed when the young woman had taken up residence.

Through a door to the right of the fireplace was a bedroom, which was as luxuriously appointed as the living room, with a mahogany four poster bed, complete with comfortable feather mattresses and pillows, linen sheets, soft woollen blankets and a silk brocade eiderdown which matched the bed hangings. There was a mahogany dressing-table from which the mirror had been carefully removed, a chest for clothes which was full of fashionable gowns, and a beautiful writing desk, which was empty of writing materials, but on which was stacked a small selection of books. In one corner of the room was a bathtub, with a ewer and basin to the side for if the occupant wished to wash herself rather than bathe.

The young woman had no need of a kitchen; all her meals were brought to her by a servant. If she wished to have a bath, she had only to ring a bell and a servant would be set to filling the tub with buckets of piping hot steamy water into which would be sprinkled lavender or rose petals to scent the water. A maid could be called for at any time to help her dress her hair and clothe her body in one of the beautiful gowns that had been provided for her, as she had had no appropriate clothing of her own when she had arrived. Overall the accommodations were delightful, and any young woman of breeding would have no cause for complaint at the quality of either her surroundings or the food.

Beth MacGregor couldn't give a fig for her accommodations. Or the food. Or the gowns.

Instead she wore her shift, over which she had tied a dressing-gown, and she braided her hair herself. The maid, after some time spent twiddling her fingers awaiting her mistress's summons, had been set to other tasks.

It was true that she did eat the food provided, and drank, though very sparingly, of the fine wines which accompanied her meals, and which she watered down, having no wish to become intoxicated. But for all the appreciation she showed for the food it might as well have been gruel; she ate purely for nourishment, because she could not afford to become weak and therefore vulnerable when her ordeal began, as she was sure it would, sometime soon. Indeed she had no idea why she had been kept waiting so long. Perhaps they hoped to bore her into submission. If so, they would not win. Whatever they did, they would not win. On that she was resolved.

In the meantime she slept for as many hours as she could, read whatever book she had been brought (she was provided with a new one every week), and then sat by the window, and waited.

And remembered.

The last thing she remembered before being in this room was running down the slope after killing the sergeant who had bayoneted Maggie. She remembered it in so much detail that if she closed her eyes she was there again, watching the look of surprise on the sergeant's face as he clutched his throat, from which her knife protruded. She hadn't actually seen him die, but she was certain that he could not have survived; she had aimed very carefully to ensure he would bleed to death in moments, and still felt a savage sense of satisfaction about it. She regretted the irretrievable loss of the knife, but she felt that her mother would have approved of the final use to which it had been put.

She would not have been allowed to keep it here, anyway. She was not even allowed embroidery materials; she had asked and been refused. Presumably they thought she might try to kill herself with the tiny scissors, or attempt to kill her guard and escape.

She remembered her head jerking back as the soldier made a lunge for her headscarf, and the sting as it was pulled from her head, taking some of her hair with it. And then she had run, bounding through the heather like a hare, the cool fresh Scottish air filling her lungs, her hands lifting her skirts so she would not trip as she tore down the slope, trying to give the rest of the women time to run in other directions whilst the soldiers were all focussed on her. She wondered now how many of them had escaped the redcoats.

And then there was nothing.

She did not remember being brought from Drumossie Moor to the Tower of London, although she knew the journey must have taken several days. She did remember waking briefly, and someone washing her face gently with warm water, but she didn't know who had washed her or where she was at the time. After that she had vague memories of a dimly lit room, and someone speaking softly to her. Then she was being burnt alive whilst just beyond the light of the flames shadows danced, laughing and mocking her agony; then the fire was gone and instead she was buried in snow, her clothes and body soaking wet, shivering violently, while someone hammered a nail slowly into the side of her head and she screamed that she would not tell, no matter what they did, she would not tell.

And then she had awoken properly to be told by a thin-faced exhausted-looking middle-aged man that the fever had broken, she was through the worst now, and it was certain she would survive her injury. She just had to be careful not to move for a day or two.

She could not move anyway; the slightest movement of her head had caused her intense agony, and even the soft light of the candles set about the room caused her pain. So she had lain very still staring at the elaborate bed hangings as the exhausted man explained that he was a physician, that he had tended her since she had been shot some three weeks previously, that she had had the worst fever he had ever known, and he had despaired of her surviving on more than one occasion. But, he had told her, she was young and strong, and clearly possessed of a great will to live, although she would not have done so without his expert care, which had all been provided by His Royal Highness Prince William Augustus, Duke of Cumberland, at great expense.

He had gone on to explain that she was now in the Tower of London and was the duke's prisoner, although she was not being kept in the main part of the Tower, but instead was lodged in the house of one of the Yeoman Warders, and was to be provided with every luxury, at the duke's express order. She was extremely fortunate; most of the female rebel prisoners were being held in Newgate Prison, in which conditions were very different, but, on account of her high birth and of the special regard in which His Highness held her, she was to have the best of everything.

Beth supposed that she should at that point have expressed her undying gratitude to the physician for saving her life and to the Duke of Cumberland for his consideration; but she did neither, and instead just remained staring at the bed hangings until the physician grew tired of waiting for a response and left her to rest.

She was not grateful. She knew that her life had not been saved because the Duke of Cumberland cared for her. Nor was she being lodged in comfort because of her aristocratic blood. She was here now, and alive, for one reason only; because she was the only person they knew who could reveal the true identity of Sir Anthony Peters, probably the most hated man in Britain, apart from Prince Charles Edward Stuart, of course. And she also knew that she would never reveal his true identity; and because of that she was most ungrateful.

She was ungrateful to the surgeon who had fought so hard to save her life; she was ungrateful to the duke, who, she was told, had been present when she was shot and who had intervened immediately; and she was ungrateful to the idiot who had shot her and missed his aim. Instead of going straight through the back of her head and blowing her brains out as he had intended, and as she now wished it had, the bullet had skated along the side of her skull, fracturing it and gouging out a deep furrow which extended for some six inches along her head, ending at the side of her eye. She would have a scar, the physician had told her, but it would fade in time, and much of it could be covered by her beautiful hair or a wig, in any case.

As though she gave a damn about how she would look as she rode to the scaffold or the stake.

It was her extraordinary hair that had saved her life, the physician had continued; due to its remarkable colour the duke had recognised her. How fortunate!

*How fortunate indeed*, she thought glumly now as she watched the sky darken and the rainclouds gather over Tower Green. As for her beautiful hair, she hated it. It had brought her to this gilded prison, and would in time, she was sure, lead her to torture, and then to death.

She must not think of that. Thinking of it would bring dread, and dread would bring weakness; and she must not weaken.

Once certain that the wound was healing well and that all danger of infection or fever had passed, the physician had disappeared and instead she had been attended by a series of servants, the men in a livery of mustard yellow, the women in striped cotton dresses with neat aprons. All of them had treated her with the utmost respect, as they had no doubt been ordered to; and all of them remained silent as they cleaned the rooms, lit the candles or the fire, and brought her her meals.

At first this hadn't bothered her; trying to speak had made her head ache dreadfully, as did any noise, so she was grateful for the quiet. Any movement at all had been agonising, especially the act of eating, as the action of chewing had made her head throb so badly that more often than not she had vomited up her food while a maid held a bowl in front of her, which was then taken away, while she lay back on the pillows, tears streaming down her face and the muscles of her neck corded as she fought the agonising pain in her head.

Over the last few weeks though, the pain had slowly diminished, and now she could eat, drink and walk about the room with the only result being a dull throbbing, which was annoying but bearable. In the absence of a mirror she had examined her wound with her fingers once the dressing had been removed, feeling the ridged and puckered skin gingerly, and remembering another ridged scar, that had snaked across a strong masculine hand, bisecting the knuckles of his index and middle finger.

Beth wondered whether the mirrors had been removed to prevent her going into a fit of hysteria about her ruined beauty, or whether her jailors had realised that, if smashed, a piece of silvered glass could be a formidable weapon or a means to end one's own life. Probably not; her enemies had always underestimated her, judging her by her physical attributes rather than her mental ones.

The highlight of her week was receiving a new book. She could now manage to read for several hours at a time, although occasionally the words would start to dance across the page, and then she would close her eyes for a time to rest them. She had no idea what was causing this, but assumed that there had been some slight damage to her brain after all.

She did not get to choose the weekly book, and her requests to read the newspapers went unheeded. She didn't know whether this was because her jailors wished her to feel isolated from the world in general, or because the supposed Hanoverian victory had not been as complete as they would like her to believe. She prayed for the latter to be true, but *did* feel isolated. She longed for news, any news, but all her questions and entreaties to the servants were rewarded with silence.

She knew she was in the house of a warder, but had no idea what he looked like, because he never visited her, although she knew he had a family because once, about a week before, there had come a knock on the door and a child had called a greeting to her and had attempted to turn the doorknob before being dragged away by an adult, his voice high-pitched and complaining as it receded down the corridor.

In the last two weeks she had established a routine. She would rise as late as possible, wash, braid her hair, put on a clean shift and her dressing-gown, and then eat breakfast, after which she would alternately read, walk around the rooms for exercise, or sit by the window looking out. In the evening she would eat her dinner and sit by the fire gazing into the flames until she felt tired enough to sleep.

Last week the much-awaited book had been *Paradise Lost*. She had read the first few pages and then had been transported to the opulence of Versailles, had felt again the lips of King Louis of France on hers as he had attempted to claim her as his mistress in front of the whole Court, had remembered Alex's explosion of rage in their room later, and her hot reaction to it. She remembered the sun on her face as she sat in the gardens, the smiling green eyes of her companion as they debated Milton's treatment of women, the prickly feel of the bushes she had hidden in as she watched those same eyes gaze into the icy sapphire depths of Sir Anthony's, before glazing over in death.

And then she had sat for a while, vacantly staring out across Tower Green, had put the book aside, and had spent the time she would normally have occupied by reading in exercising her arms as best she could with the materials to hand.

This afternoon she would be brought another book, which she awaited with great eagerness as it was the only thing she had to look forward to in a sea of ennui, although she betrayed no emotion whatsoever in front of her attendants, another skill she was practising, ready for the day when she would need it, which would come soon.

She hoped it would come soon, not because she was looking forward to her interrogation, but because she knew it was inevitable and wanted it to be over with. She was, and always had been, a woman of action, and the waiting, now she was almost healed, was driving her insane, as her jailors no doubt intended.

Patience. She must practice that too, and if she could not master it then she must appear to have done so.

And so it was that, when a new volume was brought for her that evening along with her dinner, she ignored it completely and concentrated on eating her lamb chop and vegetables whilst the servant bustled about closing the shutters, lighting the candles and making up the fire. After she had finished eating, she casually picked up the book to look at the title written in gold lettering on the spine.

*Pamela* by Samuel Richardson.

She replaced the book on the table disinterestedly and went to sit in her accustomed place by the fire, staring into the flames until the maid had left and she knew she would not be disturbed again that evening.

Then she retrieved the book and sat down again. She did not open it; instead she ran her fingers lightly along the spine and cover, feeling the slightly raised surface of the gold tooled lettering, while she remembered another time when she had needed, or thought she had needed to hide her emotions and feign indifference, a time when she had had to endure the presence of the hideous and superficial Sir Anthony as he simpered about the room while her most treasured possession at the time was burning to cinders in the library fireplace. Or so she had believed.

Beth closed her eyes and allowed herself to become completely immersed in the past, just for a short time. She saw again the twin of the book she was now holding, far too high for her to reach on a shelf in her cousin's library, and the baronet effortlessly reaching to lift it down for her. She smelt the cloying fragrance of his violet cologne, which had nauseated her at the time and which she would do almost anything to smell again now. She looked up, and saw his eyes smiling down at her as he talked about the book, revealing in doing so that he had heard the argument she had had with her brother earlier. He had such beautiful slate-blue eyes, with tiny gold flecks scattered in the irises, fringed by impossibly long lashes, in a face made hideous by lead paint and rouge.

She saw the same face, handsome this time without its makeup, the slate-blue eyes closed, the long lashes resting on his cheeks as he slept on Drumossie Moor the morning of the battle, his head resting on her lap, his arm flung out to the side, fingers lightly curled. She remembered pushing his chestnut hair back off his face, and seeing in the relaxed features what he must have looked like as a boy, innocent and carefree. She remembered looking around, seeing Duncan and Angus similarly sleeping, and her heart contracting with a love that was physical.

Frantically she tried to pull her mind back into the present, but it was too late; in her imagination she saw Alex as she never had in life, broken and dying on the same moor, the long lashes closing over slate-blue eyes that would never smile or see the beauty of an April morning again.

She stood abruptly, the book falling to the floor, and drew in a huge shuddering breath before doubling over as the agony of grief and loss consumed her, an agony far more painful than her physical wound had been, an agony that would never leave her, until she joined him in death.

He must be dead, for if he was not, why had he not come for her as he'd promised he would?

She could not bear it, to be without him, forever. But she had to. Somehow she had to pull herself together, to stay strong, to show no weakness, under any circumstances. She heard a low keening noise in the room, and realised with horror that it was coming from her mouth, and that she could not stop it. Hot tears welled up in her eyes and spilled over, pouring down her cheeks as she threw herself into bed, pulling the covers over her head and burying her face in the pillow as she wept, the sobs racking her body and making her head throb. She had to stop the occupants of the house hearing that she had given way, that she cared, that she could be broken. That she was already broken, irreparably.

\* \* \*

By the next morning she had recovered her equilibrium. She had finally cried herself to sleep, waking in the early hours of the morning, her throat sore and her pillow drenched in tears. She had risen and bathed her swollen eyes with cold water from the ewer, had drunk some wine, and then had picked the book that had inspired the torrent of memories and emotions up from the floor where she had dropped it, and had placed it under her pillow before lying down to try to get a few more hours of sleep before the servant came with breakfast.

After breakfast Beth sat calmly by the window as usual, staring out at the grass below. She would sit there for an hour or so and then would do some exercises, she decided. It was a fine day, and she would have loved to open the window and feel the air on her face; but it had been nailed shut, presumably so that she could not make a rope from her bedsheets or gowns and attempt to escape from the room. Even if she had, she would still be in the Tower grounds, and there were guards posted at all the exits.

There was a knock on the door, which made Beth jump; although she had no clock she could tell by the position of the sun that it was not lunchtime. After a moment the door opened and a maid entered accompanied by two soldiers who stood stiffly to attention in the doorway while the maid approached Beth and curtseyed, then cleared her throat nervously.

"Excuse me, my lady, but there is a gentleman who wishes to see you, and these men have come to take you to him."

Beth's pulse immediately quickened, and she felt the rush of adrenaline surge through her. *So, here it comes. Stay calm,* she admonished herself.

"Which gentleman?" she asked coolly, as though it was of no real matter to her.

The maid flushed.

"I don't know, my lady," she said. "I was sent to help you dress."

For a moment Beth was tempted to go as she was, her hair still tangled from sleep, in her shift and dressing gown; it would show her contempt for the 'gentleman', whoever he was. But if she did she would lose the possible advantage that her aristocratic background could give her. It might also give the impression that she was sexually available.

She stood.

"Very well. Please sit down. I will not keep you waiting long," she said to the soldiers, who looked surprised to be addressed by her. One of them smiled and even made a move to sit, but his companion coughed and the young man shot to attention again.

It did no harm to show kindness to a soldier; it might come in useful in the future.

\* \* \*

Thomas Pelham-Holles, Duke of Newcastle, sat behind a large desk in his office in Whitehall, awaiting the arrival of the prisoner he had been asked to question. Whilst he waited he read again the letter from his superior, which had not only requested him to conduct the interrogation, but had also given guidelines as to how it was to be done.

He hoped that the prisoner, who he had been informed was almost healed from her injury, had had time to consider her situation and was sufficiently grateful for the treatment she had received so far. He also hoped that she had spent the journey by water from the Tower to Whitehall preparing herself to behave in an appropriate manner, and that as she approached his office via a long carpeted corridor lined with alcoves from which statues of Roman Emperors frowned down imperiously on her, she would be impressed and intimidated enough to enter the room in a submissive and pliant frame of mind.

There was a knock on the door. The duke folded the letter and placed it in a drawer, issued the order to enter; the door opened and the prisoner entered, flanked by two soldiers, who came to a stop once inside the room.

"You may wait outside," the duke ordered, and the soldiers bowed and withdrew. The door closed, leaving the prisoner standing alone.

"Good morning, Miss Cunningham," he said. "Please take a seat." He indicated a chair on the opposite side of his desk, and she moved forward and sat down, carefully arranging her skirts around her while the duke observed her carefully.

By God, but she was beautiful! Newcastle had heard of her beauty, of course; it was renowned in high society, and the Duke of Cumberland had expounded on it in detail, both in person and in his last letter. He had thought the reports to be exaggerated. But now that she was sitting mere feet away from him, he was rendered momentarily speechless by her ethereal, breathtaking loveliness. She was dressed in a rose-coloured silk gown which fitted her perfectly, emphasising the creamy swell of her breasts and tiny waist. The colour complemented her flawless complexion and the delicate coral of her lips. Her incredible hair had been brushed back from her face and loosely braided, revealing the whole of the unsightly scar from her injury, which ended a mere fraction of an inch from her eye. But even that, hideous as it was, could not spoil the utter perfection of this woman.

The perfect woman, her skirts arranged to her satisfaction, now folded her delicate hands in her lap and raised her beautiful cornflower-blue eyes to his, her face impassive.

With some difficulty the duke pulled himself together. It was a long time since his head had been turned by a woman, and he was not about to be affected by this one either, lovely as she was.

He looked at her, examining her for any sign of nervousness, but saw none. Her expression was calm, neutral, and her hands were still. She gave the impression of having been invited to attend a tea party, perhaps. Well, he would soon put her straight on that.

"So, Miss Cunningham, I trust you are being treated well, and that all your needs are being met?" he began.

"I cannot complain about my accommodations, or my treatment so far. I presume that not all supporters of King James are being treated so well," Miss Cunningham replied. "Although I could wish for more diverting reading material than that with which I am provided."

Newcastle chose to ignore the reference to the Old Pretender as King James.

"I believe you are permitted to receive a book every week at the moment, but I can of course allow more. It is up to you." If she was cooperative, that was.

"No, I am referring to the fact that I am not allowed any newspapers or periodicals," she said. She smiled at him. "From which I can only infer that the war is going badly for the Elector," she finished.

"How on earth do you infer that?" he retorted.

"I would think that if it was going well, the papers would be full of the details, and that you would want me to read about it."

The duke leaned forward across his desk suddenly, expecting the prisoner to flinch, but she continued to sit calmly, waiting for his reply.

"Let me assure you, madam, that the 'war', as you call this little rebellion, is over. The rebels were thoroughly defeated at Culloden, and the prisons are now full of the survivors. King George has never been more secure on his throne than he is now. And the newspapers are full of praise for both His Majesty and Prince William, who led his troops to such a glorious victory."

She considered this for a moment.

"Is Prince Charles then dead?" she asked, as though enquiring after the health of an acquaintance suffering from a minor illness.

"The Pretender's son will be brought to account for his attempt on the throne, as will all the leaders of this ridiculous rebellion," he replied.

"Ah. Then is he held also in the Tower?" she asked. "That is where prisoners of consequence are kept, is it not? Will I see him executed on Tower Green then, or will you murder him here at Whitehall, as Cromwell murdered his great-grandfather?"

The duke reddened and opened his mouth to retort, then checked himself. What was he thinking of, about to justify himself to this chit?

"May I suggest, madam, that you concern yourself no longer with the defeated rebels, but rather consider your own situation and how you may repay the kindness of His Royal Highness, whose express wish it was that you be accommodated as befits the niece of a lord."

"Cumberland is very kind," she replied coolly. "But I am sure I will be unable to reward his consideration."

The door opened and a footman entered bearing a tray of tea. He placed it on the table, and at a signal from his master poured two cups of the beverage from an ornate china teapot, and handed one to Beth, who accepted it graciously. He held a plate of cakes out to her, and she chose an almond pastry, which she ate delicately, without dropping a crumb. She really did give the impression of making a social call. Did she have no idea how serious her situation was? Probably not. No doubt she had led a sheltered life, had always been worshipped and treated with deference due to her beauty, and was used to her every wish being fulfilled.

The duke decided to make use of the interruption to steer the conversation in another direction. She was a woman, and women, having far less wit than men, were susceptible to flattery and could be persuaded to almost anything by it. Her head had no doubt been filled with romance and nonsense by this monster Peters, and by the charismatic Charles, who had certainly wooed her in Rome. And she was very young. Newcastle softened as he looked at the young woman sipping tea on the other side of his desk. Poor deluded creature. He felt sorry for her.

"Miss Cunningham, I really do not think that you appreciate the seriousness of your situation," he began. "I have no wish to distress you. I am sure that you had no idea, when you agreed to marry Sir Anthony Peters, that he was anything other than what he appeared to be; a wealthy and fashionable man of society. Is this true?"

"It is," she replied. She replaced her cup in the saucer and took another dainty bite of her cake.

"And I am sure that when he, no doubt assisted by the Pretender's son, persuaded you to accompany him on his treasonous undertaking, he led you to believe that it would be a wild, romantic adventure, and that coming from a rural background you believed it to be merely that – an adventure, something to amaze and impress your friends with in the future."

He paused, expecting her to comment, but she did not. Perhaps she was waiting for him to ask a question.

"It is understandable that your head was turned by such an accomplished, duplicitous liar. Indeed, he fooled far wiser people than yourself, my dear. No doubt he protested undying love for you, said he would protect you, and never desert you. Was that the case?"

"Yes, it was," she agreed.

"Well, then, I have no wish to be the bearer of bad news, but I must speak plainly. The man is a rogue and a traitor, madam. He cared nothing for you. He merely used you for his own purposes, made you his whore, and now he has no further use for you has abandoned you to your fate, caring nothing for the fact that you are now ruined."

"I was never his whore," she said, her voice still calm. "Half of London society witnessed our wedding."

"Your wedding to a man who did not exist!" Newcastle responded, irritated now. "And he knew that, that the marriage was a sham. Your reputation meant nothing to him. You meant nothing to him. He was a spy, and spies are trained to be convincing. They will say anything, stoop to anything to get what they want. They care nothing for anyone except themselves and the money they will receive for their treachery. No doubt he has already forgotten you, is maybe laughing with his friends about how he cozened you."

He paused to observe her reaction to this blunt statement, but she was looking down at her lap, her facial expression hidden, and he could not tell if she was bowing her head in shame or if she was merely regarding the pattern on the teacup.

"Miss Cunningham, I am giving you the opportunity to save yourself. You can tell me about this man who used you so badly. You can give us a description of him, tell us about his associates. I am sure your information will be of the utmost value to us, and will enable us to arrest a number of traitors as well as the man who has treated you so heartlessly. Indeed, Prince William holds you in high regard and has told me to assure you that you will be treated with the utmost leniency, if you cooperate with us. I am sure that with the approval of such an illustrious friend, this unfortunate episode will soon be forgotten and you will be able to resume your place in society. Perhaps we can find an appropriate husband for you, one who will be able to overlook your folly. Come, tell me what you know, and let us put an end to this unpleasant situation."

The prisoner's head was still bent over her cup, and Newcastle waited for her to consider his words, to realise the seriousness of her situation, and come to a decision. After a moment she stood and put her cup and saucer down carefully on the tray. Then she sat again, folded her hands in her lap, and raised her eyes to his. She smiled.

"We laughed at you, you know," she said softly, so softly that the duke barely caught the words, and was sure he had misheard her. His brow furrowed momentarily, and she seemed to realise that he had not understood her.

"We laughed at you," she repeated, louder this time. "Sir Anthony and I, and Prince Charles, of course. Anthony told His Highness that you had asked him to spy for you, and they found it very amusing that you were paying for them to carouse in the taverns and attend the theatre. But I am sure this is not news to you, a man of your intelligence, who knows so much about espionage and duplicity. Although Anthony made a fool of you, and even of the Elector, didn't he? No matter," she said, waving her tiny hand in a dismissive gesture.

"Speaking for myself, I am glad you gave me this opportunity to thank you, Your Grace," she continued, using the correct method of address to him for the first time.

"It is not I you should thank, but His Royal Highness," Newcastle interrupted, believing she was about to thank him for making her see the error of her ways, and to apologise for laughing at him.

"Oh. I am sorry," she replied, and appeared genuinely to be so. "I was under the impression that you were responsible for funding our honeymoon in Rome. We really had a most delightful time, and were able to lodge in establishments far more luxurious than we could have done without your kind patronage. I also wanted to thank you for allowing me to personally become closely acquainted with Prince Charles before he actually came to Britain. This convinced me as nothing else could have done that as well as having the right by birth, he also has the intelligence, grace and ability to be a far better king than any member of that ill-bred family of German usurpers you call royalty will ever have. But if I am unwarranted in my gratitude to you, I apologise. May I impose on you to convey my thanks to the Elector's son, then? Or, if I am permitted the materials, I will write to him myself."

After she had finished speaking she folded her hands in her lap once more, appearing utterly composed as she continued to look at the duke, her face pleasant, her smile, now clearly mocking, contemptuous even, still in place.

Silence reigned for a moment as Newcastle stared at her incredulously, unable to believe that any woman, let alone a traitor's whore, would dare to address him in such a manner. Did she really not appreciate the severity of her situation, and the fate that would await her if she were to persist in her ridiculous and unwarranted loyalty to the brute who had ruined her and tossed her to the wolves? He had an almost overwhelming urge to stand and knock the smile off her face, he who had never struck a woman in his life. With difficulty he mastered himself, and locked gazes with her.

"Your cause is dead, madam, and the man you are foolish enough to call husband, if he is not already rotting on Drumossie Moor with most of the rest of the rebels, will certainly be captured, along with the Young Pretender you admire so much, and when he is, he will be hung, drawn and quartered as he so richly deserves, and if you persist in this ridiculous folly then I will ensure that you are present at the execution, before you go to your own."

He picked up a bell that stood on his desk, and rang it.

Within seconds the door opened and a footman entered.

"Tell the soldiers to escort the prisoner back to her quarters," he said. "I suggest you spend the time between now and our next interview in serious contemplation of your future, which could be long and pleasant if you decide to cooperate with me, or short and extremely painful if you do not."

The soldiers entered, and Beth stood and smoothed down her skirts.

"And I wish you luck, Your Grace, in capturing a man you know nothing whatsoever about," she said pleasantly. Then she turned her back on him and walked to the door, where the soldiers were standing.

"Shall we go?" she said, and walked briskly off down the corridor, leaving the soldiers to follow her as though they were her servants rather than her jailers.

After she had departed the duke sat for a while, deep in thought. Although it had been manifestly clear from the letters he had received from Prince William that that young man was somewhat besotted by Miss Cunningham, Newcastle had been willing to accept Cumberland's assertion that she was just another victim of the perfidious Sir Anthony.

After all, he had interviewed everyone who'd had any dealings with the man, from the Earl of Highbury down to the Browne girl, and no one had had the slightest idea that Sir Anthony was anything other than he claimed to be. Clearly the man was extremely cunning and accomplished. Of course once Miss Cunningham had married him, Sir Anthony must have revealed at least part of his true identity to her, but until now Newcastle had assumed that she had been romanced into accompanying him, and that now his deception was discovered to her, she would be only too willing to reveal what she knew about the traitor.

Now he was not so sure that she was an innocent dupe, as Cumberland believed. Newcastle was accomplished at putting the fear of God into people through his air of authority alone, yet she had sat in front of him as though at a tea party, calm and collected.

She had been incarcerated for weeks now, alone, with plenty of time to consider her position. Any normal young woman would have been terrified by the thought of what might be to come. But perhaps instead of contemplating the scaffold or the stake, she still held on to whatever romantic fantasies the man had filled her silly head with, and was expecting him to storm the Tower and rescue her. Maybe the comfort of her prison had lulled her into a false sense of security. Well, he could do something about that, at least. He would remove some of her privileges. Not too many, or Cumberland would be annoyed, but enough to make her think again about her situation.

Newcastle got out his knife and began to trim a quill preparatory to writing his report of the interview for Cumberland. He would have to word this very carefully. He dare not write that in his heart he believed Miss Cunningham to be complicit in the whole affair. Although Prince William was Commander-in-Chief of His Majesty's forces, he was nevertheless a young man of twenty-five, and young men who believed themselves in love were notoriously sensitive to criticism of the object of their passion. And the prince would certainly not take kindly to being told he was a poor judge of character. The last thing Newcastle wanted was to make an enemy of the hero of Culloden. Far better that he wait and let Cumberland interview her himself. Then he would find out for himself what manner of woman he had become infatuated with, if she persisted in her recalcitrance. Much better that the royal hatred and revenge be directed at her than at himself, the messenger.

Newcastle filled the inkwell and took out a sheet of paper, then bent to his task.

\* \* \*

Once delivered back to her apartment by the soldiers, Beth sat by the window and congratulated herself.

She had done it. She had managed to display not the slightest trace of nerves in front of her questioner. When the footman had offered her tea she had been sure that the cup would rattle in the saucer, betraying her true state, but no. Being the wife of Sir Anthony Peters for two years had served her well. She smiled.

She had also learned some information. Not as much as she would like to have learned, but some.

She had learned that Prince Charles had not been killed or captured, and therefore assumed that the rising was not over, because while he lived there was hope of another attempt to restore the Stuarts to their rightful place.

She had learned that none of the people who knew the true identity of Sir Anthony Peters, such as Cameron of Lochiel, Murray of Broughton, Lord George Murray and Graeme Elliot had been captured, or if they had, that they were keeping silence. And that John Betts, if captured at Carlisle, as he surely must have been, had not volunteered to betray Alex in return for his life.

Neither had Sarah, who must have been interviewed by Newcastle, given any description of either Angus or Duncan, both of whom she had seen more than once; and being a servant rather than a member of the nobility she would have remembered what they looked like, Duncan especially. Because if she had Newcastle would surely have told her that they knew about Anthony's accomplices. For that matter, Sarah certainly could have given a far better description of Sir Anthony than anyone else, being as observant as she was.

It was heartwarming to Beth to know that her friends remained loyal.

She turned her mind now to the question she tried not to think of; was Alex still alive? She had thought until now that if he was he would know that she had been captured by Cumberland, and would, by his cunning, have found out where she had been taken and would have got word to her somehow that he was alive. And the fact that he hadn't meant that he was dead.

If he had been unable to go back for her and the other women after the battle, then certainly Duncan or Angus, or one of the other clansmen would have gone. They couldn't *all* have been killed. And whoever had gone would have discovered that she was Cumberland's prisoner. If Alex was alive but had been injured, then he'd be temporarily unable to discover where she was, and it would be impossible for any of the other clansmen to find out, because they all spoke with Scottish accents and were unable to affect other dialects as Alex was, and so would all be treated with the utmost suspicion by the authorities. Most of them did not have the skills to dissemble in any case.

So it was possible that Alex was injured but alive; and once healed he would find out where she was and would get word to her. She had no doubt of that; he was a master of disguise and would do anything to keep his promise to her. She trusted him, and his word.

If he was alive he would come for her. And she would not give up hope, not until so much time had passed that it was futile to hope. How long would that be?

Six months. In six months a young, strong man such as Alex could recover from any injury. Two months had already passed since Culloden. Which gave her another four to believe he was alive, and to take comfort from that.

Later that day all her books were removed except for *Pamela*, which was still under her pillow.

The following morning no one came to lay the fire and light it, and it remained unlit until the evening. Instead of ten candles she now had only one to light her room after dark. The food, when it arrived was not of the same quality as it had been until now; and instead of claret, she was served small beer to quench her thirst.

She hardly noticed these small privations; she had lived for eight months outdoors in all weathers, eating whatever could be foraged for and drinking stream water or whisky, sleeping in indifferent accommodation, and often outdoors in the heather.

If he was alive he would come for her. Until October, then. She would not think beyond that.

# CHAPTER FIVE

**Scotland, June 1746**

It had been the worst spring, weather-wise, that the Highlands of Scotland had seen for years. The rain and sleet had driven down in sheets day after day, often blown horizontal by the fierce winds that had howled down the glens, tearing the heather thatch from the houses that had not been ravaged and burnt by the redcoats, and washing away the spring planting of oats and barley.

May had given way to June with no sign of the rain abating, and the MacGregors, along with many others, had spent the gloomy evenings huddled together in one house or another, singing songs and telling stories in an attempt to keep their spirits up.

There was great need to keep their spirits up. In spite of the best efforts of the occupying British Army to suppress it, news of what was happening in other parts of the Highlands filtered through, carried by young men, women, and often even children, who were as adept as their seniors at blending into the landscape, and who could hide in tiny crevices that adults could not.

So it was that the MacGregors had heard that Prince Charles had not sailed on one of the frigates that had left Loch nan Uamh for France as had at first been believed, but in fact had sent a message to Lochiel just two days after the MacGregors had parted ways with the Camerons, stating that he was in fact on the Isle of Uist, and asking if the Cameron chief could assist him. As Lochiel had not been fit to travel easily, Murray of Broughton had gone to his prince's aid instead, in the hopes of bringing him back to the mainland.

They had also heard of the horrific retribution that continued to be visited on the clans, and that was no longer restricted merely to those who had risen in rebellion; loyal clans were starting to feel the heavy hand of Cumberland's men as well, as some of their houses were looted, crops burned, and their cattle driven off. Some of the rebels who came in to surrender were shot or hung out of hand, and many others taken prisoner in spite of the letters of safe conduct they proffered to the redcoat captains.

The redcoats were still concentrating their fury in the areas within a few days' march of the forts, and they were descending on the clan lands in huge numbers that were impossible to oppose without organised resistance, which the clansmen could not muster at the moment, scattered as they were, with many of their chiefs either dead, taken prisoner or injured. Cumberland remained at Fort Augustus for the present, and at Loch Lomond the MacGregors bided their time, tried to save what crops they could, and waited for their chieftain to heal fully and decide what was to be done next.

\* \* \*

Alex and Dougal sat outside, basking in the warmth of the first sunshine they had seen in what seemed to be an age. The ground was still sodden, so they lounged on a rough wooden bench outside Alex's front door, leaning back against the wall of the house. All around the clearing the thatch of the various huts steamed as the sun's heat dried it out, and the clansfolk had all found work to do out of doors. In the middle distance could be heard the laughter of children as they splashed and swam in the loch, and the singing of women as they washed every item of clothing and bedding they possessed in the hopes of being able to dry it before the weather changed again.

Closer to hand, Graeme was instructing some very small children in the art of identifying what was a weed and what was not. In spite of the terrible weather, the small plot of land outside the little hut that the MacGregors had built for Graeme when it became clear he was intending to stay was bursting with life, carrots, cabbages, onions and potatoes all showing healthy green leaves. He had even planted nasturtiums and marigolds, explaining to the incredulous clansmen that no, he was not going soft in his old age; you could eat the leaves and flowers of nasturtiums and the seed pods tasted peppery, while marigolds attracted hoverflies and repelled pests – and the flowers could be used to make a balm that soothed midge bites. The man was a wonder. He could grow anything anywhere. Alex kept meaning to ask him where he'd managed to obtain the seeds and tubers, but kept forgetting.

Dougal's sabre wound had finally healed and he had spent the morning trying to build up his strength, making use of the rocks that Alex no longer needed. He brushed his sweat-soaked hair out of his face and stretched his legs out in front of him.

"Ye're doing too much," Alex commented. "Ye dinna need to push yourself so hard. We'll no' be going raiding yet a while."

Dougal turned his head towards his companion and raised one eyebrow.

"Aye, well, it's different for me," Alex said, correctly interpreting the look. "I'm the chieftain. I canna afford to be weakened for any longer than necessary. I've a duty to set an example."

"And as your clansman, I've a duty to follow that example," Dougal responded.

There was no answer to that, so a companionable silence reigned for a few minutes.

"Is it still paining ye?" Dougal asked finally.

"No, no' paining exactly. It aches when I've been on it the whole day, though." His leg was almost better now. The splint was gone and he was slowly regaining the heavy thigh and calf muscles he'd had before the injury. Every day, whatever the weather, he would go for a long walk, initially along the relatively flat edge of the loch, but now he could scale the mountains too, with the aid of a stick. He still walked with a limp, which was more pronounced at the end of the day, but he was now confident that he would soon recover his full strength. He knew how lucky he was, how often a man was crippled for life by a badly set broken bone, and sent up a silent prayer of thanks to God for giving him a giant of a clansman like Kenneth who'd had the strength to straighten his leg and hold it there while it had been splinted.

He sat up and looked east, as he had regularly over the past two days, in the hope of seeing his brother. Angus had been gone a week now on what should have been a four day journey at best, and Alex was starting to regret having sent him. True, Angus was a lot quieter now, and had matured considerably since Culloden; but he was still Angus. Alex hoped to God that he hadn't seen an opportunity to increase his redcoat count and embarked on some madcap raid. He sighed.

"He'll be fine," Dougal said, reading his chieftain's mind. "Ye tellt him that he was only to find out if the rumours are true, no' to actually do anything. He'll no' take any unnecessary risks, no' when he's got young Lachlan wi' him."

He had a point.

"Aye, I hope not," Alex replied. "Even so, he's taking longer than expected." He raised his face to the sun and closed his eyes, letting the warmth soothe him. It really was a glorious day. He'd just sit here for a few minutes more, then he'd go for a swim.

The sudden shout made him jump, and he jerked to his feet, instinctively reaching for his dirk which was on the bench next to him. He felt dizzy from sitting in the sun too long, and realised that he must have fallen asleep. He shook his head to clear it, and then saw Angus loping towards him, his fair hair tangled on his shoulders, his bare legs streaked to the knee with mud.

It was Dougal who had shouted as he'd seen Angus, and the other clansmen now began to converge on Alex's house, eager to hear the news from Fort Augustus. As if by magic, Morag appeared from the direction of the loch and ran to her sweetheart, who smiled and wrapped his arm around her shoulder, pulling her in to his side. They continued together until they reached Alex, then Angus released her and sank down onto the bench. She hovered by his side, clearly unsure as to whether she should sit down on the chieftain's bench without an invitation.

"Christ, I'm tired," Angus said by way of greeting. He did look tired. His eyes were red, and his face was pale and drawn with fatigue.

Alex looked round.

"Where's…?" he began.

"Lachlan? Away to his bed. I had to carry him the last bit of the way. His legs wouldna hold him up. He's fine. He did well." He scrubbed a hand over his face in an attempt to stay awake.

As eager as Alex was to hear what Angus had discovered, he could see that his brother was completely exhausted. Maybe he should have a couple of hours sleep first. He was just about to suggest it, when Angus got up again and walked round the side of the hut where Janet had left a pail of water earlier, in case anyone should want a drink. He picked it up and tipped it over his head, shook himself like a dog, and then came and sat down again, his shirt clinging to his torso, his kilt sticking to his legs. He pushed his dripping hair out of his eyes and smiled.

"I'll be fine now, for a while," he said to the eager crowd who had gathered round the bench in a semicircle, awaiting the news.

Alex sat down next to him, and indicated to Morag that she could also sit.

Angus reached up and pulled a twig of heather out of the thatch of the roof, stripped off the smaller twigs with his *sgian dubh*, and leaning forward used it to draw a square on the ground. At the corners of the square he drew smaller elongated squares which intersected with the bigger one.

"So, this is Fort Augustus," he said. "As ye ken we blew it up in March, and much of it's still a ruin. Some of the colonels and suchlike live inside the walls, and the Campbells built a wee house for Fat Billy, wi' a roof o' sods and heather and suchlike, and he lives in that. The ammunition and provisions are stored inside the bits o' the fort that we didna destroy, so we canna get at that. The food for Billy and his hangers-on is cooked inside the fort, but the soldiers shift for themselves."

"How the hell d'ye ken all that?" Alex said. "Ye were tellt to stay away and watch from a distance."

Angus was gouging out a thick line above and below the fort to show the rivers, but paused to look up and grin.

"I'll come to that. The soldiers are all camped in lines, like streets, near the River Oich, here," he pointed, "thousands o' the bastards. Too many to raid, and ye canna even take out a few here and there, unawares. Well, ye could, because some o' them sneak out at night to go plundering, but Cumberland's posted extra sentries to stop them, so the risk o' being caught's too high, and they're killing any Highland men they dinna like the look of anyway, including some of the ones trying to hand in arms and surrender.

"All of the fields around the fort are full of cattle," he continued. "Thousands upon thousands of them. The message ye got from Lochiel is right, Alex. The redcoats are driving them in from all over the Highlands. They're burning the houses, trampling the crops that have survived the rains, killing the men they can find, and then driving all the cattle away. No' just the cattle, but all the livestock, sheep, goats, horses, everything. No doubt about it, they intend tae starve us into submission. All of us, loyal or rebel."

There were murmurs of anger from the men then, but Alex raised a hand and they fell silent.

"There are dealers coming up from the south, frae Scotland and England too, and they're buying the cattle in their hundreds for almost nothing. They have auctions twice a week and the cattle are selling for about half a crown each. That's English money, they'll no' take the Scots pound."

"Half a crown?!" Iain, who knew English money, said, appalled. "That's a pound Scots, is it no'?"

"Just over," Alex said. "But aye, that's disgraceful."

"But why would they sell them so cheap?" Dougal asked. "They could get five times that wi' no effort."

"Because they're no' doing it for profit," Alex said. "They just want rid o' the cattle in case the clansmen get organised enough to raid them, and they havena paid for them so any money is better than none. Angus is right; they mean to starve us. Or have us so busy trying to find food that we've neither time nor will to continue the fight. Cumberland's a bastard, but he's no' stupid. If he was only to burn the people out, all he'd have for his trouble would be thousands of angry armed men burning for revenge. But if he takes their means of subsistence too, then he's won, because they'll no' be able to fight, even if they want to."

Everyone was silent for a moment as they took this in. They were safe for now, because they were too far south for the redcoats to easily reach, and the nearby fort at Inversnaid had been burnt to the ground and was uninhabitable. But it was only a matter of time until Cumberland's attention turned their way.

"What are ye thinking to do, Alex?" Kenneth asked.

"Ye didna find all this out by hiding down by the river, did ye?" Alex asked Angus, ignoring Kenneth's question for now.

Angus abandoned his map-drawing and sat up.

"No," he admitted. "I discovered about the cattle and where the soldiers are camped and that they're sneaking out to plunder. But it was Lachlan who found out about the auctions and the prices and suchlike. He went to one of them."

"What?" Alex said, his voice rising. "Ye let him actually go in the fort? Alone? Have ye run daft, man? The laddie's eight, for God's sake!"

Angus reddened, but met his brother's angry gaze with his own.

"No, I've no' run daft," he retorted hotly. "Ye tellt me to find out as much as I could about the livestock, and what's being done wi' them. So I did. And then I was going to come back. It was Lachlan who suggested he get closer. He wanted to do more than just sit wi' me and watch. We talked it through together, and came up wi' a plan. I still wouldna have let him go, mind, but then I managed to get a bit closer one night without them seeing me, and I saw something that made me realise that he'd every chance of learning more without much danger. So I thought some about it, and we both decided it was worth the risk."

Alex stood and scrubbed his hand viciously through his hair and all the clansmen, as one, froze. Angus stood up, his fists clenched, muscles tense. Morag scrambled off the seat and stepped away from the brothers to the edge of the crowd of men. Several of the men looked round, instinctively searching for Duncan to make the peace. Then they remembered, and sighed.

"I ken ye're fashed, Alex," Angus said, "but hear me out before ye decide I've the wrong of it."

Alex closed his eyes and held back his temper with difficulty. He knew it was his fault for sending Angus in the first place. He knew what his brother was like. If he'd wanted someone who'd have followed his orders without question, he should have sent Alasdair instead, or Dougal. And he recognised that some of his anger was frustration because he hadn't been well enough to go himself.

"Sit down," he said. "I'll hear ye out."

The men collectively breathed a sigh of relief. Angus sat down again.

"Right," he said. "While Lachlan and I were watching the

troop movements, trying to see if there was a pattern to them that might be useful in case ye're planning a raid, we saw that there were a lot of women and bairns coming in from the countryside in the evening, going up to the soldiers and talking to them, and some of the soldiers would speak to them and some would push them away. So that's when Lachlan asked if he could join them and be one o' the bairns, and see if he could hear anything useful, him having the English an' all. I thought on it, and saw no harm, because none o' the women were being hurt. So we decided to stay an extra day so he could mingle wi' them. The women and bairns are the ones that have had their homes burnt, and they're awfu' thin. They were begging for food from the soldiers, offering pennies or shoe buckles, whatever they had that they thought they could trade. Lachlan heard some of them asking if they could have the blood of the butchered animals, anything. They're desperate, Alex. It made my heart burn, when Lachlan came back and tellt me.

"Anyway, some of the soldiers gave them some meal and bread, but then Lachlan heard one of the men tell them that Cumberland had said they'd be flogged if they were caught giving anything to Highlanders, so the others were sent away. The next day they all went to the fields where the auctions were, maybe hoping to beg some food from the dealers, so Lachlan went down again to see what he could find out, just hanging around, listening to the soldiers talking. And that's where he heard everything else, from the price of the cattle to the men complaining that the officers got their food piping hot from the kitchens in the fort, while they had to make do wi' bread and cheese and what they could cook on their fires. And they were laughing about the primitive grass hut the Campbells made for Billy, saying that no doubt the Scots thought it a palace because they all lived like dogs themselves. I doubt the Campbells'd be over happy an they heard that."

After he'd finished, Alex sat for a few moments, head bent, looking at the map Angus had drawn on the ground.

"He wasna in any danger, Alex," Angus said softly after a time. "I wouldna have let him do it if I'd thought there was. And he's a sound head on him, too. I kent he wouldna do something daft. He didna go in the fort. He learnt everything from listening."

"Aye," Alex said. "Ye did well. Ye'd the right of it. I'm sorry, I misjudged ye."

"So," said Kenneth. "When are we leaving? Ye *are* planning a raid, are ye no'?"

Alex was still staring at the plan, but now he looked up at the men, who were avidly waiting for his answer. They were desperate for action, he could see that, and he had to give them some, and soon. It was driving them mad sitting here planting corn and tending cows, while a few miles to the north the country was on fire; but it could be weeks, months even before the redcoats dropped their guard and started looting in smaller groups that could be picked off a few at a time.

It would be suicide to try to raid Fort Augustus with fifty men, bristling with redcoats as it was. He needed to think. He stood up.

"Away and enjoy the sun," he said. "Come back at sunset, and I'll try to have an answer for ye. Angus, away to your bed."

He turned and went into his house, and the men dispersed slowly to chat in groups about what the chieftain might do.

Morag went with Angus to his house, where he kissed her and embraced her, and then went to his bed. Alone.

After an hour, Alex emerged from his house and called one of the children to fetch Iain. Half an hour after that, he sent for Graeme.

As the sun disappeared over the horizon, streaking the sky with gold, purple and rose, and turning the water of the loch red as blood, Alex emerged again to ask one of the children to fetch the men, but found them already assembled along with the women, who had finished their washing, all of them blind to the glories of the sunset, all of them eager to hear their chieftain's decision.

Alex came out, followed by Iain and Graeme, and sat down on the bench. After a minute, he started talking, roughly outlining his plan to them. They sat and listened, at first eagerly and then with mounting disbelief. When he'd finished, they all sat in shocked silence for a minute.

"Ye canna be serious," Kenneth, the first to find his voice, said. "Ye mean the three of ye to ride into Fort Augustus, buy two thousand cattle, and then just ride out again? D'ye think if it could be done, the Camerons or the Frasers'd no' have done it already?

They'll no' let a Scot within ten miles of the place."

"Aye, but we'll no' be Scots," Alex countered. "Graeme's English anyway, for one thing, and ye're forgetting that I was Sir Anthony Peters for over three years. I've no' got the details yet, but I'll be a cattle dealer from Yorkshire or some such place, Graeme here's my right hand man, and Iain, who canna speak wi' any other accent, is a deaf mute, but awfu' good wi' cows, as we all ken well he is, having been on so many raids an' all."

That got a laugh from the audience, at least.

"Why no' take me, then, instead of Iain?" Angus asked. "I ken the land now, a wee bit at least."

"Because I need you to lead the clan while I'm away," Alex said. "Iain canna do that, and most of the rest of you have wives and bairns, apart from Kenneth. And we're no' supposed tae ken the land. We're from Yorkshire and somewhat afeart to be in this savage land. But we canna resist the chance to make our fortunes."

"So ye're going to buy two thousand cows, and then just drive them here? D'ye no' think the redcoats'll notice? And where the hell are we going to keep two thousand cattle, or feed them?" Alasdair countered.

"And where will ye get the money tae buy so many cows, cheap as they are?" Peigi asked.

Alex and Graeme exchanged a look, then Alex nodded and Graeme spoke up.

"When Beth married Sir Anthony, she brought a dowry with her. It was held in a bank in Manchester. But when she discovered who Sir Anthony really was, she realised that if he was ever found out, her brother would try to claim the dowry. Those of you who've had the misfortune to meet Richard or hear of him know he's a piece of shit. Rather than let him have it, she withdrew all of it, and got me to hide it for her. I'm the only one who knows where it is."

"It's in England," said Alex, taking over. "We're going down to get the money we need. Then we're going to go straight to Fort Augustus and buy the cattle. We're no' bringing them here. I've heard tell of a place where they can be hidden safely, then we'll put out the word to those in need, and they can come and take them, a few at a time. The redcoats have already burnt their houses and taken everything. They'll no' come back again, they've got too many other places to plunder. We'll take a few for ourselves, but the plan is to help feed the likes of the women and bairns reduced to begging off the redcoats. I think that's a good use for the money, a use Beth would have approved of."

"Where's this hiding place, then?" Kenneth asked.

"That I canna tell ye," said Alex, "for it's no' my secret to divulge. But I'm away off tomorrow to speak wi' the man whose secret it is, and once I've his answer, we can go ahead. Or no', as the case may be."

"It's an interesting plan," Dougal said thoughtfully, "but it's awfu' risky."

"No' as risky as being Sir Anthony," Alex pointed out, "and no' as risky as being a MacGregor, but here we all are, alive."

"And we'll no' get to go on a raid," Alasdair put in sadly, to a chorus of agreement.

Alex looked up at them and smiled, something he'd done but rarely since he'd heard of Beth's death.

"Aye, I've every intention of ye going on a raid, if things go according to plan," he said. "But first I've to meet wi' the man who's got the hiding place. I should be back within the week, and I'll tell ye more then. It's about time we got our swords bloodied again, I'm thinking. I've sat on my arse for long enough. I'm healed now, and I'm ready to start fighting back, in whatever way I can. It'll no' be on a battlefield, wi' lines of us facing lines o' the enemy. But I think we've had enough of that kind of fighting, for now, anyway. It's about time we showed the redcoats why we're named the Children o' the Mist. Are ye in agreement wi' me?"

The resulting roar from the assembled MacGregors assured Alex that they were, indeed, very much in agreement with him.

\* \* \*

"No," MacIain said flatly. "I'll have no part of it. I've surrendered."

"The Grants surrendered too, and much good it did them," Alex pointed out. "A whole lot of them are rotting in jail now, and others who are trying to surrender are being shot or hung for it. Ye must have heard the news, man. It's all over the Highlands."

"Aye, I've heard the news," the MacDonald chief agreed, "But I surrendered last month, and I've been left alone since then, even though Glencoe is only a morning's march from Fort William."

"And how long d'ye think that'll last, once the redcoats have finished burning Lochaber, and the Fraser lands? Once the Campbells remember how good your land is, and how close ye are to them? The fact that ye've surrendered will mean nothing. Ye came out for Charlie; that's all that counts now."

"I'll take my chance. I'm weary, Alex. I want no more of Stuart or Hanover. I'm done wi' fighting for others. I just want to live peaceably for a time."

"We all want that," Alex said. "But the Highlands are burning, and Cumberland is trying to destroy our way of life, forever. MacDonalds and MacGregors have been reiving cattle from our neighbours for years. Now we've a chance to reive them from our true enemies. Thousands of women and bairns are starving, and we've a chance of doing something to help them. D'ye no' think it might be useful to have the goodwill of the Camerons, MacPhersons, Frasers and suchlike in times to come? If ye save them from starving ye'll have that."

"Aye, and if Cumberland hears I've helped ye steal two thousand cattle from him, all the goodwill in the world'll no' save us from his anger," MacIain pointed out.

"They were no' his in the first place, and anyway we're no' stealing them," Alex said, grinning. "We'll be paying for them, fair and square. Listen," he continued, serious again, "ye dinna have to be actively involved. Just give me permission to drive the cattle to Coire Gabhail and keep them there. We'll tend them. No one else need ken anything about it, we'll take the cattle out a few at a time tae give to those in need. And if ye've need of men later, I'll pledge my men to your cause, while I live."

"That's a generous offer," MacIain said, "and I appreciate it, Alex. But the answer's still no. It's too risky."

An hour later Alex emerged from the Glencoe chief's house, thoroughly frustrated. Nothing he had said had made MacIain change his mind, and he realised that there was nothing he could say that would do it. The man was beaten, for now at least, but this plan could not wait until his spirit revived. And they could not do it without him. He knew of no other place as suitable as Coire Gabhail, the hidden valley of Glencoe. The way up to it was steep, but then it opened out into a huge saucer-shaped green valley, completely surrounded by mountains. The opening was so narrow it could be easily defended by a few men. If it was discovered, which was unlikely. It was perfect, but none of that mattered now.

Iain and Graeme had come with him, and they were all staying with Ealasaid, but he could not face going to tell them that he'd failed just yet. He needed time to think. And he needed time to plan something else, another raid of some sort to keep the morale of his men high. Not easy, when his own was so low.

He went for a walk along the loch before going back to his lodgings, but after it was no nearer to coming up with a new plan, so he had to bite the bullet and give the others the bad news.

Any dismay Iain and Graeme may have felt at the scuppering of the plan was drowned out by a chorus of questions from the fair-haired kinfolk of Beth, who were all in Ealasaid's house at the time.

"Tell us your plan, Alex," Robert said eagerly. "Maybe we can think of a way to do it anyway."

"No," said Alex. "I tellt your chief that I wouldna reveal it to the clan unless he agreed to it. The MacIain has said no, and I accept it. I'll no' cause dissent in the clan. That would be a poor return for his hospitality. He has the right to refuse me, and I'll abide by his answer, as will all those I have power over. And so will you," he warned the young MacDonald. Robert had grown physically since he'd tried to seduce Morag in the stable, but he did not appear to have matured much emotionally. Robert subsided into a sulky silence.

"What will ye do instead?" Meg asked.

"I dinna ken. Nothing that the MacDonalds will be involved in," Alex said. He would talk about it with Iain and Graeme later. Maybe they could buy a couple of hundred cattle. Maybe if he could get a message to Lochiel…but no, the Cameron chief was still healing, and had his hands full trying to get Prince Charles to safety.

Ealasaid herself had said nothing up to this point, had listened to everything with her head bowed, eyes fixed on her hands, which rested calmly in her lap. Now she looked up.

"Well," she said. "MacIain has spoken, and that's an end of it.

Let's feed our guests, and then entertain them with a wee story and a song or two. We've no need to be downhearted. And," she continued, staring pointedly at Robert, "we've no need to cause our guests tae think less of us by pestering them wi' questions they canna answer."

Robert, who had already turned to Iain in the hopes of doing just that, opened his mouth to protest, then seeing Ealasaid's expression, closed it again and returned to his sulk.

* * *

After dinner, while they were waiting for the musicians to fetch their instruments, Ealasaid took Alex to one side and expressed a wish that he accompany her on a short walk.

"I'm feeling a need for some fresh air," she said, indicating with a wave of her hand the smoky atmosphere of the hut's main room in which a peat fire burned, the smoke hanging around in the roof space for a while before escaping through a hole in the roof. "It's dry for a change, but I'm a wee bit old and frail to be walking about alone. We can talk about family," she said, squeezing his shoulder with a firm but friendly grip that had nothing frail about it.

Alex had no wish to talk about 'family', which to him could only mean Beth, but nor did he wish to join in the merrymaking. He wanted nothing more than to lie down and turn his face to the wall, but he knew that was something he must fight against. And Highland courtesy demanded that he acquiesce to his hostess's wish, so he took her arm and they walked slowly out of the hut and through the village in companionable silence. Although the evening was advanced, it was still light; at this time of year the nights were very short.

He expected her to turn around at the end of the village, but to his surprise she continued on, striding up the grassy slope with an agility that belied her professed feebleness. She continued until they were a good way up the mountain, where there was a large flat rock upon which she spread her shawl.

"Sit yourself down, laddie," she said breathlessly. "Ye're doing well, outwardly at least."

Alex sat down gratefully, stretched his legs out in front of him and smiled.

"Ye fooled me there for a minute," he said. "I should have remembered how 'frail' ye were at our wedding feast." As soon as the words were out of his mouth, he cursed inwardly, thinking that Ealasaid would use them as an introduction to talking about a subject that would bring him nothing but pain.

"It takes me a wee bit longer to get moving in the mornings," she said instead, "but I'm blessed, I think. Most people of my age are lying in their beds waiting to die."

"There are no' many people of your age at all," Alex responded, knowing that Ealasaid, in common with her granddaughter, would prefer blunt truth to flattery any day.

She laughed, and it sounded so like Beth's laugh that his heart twisted.

"Good," she said, still gasping a little from the effort of the climb. "The truth. That's what I've brought ye here for."

He looked around appreciatively, waiting for her to regain her breath. In the valley below, the village nestled by the shores of Loch Leven, which appeared blue and peaceful in the soft light of evening. Along the banks of the loch the mountains rose, the lower slopes forested, the higher ones displaying the hazy purple of early-flowering heather in places. To the north on the far side of the water were the mountains of the Cameron lands, rendered slate blue by distance. He wondered idly where Lochiel was right now, and hoped that he was safe.

"Aye," she said, her breath back. "It's a bonny view. I used to come here to think when I was a wee lassie wi' a head full of dreams but no common sense at all. But we're no' here to admire the view. We canna be overheard here. Tell me your plan."

"There's nae point to it," Alex countered. "He said no."

"Even so," Ealasaid said. "I've an urge tae ken how my grandson-in-law thinks. And I pride myself that ye think me trustworthy. I take it there was a raid involved?"

He did think her trustworthy.

"Aye, there was," he said, still gazing into the distance. "My men are restless, they've a need to release their energy, and I thought this was a way to do it, to fight back against Cumberland, and to help those in need."

He explained the plan, and she listened without interrupting until he'd finished. And then she remained silent a while longer, thinking.

"And ye think ye can carry this off, impersonating an English cattle dealer?"

"I do," he said. "I've done something of the sort before." Although he was willing to reveal an aborted plan, he was not about to tell anyone who didn't already know about Sir Anthony.

She nodded.

"Well, it's different, and there are risks, but no' as many as when Charlie arrived wi' his seven useless men, the wee gomerel," she commented irreverently.

Alex laughed, his first genuine laugh in a long time.

"It's good to hear ye laugh, laddie," she said, laying her hand on his arm. "Your leg's healing well, I can see, but your heart isna. It shows how well ye loved her, but it's a sadness to me."

"Ye tellt me when I was here last that I shouldna blame myself, and you were right. But I canna stop loving her, and I never will. I tellt her once that I was hers until I die, and I meant it. I'll not take another."

"Not even to give the clan an heir?" Ealasaid asked.

"No. If I couldna have bairns wi' Beth, I'll no' have them at all. Duncan is gone, but Angus will make a good chieftain in time, and there's no reason he shouldna have bairns. He's a sweetheart waiting to marry him. They've put the wedding off for a while until things settle down, but she wasna happy about it. Angus is intent on fulfilling his blood oath, but she's growing impatient."

"Is this wee Morag, that Robert tried to seduce in the barn?" Ealasaid asked.

"Ye remember that. Aye."

"I'm old, but my mind's as sharp as it ever was," she said. "Let's away back down the hill. Ye've had a long day."

They made their way back to the village, slowly, because his leg ached more going downhill than up, and because the dusk made rabbit holes and stones harder to see, and the last thing he needed now was to twist his ankle, when he was healing so well.

When they got back to the cottage, the others, apart from Iain and Graeme, had disappeared, to Alex's relief. The two men were sitting at the table playing cards, but both looked up at him when he entered.

"I'm tired," said Alex brusquely, to forestall conversation. "I'm away to my bed. We can get an early start in the morning."

He would put his disappointment to the back of his mind, try to sleep, and come up with another plan on the way home.

\* \* \*

Although Alex was awake before dawn the following morning, when he wandered into the living area of the house Ealasaid was already up and about, and clearly had been for some time.

"There's bread and butter, and cheese on the table," she said. "Would ye like some tea?"

"Do ye never sleep?" Alex asked. "I would love some tea." He sat down at the table, rubbing his eyes to wake himself up.

"When ye get to my age, ye dinna need much sleep," she said. "And when ye've so little time left, it's a shame to spend it sleeping, in any case." She bustled about with the kettle, and soon there was a steaming cup of the fragrant brew sitting in front of him.

"I didna offer ye any last night, because Robert was here, and if he kent I'd got some, he'd find it and drink it all. He's awfu' partial to it."

It was Alex's view that Robert needed a good thrashing, but he kept silent and instead took a sip of tea, sighing blissfully.

"I'll let Iain and Graeme sleep yet awhile," he said. "But I'd like to get an early start for home, all the same."

Ealasaid poured herself a cup of tea and came to sit down opposite him.

"The MacIain'll no' be out of bed yet awhile either," she said. "He was up late last night. Enjoy your breakfast, laddie. Ye'll no' be making any start for home at all today. Ye've a raid to plan."

Alex stopped drinking and stared at her. Her blue eyes were sparkling with mischief. She looked exactly as Beth would have done had she lived another sixty years.

"But…MacIain said no. He was verra adamant," he said, puzzled.

"Aye, well. We had a wee chat last night after ye were snoring, and ye'll find him of a different persuasion this morning, I'm thinking."

"What the hell did ye say to him?" Alex asked, astounded. Was she serious?

"Let's just say I've a persuasive tongue, and leave it there." She winked. "I've a favour to ask, though."

She was serious. He felt the heady rush of excitement flood his veins, as he always did when faced with the prospect of danger.

"Name it," he said rashly.

"If all goes well, and ye have the wee stramash that ye're planning, MacIain's said that he'll no' stop anyone who wants to join in from doing so, although he'll be staying at home himself. He's no' a well man, Alex, in fairness, and although he doesna remember the massacre in '92, it weighs heavy on him all the same."

"You do remember it though, yet by the look on your face ye'd be fighting wi' us, were you able," Alex pointed out.

"True, but I've always been impulsive, and I'm no' the chief. It's a heavy burden he carries, as ye ken well. But it's different for you, your name and lands are forfeit anyway. Ye've got nothing to lose but your lives if it miscarries. He could lose his lands and his name, and the clan's future."

Alex could not dispute this.

"What's the favour, then?"

"I want ye to let Robert be in the raiding party. Aye, I ken ye think he's no' ready, and maybe you're right. But he was sore hurt that he couldna go wi' the clan to follow Charlie. MacIain wouldna let him go, and now he has to listen to the men boast of their exploits, knowing that he's unlikely to get a chance to fight for the cause for a good while, if ever."

"It's no' over yet," Alex said. "Charles lives, and there are many who would rise again for him, if he can get French help this time. He's proved he can raise an army, and lead it. Maybe Louis will take him more seriously now."

"I hope so. But in the meantime, Robert's burning up to do something worthwhile, so he can feel like a man. He *is* a man in most ways."

Alex nodded.

"There was a laddie along wi' us, same name. Robbie Og. He was fifteen and I wouldna let him come, for the same reasons as I think MacIain didna let your Robert go, although his age was a factor too. Some of the men went home for a visit after Prestonpans, and Robbie came back with them. He *did* grow up in the end, although he nearly got himself hung in the meantime."

"Well, then," Ealasaid said. "Maybe –"

"He's dead," Alex interrupted. "He was killed at Culloden. I heard him scream, but I couldna go back to see to him because we were charging, and it wasna possible. And afterwards…" He paused, and scrubbed his hand through his hair. "I like to think he died quick and clean, but I dinna ken. He could have died slowly wi' all the others who were left to bleed and freeze to death for two nights on Cumberland's orders. What I'm saying is that if Robert wants to come so badly, then I'll accept him, but he'll have to listen to whoever I put in command of the raid, because it'll no' be me, and if he doesna and gets himself in trouble, I'll no' risk my men's lives to try to save him. And if he does something that puts the rest of us at risk, then I'll kill him myself. Are ye willing to risk his death? And will ye blame me if I'm the one to kill him?"

She sat and thought about it for a few minutes.

"Aye, I'll risk it, if ye'll give him the chance. And ye're a fair man. I'll no' blame ye if ye have to make a hard choice," she said. "For if he doesna learn the hard way, he'll no' learn at all. He's like myself in that. I'll make it clear to him what ye've tellt me, and that you're serious, and then it's his choice. And now," she added, eyes sparkling once again, "Do I get a wee hug for my trouble wi' MacIain? I'm no' too old to appreciate being held in the arms of a handsome young man."

She was clearly joking, but Alex took her at her word, and swept her off her feet in a tender, loving, yet respectful embrace. She laughed again, in that way that was so like Beth, and wrapped her arms around his neck.

"Ye're a fine laddie," she said into his ear. "I'm proud of ye. Beth couldna have chosen a better, had she searched the whole of Scotland first."

And it was at that moment that Iain and Graeme chose to make their entrance, and found Alex and Ealasaid embracing like lovers while tears poured down their cheeks, as they took, although they did not know it, their last farewells of each other.

# CHAPTER SIX

**London, July 1746**

Sarah moved about her living room, cradling the baby in one arm whilst preparing her evening meal with the other. She had cut herself a slice of chicken pie, which she'd prepared early that morning and had just finished baking in her Dutch oven. It was the first time she'd tried this recipe, which included wine and spices, and it smelt wonderful. Her stomach rumbled in anticipation.

It had been a long day. In the morning she had made a house call, and the whole of the afternoon had been spent dressing the hair of a group of chambermaids who had been allowed an evening off and were heading to Vauxhall to try to meet the man of their dreams. She thought them more likely to meet a rake who'd give them the pox, but it was her job to encourage their dreams and do her best to help them fulfil them, not to destroy them.

The baby's eyes were closing now, lulled by the rocking motion of Sarah's arm and the warmth of the room, fragranced with the scent of cloves and nutmeg. She popped the baby in her cot, and went back into her living room, leaving the bedroom door ajar so she could hear if Mary started grizzling. She picked up the bucket in which she put her slops; hair clippings, dirty water, vegetable peelings, and opening the back door, which led on to a dark alley, threw the contents out to join the other refuse which covered the ground.

It was while she was shaking the bucket, trying to dislodge some cabbage leaves which had stuck to the bottom that she heard her name called, and instinctively looked up the alley in the direction from which the voice had come.

About twenty yards or so away could be seen the figure of a man who was making his way toward her, and who appeared to be limping. It was too dark and he was too far away for her to see his face, but she wasn't about to wait for him to get any closer. As quick as lightning she jumped back into the room, shut the door, turned the key in the lock, shot the bolts at top and bottom, then stood with her back to it, her heart thumping in her chest.

She didn't know any men. Well, of course that wasn't true. She did know *some* men; she had exchanged words with several of her clients' husbands, and with tradesmen. But she didn't know any men who would approach her by way of a filthy back alley, unless they were hoping to rob her or worse. Her pistol was in the shop under the counter, but she was confident that the locks would hold if he attempted to break in. It was a sturdy door. She started to relax a little.

There came a knock right behind her head, and she gave an involuntary scream then stepped back, away from the door. She went and quietly closed the door to the bedroom so as not to wake the baby, then returned.

"What do you want?" she said in a clear, firm voice.

"Sarah? Sarah Browne?" the voice answered.

"Go away," she replied, "or I'll call the watch."

"You were Beth's kitchen maid in Didsbury? Beth Cunningham?"

*What the hell?* Although it was known to many that she had been Beth's maid in London, and that she had accompanied her from Manchester, nobody, apart from Beth's servants in Didsbury knew that she had started her career as a kitchen maid. Except Richard. But this man, whoever he was, was not Richard.

"Who are you?" she asked, intrigued in spite of herself.

The silence that followed this question went on for so long that Sarah thought the man had given up and gone away. She was just about to return to her pie when the voice came again, this time from the keyhole, and much softer.

"It's John," he said. "John Betts. The stable boy."

Sarah's first instinct was to open the door. Although she had hardly known John, Beth had always spoken highly of him. He had defended her against Richard, and had had to leave. But what was he doing here, and how did he know where she lived? It was a ruse of some sort.

"Why have you come here?" she asked.

"I need help. I didn't know where else to go," he said. "Please, let me in. I'll explain everything."

She thought, rapidly.

"Tell me some things about Didsbury. Things other people wouldn't know," she said.

Another silence, then a torrent of low-voiced words, spoken with some desperation, came from the other side of the door.

"I didn't know you for long. Richard brought you to replace Martha and spy on Beth for him. We all hated you. Graeme was the gardener, Thomas and Jane were the steward and cook, Grace was Beth's maid, Mary and Ben were the scullery maid and odd job boy. Beth told me that you turned out to be one of her best friends. You saved her when Lord Damien tried to make her marry him."

"Daniel," Sarah corrected automatically, then cursed herself. She came to a decision.

"Wait there a minute," she said.

She ran into the shop, retrieved the pistol from under the counter, checked it was primed and cocked and ready to fire, and then went back to the door. She undid the bolts, turned the key in the lock, and then stood back.

"Come in," she said, "slowly."

The door opened very slowly, to reveal the filthiest individual she had ever seen in her life. He made to step in the room, but then saw the pistol levelled at his head and stopped, his eyes widening. He raised both his hands in the air and swallowed audibly. The sleeves of the torn and ragged shirt he wore slid up his arms, revealing wrists that were a mass of sores, writhing with maggots. His ankles were in the same state, which explained why he had limped down the alley. The smell emanating from him was worse than that in the alley had ever been, even in the height of summer. Apart from his height, there was nothing left of the handsome youth she'd last seen mucking out the stables in Didsbury. The emaciated wreck standing in front of her now could have been fifty.

"Dear God," she said, lowering the pistol and involuntarily retching at the stench. "What happened to you?"

He kept his hands up, but glanced behind him at the open door. She got the message and motioned him further into the room, then walked behind him, shut the door and locked it. Then she looked at him again, assessing him. His eyes were wild as he watched her warily, his chest heaving as though he'd been running, although he'd been standing outside her door for a good few minutes. He was certainly capable of violence, she realised, but only in the way of a cornered animal that must fight or die.

"It's alright," she said. "I won't shoot you unless you try to hurt me. But if you do, I will."

He nodded.

"What happened to you?" she asked again.

"I escaped from Newgate," he said. "I didn't have anywhere else to go, and if I stay like this, they'll catch me. I'm sorry."

"Why were you in prison? Tell me the truth."

"I was taken prisoner when Carlisle fell. I was in the Manchester Regiment, fighting for Prince Charles."

"I thought you'd joined the militia," Sarah said, wary again. "How did you end up as a rebel?"

John smiled, displaying a set of teeth white enough to show he was a lot younger than he appeared.

"I thought joining the militia was the quickest way to learn to use a sword. I wanted to kill Richard. From what I've learned about him since, I wish I had," he said.

Sarah warmed to him instantly.

"How did you know I'd saved Beth from Lord Daniel?" she asked.

"I met her when…" His voice trailed off. "Are you going to call the watch?" he asked.

The fact that he'd been about to reveal incriminating evidence about Beth and had stopped in case she betrayed him, and in doing so betrayed Beth, committed Sarah to a course of action that the sensible part of her had already dismissed as insane.

"No," she said. "I'm going to get you clean enough so that we can talk without me wanting to be sick. Come through to the shop. I've not long closed, so the water will still be warm."

She led him through the room and to a corner of the shop,

where there was a brazier and on top of it a large pot, half-full of water. She handed him a bar of rose-scented soap, a comb and a cloth to dry himself, then went and got a blanket from the chest at the foot of her bed.

"I'll leave you to wash," she said. "When you're clean, wrap yourself in the blanket for now. I'll get you some clothes tomorrow."

He looked at her, shocked.

"I don't expect you to let me stay here," he said. "It's too dangerous. I'll just wash these clothes as best I can, and if you can lend me a little money, I'll find somewhere to stay until I can get a coach out of London."

"Did you tell anyone you were coming here?" she asked. "Did anyone see you come into the alley?"

He shook his head.

"Well, then. Wash yourself, then have something to eat, and I'll get something to dress your wounds."

For a moment he seemed not to know what she was talking about, then he followed her gaze down to his wrists.

"I'm not wounded," he said. "It's just –"

"A mess," she interrupted. "Come back in when you've finished."

It was nearly half an hour before he returned to the cosy living room. In his absence Sarah had been busy. She'd opened the door for a few minutes to let the smell out, and then had sprinkled rosewater around the room. On the table was a jug of warm spiced ale, a large slice of the chicken pie, and an assortment of bottles of varying sizes.

She looked up at him as he came in, and whistled softly through her teeth. He was a lot thinner than when she had last seen him, his hair, light brown again now it was clean, was longer, and he had a thick beard, but nevertheless she now recognised the youth she had known briefly in Didsbury.

"Sit down," she said, and motioned to the pie.

He needed no second invitation and fell on the pie like a starving animal, which, she supposed, he was.

Afterwards, while he told her his story, she combed powder of staves-acre through his hair to kill the lice, and then went to work on his wrists and ankles, picking off the maggots with tweezers and throwing them in the fire, her nose wrinkling with disgust.

"When the prince went back into Scotland," John said, "he asked the Manchester Regiment to hold Carlisle Castle for him, for when he came back. Most of us stayed. Graeme went with the others on to Scotland though. I wish I had too, now."

"Graeme?" Sarah said. "The gardener? But he's an old man!"

John laughed.

"Don't let him hear you say that," he said. "He joined the army when Charles came to Manchester. That's where we met Beth. I threw a knife at her."

Sarah stopped what she was doing, abruptly.

"I'd been learning to throw knives," he continued hurriedly, realising how his last sentence had sounded. "I wanted to be as good as her. I never was, but I was pretty good all the same. I was showing off, and threw a knife at the door she was sitting against. Anyway, then we stayed together down to Derby, then all the way back to Carlisle. When Cumberland took the castle, we were all arrested and we've been in prison ever since. The officers were brought to London, and we were tried two days ago and sentenced to the traitor's death."

"Hanging, drawing and quartering," Sarah said, shuddering. "Some of my clients told me about the crowds outside the New Gaol. You were marched there through the streets. Is that how you escaped?"

"No. After the trial they took us back to Newgate. Three of us were in a tiny cell, and we were just left there for two days with no food or water. No one came to look at us; I think they'd forgotten about us, to be honest. Which gave us time to find a loose brick and to work all the mortar away from round it." He held up his hands; the nails and ends of his fingers were ragged and bloody.

"It was really damp in there," he continued. "The water was running down the walls, so the mortar was very soft, and we all had long nails by then so we took turns to scrape it out. Then Jack found a rusty bit of metal in the corner of the room, and we used that, too. Anyway, once we'd pulled out the brick I had a look through to see what was on the other side, thinking it would probably be another cell, but we couldn't believe our luck because it led straight out onto the street. We'd been kept in irons until our trial, and they chafe a bit," he said with spectacular understatement, "but the wardens didn't bother to put them back on again afterwards. Newgate's full to bursting with rebel prisoners, so the guards are run off their feet. There was only one tiny window high up in the wall of our cell, so I suppose they didn't think there was any danger of us escaping. All three of us got away, me, Jack Holker and Peter Moss, although Peter and me had to pull Jack through the hole, because he had been a portly fellow, and still had a bit of weight on him. Then we all split up, because we thought we'd have a better chance separately. Jack said he was heading for the coast to try to find a ship for France. I don't know what Peter's going to do. And I thought I'd come here and see if you'd lend me the money to get back to Manchester. Thomas and Jane'll look after me until I can find somewhere safer. Graeme might even be there, if he lives," John mused.

The maggots gone, Sarah opened a pot and rubbed salve all over the festering wounds. Then she poured some more ale for them both.

She'd just sat down, when a thin wail came from the adjoining room. John looked round in surprise.

"You have a baby?" he asked.

"She's my sister's child," Sarah explained. "She died in childbirth, and there was no father so I took her." She went through to the other room, returning a few minutes later.

"You said you were with Beth. How is she?" Sarah asked. "I was so worried about her when her and Sir Anthony vanished."

John's brow furrowed.

"Sir Anthony?" he said. "Oh! You mean A –"

"NO!" Sarah shouted, making John jump so violently that he spilled some of the ale he was about to drink on the blanket he was wearing. "I'm sorry," she said. "I didn't mean to frighten you, but if you were about to tell me Sir Anthony's real name, I don't want to know. I've already been interviewed by the Duke of Newcastle. Sir Anthony's one of the most wanted men in Britain. I don't know whether I'll be interviewed again, but the less I know, the better."

John nodded.

"They won't interview me about him, because no one knows I had any connection to Beth or…him. She was well the last time I saw her, at Carlisle. She tried to stay there, with Graeme and me because she'd had an argument with…er…"

"Just call him Sir Anthony. That's what I knew him as," Sarah said.

"She'd had an argument with Sir Anthony, then. I don't know what it was about, but it must have been serious, because I never saw two people so much in love with each other. But he just stopped talking to her completely, wouldn't even look at her. She was very unhappy, and when Prince Charles asked us to stay in Carlisle she decided to stay as well. But Sir Anthony wouldn't let her. He sent An…another man to make her go on with them to Scotland. So Graeme went too, to keep an eye on her. I hope they made up," he finished wistfully. Suddenly realising that the blanket had slipped while he'd been talking, exposing his nakedness, he pulled it tighter round himself before casting an embarrassed glance at Sarah.

She hadn't noticed. She was staring at a point somewhere over his left shoulder, but the misty expression in her eyes told him that she was far, far away from this room. He waited for a while, then for a while more. And then he coughed softly.

Her eyes cleared, and her focus shot back to him.

"Sir Anthony had two servants," she said, her voice uncharacteristically hesitant. "I knew them as Jim and Murdo, and I don't want to know their real names either. But one was tall and fair-haired, and the other was a bit smaller, with dark hair and grey eyes."

John smiled.

"Yes," he said. "I know who you're talking about."

She leaned forward eagerly, then checked herself and sat back again.

"Were they well, when you last saw them?" she asked.

"Yes. Both of them were in excellent health when I last saw them. But that was in December," he added softly. Clearly one of these men meant something to her, but he didn't want to raise her hopes. "A lot has happened since then."

Sarah looked at him, and tears sparkled on her lashes.

"I know," she replied. "You're right." She brushed her hand

across her face, and stood. "You can sleep in here. It'll have to be on the floor, I'm afraid, but there's a bit of carpet, and I'll get another blanket for you. I'll go out in the morning and get you some clothes. I'll go where no one knows me," she added.

"I really appreciate this, Sarah," John said. "After all, you didn't really know me, and when you did I made it very clear that I hated you."

She laughed.

"You were right to, then," she said. "I was a bitch. I still can be. But you say Beth spoke highly of me. Well, she spoke highly of you too, and that's enough for me. Here," she said, handing him the pistol. "Keep that with you tonight. Just in case anyone did see you coming into the alley."

"They didn't," John said, checking it was all in order and ready to fire if necessary. "I was very careful. I don't really know London, though. Is this a dangerous part of town, then?"

"No," Sarah replied. "I bought that and learned how to use it, so that if Richard ever comes to see me again, I can blow his fucking brains out."

And with that she went to bed, leaving John not knowing whether to be more shocked by the expletive she had just uttered, or by her tone of voice, which left him in no doubt that if Richard Cunningham was at any time to enter her premises, it would be the last thing he ever did.

* * *

When Sarah got back from the market the next day, carrying a parcel of clothes, the baby carefully swaddled against her chest by means of a cleverly-tied shawl, John had cleaned the small room and got a fire going, and two pots of water were boiling over it. He looked up as she came through the door from the shop and smiled at her. He was still wearing the blanket from yesterday, as whilst he had been washing the previous evening she had unceremoniously burnt all his vermin-infested clothes. However, with the aid of a piece of rope, he had now tied the blanket around him in an interesting fashion, which left the lower part of his legs bare, but which covered the upper part and most of his torso.

Sarah placed the parcel of clothes on one chair, then untied the shawl from round her waist. An ominous smell came from the baby, which competed with the spicy smell from the remains of yesterday's pie, which was reheating in the Dutch oven. She placed the baby on the chair and massaged the small of her back with her hands.

"She doesn't seem to weigh much, until you've been carrying her round all day," Sarah said. She looked around the sparkling room. "You've been busy. You didn't have to do this, you know."

"I wanted to," John said. "It was nice to be active, after being stuck so long in a cell. I used to walk round and round it, just to keep my legs strong. I hope you don't mind," he added, gesturing to the fire, "I put some carrots and potatoes to boil, I thought you might appreciate not having to cook."

Sarah picked the baby up, who was now awake. Her little face puckered up as she prepared to howl at the double discomfort of a dirty bottom and an empty stomach.

"You'll make someone a wonderful wife one day," she joked. "I'll go and change her clout and feed her," she continued. "I won't be more than a few minutes."

When she came back, minus the baby, John was busy putting the food out on plates. Sarah sat down at the table with obvious relief.

"There," she said. "She's all clean and fed and should sleep for a couple of hours now."

"What are you feeding her?" John asked unexpectedly.

Sarah instantly blushed scarlet, to his surprise.

"I'm sorry," he said. "It's just…I wondered if you had a wet nurse for her, that's all."

"No," Sarah replied. "I feed her myself. Cow's milk, or goat's when I can get it," she added hurriedly. She focussed all her attention on cutting up a potato. "These are perfect."

It was clear from her tone that she was very surprised he was capable of the simple act of cooking a potato.

"The Highlanders aren't like us," he explained. "The men don't think cooking is woman's work. In fact it's really common for the men to cook. I learnt from them, and it seems natural now. After all, the women work really hard, doing all the cleaning and washing and so forth, and when there are no battles to be fought, there's often not a lot for the men to do, so they cook."

"Did you learn your interesting way with a blanket from the

Highlanders too?" she asked indistinctly, her mouth full of potato.

Now it was John's turn to blush as he looked down and realised how scantily covered he was, by English standards.

"I'm sorry," he said again.

Sarah waved a hand in the air to indicate that she was intrigued rather than offended by his attire. She chewed briskly and swallowed.

"It's very clever," she said.

"The Highlanders have more material in theirs. They call it the *féileadh mhór*. They wear it a bit like this," he indicated the knee-length skirt he'd fashioned, "but they gather it at the back, so it allows them to move freely, and then the part that hangs over the belt," he pointed to his bit of rope, "can be worn like a cloak, or over one shoulder…all kinds of ways. They use it as a blanket too, or even a tent, sometimes. Sorry, am I boring you?"

He had to admit she didn't look bored. If anything she looked entranced. She had been still, her forkful of pie poised halfway to her mouth the whole time he'd been speaking.

"No," she confirmed. "It's really interesting. I only know what the newspapers say, since I learned to read; that the Highlanders are all savage barbarians who kill each other at the drop of a hat, are dirty and ragged, speak with grunts, and rape and murder at will. But I met Murdo and Jim, and Sir Anthony, of course, and I'd love to know more about what the Highlanders are really like, because the newspapers are full of lies. Beth told me that the king is dull and boring, and Cumberland spoke only to her breasts, and that most of her friends don't like King George, even the ones who support him. And that's nothing like what the Gazette says. But let's eat first, and you need to be careful about what you tell me, because I really don't want to know their proper names, or where they come from, or anything that could help them be arrested."

"Is the Duke of Newcastle that frightening, that you think you'd give information away to him?" John asked.

"No. But what I don't know I can't tell, whatever happens," Sarah pointed out logically.

So they ate, and he thought, and then he told her that he'd believed the same as her until he'd met Highlanders in the flesh, when he'd found those he'd met to be, in the main, highly civilised people. Even on campaign they tried to keep as clean as possible; they respected women and cared for children, and he hadn't seen one instance of rape in the whole time he'd been with the Jacobite army. Although he couldn't understand their language, far from being a series of grunts, it had a musical lilting tone to it that was beautiful.

"Did you learn any?" Sarah asked.

"*Tha gràdh agam ort, mo chridhe,*" he said.

"Oh, that sounds lovely. What does it mean?"

John grinned.

"Jim told me it meant, 'a good morning to you', but after I'd said it to half a dozen burly men who gave me very strange looks, Ke…one of Sir Anthony's friends, when I said it to him, started laughing, and knew straight away that Jim had taught me. Believe me, this man was not someone you'd want to say *tha gràdh agam ort* to, not if you were a man, anyway, and wanted to live long."

"What does it mean, then?"

"I love you, my heart. I told Jim I'd skin him alive if he taught me any more things like that. I could have died of embarrassment."

Sarah tried not to laugh for all of five seconds, then gave in. She laughed until the tears ran down her face, and then she gave a great sobbing sigh, and John realised that somewhere along the way the mirth had given way to sadness. Instinctively he stood and moved to comfort her, but she waved him away, so instead he hovered uncertainly near her, not knowing what to do.

"I miss them," she said finally, when she'd got her emotions under control a little.

"I'm sure Beth's all right," John assured her, not sure who she meant by 'them'. "I'm sure she made up her argument with –"

"Not just Beth," Sarah interrupted. She hesitated for a moment, as though about to reveal something, then changed her mind. "I miss Sir Anthony too. He was different."

"I know, Graeme told me. He called him the Purple Popinjay."

"No, not that. Yes, everyone thought he was an incompetent flowery fool, that all he thought about was fashion, gossip and himself. But there was more to him, I knew that the first time I met him. Of course I didn't know what it was." She blew her nose, sniffed, and gave John a watery smile. "But he always treated women with respect, even servants and beggars. And when I saw his reaction when I ran into Lord Edward's card party and told him Lord Daniel had abducted Beth, I knew then that he loved her, even if she didn't. You could see it in his eyes. His voice was different too. It was as though he forgot to be Sir Anthony for a moment, forgot everything except that Beth was in danger."

"He loves her," John agreed. "And she loves him. I never saw anything like it. At first I thought I'd love to find someone I could care that much for, but later I changed my mind."

"Why?"

"Because I can't imagine either of them being able to live without the other one. They might go on breathing and walking about and suchlike, but I think if one of them died, the other would never recover."

"I hope they're both alive, then, and together," Sarah said.

"So do I. Or if not, that they died together, and quickly."

They sat and thought about this for a minute, then Sarah stood suddenly.

"Right," she said briskly in an obvious attempt to dispel the melancholy mood that had overtaken them both. "Let me show you the clothes I bought for you. As fetching as you look dressed in your faila….in that," she pointed to his blanket, "I think you'll be noticed if you go out in it." She picked up the package and started to unfold the clothes. There was a pair of grey woollen breeches with a buckle at the knee, two pairs of black cotton stockings, a woollen waistcoat, three white shirts, a grey wool tabby frockcoat, a jaunty red and white neckerchief, a hat and some slightly scuffed black leather shoes decorated with silver-plated buckles.

"They're not new. I thought you'd stand out more if you had a whole suit of new clothes, and you don't want that, but they're in good condition and they've all been washed, and I think they'll fit you," she said. "But if not, I should be able to alter them so they'll pass. I was pleased with the shirts and coat," she added. "The shirts are linen, and the coat was a bargain. It's hardly been worn at all, and the cuffs are really long, so they should hide your wrists. Once we've got you shaved and dressed, you'll look like a respectable tradesman. You're very pale, but you can tell anyone who mentions that that you've got the consumption and you're going to stay with some friends in the country for a few days to get some clean air. That should keep people away from you too. You'll just have to be very careful not to let anyone see your wrists." She looked at his hands. "And your fingers. I didn't think about them. I should have got you some gloves as well. Damn!" she said. "I'm sorry."

John looked at her in amazement.

"You're sorry?" he said incredulously. "You've saved my life, fed me, let me sleep here overnight, spent your hard-earned money on buying me clothes when you hardly know me, and you're sorry?"

"Now," she continued, blushing slightly at his praise, and brushing it off, "there are no posters or anything of that sort out about anyone escaping from the New Gaol, and the Gazette hasn't published an extraordinary about it. I assume that's because they don't want everyone to know it's possible to escape from prison, and that there are murderous rebels on the loose. But at the market I was told that the watch are knocking on doors and asking in the streets if people have heard or seen any dangerous-looking strangers, and to report to them if they do.

"I also heard that the Duke of Cumberland's due to arrive back in London tomorrow. They're already building bonfires and people are out cleaning the streets and putting candles in their windows. There'll be thousands of drunks on the streets tomorrow night, and it'll be chaos. It'll be a perfect time for you to slip away, while everybody's out cheering for the hero of Culloden. So I think you should stay here tonight. I'll keep the shop closed again tomorrow, and everyone will think it's because I'm overcome with excitement about the duke. I can get you some gloves in the morning, and then you can leave in the afternoon. I'll give you the money for the coach. Do you know how much it costs to get to Didsbury?"

She looked across at him. He was running his hand over the wool of the coat, deep in thought. He mumbled something, too low for her to hear.

"What?" Sarah asked.

"I can't go tomorrow," he said more loudly. "I-I have to do something."

"What do you have to do?" she asked, puzzled. Her tone clearly indicated that she couldn't think of anything worth missing this golden opportunity for. "If you want to say goodbye to somebody, you can write a letter and I'll deliver it for you. Or if you can't write, I can do it for you. I learnt how to write, I can do it quite well now," she finished, with pride in her voice.

"No, it's not that. But…can you lend me a few shillings to find a room, just for a week, that's all? Then I can leave. I'll send you the money back, I promise, once I find work in Didsbury."

"I don't understand," she said. "You can't stay in London another week, John. The people already know there's something amiss. News travels like wildfire on the streets. Within a couple of days someone in the watch or one of the prison guards will let something slip and everyone will know *exactly* what happened and probably what you look like too. You have to get away now, while you can."

He looked down at the clothes again. A full minute passed in silence.

"John, talk to me. You've trusted me this far. What do you have to do that's worth risking being captured for?"

"You'll think I'm an idiot," he said, still looking at the frockcoat.

"No, I won't. Tell me."

"The men that were convicted with me, Colonel Towneley, George Fletcher, Tom Chadwick, John Berwick, Tom Syddall, Jemmy Dawson…" his voice trailed off, and he swallowed, hard. "And others," he continued after a minute. "Tom Deacon, Andrew Blood, Dai Morgan. They're all going to die next Thursday. I should have been with them on the scaffold. But I'm going to be there to watch them die, and if any of them see me, to let them know I'm there for them. I'll pray for their souls every day for the rest of my life. And if Maddox has been released yet and I see his smug face in the crowd, I'll break his neck, and gladly hang for it."

Her expression told him that she did indeed think he was an idiot. She sat down and ran a hand over her face.

"John," she said, "you can't do this. There will be soldiers everywhere, and guards from the prison, who know what you look like. There'll be thousands of people watching. Your friends won't see you, they won't even know you're there. You can pray for them all the way to Didsbury in the coach if you want. I don't know who this Maddox is that you hate so much, but surely he's not worth dying a traitor's death for?"

John finally looked up from the coat, and at her. His brown eyes were full of tears, but his mouth twisted in a cruel parody of a smile.

"Yes, Maddox is worth dying for," John said. "I don't think they'll release him yet though. But I have to do this, Sarah. This is the least I can do for them. If I just turn my back and run, I'll never forgive myself. I can't explain it, but I have to."

Sarah bit her lip and thought.

"All right," she said. "I think you're wrong, but if you have to do this, you have to."

John let out a great sigh of relief. He wasn't sure why, but it really mattered to him that he had her support, if not her blessing.

"But I'm not giving you money for lodgings," she added. "You can stay here. It'll be safer."

"I can't stay here for a week!" he protested. "What will people say?"

"They won't say anything," she replied. "There's nothing wrong with a brother who's been in the militia and has only just heard of his sister's death coming to visit his other sister, and his baby niece. That's what I told people at the market today. Well, not the militia bit, but as you've actually *been* in the militia, if anyone asks you, you'll be able to talk about it. My customers are unlikely to ask. Emily would but she's worked very hard this last year, so I'll give her a week to go home and see her family. The only other person who might call round and show an interest is Anne, but I'm sure we'll be able to convince her. Anne's the poor cow who married Richard," Sarah elaborated. "She's lonely, and she's become a sort of friend, even though she's a lady, and was very rich until she married that bastard and let him take control of her fortune. Strange how Richard, who hates women so much, manages to bring them together. Beth, me, Anne, even Caroline, in a way."

"Who's Emily? And Caroline?" John asked, thoroughly perplexed by this torrent of words about people he'd never heard of.

"I'll tell you later. Put your clothes on, then we can go into the details, get our story straight. You're going to have to pretend to like babies, I'm afraid. But Mary *is* very placid, at least."

"I love babies, placid or not," John said. "I haven't asked to hold her because I wasn't sure you'd want me to, a stranger and all."

Sarah smiled and turned to leave the room and let him dress, but he put his hand on her arm to stop her, felt her flinch instinctively, and remembered what Beth had told him about Sarah's past. He let her go, but she turned back to him.

"I know you're making light of it," he said, "but you're taking a big risk, sheltering me, pretending I'm your brother. Why are you doing it?"

Instead of answering his question, Sarah asked one of her own. "Did you know there was a big reward out for information leading to the capture of Sir Anthony?"

"No," said John. "But I'm not surprised. Graeme told me a bit about him, about the fact that after he married Beth they went to Rome and spent time with Prince Charles, and over here he was part of the cou….never mind, you don't want to know. But yes, Graeme told me you'd written to warn them you'd been questioned by the Duke of Newcastle, so they could get their stories ready. Graeme really likes you, you know. He told me he couldn't have been more wrong about you. So yes, I know that the authorities really want to find Sir Anthony."

"And did you realise that if you'd told them that you knew who he was, and what he looked like, you'd probably have been offered a full pardon?"

He stared at her, aghast.

"Maddox," he said cryptically. "You said you don't know who Maddox is. Sam Maddox. He was an ensign, like me. And he turned evidence. He hates Colonel Towneley; a lot of us didn't like him, to be honest. He's brave and loyal to the Stuarts, but he's got no sense of humour, and thinks himself above his men. I don't know what he did to make Maddox hate him so much, but whatever it was, it's not worth turning traitor for. I'd kill him for that alone. But he gave evidence against a lot of other men too, just out of spite and cowardice. I can't think of anyone I despise more, except perhaps Richard.

"I didn't know about a reward, but yes, I suppose I should have realised that if I offered information about Sir Anthony I'd probably get a pardon, although I never thought about it until right now, when you mentioned it. And I'll tell you this; they could torture me for the next ten years and I wouldn't tell them *anything* about Sir Anthony. I love Beth like a sister, and Sir Anthony was good to me in the time I knew him. I have enormous respect for him, and for his…friends. I wouldn't betray any one of them, for all the pardons or gold in the world. How could you even think I would?" His voice had risen in anger, and his face was flushed. From the bedroom came a wail. The baby had woken from her nap.

To his surprise Sarah laughed, and then to his astonishment she enfolded him in her arms in a quick hug, before letting him go and stepping back.

"I don't," she said simply. "I don't think for one minute that the John Beth told me about would betray Sir Anthony, or anyone else, no matter what. And there's your answer too. How could you think I'd let such a man as you go out and risk being recaptured, when I can do something to stop it? And anyway, we have something in common that makes you as dear to me as if you *were* my brother."

"What's that?"

"You love Beth, and you hate Richard. That's enough for me." She turned to go into the bedroom, from which the wails were growing louder, then looked back at him. "I never thought I'd go to an execution," she added. "But I guess there's a first time for everything."

"But –" John started.

"Do you think I'd let my brother go through an experience like that alone?" she interrupted. "What kind of a sister would that make me? Now get dressed, will you?"

Before he could say another word she left the room. He stared after her for a moment. And then he shook his head and smiled. He could see why Beth loved her. They had a lot in common.

He picked up the stockings and started to put them on.

# CHAPTER SEVEN

**Fort Augustus, July 1746**

The three men approached Fort Augustus by way of the track that followed the river, slowing as they neared the entrance to the streets of tents in which the bulk of the British Army was housed.

As they arrived at the first of the tents they were approached by a small boy, barefoot and dressed in rags. The man at the front reined in his horse, a bay mare, thereby causing his companions to do the same, then leaned down to the boy, who reached up earnestly to him in the classic gesture of the beggar. The man rummaged in the pocket of his brown woollen frock coat and produced a coin, which he placed into the outstretched hand. The boy smiled and released a torrent of Gaelic, presumably by way of saying thanks, although the precise meaning of the speech was clearly incomprehensible to the recipient of it.

"You shouldn't encourage them, sir. Before you know it you'll have a hundred of them round you, pawing at you with their filthy hands. We're forbidden to give them food or money now. They've become a real nuisance."

The philanthropist removed his attention from the boy and placed it on the owner of the voice, a young soldier dressed in buff breeches and a white shirt, who was sitting on a rock outside his tent, vigorously polishing a pair of black leather boots.

"Like as not you're right," replied the horseman."I'm too soft for my own good, but he looked in need of a meal, and it was only a copper I gave him."

The soldier put the boot down on the ground and stood.

"Have you come for the cattle auctions, sir?" he asked.

"I have indeed." He swept off his hat and bowed his head. "Tobias Grundy at your service, sir." He gestured to his two companions. "This is my assistant, George Armstrong."

"Your servant, sir," said George. The soldier smiled up at him, his face briefly registering his shock at the sight of George's mangled face before settling back into a neutral expression.

"And this," Tobias said, gesturing to the third man, who loosely held the reins of a fourth horse, laden with provisions for the journey, "is John."

John had paid no attention to this exchange of greetings, but instead was gazing out across the fields surrounding the fort, which were covered with thousands of grazing cattle.

"You'll excuse John's manners, sir. He's deaf, and cannot speak, although I daresay if he could, he'd have nowt worth saying in any case. But he's steady and good with cattle, and that's what matters to me."

"Pleased to meet you, sirs. Private Thomas at your service." He sketched a bow. "If you're here for the auction, you'll need to speak with Sergeant Williams. He's in charge of those. If you'll care to follow me, I'll take you to him."

While the young soldier was putting on his boots and jacket, Tobias and George dismounted, and John, belatedly noticing this, dragged his gaze away from the cattle and followed suit. By a series of elaborate gestures Tobias managed to communicate to John that he was to stay with the horses, and then he and George followed Private Thomas as he led them down one of the makeshift streets in the direction of the fort itself.

"It's a tidy operation you've got here, and no mistake," Tobias commented, admiring the neat rows of tents, the front flaps of which were mainly tied back due to the warmth of the day, revealing neatly ordered interiors. Men in various states of undress were sitting about on the grass, polishing boots or equipment, smoking pipes, or playing at dice or cards. They took little notice of the visitors; clearly it was not unusual for strangers to appear amongst them seeking directions.

"We have to, sir," Private Thomas replied. "The duke is very particular about order and cleanliness, and runs a tight ship."

"The duke?" exclaimed Tobias. "Are you talking about the Duke of Cumberland, sir? There's a man I would dearly love to –"

Whatever Tobias would have loved to do to the Duke of Cumberland was left unsaid, as their guide stopped and pointed to a man who was walking in their direction.

"Ah, here's Sergeant Williams, sir." He saluted smartly to the approaching figure, who made his way toward the group. "These men have come for the auction, Sergeant. I was bringing them to you," he said to the tall middle-aged man, who was dressed in full uniform and sweating freely in the heat.

Greetings were exchanged, after which Private Thomas returned to his boot-polishing and the three men made their way to the fort, where Sergeant Williams had set up a makeshift office in one of the rooms not wholly destroyed by the rebels. He asked them to take a seat and then sent for some refreshments.

"So, you're here to buy cattle, Mr Grundy," Sergeant Williams said, addressing the young man sitting opposite him.

"That I am, sir. I was at the county fair a few weeks ago, and was told that you were selling cattle at a rate worth riding up to this godforsaken place for. Begging your pardon, Sergeant," he added belatedly.

Sergeant Williams assessed the man; good quality but practical clothing, somewhat travel-stained; a decent sword, but the basket hilt showed signs of rust, so probably carried to deter thieves rather than because the wearer was a swordsman. Tall and well-built, and clearly used to an outdoor life. The eyes behind the brass-rimmed spectacles he wore were blue and his eyebrows black, as no doubt was his hair, currently hidden under a cheap bagwig, which he wore somewhat uncomfortably, as though unaccustomed to it. Trying to make a good impression then, and a countryman rather than from the city, as neither the clothes nor the wig were of the latest fashion.

"No need to apologise, sir. I share your feelings. The sooner we can get the job we're here to do done with and I can get back home, the happier I'll be. You're from the north of England then, Mr Grundy? Your accent, sir," the sergeant added, noting the young man's surprise at him knowing this.

"Oh! You have a knowledge of accents? I can't tell one from t' other myself, for the most part. If they don't speak like me, they're foreign. That's as far as it goes with me. Yes, I'm a Yorkshire lad, sir, born and bred and proud of it. I've a farm over on't moors, near Haworth. You'll likely have heard of it, if you're from those parts yourself, though you don't sound like it, I must say."

The sergeant smiled, realising that he'd just been designated as 'foreign' by the Yorkshireman, who probably had never travelled more than a few miles from his home town in his entire life. This must be an enormous adventure for him.

"No, I'm from the midlands," Sergeant Williams responded, "but my father's family were from Yorkshire. Never been there myself. Now, Mr Armstrong, is it?" he said, addressing the other man.

"Indeed sir, George Armstrong."

"Can I ask you, Mr Armstrong, how you came by that injury?"

Armstrong bristled noticeably, and his face reddened.

"I had the misfortune to be in Carlisle when the rebels came through, sir. One of the bastards took offence to something I said. I'd been drinking, and looking back, it probably wasn't the best time to toast the health of the king. Even so…I'd rather not talk about it, if you don't mind."

"Are you from Carlisle, Mr Armstrong?" the sergeant persisted, ignoring the man's request.

Armstrong shook his head.

"Cumbria. I was up there on business. I'd never have gone, but we'd had word that the rebels were headed for Newcastle rather than Carlisle, so I thought I was safe to go ahead. I nearly died that day sir, and I still have bad dreams about it. You'll be accustomed to such things, no doubt, being a fighting man, but I'm a man of the soil, and have never courted any trouble."

At first glance he didn't look like a man of the soil, the sergeant thought; but in retrospect that was probably because of the horrific injury, which, apart from taking the man's eye, had disfigured him badly, making him look very ferocious. But looking beyond that, he could see the weatherbeaten lined skin of an outdoor man; and the gnarled and swollen joints of his fingers indicated rheumatics. Yes, a man of the soil who'd been in the wrong place at the wrong time, he concluded.

"I'm sorry to bring back bad memories for you sir, but we can't be too careful. As I'm sure you've seen, we have thousands of animals here that have been brought in from the rebel lands during the pacification. Many of the rebels have now surrendered their arms, and their houses and lands are burnt, but there are still a stubborn few skulking in the mountains, determined to fight on."

"What, you think they might attack the fort?!" Mr Grundy said, thoroughly alarmed. Mr Armstrong's expression was more difficult to read; no doubt the man's nerves had been damaged by the sword cut, and the strange twisting of the mouth denoted fear rather than the anger it appeared to show. The sergeant held up his hand.

"No, no, you mistake me. The rebels would never dare to attack the fort. We have thousands of men here. But they might attempt a raid to retrieve some of their cattle. To that end we have a strong guard around the area, day and night. And then of course there is the danger of spies being sent to assess our numbers and arms, which is why I had to question where you came by your injury, Mr Armstrong. I appreciate now that you probably despise the rebels even more than I do."

"You can't imagine how I feel about the rebels," Armstrong replied, tight-lipped.

"Perhaps not. My apologies if I caused you any offence, sir. Anyway, let us get down to business. How many cows are you hoping to buy, Mr Grundy?"

"Please, let us not stand on ceremony, Sergeant. I'm a plain man. Call me Toby, sir. I'm after about two thousand beasts, if the price is right, of course."

The sergeant's eyes widened.

"Two *thousand?*" he repeated.

"That's right. You've a good many more than that, by the looks of it. I should think you could spare them."

"We can. But most people are buying two hundred at best, sir."

"Maybe they are. But I've not ridden for two weeks through bogs and rain in mortal fear of being killed by savages just to make a few guineas. I'll speak plain, for I'm a plain man, as I said. I'm here to make my fortune, sir. It's a clever plan you've got, to starve the bastards so they can't fight even if they would, and judging by the beggars we met at the gates, it looks like you're doing a fine job of it. I've no doubt you're wanting to be rid of the beasts as quick as you can sir, to make sure they're out of reach of anyone desperate enough to try to take them anyway, in spite of the guard. I'm sure your men have got better things to do with their time than guarding cows."

The orderly returned with bread, butter and beer, and the sergeant sent him off again, this time for a bottle of good brandy. These guests were worth more than ale.

"You speak the truth, Mr…er…Toby," said the sergeant. "Do you mean to drive them back to Yorkshire?"

"I do indeed. They can fatten up along the way. There's plenty of grass for them at this time of year."

"How many men have you got with you, to drive them?"

"Just three of us. Me, George, and John, who's with our baggage. I did employ a couple of guides to show me the way, but I've sent them on their way now. I was hoping that I might be able to pay for some of your men to help us drive them." The sergeant opened his mouth to speak, but Toby continued quickly. "Only as far as Glasgow, Sergeant. I've already written to some friends there, who have men willing to help us take them the rest of the way. Once we're south of Glasgow I think we'll be safe from attack, and we'll have no more need of soldiers, just cattle men. I saw no point in paying for militiamen to come all the way from Yorkshire, sir, when I knew there were a lot of experienced soldiers here."

"The British Army is not here to escort cattle across country, Mr Grundy. We are here to fight the rebels!" the sergeant protested.

"Oh. I'm sorry. I thought the rebels were defeated. I'm sure that everyone in Yorkshire thinks so. Why, they were ringing the bells day and night for nearly a week in April when we heard of the Duke of Cumberland's great victory. Right bloody racket, it were. And it were in all t'papers too. The duke's a hero – everyone's saying as how he's saved us from popery and tyranny. In fact, I was only saying to Private Thomas there, that I'd love to meet the duke, if it were possible. I'd give my right arm to see him, sir, that I would. I'd no idea the war was still going on. Maybe I'll just have a hundred cows then. It'd be a shame to come so far and go home with nowt to show for it. But I'm right disappointed, and that's a fact. I've no idea what I'll tell my friends when I get back without my cows, and tell them the war's still going on after all."

The man did look completely crushed, even tearful. He took off his glasses and polished them briskly on the sleeve of his coat, clearly trying to compose himself by doing something. His companion remained silent, but seemed equally crestfallen, and was looking down at the floor, presumably trying to appear as though he hadn't noticed his master's embarrassing emotional state.

The orderly reappeared with the brandy and three glasses, and while he was pouring, the sergeant thought, hard. His captain would have his balls for breakfast if he lost such a huge sale. More cattle were coming in daily, and it was a real problem finding room for them all, in spite of the twice-weekly auctions. Two thousand was a lot, and if Grundy got them back to Yorkshire safely, others would hear and hopefully head up to buy more. The sooner the cattle were sold, the sooner he could leave this place and head home, hopefully before winter. Because without food the rebels would starve, and if they were starving, they couldn't fight. The thought of spending another winter in this shithole of a place made the sergeant's blood run cold.

"Let me reassure you, Mr Gru….Toby," the sergeant said, the second the orderly had left the room. "The rebels are most certainly defeated. Most of their leaders are either dead or captured, and the Pretender's son is within an inch of being caught." Seeing Toby's teary-eyed look of doubt, the sergeant hurried on. "In fact, His Highness the Duke has departed for London, so sure is he that the rebels will not rise again. He takes his responsibilities very seriously, and was determined not to leave Scotland, in spite of the calls for him to do so, until he was certain that the rebellion was entirely crushed."

"Ah. That's good news, sir, although I would very much have liked to meet –"

"I'm sure the duke would have been delighted to allow you to kiss his hand, had he been here," the sergeant said insincerely.

Mr Armstrong, who had been sipping his brandy, suddenly choked. Toby patted him absently on the back while he pondered the sergeant's words.

"I'm very glad to hear that the war is over, but you said –"

"What I meant," the sergeant interrupted, "was that the men are very busy pacifying the Highlands. However, you said that you have friends in Glasgow who can help you from there." Glasgow was a loyal Whig town; there was no danger of an attack by Jacobites that far south.

"I do, sir. Good stout men."

"Well, then. If you are willing to lengthen your journey a little, I have two hundred men going to Fort William in three days to join the garrison there, in preparation for… I am sure they will be happy to help drive the cattle for a small consideration, say sixpence a day?"

"Tuppence," Toby responded automatically.

"Threepence," the sergeant replied.

Toby nodded, and the sergeant cursed inwardly. He probably could have got fivepence. He had been given the task of cattle-dealing because of his administrative skills. He hated haggling.

"And from Fort William?" Toby asked.

"How many men will you need?"

Toby thought for a minute.

"I'd say thirty, if they know about cows."

"I'll have a word with the captain. I'm sure we can sort something out. Now, about the auction…"

\* \* \*

By the time Toby and George got back to their horses it was dusk and their companion had set up the tent they were to share, out of earshot but not out of sight of the soldiers' tents, had unpacked their bedrolls, made a fire, and was in the process of cooking a meal. He had his back to them as they approached, and when Toby clapped him on the back by way of greeting he jumped a foot in the air, to the amusement of a group of nearby soldiers. After a short discussion, using hand signals which conveyed to John in simple terms the plan they'd discussed with the sergeant, and which confirmed to the soldiers that John was not only deaf and dumb, but something of an idiot as well, Toby wandered off towards the river, announcing that he needed a piss, and maybe more than that, and might be a few minutes.

If anyone else had happened to be down by the river a few moments later, they would have seen that Private Thomas had been right; the young beggar boy clearly had been encouraged by Mr Grundy's generosity earlier in the day, and had no qualms about approaching that gentleman, even when he was squatting with his breeches round his ankles. There proceeded a low-voiced discussion, after which Mr Grundy gave the boy a cuff round the ear and sent him on his way, apparently empty-handed.

He returned to the tent a few minutes later, where he and his colleagues ate and then, declining an invitation from the military men to join them in a game of cards, they turned in for an early night, having been on the road all day.

"Did ye meet wi' Lachlan?" Iain whispered once they were inside the tent with the flaps down. Although they had no candle the light from the nearby cooking fires of the soldiers illuminated the interior of their accommodation enough for Iain to see Alex put his finger to his mouth, and he immediately fell silent.

"The soldiers won't hear our words if we whisper," he said, still using the flat vowels of Toby Grundy, Yorkshireman, "but Scottish accents have a different cadence, even when whispered, that they might pick up on if they're astute. We can't be too careful."

Iain nodded.

"But yes, I did. I told him that we'll be leaving in three days, and to tell Angus to wait for further instructions once we get to Fort William. If he's quick, he should be back with us before we reach there, and we can tell him more then. We can't go ahead with the plan while there are two hundred soldiers with us. I hadn't planned on that many. But it's good that we'll be heading down the country from Fort William, because we won't have so far to go to drive the cattle to Glencoe."

"Unless they send the two hundred soldiers to Glasgow with us," Graeme commented.

"I'll deal with that as I come to it. I'll think of something. Did you hear anything useful, Iain?"

Iain shook his head.

"Tomorrow go for a walk round, be interested in everything, but understand nothing. You're really good at being a deaf idiot now. The way you jumped when I touched you, if I hadn't known better I'd really have had no idea you heard us coming a good minute before."

The deaf idiot grinned and winked, but kept silent.

"You're a good teacher," Graeme whispered. "I knew you could act a role, I mean I saw you as Sir Anthony twice, remember?"

"I'm not likely to forget you and Thomas running down the garden to kill me for attacking Beth," Alex said, smiling at the memory and then trying to dismiss it quickly before the pain came.

"But I didn't realise just how good you were until today. Everything about you was a blunt northern Englishman, a man who likes to think he's plain, but is so desperate to make a fortune and rise in the world that he's moved to tears when he thinks it won't happen. You were so good I was actually disappointed for you that you weren't going to get to kiss Cumberland's hand and dine out on it in Haworth for the next twenty years."

Alex laughed softly.

"Not as disappointed as Cumberland'd be if he knew that Sir Anthony Peters was lying within a few feet of thousands of redcoats right now, feeling safe as if he was in his own house."

"Do you really feel that safe?" asked Graeme. "I'm damned if I do."

"I do. I have to, or I'd be nervous all the time, and men can sense nervousness. I spent over three years living a lie every day. I had to learn how to relax. We all did. That's why Iain wouldn't have choked on his brandy like you did. You covered it well, though. And your story about the injury sounded convincing."

"I'm a plain man," Graeme said, grinning. "I'm not used to lying. I'm glad we had the time for you to teach me while we were riding down to Cheshire to get the gold. I'm sorry we couldn't go to see Thomas and Jane, though. I'd like to let them know I'm well."

"I'm sorry. But we couldn't risk it. If you'd been recognised by someone who knew you'd joined the prince…maybe in time you'll be able to, but it's too soon now."

"I know. But at least now you know where the money is, should anything happen to me. It's worried me ever since Beth…" His voice trailed off into silence and he closed his eyes for a moment, compressing his lips into a tight line to try to contain the grief that had risen in him at the mere thought of her death. "I didn't want to be the only person who knew where it was," he continued after a moment. "What would you have done if Cumberland had still been here and agreed to let you kiss his hand?"

"I'd have kissed it. Then one day, when I was sure I was safe, I'd have written to him to let him know how close he was to Sir Anthony this day. Now, let's get some sleep. I want to look at the cattle tomorrow, pick out the best, and find out more about how the auction's run. In fact in view of how many I'm buying, I'm hoping to bypass the auction altogether. And I'd rather pay for the cows and get rid of the money before the soldiers find out I've got five hundred guineas in gold with me."

\* \* \*

## 25th July, 1746

It was a glorious day. In London Prince William Augustus, Duke of Cumberland was arriving in London to a tumultuous welcome from its grateful citizens. Much further north, Prince Charles Edward Stuart, back on the mainland of Scotland had, four days earlier, successfully broken through the extremely tight cordon around Moidart set up to capture him, by passing silently between two sentries, and was now safely resting in a cave in the Braes of Glenmoriston in the loyal company of the famous (or infamous, depending on one's viewpoint) Glenmoriston men, who had vowed to fight on regardless of the Elector's son's 'great and complete victory'.

Meanwhile Tobias Grundy, plain man of Yorkshire, was riding, as proud as though he himself was a prince of the blood royal, along the banks of Loch Ness at the head of the newly bought cattle which were to make his fortune, as he declared loudly to anyone willing to listen. From time to time he would remember that he was in a barbarous country peopled with savages, and would look around nervously as though expecting a horde of tartan-clad fiends to fall upon them at any moment.

Noticing this, Captain Matthew Sewell, who was leading the two hundred soldiers currently doubling as cattle-herders to Fort William, cantered up to join the Yorkshireman and his two companions.

"You need have no fear, Mr Grundy," he said reassuringly when he reached them. "We are riding through the Fraser lands, or what were the Fraser lands. But we will have no trouble from the clansmen, sir. Those who are left will no doubt be in mourning. Their chief Lord Lovat was taken a couple of weeks ago. Hiding in a tree, he was, but now on his way to London and to execution, if justice be served."

Mr Grundy was clearly extremely relieved to hear this news.

"I'll tell you, Captain, I've heard people say that the dales of Yorkshire are wild and barren, and it's true that in the winter they can seem to be. But it's good fertile land, and in the summer there's no finer place in the whole of His Majesty's realm, sir. But this," he made an expansive hand gesture which took in the waters of the loch, sparkling in the sunshine, the craggy mountains lining it, and in fact the whole of Scotland, both north and south, "I don't know how anyone can live here. I've never been in such a dark and gloomy place in my life."

"It's a fine day today, Toby," his hideous-looking companion observed. "The water looks very inviting. I was thinking to go for a swim later, when we stop for the night."

"I wouldn't swim in that for all the tea in China," another soldier commented. "It's said to be bottomless, and there's a sea monster lives there. Even the Highlanders themselves won't go in it in case they get eaten."

Tobias and George looked at the stretch of water with horror, while John, as was his way, stared vacantly off into the distance.

"That's nonsense. I'm surprised at you, Barker, and you a good Church of England man," scoffed the captain. "Old wives' tales, just the sort of thing an ignorant papist savage would believe. I've swum in there several times myself since I've been here, although the water's a bit murky. It's not often we have a day warm enough for swimming though, but it's a lovely day today. I'll happily accompany you in a swim, Mr Armstrong," he continued, "as I daresay will many of the men. Just the thing to cool down. You can sit on the bank and watch for sea monsters and mermaids, Barker."

There was a general chorus of laughter at this, and the hapless Barker reddened and fell silent.

"You are in the right though, Mr Grundy," continued the

captain. "I don't know why anyone would choose to live in such a place. I'll admit that when I first went out to help clear the lands – the Cameron lands, sir, up ahead of us – I was shocked by how poorly the people lived. Little huts they have, with no furniture to speak of and a ragged sorry bunch they were when we drove them out. Not a one of them speaks the King's English, and no doubt they'd think a book was something to light a fire with. All they know to do is kill, and they'll follow their chief before God. Not that the Camerons'll be following theirs any more. He was wounded in the heel at Culloden and has since died of it."

"Died of a wounded heel? I never heard of such a thing!" exclaimed Mr Grundy, who had clearly never been within a hundred miles of a battle and seen how a seemingly minor wound could fester and blacken, and in spite of all the doctors could do, kill an otherwise healthy man in a matter of days.

"Indeed, it's more common than you'd think. It's said by many, on both sides, that Lochiel – that's the chief's name – was a man of honour. He certainly had a fine house. I saw it before it was burnt. All made of wood it was, and beautiful gardens round it too."

"I don't see how anyone could fight against his rightful king and be called a man of honour, Captain," Mr Grundy said indignantly.

"I take your point, sir. But it doesn't matter now, because he's dead and his clan scattered. Our job here is almost done, I think."

"You must be looking forward to going home then," Mr Grundy remarked.

"Not yet," Captain Sewell said, with obvious regret. "We have another task ahead of us, which is why we're on our way to Fort William."

"And I'm glad you are, sir. Your men are doing a fine job of keeping my cows together. They'll make my fortune when I get them back to Yorkshire." He beamed. "You don't seem happy about this task of yours, Captain. Is it a dangerous one?"

"Dangerous? No, I don't expect it to be," he replied.

"Is it building work you're doing then?" Mr Armstrong put in. "I remember the fine roads that Wade built, back when I was a younger man. They made getting here easier, that's for sure."

"I heard that too, George, though I don't remember them

being built, being just a sprat at the time. Didn't the rebels use them to bypass the army on their march south, though?"

Captain Sewell cast a venomous look towards Mr Grundy, who returned it with a look of the utmost innocence. No, ignorance. The man obviously had no idea that it was not politic to bring up such things as the enemy using your own roads against you.

"Well, they will not be using them again. No, it is not building work we'll be engaged in, Mr Armstrong, although I'm afraid I cannot say what we will be doing. Orders, you understand."

"We need to find out what they're intending. Glencoe is only a morning's march from Fort William, and we're only a couple of days further," Alex muttered as the three men stood by the lochside later that evening. A little way back from the shore the men had set up camp for the night. A number of them, undaunted by the prospect of being devoured by a sea monster, were splashing and swimming in the loch fifty yards or so away. No one was in earshot, but they were in sight. With this in mind, Graeme was stripping off in preparation for his swim, while Alex had only gone so far as to take off his stockings with the intention of merely washing his feet, and demonstrating trepidation even at that. Iain was sitting on a rock between his two companions, throwing pebbles into the water in a deliberately inept attempt to skim them across the surface.

"It'll take more than two days for the redcoats though," Iain said, his face turned to the west so that no particularly keen-sighted observers would see his mouth moving. "Five, maybe."

"That depends if they're riding or marching, and how many they are. If they're gathering in such numbers though, they're up to something big. The question is, is it something big north, or south?"

"What do you think about Lochiel?" Graeme asked as he pulled his shirt over his head, revealing a white but surprisingly well-muscled torso for a man of his years. He was indeed a man of the soil, and his years of outdoor toil had left him with the athletic body of a much younger man.

"I dinna ken what to think. I heard he'd died at Culloden, then that he'd escaped to France, and neither of those rumours were true. His wounds were healing when I last saw him, but that was a while ago. But we canna do anything about that. Iain, I want ye to split away from us the morrow. Watch the cows, and if ye can, when we get to Fort William wander about and see if ye can find anything out. The soldiers are bound to talk amongst themselves."

"It's a shame Angus isn't here," Graeme commented, taking off his breeches and standing in all his naked glory, ready to go into the water. "He could have gone to the tavern and drunk them all under the table. They're most likely to talk when they're drunk."

Folding his breeches carefully and placing them on top of his shirt on the rock, he strode fearlessly into the water. Alex followed more slowly, stopping when the water was up to his shins.

"How's the water?" he called to Graeme, all Yorkshire again.

"Bloody freezing, till you get used to it. Then it's lovely," Graeme called back. He swam away strongly in the opposite direction to the soldiers, and was soon a mere speck in the distance.

Alex stood in the shallows, doubt and apprehension in every line of his body.

"Come on in, Mr Grundy!" one of the soldiers shouted, swimming a bit closer to them. "We'll save you from the sea monster!"

There was laughter from the other men, who were also drawing nearer. It became evident that they were intending to compel Mr Grundy to take a dip.

"That's very kind, but I cannot swim, sir," he called back. He didn't want these military men to see him undressed, and if they dragged him in fully clothed as they clearly intended to, they would certainly expect him to take off his sodden garb when he emerged from the loch. You did not achieve a body like his by being a cattle dealer in the Yorkshire dales. Maybe the legs, yes; walking for miles around the moors would certainly build calves and thighs. But it would not give you a massive solid torso, nor would it give you shoulders and arms knotted with heavy muscle, gained from years of practice with weapons of all kinds. They were trained fighters; they would recognise a warrior's body.

He turned and began to walk out of the water, hoping that they would give up once he was on dry land, although from the looks of them, he doubted it. They were clearly amused by his apprehension and were egging each other on. He didn't blame them; it was just high spirits, the sort of thing the MacGregors would do if faced with a timorous Englishman. He would have to improvise a pugilistic background. He was a keen boxer in his native dales, and had once defeated the champion of somewhere…Harrogate? York? Although that would not explain the sword cut on his side, nor the scar on his chest inflicted by a MacFarlane dirk on a cattle raid across Loch Lomond some ten years previously. Nor would it explain why his eyebrows were black, but his hair red-brown. Damn.

A rock flew over his left shoulder and landed in the loch with a loud splash, and then the deaf mute idiot behind him stood suddenly and ran fully dressed into the water, eyes fixed on the opposite shore, oblivious to either the shouts and hand gestures of Mr Grundy on his left or the jeers and laughter from the soldiers on his right. It was clear that he had seen something on the other side of the loch that appealed to his dim mind, and was determined to go to it.

"John! John!" Mr Grundy bellowed, to no avail. John, now up to his waist, fell forward in the water, preparing to strike out for the other side. Mr Grundy walked back into the loch up to his knees, then stopped. "Please, bring him back!" he begged of the soldiers who, faced with this new diversion, had temporarily abandoned their plan.

"There's no sea monster, sir!" one of them called mockingly. "He won't be eaten."

"He can't swim!" Mr Grundy shouted back desperately. "He'll drown! Please, I beg you, bring him back." He was almost in tears now as he watched his servant, who had in fact managed to swim with some skill until Mr Grundy made his plea, suddenly flounder and go under the water before resurfacing a moment later, arms and legs flailing in all directions. Mr Armstrong, having observed the commotion from afar, turned and began to swim back, although there was no doubt he would be too late to save his companion.

The soldiers hesitated, clearly torn between watching to see how long it took the idiot to drown, and rescuing him. One of them called out, "Sixpence that he lasts to the count of two hundred!"

"A shilling for the count of one hundred!" another replied. All thought of rescue was forgotten in the excitement of a wager.

"One, two, three, four…"

"Ten shillings to the man who brings him safe to shore!" called the Yorkshireman, beside himself with anguish.

Two minutes later a reluctant John, still intent on making it across the loch, was dragged unceremoniously out of the water and deposited at his master's feet, shivering and dripping from head to toe.

"Thank you," said Mr Grundy earnestly, clasping the rescuer's hands in gratitude. "I'll get him back and out of those clothes, or he'll catch his death. Come to my tent in an hour, sir, and I'll give you your reward."

He helped John to his feet, and taking a firm grip on his arm to stop him making a second attempt to cross the loch, led him away in the direction of the tents.

* * *

It was really amusing. The idiot seemed to actually think they were his friends, just because they'd dragged him out of the loch. He had no idea that if that pathetic coward Grundy, too scared to get wet himself, hadn't bribed them to drag him out, he'd have been feeding the fishes now. Or the sea monster, if it really did exist.

Instead he had followed them everywhere for the last three days, grinning inanely at them and generally getting under their feet. He had even tried to follow them into the fort itself, no doubt intending to sleep in their barracks, but luckily that grim-faced ugly old fart Armstrong had come along and dragged him away to the room they'd managed to get in the remnants of Maryburgh, which had been burnt in March but was now being repaired.

Since the incident by Loch Ness Grundy had been subdued and had kept himself to himself, no longer boasting about his future fortune, which was currently grazing in the meadows near the fort, guarded by a detachment of forty soldiers, who were to accompany the three men down to Glasgow. No doubt he knew that the soldiers held him in contempt for his fear of the mythical monster. How the hell he'd had the balls to ride all the way from Yorkshire to Fort Augustus with only an idiot and a decrepit old man for protection was beyond them. But then, the lure of money was a powerful incentive and could cause a man to take all manner of risks.

A case in point being the five men now entering the tavern, shadowed by the idiot. They had initially done their utmost to avoid being picked to herd the cattle down to Glasgow, aware that to do so they would have to pass through rebel territory; until they had been informed that Mr Grundy was willing to pay two shillings per man per day for the journey south from Fort William. For less than half of that they had stood on the battlefields of Dettingen, Prestonpans, Falkirk Muir, to name but a few, while the enemy shot and slashed them to pieces. All of a sudden taking cows to Glasgow seemed positively harmless. They had leapt to volunteer, telling themselves that they would only be passing through a few miles of enemy territory; most of their way led through the friendly Campbell lands.

Captain Sewell had told the men that herding the cattle for Grundy would give them an ideal opportunity to survey the territory. They were not expected to engage with any rebels, although of course if they came across a few isolated villages they could use their initiative. The main foray would come later, once Mr Grundy and his companions were safely on the road to England.

As far as Matthew Sewell was concerned, this whole exercise promised to be a waste of resources; the bulk of the rebels had come from the areas already ravaged. Further south support for the Pretender had been far more sporadic.

For his part Captain Sewell would have preferred to head north in search of the Young Pretender and those sheltering him. Thirty thousand pounds was a powerful incentive, to say nothing of the glory and praise that would be showered on the lucky man who captured the Stuart upstart.

But he had his orders, and they were to disarm that part of Dumbarton which lay on the east, west and north sides of Loch Lomond. And orders had to be obeyed.

The five soldiers, with money in their pockets and the promise of much more to come in the next days, embarked upon their night of drinking in high spirits, which soon became even more elevated when the idiot produced a golden guinea, which he surely must have pilfered from Grundy, giving it to the barmaid with one hand whilst with the other making a sweeping gesture which took in the whole table, followed by a reasonable mime of drinking. The soldiers gave a great cheer, and John the idiot became their best friend for the evening.

They had determined to have some sport with him, but he had no head for liquor and after two tankards of good ale and a brandy he fell asleep slumped over the table, his head pillowed on his folded arms. Feeling magnanimous in view of the fact that he was paying for the evening's drink they left him there, and set to discussing the days to come, and seeing if they could drink a whole guinea's worth of alcohol between them.

It was after midnight by the time George Armstrong found them, by which time the men had made considerable inroads into the guinea. He took one look at the snoring figure of John, and sighed.

"What the hell are you up to, letting him get like that?" he said accusingly to the bleary-eyed redcoats. "You know he's soft in the head."

"We din't do nuffin' to 'im, you ugly old bugger," one of the men slurred, swaying in his seat. He waved an arm around the table to indicate the innocence of his companions and in doing so lost his balance, toppling backwards off the bench and landing on the floor, giggling.

Armstrong looked at the group and seemed to realise he'd get no sense from any of them.

"Come on, lad," he said instead, grasping John round the chest and lifting him bodily from the seat. "Let's get you home."

The deaf man seemed to rouse for a moment, opening one eye and attempting to get his legs to support him, before collapsing onto the bench again. It was with some considerable difficulty that George managed to stop himself from landing on the floor with the soldier who had insulted him and who was now subsiding into sleep, his mouth hanging open.

"He's bloody heavy for a bony bastard," George said to no one in particular, and taking John by the shoulders, shook him hard, which met with more success in that he woke up enough this time to stagger to his feet. George put his arm round the idiot's waist to support him, and John, finally realising that he was going to have to walk, slung his left arm over the older man's shoulder and attempted to stand upright, while with his right he fumbled with his breeches.

Those of the soldiers still sober enough to notice what John was doing, started laughing.

"Watch out old man, he thinks you're his doxy," one of them said.

"Only chance you'll ever get to be fucked, face like that," another one mumbled, to general hilarity.

John took out his penis drowsily and then proceeded to urinate, aiming with deadly accuracy into the collapsed and now comatose soldier's open mouth.

George's mouth twisted in that strange sneer he had, and then he tightened his grip round John's waist and attempted to head for the door, clearly intending to get out quickly before the others realised what was happening. John, penis still in hand, lurched round in George's grip, spraying the table and the soldiers sitting at it in the process, before staggering across the room and out of the door.

They continued to weave their way drunkenly down the street until they rounded the corner, where John miraculously and instantaneously sobered up and the two men slumped against the wall, laughing hysterically.

"I can't believe you did that," Graeme said, once he could speak. "You could have got us both killed."

"No, they've been drinking solid for four hours. I doubt a one of them could even stand up, let alone draw his sword."

"Well, you made good use of *your* sword, so to speak," Graeme spluttered, giggling like a five-year-old. "And they say Angus is the reckless one."

Iain grinned.

"I couldna resist. My ma would hae washed my mouth out wi' soap, an I'd insulted an elder like that wee gomerel insulted you. I just didna have any soap to hand, so I improvised. I doubt they'll remember, come morning," he said.

"They might, when they wake up stinking of piss," Graeme said. "Come on, let's get back to the room."

Five minutes later they walked into the small, sparsely furnished but more importantly private room they were sharing, still giggling. Alex, occupying the only chair, looked up in surprise at the unexpected hilarity.

"Christ, man, how much did ye drink?" he said, instantly concerned. Iain was no Angus where liquor was concerned.

"Enough to give a Highland baptism to five redcoats," Iain said cryptically.

Alex watched with astonishment as the two men, neither of them normally prone to such childish behaviour, collapsed into laughter again, grinning in spite of the fact that he had no idea what this Highland baptism of Iain's was. It was good to see him laugh again. He had barely even smiled since Maggie's death.

He waited until the laughter subsided, and then put the question he'd been intending to ask when they'd first come in.

"Did ye find anything out about the redcoats' mission?"

Iain looked across at his chieftain, and his face grew serious.

"Aye," he said. "They mean to disarm the MacGregors. The soldiers have been told tae spy out the land while they're guiding us. And then once they report back, they're sending more down to wipe us out, once and for all."

"How many more?" Alex asked.

"They dinna ken, but a lot. More than we can fight, anyway. They've over two thousand men in the fort, and more coming."

Alex nodded then swept his hand through his hair, absently combing through the tangles with his fingers. He sat for a few minutes, silently.

"Well," he said finally. "At least we're forewarned, which is more than the Camerons and Frasers were. Ye did a good job tonight, Iain."

"What will you do?" Graeme asked.

"Run," Alex said bluntly. "I canna fight an army wi' fifty men. Lachlan is back. I saw him this morning. And Angus tellt Jamie, Hector and Donald to spread out along the way home, in case we need to get a message through quickly. If I speak wi' him in the morning, the news will be wi' Angus by the following day. That will give the women time to move everything out and away up into the caves."

"Caves?" said Graeme.

"Aye. There's a reason the MacGregors are called 'The Children of the Mist'," Alex said. "Over the years we've grown accustomed to disappearing from time to time. But as we're no' magical, but flesh and blood, we've found places we can disappear to. Places where the redcoats'll no' find us. And if they do, we'll be able tae kill an awfu' lot of them before they take us. We're no' in the habit of showing Sasannachs where those places are. But I guess we'll make an exception for you." He winked.

"I'm honoured," Graeme said, intending it as a joke, but then realising that he actually was. It was no small thing to earn the trust of a clan that had learned, over a hundred and forty years of proscription, to trust no one.

Alex looked at his companions and smiled, a real smile that lit up his eyes.

"At least we can be sure we'll no' starve while we're in hiding," he said. "We'll have plenty of meat, at least. And," he continued, "before we go we'll gie the bastards a leaving party to be proud of."

He stood, stretched, and yawned.

"Let's away to bed," he suggested. "We've a busy few days ahead. I've a fancy for a wee bedtime story tae send me to sleep though."

Iain grinned.

"Ye'll be wanting the one about the deaf idiot and the ugly old bastard and the Highland baptism then, I'm thinking," he said.

"You read my mind, laddie."

* * *

It was a dull morning, but one that promised to be fair once the sun had risen high enough in the sky to burn off the haze. Mist shrouded the mountains which surrounded them on all sides, and the path which snaked between them that they were to head down today was visible for only a few yards, as were the tents of the soldiers, from which they were sleepily emerging in various states of undress.

Some particularly early risers had already lit fires and started to cook breakfast, while Mr Grundy, perpetually afraid that someone would steal his cattle in the night, had risen and breakfasted before sunrise and had ridden off, dragging the sleepy Mr Armstrong with him, to attempt to count his fortune, which could be heard but not currently seen, lowing all over the valley.

The deaf idiot had dutifully taken down the tent and packed all their belongings and was now sitting on the grass, seemingly oblivious to the heavy dew soaking through his breeches, all his attention concentrated on a small chestnut-coloured squirrel which was currently some three feet away from him, but edging slowly closer, enticed by the piece of bread that he was holding out to it. It moved forward again, now only two feet away, and sat up on its back legs, its bushy tail fanning out behind it, watching him warily with large brown eyes.

John continued to hold the piece of bread between his thumb and index finger, his arm outstretched. A short distance away a small group of soldiers looked on, equally entranced, but more by the preternatural stillness of the man than by the squirrel, who was now chattering at him before edging closer still, then even closer. It stretched its neck to take the bread, its mouth a mere inch from John's fingers.

A shot rang out, echoing off the surrounding hills, and the squirrel exploded, spattering John's arm and the grass with blood and fur. John started at the animal's sudden transformation from living creature to red mush, and then he turned his head slowly to look at the soldier, who looked back and grinned, before slinging his musket across his shoulder.

"Vermin, they are," he said. "Carry all sorts of diseases."

John did not react, but continued to stare at the man in shock, his mouth hanging open slightly. The soldier's comrades had all jumped and uttered expletives when the shot was fired, but now they started laughing at the expression on the idiot's face.

Somewhere down the line of tents could be heard a commotion, and appearing through the mist to the left of John came Sergeant Applewhite, his face almost as red as his jacket. All the soldiers shot to attention and saluted instantly, but he ignored them, instead briefly surveying the remains of the squirrel and blood-spattered deaf mute before grabbing the unfortunate marksman by the throat and shaking him like a rat.

"You fucking idiot!" he roared, spraying the man's face with spittle. "You never fire your weapon unless ordered to, and then only at an enemy! You could have killed the man, for God's sake!"

"It was only a squirrel, Sarge," the hapless private managed to splutter. "They're vermin. He's not harmed."

"A month ago you didn't know one end of a gun from the other and now you're telling me you're an expert? You're lucky you didn't blow the man's head off! If Captain Sewell gets to hear of this, you'll hang!" He looked over at John, who was still staring at the humiliated private, now looking down at the ground and clearly wishing himself anywhere but in His Majesty's Army.

"Wouldn't be much of a loss if he had," one of the other soldiers muttered.

The sergeant threw the man he was holding away from him and rounded on the mutterer.

"I know the man's deaf and an idiot," he growled. "But he's also the servant of the man who's paying all you lumps of shite a shilling a day for strolling through the mountains, money that none of us have seen yet, and won't till we get the cattle safely to Glasgow. Do you think he's going to pay us if one of you kills his man? Both of you report to me when we camp this evening. A hundred lashes for the pair of you."

"But Sergeant, it was just –"

"Two hundred."

A deathly silence fell over the group of men.

"You'll get your chance to shoot real vermin soon enough, on the way back from Glasgow. That's what I was coming to tell you, when I heard this idiot firing his gun."

The men instantly brightened.

"I thought we were just spying out the land, sir," a private from one of the other tents said.

"Yes, we are, on the way down. But I've just been told that the general's sending a regiment on after us in a few days, and we'll meet them coming back up Loch Lomond. We'll trap the rebels between us, and then you should get some real action. And maybe next time you shoot a squirrel, it'll be through skill rather than luck. In the meantime, keep your eyes and ears open on the way. We're not out of MacDonald territory yet."

He strode off back the way he'd come, to general applause and cheers.

John, oblivious, stood and tried to brush the bits of sticky orange fur off his shirt and breeches.

The sun rose higher in the sky and the mist started to lift, so that by the time they'd travelled a few miles up the track, only the tops of the mountains were still invisible. Mr Grundy and his companions rode at the head of the column of soldiers along with Captain Sewell and Sergeant Applewhite. As they walked behind the riding officers, making slow progress due to the cattle, the soldiers glanced left and right from time to time at the hills that hemmed them in. The lower slopes were lush and green, providing food on the go for the cattle, the higher slopes thickly covered with heather, now in full bloom and clothing the mountains in hazy purple. Waterfalls cascaded down over the rocks to swell the stream which bubbled merrily along at the side of the track. Some people might have thought the landscape beautiful.

Mr Grundy clearly was not such a person. He regarded the looming mountains with an expression of terror on his face, swivelling his head from left to right as though expecting the whole Jacobite army to appear on the horizon at any moment.

"You need have no fear, Mr Grundy," Captain Sewell said reassuringly. "You are perfectly safe."

Mr Grundy remained unconvinced.

"When I heard that shot I nearly had an apoplexy, sir. How I kept my seat, I will never know. I thought we were being attacked."

He had in fact come galloping into the camp a full five minutes after the incident, and must have been half a mile away when it happened. The captain sighed inwardly. The sooner he could pocket his money and be rid of this cowardly fool the better. And his companions. God, Armstrong's face could curdle milk, and the idiot, far from being 'good with cattle' as Grundy had claimed, seemed only to be good at trailing along behind others and staring blankly around him.

"And one of the men, Private…er…Johnson?" Grundy rambled on. "Anyway, he told me that we're in MacDonald country and the MacDonalds are rebels, are they not?"

"Were rebels, sir," Sergeant Applewhite put in. "No more. They were among the first to submit to His Majesty. Their chief made a grovelling apology, and they're no longer a threat to anyone. In just a few minutes we'll be in Campbell land, and they're loyal to the king. That's right, isn't it, Corporal?" he called to a man behind him, who ran up to join the company.

"What's right, sir?" he asked.

"That we're almost out of MacDonald country."

"Damned if I know, sir. All looks the bloody same to me."

"Well, in any case," continued the sergeant, dismissing this unhelpful comment, "you need fear nothing from the MacDonalds."

"Even so," replied Mr Grundy, "I will be most relieved when we are away from their land."

In fact they were already away from Glencoe's land, and had been for about five minutes, as the plain-speaking Yorkshireman and the deaf idiot well knew.

They rode for a couple of minutes in silence, to the captain's relief. Bees buzzed in the wildflowers and occasionally a butterfly flitted past their faces. A large horsefly landed on the sergeant's cheek and he raised his hand to squash it before it could bite. High up on the hill to the right a figure dressed in dark purple and green appeared and started to run down towards the redcoats, before suddenly halting and then dropping like a stone to the ground and disappearing in the heather.

Mr Grundy let out a screech and reined his horse in so suddenly that George, riding directly behind him, cannoned into him. The captain's horse reared up at the sudden noise right next to his ear and Sewell swore fluently as he brought it under control. The Yorkshireman barely noticed. He was pointing up the mountain on the left, a look of abject terror on his face, his eyes enormous behind his brass-rimmed spectacles.

"Look!" he cried. "It moved!"

Everyone stared up at the spot on the hillside at which Mr Grundy was pointing. Except John, who was, as was his way, staring vacantly all around him.

"What is it? What can you see?" asked the captain. All he could see was grass and heather.

"There!" Grundy persisted. Protruding from the heather some three-quarters of the way up the mountain was a large black rock. "Is it a bear?" he asked fearfully.

Everyone within earshot started laughing, except Captain Sewell, who was thoroughly sick of this man who had grown increasingly fearful as the trip had progressed and would soon no doubt be terrified of his own shadow.

"There are no bears in Scotland, sir," he said, holding on to his temper with some difficulty.

"Except the ones that go down to Loch Ness to dance with the sea monster at the full moon," a wit cried out from further back. More laughter.

"Are you sure?" asked Mr Grundy, unconvinced. "It looks like a bear to me."

"It's a rock, Toby," Mr Armstrong said reassuringly, aware that the captain was close to saying something unforgivably rude.

Mr Grundy took his glasses off, cleaned them on his coat sleeve, put them on again and peered up the mountain once more.

"Oh," he said, a little shamefacedly. "So it is."

The cavalcade started moving again. John seemed to be having some trouble getting his horse to move, with the result that he dropped back a little and ended up riding almost level with the soldier who had shot the squirrel earlier.

They rode for maybe five more minutes. The mist had cleared completely now and it was becoming very warm. Mr Grundy twisted a little in the saddle, reaching his left hand up his back in an attempt to scratch between his shoulder blades. Mr Armstrong moved up level with him, so they were riding three abreast; Armstrong to the left, Grundy in the middle and Captain Sewell on the right. Directly in front of Armstrong rode Sergeant Applewhite.

Mr Grundy gave up trying to reach the itchy spot and instead took his hat off with a great flourish, mopping his brow and dislodging his wig in the process, which fell to the ground. His natural hair, which had been tied at the nape of his neck and then pushed up under the wig, was revealed in all its chestnut glory.

Captain Sewell just had time to register that Mr Grundy's hair was a completely different shade to his eyebrows before the man drew his sword with lightning speed, raising it high in the air.

"*Ard choille!*" he yelled, and then turning, drove his blade deep into the captain's chest. The man slid sideways off his horse and was dead before he hit the ground, a look of puzzlement still on his face.

Graeme meanwhile had buried his dirk between the sergeant's

shoulder blades, pulling it out again, and the man backwards with it.

Before the other redcoats could register what was happening at the front of the line, the mountains on both sides erupted into life as a horde of kilted Highlanders materialised out of the heather and began to charge downhill at terrifying speed, straight towards the soldiers.

Some of the soldiers panicked and attempted to run on, or back; but more Highlanders were running up the track towards them in both directions. There seemed to be hundreds of them, and as they charged they drew their swords and roared their fury, made all the more terrifying because the language they spoke was incomprehensible to the redcoats.

The soldier who had shot the squirrel was already dead, stabbed through the throat by Iain as he tried to unsling his musket from his shoulder. Ahead Alex was laying waste to everything around him, slashing and hacking in all directions. Graeme spurred his horse ahead in an attempt to catch up with a couple of officers who were riding on at a dead run hoping to ride straight over the oncoming Highlanders and on to freedom.

No one could live to tell the tale; that was the most important thing. He kicked at his horse, forcing it to even greater effort, and then there was a series of loud cracks from partway up the hill and the soldiers jerked and fell from their horses, which carried on riderless at a dead run. One of the men's feet had caught in the stirrup as he fell, and he was dragged along beside the horse like a rag doll. Graeme reined in hard, and his horse reared, almost throwing him from the saddle. He fought to control it as the running Highlanders parted like the Red Sea to let the horses and Graeme through, one of them slashing at the stirrup to release the tethered man, then neatly cutting his throat, before joining his comrades in what became within seconds a bloodbath.

By the time Graeme had brought his horse to a standstill, then turned and ridden her back, it was all over. Scarlet-coated bodies lay everywhere, and the stream, still bubbling merrily along, ran red with blood. The Highlanders, dressed in muted shades of purple, brown and green, which blended perfectly with the terrain through which they had, mere minutes ago, charged with such devastating effect, were now examining the redcoats, ensuring that none of them lived.

Graeme rode up to where the MacGregor chieftain and his brother stood deep in conversation. All around them men were laughing and congratulating each other on what had been, without doubt, an unqualified success. Forty redcoats dead, and not one Highlander lost. A couple of minor wounds, but that was nothing.

In a few minutes the hard work would begin. The cattle, which had run off all over the valley, had to be rounded up again; and all the redcoats had to disappear. But for now there was general celebration. MacGregors and MacDonalds sat themselves down and rested while they waited for further instructions. Someone produced a leather skin full of whisky which was passed from hand to hand.

"Looks like I missed most of the party," Graeme commented wryly, swinging himself down from the saddle and massaging his knee, which was giving him problems at the moment.

Angus, uncharacteristically grim-faced, looked across at the older man, and then over his right shoulder. Graeme glanced back and saw Allan MacDonald approaching them. His silver-blond hair had come free from its leather thong during the skirmish, and blew around his face. He pushed it back impatiently and then spoke.

"Where is he?" he said.

Alex made to move forward between the two men, but Angus stopped him.

"Up there, near the rowan," he said, pointing to a spot at the top of the hill some way in the distance.

"Aye, well, let's go and get the wee gomerel, then," Allan said. "Aunt Ealasaid'll break his neck when she finds out what he did."

Alex called to Iain, who was heading their way.

"Let the men have a couple of minutes, and then we need to start cleaning up, fast. We have to do it all and be gone before sunset. Did ye bring the tools?" he asked Angus.

"Aye, we left them at the top when we charged."

"Good. Iain, leave the cattle for now, they'll no' go far. Get all the bodies together, and then I want everyone to start digging up there." He pointed to a heather-clad part of the mountain. "Dig up the heather first, and put it to one side, then we need a hole, big enough to bury everyone. Afterwards we can put the heather back, so it'll no' be seen from a distance."

Iain nodded.

"Where are you going?" he asked.

Alex pointed to the rowan.

"I'll no' be long," he said in a low voice. "You did well today," he shouted across to the men of both clans seated on the grass all around him. "It does my heart good to see us fighting together again!"

Judging by the resounding cheers that followed the three men as they started to climb up to the rowan tree, they agreed with him.

\* \* \*

"Oh, shit," Angus said, softly but with great feeling a few minutes later. He had run on ahead of the other two men, anxious to see the results of his earlier action.

Robert MacDonald lay in the heather where he had fallen, felled by the rock thrown at his head by Angus some twenty minutes before. The beautiful flaxen hair that he shared with several members of his family, including the brother now toiling up the hill behind him, moved gently in the soft summer breeze. His equally beautiful cornflower-blue eyes were open, gazing sightlessly at the sky. One arm was outstretched, the fingers still curled around the hilt of his sword, which he had drawn as he had charged prematurely over the brow of the hill, in flagrant disobedience of Angus's orders.

Angus knelt down by the side of the boy, and gently stroked the hair back from his face.

"Christ, laddie," he said softly. "Why could ye no' listen, and do as ye were tellt?"

Alex trotted up to join him and stopped.

"Shit," he said, echoing his brother, and turned, seconds too late to shield Allan from seeing his brother's lifeless body splayed across the heather.

Allan stopped dead and stared for a moment, as though unable to believe what his eyes were telling him. Angus started to rise, holding up a placatory hand.

"Allan, I didna mean to…" he began, but the young man pushed past him, intent only on reaching his brother, and dropping to the ground, he wrapped his arms around Robert, lifting his upper body across his lap and cradling him as though he were a small child.

"No," he said breathlessly. "No, oh God, no, no, no." He crushed his brother's face against his chest, rocking back and forth, tears streaming down his face.

Tears sprang to Angus's eyes as he watched the young man mourn the death of his brother, remembering how he had felt when his own brother had died on the battlefield of Culloden. His heart clenched in his chest and he felt the grief well up in him, grief for Duncan, who was lost to him forever, and grief for this reckless youth whose life he had taken away almost before it had begun.

He turned, unconsciously seeking comfort from his remaining brother, but Alex had moved away and was leaning against the tree, his face in shadow, whether to give Allan space to grieve or because he couldn't bear the visual reminder of his dead wife in the features of her cousins, Angus couldn't tell.

He stood frozen, utterly at a loss for what to say or do to make this right. He could not make this right. The MacDonalds would never forgive him. The cheerful laughter and banter of the mingled clansmen drifting up the hill would, once they found out what he'd done, turn to hatred and bloodshed. More bloodshed.

It seemed that he stood there for hours, but when Allan finally stopped keening and rocking and gently closed his brother's eyes before laying him back down in the heather, the sun had barely moved in the sky.

Allan stood up and looked across at Angus, his eyes red-rimmed, the tears still pouring unheeded down his cheeks.

"It wasna your fault," he said in a choked voice. "He never did listen when his blood was up, no' even tae MacIain. It wasna your fault. I saw him run. Ye had to stop him or he'd have killed us all."

"I didna mean to kill him, man. I swear to God," Angus said earnestly.

Allan walked over to Angus on shaky legs and gripped him by the shoulder.

"Dinna fash yerself. I'll tell them." He nodded down towards the men below them, who were now moving to drag the redcoat corpses to the burying spot Alex had pointed out. "I loved him," he added softly. "MacIain was right no' to let him fight for Charlie. But he couldna protect him forever, and he'd have died anyway, the first time he fought. At least it was quick, and clean." His voice broke then and he closed his eyes for a moment, breathing hard through his mouth to force back the emotion. "I'll tell them it wasna your fault," he repeated. "I just need a minute, alone."

Alex moved forward now, out of the shade of the tree.

"Take all the time ye need, laddie. We'll bury the redcoats and gather the cattle together. And then we'll take Robert home, the three of us."

Allan nodded, then walked back to his brother and knelt down beside him.

Alex jerked his head at Angus, and the two MacGregors started to make their way back down the hill, leaving Allan alone to say goodbye to his brother. Both of them felt drained and utterly weary, as men do when grief has swept unexpectedly over them, a grief rendered all the more potent by contrast with the euphoria of a few moments before.

And both of them were remembering the brother who had united them, the gentle soft-spoken peacemaker who had stepped fearlessly between his hot-headed siblings from the moment they'd been old enough to fight each other. They had not had time to say goodbye to Duncan, had no idea where his body was, whether buried or left for the crows to pick clean, and both of them felt that keenly. The least they could do was give Allan what they had not had.

"If Duncan's killer had come to apologise to me," Angus said as they approached the valley, "I couldna…" His voice trailed off. He was stunned by the generosity of spirit of the young MacDonald.

"Aye. It takes a brave man to say what he said there to ye, to be so fair, wi' his brother lying dead next to him. He's a fine man, worthy of his kin. Ealasaid must be very proud of him. And he was right. It wasna your fault. I saw him come charging over the hill. I managed to distract the redcoats by pretending I'd seen a bear over on the opposite side of the glen, but if he'd made it another few feet the redcoats would have seen him. They'd probably have killed at least a few of us, and I doubt we'd have been able to stop some of them making it back to Fort William. I ken we promised MacIain that we'd get onto Campbell land before we ambushed them, but the British are no' stupid. They'd have wiped out Glencoe anyway, just to be sure. I feel sorry for the laddie, but he was a fool, and if you hadna killed him someone else would have, soon enough."

"D'ye think Ealasaid will believe that I didna kill him because I still bear a grudge over Morag?" Angus asked.

"Aye. She likes you. And she kens that ye were angry that night, but that ye didna see him as a real threat. Is that what's worrying ye?"

"A lot of things are worrying me. Whether MacIain'll accept it was an accident or declare a blood feud. Whether the other MacDonalds'll accept it was an accident, regardless of what Allan says. And whether I can forgive myself for killing an innocent wee laddie, just because he was a loon."

Alex stopped, forcing Angus to stop with him.

"Whatever MacIain and the MacDonalds think, we'll find a way to make them see the truth of it. I think they'll accept Allan's word and yours, to be honest. MacIain's no' in the mood for a blood feud anyway, I'm thinking, and neither am I. But there's nothing for you to forgive yourself for. He was seventeen, Angus, no' a wee laddie. When ye were seventeen ye were reckless and ye grieved me at times, but ye never defied a direct order from me, even when ye believed I was in the wrong. He wasna innocent, he was defiant and heedless of the consequences. Far better ye killed him than let him be the cause of his whole clan dying. MacIain will see the sense of that, as will Ealasaid. I warned her that I'd kill him if he defied me, and she accepted that. You were acting as chief for me. Dinna waste a second on remorse for what ye did. Ye were right, and I'll stand by ye."

Angus took his brother in a sudden bear hug, and they clung to each other for a moment.

"I'm sorry I grieved ye," he said.

"Aye, well, ye're grown now, and no mistake. If anything were to happen to me, I'd leave the clan in good hands. But I'll only say that the once, mind." Alex clapped his brother on the back, then released him. "Now," he said, "there's a burying to be done, cattle to be taken to Coire Gabhail, and then we can make things right wi' Glencoe. And after that I've a mind to head north and find out if Lochiel really is dead, as the redcoats seem to think. I'll no' believe it till I hear it from someone I can trust."

He carried on, down to the valley. He would wait until Allan came down before he told the MacDonalds what had happened. They could not afford to stop for an argument now; burying the redcoats and rounding up the cattle was paramount, and they needed to work together to do that, and quickly.

In spite of the emotional scene of a few moments ago, as he joined the others he felt a weight lift from his heart. It was good to have a sense of purpose again, to be fighting. It stopped him sinking too deeply into memory and regret. He would have to keep active and focussed on revenge, put everything into that. He knew it was highly likely that at some point he would be taken or killed, but at least he would die doing something Beth would have approved of. And that was worth something.

# CHAPTER EIGHT

**London, July 25th, 1746**

Beth sat in her customary place by the window, her mouth drawn tight in a grimace of pain. Her right arm was held out sideways at shoulder height, in her hand the book *Pamela*. She had not changed position for eight minutes, hence the facial expression. One more minute and she would have beaten yesterday's time. She watched as the clock on the wall ticked away, the large hand taking forever to move one click round the face. Then she dropped the book in her lap and rotated her shoulder, massaging it with the fingers of her left hand.

Without either company or access to the outdoors, she was finding it increasingly difficult to keep her spirits up. Deprived of reading material, with the exception of the volume now resting on her knee, which had been under her pillow and therefore missed when the servants came to take away all her books, she had searched for something else to do to stop her spending all her time agonising over whether Alex was alive or dead, and had finally decided to build up her strength. She reasoned that whatever the authorities intended to do with her, having a strong body would stand her in good stead and achieving it would pass the time. So she had started walking briskly round her room and running on the spot, firstly for minutes at a time, and now for hours, no doubt to the annoyance of the unseen warder's family living below.

She had reread *Pamela,* twice, and had not changed her mind about her opinion of the hero and heroine from the long-ago night at the Cunningham dinner table when she had thrown wine in Edward's face for insulting her mother.

In her view, building up the muscles in her arms was a far better use for the novel than reading the damn thing had been. She rotated her right shoulder again, and then picking the book up in her left hand, shifted position in the chair a little so she could hold her left arm out without hitting the window frame.

She had been sitting like this for some five minutes when all of a sudden the cannons near the Tower started firing one after the other, causing her to jump violently and drop the book on the floor. No sooner had the cannons stopped than all the church bells in London started ringing.

Something was happening. She stood up and looked out of the window, but in the Tower grounds at least, everything seemed to be as normal. She looked at the clock. Two thirty. It was probably the Elector's birthday or some such thing. She sat down again, picked up the book and continued with her exercise regime. The clamour continued.

The Elector's birthday was on the ninth of November. Cumberland's birthday was on the fifteenth of April. That birthday she would never forget; the day before Angus's and the day before Culloden and the last time she'd seen Alex. What date was it today?

She had taken to making marks on the window frame, one for each day. The doctor had told her that she'd been unconscious for about three weeks, and since then she had made seventy-eight marks. Twenty-third of July then, approximately. When was Prince Frederick's birthday? She racked her brains but couldn't remember.

Could they have captured Prince Charles? When he'd interviewed her Newcastle had let slip that the prince was still at large. Surely he would have found a way to get to France by now? She closed her eyes and sent up a silent prayer that whatever the reason for the salutes and the bell-ringing, it was not the capture of Prince Charles Edward Stuart. King James was too old and dispirited to fight for his throne, and Prince Henry too weak; the success or failure of the Jacobite cause rested on the shoulders of Charles alone. If he was captured, the cause was dead.

She opened her eyes again and told herself that there could be any number of reasons for the celebration; it was silly to worry when she had no idea what was happening. She abandoned the book and, standing, began her brisk walk around her chambers. She would walk for two hours today then run on the spot for an hour, just before dinner. That would disturb the warder's evening. It was a small victory, but small victories were all she could enjoy for now.

But as day turned to night, the sky turned orange from the light of the bonfires, and the sounds of revelry could be heard even in her rooms, she began to doubt again. This was no annual celebration; this was something extraordinary. What could it be, if not the capture of the heir to the Stuart throne?

In spite of her resolution not to worry, she spent all of that night and most of the next day pondering the consequences of his capture, with the result that the following night she was completely exhausted when she went to bed, and slept late, being finally woken by a serving-maid, who was forced to break the rule of not speaking to the prisoner by calling to wake her, after clattering around the room and opening the curtains and shutters had failed to do so.

Having broken her silence, the maid seemed happy to continue chatting as she set out the breakfast things while Beth yawned and stretched and got out of bed.

"After you've breakfasted, my lady, I'm to help you dress. Would you like to choose a gown to wear?" she said while pouring Beth's chocolate.

"What's your name?" Beth asked, startling the maid. No one of consequence had ever asked her name, and although this woman was a prisoner, she was also of very great consequence; everyone in the house knew that, although not why.

"Kate, my lady," she replied, bobbing a curtsey.

Beth smiled.

"It's a pretty name. Is it short for Catherine?"

"I don't know, my lady. Everybody has always called me Kate." She blushed. "Would you like me to help you choose –"

"I'm sorry you had to wake me," Beth interrupted. "The noise of the celebrations kept me awake, and I was catching up on my lost sleep. Was it Prince Frederick's birthday?"

"Oh no, my lady. It was for Prince William. He came home on Wednesday. There were bonfires in the streets and dancing, and everybody put candles in their windows. Half of London is at Kensington Palace, hoping to see him. You are very honoured, my lady."

Beth had been silently sending up a prayer of thanks that the celebrations had not been for the arrest of Prince Charles, and only registered this final sentence belatedly.

"Honoured?"

"Yes, my lady. He has asked especially to see you, at eleven o'clock."

Beth glanced at the clock. Nine.

"We have plenty of time, then. Sit down. Would you like some chocolate?"

The maid seemed completely at a loss, but whether it was because of Beth's obvious indifference toward meeting Prince William, or because she'd just been invited to sit and drink chocolate with her, was unclear. It seemed that the warder, whoever he was, had the same feelings about the serving classes as Lord Edward did. But as far as Beth was concerned, the maid was the first person to have actually spoken to her in two months, a potential source of information, and a possible ally.

Kate hovered over the chocolate pot, clearly torn between her duty to her master and her wish to taste the expensive beverage.

"Have you ever tasted chocolate, Kate?" Beth asked.

Kate shook her head.

"Well, then. Here's your chance. I won't tell anyone, I promise. We can discuss what I'm going to wear while you're drinking it, and then if anyone asks you can honestly say you were following your orders."

Kate sat down awkwardly on the edge of the chair and Beth stood, briskly refilling her cup and then passing it over to the maid, who looked at the beverage as though it might rear out of the cup and bite her on the nose. She reminded Beth a little of Grace; not in her looks, but in her attitude. She abandoned the idea of using the maid to possibly acquire writing materials for her and to smuggle a letter out. Kate seemed innocent, unworldly; Beth would not be the cause of her losing her job, or worse. But the information…

Kate had now started sipping at the chocolate, a look of bliss on her face.

"When I heard all the bells, I thought the Pretender's son had been captured," Beth said conversationally.

Kate looked up from her cup.

"Oh no, my lady. They say that he is in the Isle of Skye, and is hiding there dressed as a woman!"

Beth took in this piece of unlikely information, trying and failing to imagine the six-foot-tall athletically built prince passing himself off as a woman. This could not be true, surely? But at any rate, he was still free.

"Who are they? The ones who say this?"

"Oh, it was in the papers, my lady. Mr Staines, he's one of the footmen, you know, he can read, and he told us. He said that there are a lot of soldiers, hundreds of them looking for him now, and it can't be long before he's taken, for there's a thirty thousand pound reward out for him. And then we'll all be able to sleep in our beds at night again."

"The Isle of Skye is a very long way away, Kate. I doubt the pri…Pretender's son would come all the way here just to murder you in your bed. And if he could he would not. He is a kind man, a gentleman. Do not believe everything you hear from the newspapers."

The maid stared at Beth, wide-eyed.

"Have you met the Pretender's son, my lady?" she asked, awestricken.

"I have. And he treats women, and men too, with the utmost honour. He is not the man they would have you believe him to be. Nor is Cumberland."

Kate blushed again, and seemed to suddenly realise the enormity of her situation, agreeing to share breakfast with someone who was not only acquainted with the Stuart prince, but also with the hero of Culloden, who everyone in London would die to meet. She had finished the chocolate and was about to stand up, but Beth waved her back down and poured her another.

"We have to get you ready to –"

Beth raised a hand imperiously.

"We have plenty of time. It won't take me long to dress."

"Oh, but you will want to bathe, and wash your hair, and then I have to dress it, and –"

"I can wash, that will be quicker, and I do not need to wash my hair, nor do I wish to dress it. A simple braid will be enough."

The maid opened her mouth to protest.

"My injury still pains me greatly," Beth lied smoothly. "I cannot wear my hair any other way. I'm sure the prince will understand." She couldn't give a damn whether Cumberland understood or not, but she was not dressing up any more than she had to for him.

She had no choice about the dress; all the gowns that had been provided for her were costly and richly embellished with embroidery. She would have liked to arrive at his door in the dress she had worn on the day of Culloden, but she supposed it had been thrown away.

In the end she let Kate decide, who considered it a great honour to do so, and by prevaricating over her choice of shoes and jewellery contrived to arrive fifteen minutes later than 'asked' to do so, thereby insulting the prince before she even arrived at Whitehall, where he was waiting to see her.

Small victories.

\* \* \*

Prince William, Duke of Cumberland, did indeed consider himself to be insulted as he sat behind Newcastle's desk, waiting for Miss Cunningham to arrive. But when she was shown in by her military escort who, on his signal, bowed and retreated, leaving them alone, he forgave her instantly.

After the soldiers had left she remained standing by the doorway, dressed in sky-blue brocaded satin, tiny, fragile and looking very vulnerable. He stood and came around the desk to meet her, taking her hand in his and raising it to his lips, ignoring the fact that she did not curtsey to him as she should have done. No doubt she was overwhelmed by her situation.

He had wondered how she would respond to his gesture. He had hoped she would curtsey, blush, smile. He had dreaded that she would pull her hand away, slap his face. But she did not respond in any way at all, which left him with no idea as to how she felt toward him. He invited her to sit down and she moved forward silently, taking the chair he indicated.

He returned to his seat on the opposite side of the desk. He had taken great care in dressing today and had abandoned military uniform in favour of a sage green silk suit with lavish gold embroidery, not wishing by displaying his scarlet coat to bring back unpleasant memories for her of the battle and the last time they had met. He wondered if she did in fact remember him leaping off his horse and bending to lift her gently from the ground. She had moaned softly as he had gathered her to his chest, and he had known then that she was alive, had sprung into action immediately, doing everything in his power to ensure she survived.

He told himself and everyone else that he had taken such pains because she was the only person who could definitely identify the traitor Sir Anthony, but looking at her now, sitting calmly and demurely opposite him, he realised that he'd had other motives for saving her life.

She looked lovely in spite of the livid scar that marred her left temple; the doctors had done their job well, and she seemed to be blooming with health. He stopped himself from leaning over the desk, not wishing to appear too eager, and instead sat back in the chair.

"I trust you are being treated well?" he asked.

"Yes," she replied simply.

"Do you need anything to make your stay more comfortable? You have only to ask."

"No."

"Does your injury still pain you?"

"A little."

He was instantly all concern.

"I will get my personal physician to attend you. I am sure he can give you something to relieve the pain."

"No thank you."

There was a short silence while the duke tried to think of a question that would require a longer answer and she sat calmly looking past him and out of the window. He felt gauche, wanting to say something that would elicit a favourable response, and at a loss as to what that might be.

This was ridiculous. He was the victor of Culloden, commander of the British Army, favourite son of the king, and she was the cousin of a minor aristocrat. He pulled himself together, and decided to get to the point. Well, to start to make his way to the point, at any rate.

"I am sure you know by now that the rebels have been utterly defeated, and that the rebellion is over."

"Yes, your sergeant told us, just before he murdered an innocent woman and baby," she replied calmly, still looking over his shoulder. He resisted the urge to turn and follow her gaze, and ignored her reply.

"Many of the leaders of the rebellion are killed or taken. Two of them are to be executed tomorrow."

"And yet Prince Charles is neither killed nor taken," she responded.

"It is only a matter of time before he is. There is a thirty thousand pound reward for information about him, and we are closing in on him. As I said, it is –"

"And yet no one has claimed the reward," she said softly, as though unaware she had interrupted him. "It is not over, then."

He reddened, betraying the fact that she had hit a sore spot. This was not going at all as he had imagined. He must end her delusion, now.

"Elizabeth," he said, leaning forward in spite of his resolution not to appear eager. "The rebellion is over. The clans are scattered and more and more surrender their arms every day. You have been abandoned, both by Charles and by your husband. I understand how persuasive my cousin can be, and how clever Sir Anthony was. I am sure you believed him to be in love with you, believed yourself in love with him. What woman's head would not be turned by such sophisticated liars? But now you see what it has brought you to. You must think of yourself, for I can assure you the man who ruined you certainly does not."

"You speak of him in the present. You know him to be alive then?" she said.

Was she mocking him? He observed her expression, but it was completely neutral.

"If he fought at Culloden, then he is almost certainly dead," Cumberland replied brutally, nettled by her lack of emotion. "If not, then he may be in prison or skulking in the mountains."

"Or in France, raising troops for another rebellion," she said.

"Wherever he is, madam, he cannot help you. Whereas I desire nothing more than to help you. Tell me what you know of this man who has treated you so badly, and I promise you we need never speak of it again. I can obtain a full pardon for you and will purchase a fine house, in the countryside perhaps, but not too far away. You will want for nothing, I assure you. And when I visit you I will be very discreet."

Now, finally, she turned away from her perusal of the view and looked at him.

"Are you asking me to be your mistress?" she asked coolly. "And I a ruined woman and a traitor?"

"You are no more a traitor than I am, Elizabeth," he said passionately. "We were all deceived by him, but you most of all. Of course you, who are so beautiful, so spirited, could not resist such a man, who promised you wealth, romance, adventure! I understand that, of course I do. Society may consider you a ruined woman, now. But once under my patronage, your reputation and that of your family will be restored. Whether Sir Anthony is captured or not, I will ensure that everyone knows you cooperated willingly and fully with us, and that you have atoned for your weakness in being bewitched by him. Given time you will be able to resume your place in society. And I assure you, you will find no one more…"

His voice trailed away into nothing as he noted that now, for the first time since she had been escorted into the room, she had an expression on her face. He looked away from her, unable to bear the mocking smile and the contempt in her eyes. Was she aware that he had been about to declare his devotion to her? He hoped not.

"The reputation of my family should not have been affected by my actions, nor by Anthony's. Everyone was taken in by him, even you. If my family's reputation is tarnished, then so is the whole of society's. My cousins knew nothing of what Anthony truly was, nor of my own political views. In fact Edward thinks women incapable of having any views at all.

"As for yourself, let me disabuse you once and for all of this notion you have that Anthony bewitched me. It is true I married him reluctantly, but once I found out his true nature, and that he wholeheartedly supported King James, I followed him in everything willingly, and if I could have my time over, would do so again without hesitation. I do not consider that I have done anything dishonourable in supporting the cause of the rightful monarch over a pack of German usurpers."

He flushed scarlet with anger and opened his mouth to speak, but she held up a hand, and to his astonishment he found himself obeying her signal to let her continue.

"You ask me to betray everything I hold dear, and for what? To be your mistress? Never. I don't care a fig for what society thinks of me, but I could never look at myself in a mirror again if I were to become your whore, and you insult me by even suggesting it."

"Elizabeth, I cannot marry you, you know that," he said, appalled that she could think he was insulting her by suggesting she become his mistress. That was the furthest thing from his mind.

"I have no wish to marry you. I have a husband already."

"He married you under a false name. Your marriage was not legal. And in any case, if he was at Culloden, which I assume he was, then he is almost certainly dead, as I said earlier."

"If that is the case, then any information I could give regarding his true identity would be worthless, and I will happily die a widow, knowing my *husband* was a man of courage and honour. And in the meantime I am proud to be a Jacobite prisoner, which I consider a far more honourable condition than being either a cowardly traitor or a whore. You dishonour both yourself and me to even suggest such a thing."

For a moment he felt completely humiliated. Then indignation took over. How dare she speak to him thus! And she had not used his title once, in spite of knowing the proprieties! He had offered her, a fallen woman and a Jacobite to boot, the highest honour he could, an honour many women would give anything for, and she had the temerity to accuse him of dishonourable behaviour?

By God, he would bring her to her senses! Before he could weaken and change his mind, he shouted for the guards.

"You will escort the prisoner directly to Newgate," he ordered. "She wishes to be treated as any other rebel prisoner. Ensure that she is."

He looked at her again, hoping that she would be horrified by the mere suggestion of incarceration in a prison whose reputation was known throughout the land. But her face was once more calm, expressionless. She stood, and turning her back on him accompanied the guards from the room without another word.

After she had gone he sat for a moment, letting the conflicting emotions she had roused in him wash over him. Anger, humiliation, outrage…

Love.

He loved her. And she had once led him to believe that his feelings were reciprocated. What evil spell had that traitor Anthony cast over her, that even now, after all that had happened, she still fancied herself in love with him? Let her see what happened to ordinary rebels, what could happen to her if he withdrew his protection. Although…

He sat for a minute, deep in thought, and then rang the bell and summoned a footman to carry an urgent message to the keeper of Newgate Prison.

\* \* \*

Upon arrival at Newgate Beth was taken into a dank, cold room underneath the entrance gate. Through the middle of the room ran an open sewer which discharged its foul-smelling contents into the Fleet river. The smell was overpowering, and it took all Beth's willpower for her not to vomit at the stench.

A stout wall-eyed man with lank greasy hair whom she supposed to be the keeper, eyed first her and then her clothes with appreciation.

"Welcome, Mistress Cunningham," he said. "I'm told you're to be put with the rebel prisoners. But first we have to measure you for your irons. What do you think, Mr Twyford?"

A figure materialised from the shadows, and moved forward.

"I would think twenty pounds should be sufficient to subdue her, Mr Jones," Twyford commented. "Although it would be a shame to shackle such a beautiful woman. You know what a mess the irons make of them; scars them for life. Why, only last week a young lady had to have her arm cut off. The irons cut her to the bone, they did. Went bad."

"You speak true, Mr Twyford, true indeed," intoned the keeper sadly. "Of course, Mistress, for a small consideration I daresay we could come to some accommodation."

"You can save your breath, sirs," Beth said as calmly as she could, trying not to remember the hanging Alex had insisted she attend, and the woman's wrists, which had been raw and infected. "I have no money, nor have I any friends who would pay you your 'small consideration'. So do what you must, and have done with it."

"Come now, surely a young woman as beautiful as you and dressed so expensively, must have access to funds? In fact I daresay that your dress could fetch a reasonable sum, if –" He got no further before there came a banging on the door. It opened, and a young man dressed in the livery of the Duke of Newcastle entered.

"An urgent message, sir, regarding the prisoner," he said breathlessly. The wall-eyed man stepped outside, returning a few minutes later with a completely different attitude.

"Well, it appears that you do have friends after all, Mistress Cunningham," he said. "No shackles, Mr Twyford."

"Shall I take her to the press yard then, Mr Jones?" asked his companion, who had clearly recognised the livery.

"No. No shackles, but she's to be confined with the other rebel women."

Mr Twyford appeared confused by this. In fact both men did. Beth wondered what the press yard was, and what the footman had said to puzzle them. Maybe Cumberland still hoped she would relent and become his mistress after all, and did not want her to be scarred any more than she already was. Whatever it was, she was grateful not to have to wear irons, although it would be a cold day in hell before she gave herself to that fat usurping slug.

She was led out of the foul-smelling room, up two flights of narrow stone steps, then down a corridor lit with candles placed in sconces, to a door at the end. Mr Jones opened the door with an enormous key and waved her in, before closing and locking it behind her.

She found herself in a room lit only by a narrow barred window high up in the wall. It was completely bare of furniture, and very cold, in spite of the fact that it was summer. She stood a moment and let her eyes become accustomed to the gloom, upon which she began to make out the shapes of several women, most of whom were sitting on the wooden floor, leaning against the stone walls which were glistening with moisture. The air was heavy and fetid with the smell of unwashed bodies, urine and excrement, and Beth breathed through her mouth in an attempt to reduce the stench assailing her nostrils. *I will become accustomed to it*, she told herself desperately.

There came the sound of flint and tinder, and suddenly a candle was lit, banishing the shadows to the corners of the room. Someone started to protest in a soft Scottish accent at this waste of what was apparently a luxury, but was immediately hushed. The bearer of the candle stood and made her way over to Beth, who was still standing by the door.

"Well, what 'ave we 'ere?" she said. "A bloody lady!" She curtseyed deeply, then laughed raucously and held the candle up to get a better view of the newcomer.

Beth took advantage of the illumination to take the measure of this woman who was undoubtedly the self-styled chief of the room. She was nearly a head taller than Beth and would probably have been described as 'strapping', before prison life had stripped her of some of her muscle. Even so, she was still formidable. And filthy. Her dark hair was tangled and her face greasy and milk-white from lack of sunlight.

"And you're a whore, I take it?" Beth replied calmly, eyeing the red ragged petticoat and very low-cut bodice the woman was wearing. At one time they would have passed for stylish, at night, anyway.

The woman laughed again, clearly not offended by Beth's observation.

"Make my livin' whatever way I can, don't I?" she said.

"Not very well at the moment, it seems," Beth commented. She heard the gasp of horror from the other women, and watched the anger kindle in the woman's eyes. Yes, she was right. This woman was a bully, and had succeeded in cowing the other occupants of the room. And yet these were rebel prisoners, and the Jacobite women Beth had met en route to Culloden would not have been easily subdued by just one bully, no matter how dominant. She probably had the assistance of one of the turnkeys then, perhaps in exchange for sexual favours.

Oh, well. She would worry about that later. One thing at a time.

The woman was looking at Beth's dress now, the blue brocaded satin shimmering in the candlelight. She whistled appreciatively.

"Look at this, girls!" she said, taking a handful of the skirt and lifting it. Beth made no move to stop her, and she smiled triumphantly at her easy conquest of the new prisoner. "We could live like queens for a year on this, couldn't we?"

There was no answer from the 'girls'.

"You a whore too, then?" she asked Beth mockingly. "Or one of them scullery maids who gets an 'and-me-down from 'er mistress then goes down Vauxhall and gets 'erself swived by some footman under a tree?"

"Well, whatever I am, I'm clearly better at it than you, aren't I?" Beth replied, looking her adversary up and down with deliberate contempt. A deathly silence fell over the room, and before the woman could react to this insult Beth punched her in the stomach with both fists as hard as she could, silently thanking Richardson for writing such a weighty tome.

Unprepared for the assault the whore doubled over instantly, badly winded, and Beth followed through, bringing her knee up hard into the woman's face. She felt the crunch as the nose broke, and then the bully dropped the candle and crumpled onto the floor, clutching her face and gasping for breath. Miraculously, the candle was not extinguished, and bending down, Beth picked it up and briefly examined her victim. Once sure that the woman was actually managing to pull a little air into her lungs, she straightened up again and smiled at the other occupants of the room, who were all looking at her with identical expressions of shock.

"That wasn't quite the greeting I expected, but I do have a reputation for making memorable entrances, so I suppose I shouldn't have been surprised," she said pleasantly. "*Halò, is mise Beth. Tha mi toilichte ur coinneachadh.*"

There was a stunned silence for a moment as the women tried to take in the fact that someone who was clearly a Sasannach and, what was more, both looked and spoke like a lady, nevertheless had the Gaelic. Then one of them started to clap her hands, and then another, and within a minute all of them were clapping and smiling, and the bully, still gasping and struggling to sit up, was forgotten as they stood to greet the newcomer who had made such a spectacular first impression.

\*  \*  \*

## 29th July 1746

"God, I'm tired," Edwin said by way of greeting to his wife as he entered the salon. He gave his coat and hat to a waiting footman, then threw himself into a chair.

Caroline looked up from her desk, where she was finishing off a letter.

"It's wonderful to see you too, darling," she commented drily, folding the paper and carefully pouring sealing wax onto the join.

"I'm sorry. It is wonderful to see you, really. I've missed you. How's Summer Hill coming along?"

"Extremely well. I arrived back this morning. Some of the rooms are habitable now. I was just writing to William to arrange a meeting." She stamped the brass seal into the wax.

Edwin looked across at her in surprise.

"I think he'll be very busy for a while. Half of London is begging to see him. What do you want to meet him for, anyway?"

"He's designing the garden. I told you last week. And I know I had to fight to prise him away from Henry, but why is half of London begging to see him?"

"Cumberland's designing the garden?" Edwin replied, thoroughly bemused.

Light dawned.

"Edwin, there is more than one person in the country called William, you know," Caroline said gently. "You really need to get away from parliament now and again. William Kent is designing the garden. I think Cumberland is somewhat busy basking in the adoration of Britain at the moment. Shall I call for some food for you? It's a bit late, but cook should be able to put a cold collation together."

Edwin yawned hugely, and glanced at the clock.

"I had no idea it was that late," he said. "No, I'm not hungry. I dined at my club between sessions."

"What kept you so late?" his wife asked, getting up and coming to stand behind him. She gently massaged his shoulders, knowing how much he loved her to do that. The muscles of his neck and upper back were solid. A hard day, then.

"You know the Dress Act has been passed into law now?" he said.

"The one denying Highlanders the right to wear their traditional clothes?"

"Well, it denies anyone in Scotland the right to wear them or in fact to even possess a piece of tartan at all. But yes, it's aimed at the Highlanders. Well, now we're thrashing out the details of the Heritable Jurisdictions Act, which will effectively take away all the powers of the clan chiefs. And debating what to do about the prisoners."

Caroline whistled through her teeth.

"So the king really does mean to destroy the clans then?"

Edwin nodded.

"Something drastic has to be done, Caro, otherwise, unless Charles is captured, it'll only be a matter of time before there's another rising. And if the French invade as well this time…"

"It seems pretty drastic though, destroying their whole way of life."

"Not as drastic as one proposal, to transport whole clans like the Camerons and MacGregors. But it was thought to be too expensive and impractical, and in any case, a lot of them would have probably found a way to return. Instead they're being systematically disarmed. There are still pockets of resistance but the military presence there is making sure that they can't assemble enough men for another rising at the moment. And the laws we're bringing in will hopefully make sure that they finally come into line with the rest of Britain. It's ridiculous that half the country still lives under feudal law, in these times!"

Caroline nodded at the wisdom of this.

"What's the problem with the prisoners, then?"

"The sheer numbers of them, really. The prisons are overflowing, so we're going to turn some of the hulks into floating prisons for them. They'll be docked at the mouth of the Thames, and then the prisoners will draw lots. One in twenty will be tried and the rest will probably be transported, in time. It would take us years to try all of them."

"I thought William was for executing them all? Cumberland that is, not Kent."

He tipped his head back and eyed her sceptically.

"I don't know. He certainly believes in teaching them a stern lesson in Scotland, but here it seems that sending them to the Colonies will be the most practical solution. The only ones the king is determined to make an example of, apart from the leaders of course, is the Manchester Regiment. Manchester was the only English town that raised enough men to form a regiment of its own. I think he wants to make sure that the English at least will never rise for Charles again."

Caroline gave up trying to loosen the knots of tension in his muscles, and sat down opposite him.

"If you're not hungry, let's go to bed instead. At least you can sleep late tomorrow," she said. "Parliament isn't meeting until two, is it?"

"I can't," he said, standing and allowing her to lead him from the room. "That's what I was about to tell you. I'm attending the hangings of the Manchester rebels tomorrow. They're at eleven, but I'll have to set off very early."

Caroline stopped part way up the stairs and turned to him, shock written all over her face.

"You're attending the hangings? Whatever for? You've never shown the slightest inclination to go to one before. You *hate* violence! And these aren't just normal hangings. I was brought up going to such things, but even I have no wish to see men drawn and quartered. What are you thinking of?"

"We drew straws," Edwin said tiredly. "I lost. Or won, in the eyes of some of the others."

"Let one of them go, then," Caroline retorted. "You sleep in."

"It's too late. I've already agreed. And the king expects at least one of his new knights to attend."

"But that's ridiculous! There will be so many people there that no one will notice whether you…wait…what did you just say?"

He looked up at her, standing above him on the stairs, still holding his hand.

"As of next month, you will be married to Sir Edwin Harlow. The king has awarded me a knighthood to compensate me for all my hard work during the rebellion. And for the loss of my family life," he added, although Caroline knew well that the king did not consider a man's family life to be of any importance where war was concerned.

Caroline squealed in a most unladylike manner and threw herself at her husband, which, as they were part way up the stairs, resulted in them toppling backwards and landing in an undignified, though thankfully uninjured heap in the hall.

"That's wonderful news! Why didn't you tell me as soon as you came in?" she asked, hugging him.

"I was going to wait until we had time to celebrate it, but then I found I couldn't wait to tell you after all." He beamed up at her, and she kissed him ecstatically. In spite of his fatigue he felt a stirring in his breeches, and realised that it had been a long time since he and his wife had made love. Too long.

"Er…Shall we continue this in private, Caro?" he suggested.

She grinned at him so lasciviously that he blushed.

"No," she said. "Tonight you need to sleep. Tomorrow we have a hanging…several hangings to attend. And then you are taking a few days off to come and see Summer Hill, even if I have to petition the king myself."

"But-"

"No arguments. You work too hard and deserve a holiday. Now bed, for both of us."

He had been going to protest against her attending the executions with him rather than the holiday, but as she pulled him firmly up the stairs again he realised that he was dreading tomorrow, and really would appreciate her support during what would be for most Londoners a wonderful day out, and for him a terrible ordeal.

\* \* \*

Sarah insisted that she and John set off bright and early for Kennington Common on the Wednesday morning.

"It's going to be very crowded," she said, "and if you're determined to do this, then you want to stand near enough that there's a slight chance at least of one of your friends seeing you."

"I really appreciate this, but you don't have to go, you know," John said.

"Yes, I do. I'm not letting you face this alone. I'd never forgive myself if I did."

Initially John had planned to get the stagecoach to Manchester straight after the executions, but Sarah had pointed out that the crowds would be so dense it would take him hours to get away afterwards, and that in any case he would have to carry both his spare clothing and the money she was lending him for his fare – a crazy thing to do when London's most accomplished pickpockets would be enthusiastically plying their trade.

Privately she also wanted him to spend another night with her, because over the last week that he had stayed with her she had come to know him well, and both liked and respected him. She could see why Beth was so fond of him. He was both passionate about the Jacobite cause and sensitive, and Sarah was sure that seeing his friends die in such an awful way would affect him profoundly. She wanted to be with him tonight so that she could try to help him come to terms with what he was about to see.

And she would miss him. In the last week they had grown close, and she had come to think of him like a brother, which made the pretence that he was to inquisitive customers easy to maintain. He was wonderful with Mary too. In fact she would be quite happy were he to stay with her indefinitely, but knew that it was too dangerous. He had to get out of London as soon as possible. Thomas and Jane would look after him until he was completely healed of his fetter wounds, and then he could find a place to go where no one knew him, and make a new life for himself.

Although they set off very early there were already plenty of people out on the streets, heading in the same direction. They were about halfway there when a coach passed them and then stopped. As they drew level, the door opened and Caroline leaned out.

"Sarah!" she said brightly. "Are you going to Kennington?"

Sarah looked up. "Good morning. Yes, we are," she replied.

"Jump in then. We'll take you," she said. The footman jumped down from the back of the coach and lowered the steps for them to climb in. Sarah hesitated.

"It's very kind of you, but we can walk," she said.

"Nonsense!" Caroline replied briskly. "It's coming on to rain. There's no point in you both getting wet before you need to."

Realising that it would look churlish at the least, and suspicious at the worst if they were to refuse this kind offer, she capitulated.

John handed Sarah up into the coach, then climbed in after her. They sat down opposite the Harlows, and the coach started off again. Caroline looked expectantly at John.

"This is my brother, Jem," Sarah said. "He was in the militia and was away when my sister…when Mary was born. He came down here to see her and he's been staying with me for a few days. Jem, this is Mr and-"

"This is Edwin, and I'm Caroline," Caroline interrupted.

Edwin, who had been sitting back in the coach looking uncharacteristically morose, now leaned forward and offered his hand to John, who shook it, very glad that he had remembered to wear gloves today. His fingers were healing, but were still raw enough to excite curiosity.

"I'm very sorry for your loss, Jem," Edwin said. "It must have been a terrible shock for you."

"It was, sir," John replied, then fell silent, hoping that the couple would think he was too overcome with emotion to elaborate on the death of his fictional sister.

There was a slightly awkward silence.

"So what do you think of London, Jem?" Caroline asked. "Have you been here before?"

"No, and I hope never to again," John replied without thinking, then reddened.

"Jem's a country boy," Sarah leapt in immediately. "He finds the noise of the city difficult to become accustomed to."

"To say nothing of the smells," Caroline put in, to John's surprise. "Although you get used to those, for the most part. We've lived in London for five years, and it can be an exciting place to be, but it's also very tiring. We've got a house in the country now, Sarah. I'm furnishing it at the moment. When it's finished, you must come and visit. Both of you."

John looked at this obviously aristocratic woman, astounded. There was no condescension in her invitation to this couple who were so far beneath her on the social ladder. Edwin and Caroline. He vaguely remembered Beth telling him that she didn't give a fig about deceiving her family, but she felt bad about two of her friends. She had written to one of them about Martha. Was this her? Her husband was in the government or something.

"Do you work in the city, sir?" John asked Edwin impulsively.

"Yes, for my sins," Edwin replied.

"Edwin is a Member of Parliament," Caroline explained. "He is attending the executions today because he is obliged to. He has no wish to go, and neither do I. But of course there is nothing wrong with going to such an event, if you want to," she amended hurriedly.

This *was* the woman Beth had spoken so highly of! He warmed to her instantly, smiled, and was a hairsbreadth from mentioning that he knew Beth when Sarah squeezed his arm warningly, and he remembered that he was supposed to be Sarah's brother. He had never met Beth, had no idea she existed.

He hated lying. He was no good at it. They should have insisted on walking.

"Jem has never been to a hanging before," Sarah said quickly. "I don't think he'll enjoy it, myself, but he insisted on coming, so I decided to come with him."

"Well, it is certainly a memorable experience," Caroline said brightly. "But I hope Sarah has had the time to show you some of London's more pleasant attractions. St Paul's, Vauxhall or Ranelagh Gardens, perhaps?"

"Sarah works very hard," John said. "I came to see her and the baby, that was enough for me. I didn't come to see the sights."

*If you only came to see your family, why are you so eager to go to an execution?* The question hung in the air between them. Damn.

"I didn't have time to show him anything else," Sarah said somewhat frantically, John thought. "And Vauxhall and St Paul's will be there next time he visits me. But there will never be another execution like this."

"God, I hope not," Edwin said with great feeling.

The carriage came to a halt and Edwin jumped down, followed by John, who then helped the ladies down. That done, he looked around and discovered to his horror that the coachman had managed to work his way almost to the front, and there were only a few rows of people between him and the gallows. Sarah had told him that people would have been arriving there since the previous evening, and in his heart of hearts he had hoped to be able to satisfy his conscience from a great distance, and maintain some level of emotional detachment.

"Edwin did not purchase tickets for the stands," Caroline was explaining, "but we will be able to see everything from here."

In front of the gallows a block had been set on which the bodies would be dismembered, and next to it a pile of faggots on which their hearts and intestines would be burnt.

They stood and waited. People pushed their way through the crowd selling pies, oranges and printed copies of the dying speeches of the men, who had not even arrived yet, let alone spoken.

"The crowd is very quiet," Caroline, who had attended many executions as a girl, said. "I hope there will not be trouble."

"Why, are they not normally like this?" John asked. He had thought this normal. Seeing men being executed was not a reason to celebrate, in his view.

"No. For most people this is a day out, an entertainment. It's like going to the fair would be in smaller towns. This is unusual. Perhaps it's because they are to suffer a traitor's death."

A great sigh suddenly arose from the crowd as a detachment of soldiers came into view, their scarlet coats a bright splash of colour. Between them were three sledges drawn by shire horses, and on each sledge three men were strapped on their backs facing the sky, the rain, which was now falling heavily, splashing onto their faces. The sledges stopped, the men were untied, and the soldiers formed an oval around the gallows, bayonets fixed, watching the crowd intently for any sign of an attempt at rescue. They too were clearly unnerved by the abnormally quiet crowd.

"Where is the minister?" Caroline asked, puzzled. John hadn't thought about that, but others clearly had, and murmurs of indignation arose from the people near to them.

"This isn't right," one man to the left of John said. "They should have a man of God with them to help them pray and repent of their sins. Even papists deserve that."

John opened his mouth to tell the man that they were not papists but Episcopalians, as was he, but Sarah took his arm in a death grip, and he subsided.

The faggots were lit with some difficulty due to the rain, and the nine men who were to die that day were helped up to the scaffold and left there to make their last statements.

Colonel Towneley spoke first, the man who John had said was humourless and thought himself above his men, but who was brave. He certainly showed his bravery, speaking in a clear, calm voice about how honoured he was to give his life for his rightful king and prince.

After him came Dai Morgan, who tried the patience of the crowd by taking out a book and reading aloud from it for a full half hour. He also made a vicious attack on the Roman Church, to the astonishment of the man to the left of John, who had obviously believed the Hanoverian propaganda that Jacobites were papists to a man.

The other seven condemned men made shorter speeches. Thomas Deacon suddenly lifted his arm and threw his hat into the crowd, and John made a desperate leap high into the air as it flew over his head, snatching it from the eager fingers of three other men, who would have perhaps made something of it had John not shot them a look of such hatred and venom that they thought better of it and let him keep his prize, which he clutched to his chest.

"I'll give it to his father, when I get home," he said softly to Sarah.

Caroline looked at him strangely, but anything she was thinking to say was drowned out in the sudden roar of the crowd as, finally, the men stopped speaking, and the hangman adjusted the nooses around their necks then pulled hoods over their heads, before pushing them one by one off the cart, where they dangled, their limbs twitching and jerking as they strangled.

John made a sudden move forward in an instinctive gesture to rescue his friends, and Caroline, noticing, put a hand out, and he stopped himself. Edwin had closed his eyes momentarily, but now opened them again, and forced himself to look as the men's struggles became weaker.

After a few minutes, the men's clothes were removed and Francis Towneley's body was cut down and laid on the block, while the others were left to hang naked. The hangman lifted a butcher's cleaver and bent over Towneley's body, which twitched feebly.

"Dear God, this is terrible," Edwin breathed. He was as white as a sheet. Caroline put her arm around his waist, and he leaned into her.

John was breathing heavily through his mouth, tears streaming down his face unheeded, and white flashes swam at the edge of his vision. By a sheer effort of will he forced himself not to faint, nor to look away. It had been cowardly of him to hope that he would be too far away to see their suffering. He should have been on the scaffold with them, strangling slowly, gasping for breath. The very least he could do was witness it, to tell others that even if they had never had the chance to show their bravery in battle, they had shown it on the scaffold.

John expected the hangman to slit open Towneley's chest and tear his heart out, still beating, but instead he hacked off the man's head first, holding it up to the crowd, who cheered, and only then did he cut open the chest and draw out the bowels and heart, which were thrown on the fire.

It seemed to John to take an eternity for the process to be repeated with the other eight men, but finally Jemmy Dawson's heart was thrown into the fire and the hangman shouted to the crowd, "God save King George!"

The crowd roared back, and then it was over. The coffins, containing the severed heads and corpses of John's brothers-in-arms were drawn away, and the crowd began to disperse. John stood, rooted to the spot, while a wave of hatred for this so-called king and all his family washed over him so strongly that he thought he would never feel anything again but a burning desire to be revenged for the undignified, brutal way these young men had died for the entertainment of a mindless mob, the same mob who would have no doubt cheered for Prince Charles had he continued on to London and victory, instead of turning back to Culloden and defeat.

He felt the hot bile rise in his throat, and swallowed it back. If they, who had suffered and died, had not shown weakness, then he was damned if he would.

He felt a tugging on his arm, and looked down into the worried eyes of Sarah. Incapable for the moment of speech, he nodded to her to let her know he was alright, although at that moment he thought he would never be alright again. He let her lead him back to the coach, and he handed her in and then climbed in after her, hardly aware of what he was doing.

The coach trundled along, slowly at first, and then faster as they started to move away from the crowds.

"Dear God, that was awful," Edwin said, half to himself. "This is not right. How can people enjoy seeing men suffer so?"

"They were traitors, Edwin," Caroline said softly. "That is the penalty for high treason. At least their heads were cut off before their parts were thrown on the fire. It was not always so. And women can still be burnt at the stake for treason, which can be far more prolonged and painful."

"I know they had to die, and be made an example of, to deter others. But to take children…I would never take Freddie to such a horror," Edwin said. He took out his handkerchief, wiped his eyes and blew his nose.

Caroline looked across at Sarah's brother, who hadn't spoken and was still clutching the hat to his chest. He looked ghastly.

"You knew some of them," Caroline said. It was not a question, and John felt too sick at heart to deny it.

"Yes," he replied. "I did."

"Jem lived in Manchester for a time, like me," Sarah jumped in. "A short time. He got to know quite a lot of people, but only a little. A very little."

Caroline nodded.

"Well," she said. "I hope that you will take something useful away from this experience."

She was looking at the hat, but John had the uncomfortable feeling that she was not referring to that.

"I certainly will," he said bitterly.

Caroline had instructed the coachman to drive straight to Sarah's shop, and once there, John and Sarah thanked them and climbed out. Sarah went to open the door, but as John turned to follow her, Caroline leaned out of the coach again and beckoned him closer.

"Jem," she said very softly, so only he would hear. "May I say something, as a friend of your…sister?"

He nodded and waited, very aware of the pause she had made in her sentence and its implications.

"Do not take offence, but you are not a good liar. Which is to your credit, but I think you should leave London as quickly as possible, and perhaps refrain from any more outings in the meantime. I am sure your friends would have appreciated your gesture today, had they known, and that Mr Deacon's father will take great comfort from the return of his son's hat. It was a reckless thing to do, but a brave one. I wish you well, but there are many who wouldn't. It would not be wise to linger here, I think, for your sake and Sarah's."

Before he could respond she sat back in the coach and tapped on the roof, and the driver set off down the street. John watched as it disappeared round the corner, then slowly turned and followed Sarah into her shop.

He would leave tomorrow, as early as possible.

They rode on in silence for a few minutes, Edwin looking out of the window, deep in thought.

"You said the crowd were quiet today. What are they normally like?" he asked suddenly, making Caroline jump.

"They're normally a lot noisier than that, but their mood depends on who's being hung," she replied. "If it's an unpopular criminal, then they'll jeer and throw things. When Jonathan Wild was hung twenty years ago there was nearly a riot, he was so hated. On the other hand if it's someone popular, like Jack Sheppard, or some of the more famous highwaymen for example, then the crowd might be more sympathetic, especially if he or she gives a good speech. That can be more dangerous in a way, because the sympathy is for the criminal, not the authorities. It's a great entertainment for them, in any case."

"I really cannot comprehend how people can be entertained by watching others die horribly. I have no sympathy for murderers and robbers; they know the risks they run if they are caught. The law of the land must be upheld or we would have anarchy, and of course such people have to die. I understand that. But I have always thought executions to be a lesson to the spectators, not an amusement! And now you tell me that rather than learning from their grisly end, people actually have sympathy for footpads and highwaymen?" Edwin asked, bemused.

And traitors. Caroline had been about to mention that when Sarah's brother had leapt up to grab the hat his coat sleeve had fallen down his arm, and she had seen the unmistakable fetter wounds on his wrist. Three men had escaped from Newgate a week ago. Three men who should have been hung today.

No. Now was clearly not the time. Maybe there would never

be a right time to tell him that where he would see a traitor in Jem, she saw a brave if misguided young man, who had risked recapture to make a gesture of support and loyalty to his friends. She was almost certain that Thomas Deacon had seen him, had aimed the hat at him, had hopefully taken comfort from the fact that he'd caught it. She could not bring herself to turn him in, and in doing so also condemn Sarah, who she considered to be a friend.

She knew that good people could do bad things. And whilst she agreed with upholding the law she was nevertheless willing to bend it for those misguided people who happened to be her friends, as she had just now. But Edwin was an innocent in many ways and took comfort from seeing things in black and white. Good, evil. Legal, illegal. The discovery of Anthony and Beth's treachery had shaken him to the core, as did the fact that he could not, no matter how hard he tried, find it in his heart to hate them. Caroline forced herself back to the question he had asked.

"Some highwaymen behave like gentlemen, are polite to their victims. And remember, most of the people who attend executions are poor and powerless, and they see highwaymen as people like them who are fighting back and who are, however temporarily, winning a victory over those in power. If the criminal then stands on the gallows, defiant, and makes a good speech, he will be the hero of the day."

"So you are saying that public executions glorify crime and lawlessness rather than acting as a deterrent?"

"Well, I hadn't thought of it like that, but yes, I suppose they can. Some criminals redress the balance between the powerful and the powerless, at least for a while, and win the hearts of the crowd."

Edwin thought for a moment.

"I need to go to another execution," he said. "Maybe more than one. I want to see for myself what a normal hanging is like."

Caroline stared at him, shocked.

"Edwin, you're grey. I thought you were going to faint at one point today. Why would you want to put yourself through that again? Leave it to those who enjoy such things."

"No, you mistake me. As far as the government is concerned, executions act as deterrents. Look what will come of you if you break the law, look how horrifying it is to die by hanging, in public. But you're telling me that the criminals are glamorised by the mob, who see it as a great entertainment rather than a terrifying lesson. I need to see this for myself."

"Why? Isn't it enough to see one?"

"No, it isn't. Because if I am going to campaign for a change in the law regarding public executions, then I need to know if I am right in believing that many criminals are encouraged in their crime by the knowledge that if they're caught they will have their moment of fame, and that the crowd learns nothing from witnessing their end."

"You think that we should not execute criminals and traitors?" Caroline said.

"No. I think we should execute them, but quickly and privately."

"You are upset, Edwin. This has shocked you terribly. I knew it would. But people need to know the consequences of treason. Will they learn that without seeing the end they could come to?"

"Do you think that Anthony and Beth didn't know the consequences they would face if they were caught? But did it stop them?"

Caroline sighed.

"No, it didn't. Because in their minds, it was worth the risk of dying in such a manner to see the Stuarts restored to the throne."

"Exactly. In which case making such executions public is pointless, because it acts as no deterrent at all to those who are determined to pursue such a path."

"I agree. It will not stop those who are determined, or desperate. But for those who are thinking about it, seeing what they might come to if they continue might stop them embarking on a life of crime in the first place. We live in a brutal world, Edwin, and sometimes brutal means are needed as a deterrent."

"You are right. I need to think about this. You told me once that I was gentle and caring, and fight with words, not fists."

"I remember. When I threatened to shoot Richard. Part of me still wishes I had."

He smiled.

"Today I've realised that there's a whole world out there that I know almost nothing about. And I *should* know about it. I am lucky enough to be in a position where I can influence policy decisions. But I need to see the consequences of those decisions, and I cannot do that by hiding away from them. There is something deeply wrong about what I witnessed today, but I'm not sure what it is, or how it can be changed. I need to find out."

"Then you must. But not now, while you're so upset. And not for the next few days, either. Because you are coming to Summer Hill with me and Freddie, to see what I've been doing there. I need you to see the consequences of *my* decisions, and to influence my future ones. And then when you're calmer and relaxed, you can think about changing the rest of the world. And I will support you in that, if I can."

He put his arm around her.

"What would I do without you, Caro?" he said.

"The same as I would do without you, Edwin," his wife replied. "Fall apart. So let us enjoy the time we have together."

# CHAPTER NINE

**Scotland, August 1746**

It was a glorious summer day when Alex finally returned to Loch Lomond, some four weeks after the personas of the plain-speaking Yorkshireman Tobias Grundy, the ugly old bastard George Armstrong, and the deaf idiot John had been buried, along with the all-too-real corpses of forty soldiers of His Majesty's Army. Their weapons and most of their clothes, with the exception of the instantly recognisable and therefore incriminating scarlet coats, had been redistributed amongst those Highlanders in need of clothing and in want of arms to continue the fight, and the cattle were now being slowly and very discreetly delivered to those in need of food. All things considered it had been a great victory and an excellent start to the war of attrition that Alex intended to wage on the redcoats, along with those men who wished to fight with him.

Normally when a chieftain returned to his clan after an absence, particularly one with the potential for news gathering this one had, he would expect to be loudly and joyously welcomed by his clansfolk. However Alex had neither wanted nor expected such a welcome, and so was not disappointed by the profound silence that greeted his return to the settlement.

Of course the silence was not *really* profound; birds sang in the trees, bees buzzed in the heather and clover, and the waters of the loch lapped gently against the shore. But there was no human sound at all, and no sign that humans had inhabited the area for some considerable time.

Angus had excelled himself, if this was indeed his idea. Alex had told the MacGregors to abandon their houses, but they had done far more than that. The heather thatch and roof timbers were gone and the stones of the houses collapsed, as if they had fallen in over time. Some of them had been removed completely, as though pillaged by another clan for building materials. All the clansfolk's belongings were gone. Graeme's garden had been obliterated. Even the cowpats, a sure sign of recent occupation to an observant soldier, had disappeared. The only thing they had not been able to do was replicate the encroachment of nature; there were no weeds growing up through the floors, no ivy creeping over the abandoned houses. But all in all, the village gave a good impression of having been abandoned some time ago.

Alex smiled to himself and began to make his way up the mountain to the place where he knew they would all be waiting to hear his news. It had been a very tiring few weeks, first emotionally and then physically, and he couldn't wait to get home and relax for a day or two.

The emotional part had been the worst. Taking Robert MacDonald's body back to his chief had been not only very upsetting, but potentially dangerous too. Alex knew that the Glencoe chief had wanted no part of the raid and had only agreed to let them use his valley as a hiding place because of some favour he owed Ealasaid. Alex had prayed that MacIain would accept Allan's word as to the circumstances of the killing.

If he had not, then a blood feud would have been declared between the clans, because Alex could not, would not have accepted the alternative, which would have been to sacrifice Robert's killer in atonement. He had already lost his wife and one brother; he would not lose another, no matter what the price he had to pay.

But in the end the MacDonald chief had accepted Allan's story, and that it was better to lose one reckless clansman than risk the wrath of the British Army coming down on them.

"Ye ken well, I wanted no part of this raid," he had said sadly, "but once I agreed to it, I wouldna go back on my word, and in truth I'm glad I changed my mind, for surrendering as I did pained my soul and this has gone some way to appeasing that. But when some of the men came to me and asked to join you in the venture, I tellt them then that if they did they must accept you as their chief for the duration of the raid, or face the consequences. And they agreed, all of them, including this wee loon." He looked sadly down at the shrouded figure of his clansman, and then at Angus, who was standing, pale and anxious, in the corner of the room. "I'll no' have bad blood between us over it. Ye did right, laddie, but I'm sorry ye had to."

"Will ye let me be the one to tell Ealasaid?" Alex asked. "As her kinsman by marriage and the one who proposed the raid, I feel it should be myself who breaks the bad news to her."

MacIain looked up then, and to Alex's surprise the chief's eyes filled with tears.

"Christ, ye dinna ken. Of course, how could ye?"

"Dinna ken what?" Alex asked.

"She's dead. She died three days ago. She just went to bed and didna wake up. I'm sorry, man," he added, alarmed by the sudden pallor of Alex's face as he heard the unexpected news. "Sit down."

Alex sank down into a chair, and rubbed his hands over his face as he fought to control the surge of grief that threatened to overwhelm him.

"I'm sorry," he said after a few moments. "I shouldna be so shocked. I mean, she was a great age, but –"

"But ye thought she'd live for ever," MacIain finished sadly. "Aye, we all did. She'll be sorely missed. But it was the way she'd have wanted to go, peacefully and surrounded by her family. Well, being the woman she was, maybe she'd have preferred to die in battle, given the choice, but in a manner of speaking she did. She fought a fierce battle of words wi' me to get me to agree to your plan. It's a fitting tribute to her."

It had indeed been a fitting tribute to her. And a fitting start to the revenge for the death of her equally feisty granddaughter, who *had* died in battle, killing the soldier who had killed Maggie. Angus, Alex and Iain had all made some headway into fulfilling their blood oath to Maggie.

At Glencoe he had left Angus to make his way home, and had continued north alone to try to find out if Lochiel was dead, and how things stood with Prince Charles. And now, three weeks later he had a lot of news and couldn't wait to tell the others. And to rest his leg, which had taken some punishment in the last weeks and was aching dully but constantly now. But it had healed very well, and no doubt the sporadic aching in the bone would eventually stop too. Hopefully.

Halfway up the mountain was a large saucer-shaped hollow, which could not be seen from the loch side. The cave where the MacGregors should all have been hidden was in the side of the mountain on the opposite side of the hollow, the entrance concealed by carefully draped foliage. Alex expected to see some of his clansfolk out in the hollow, it being such a fine day, or at least to have spied a couple of the sentries, who would surely have been watching out for him. But there was nothing; no sign of any life at all.

Deeply concerned now, he unslung his targe from his back and drew his sword. Before pulling back the foliage he listened, hard. Apart from the sound of a nearby waterfall, which trickled down the side of the mountain and provided a useful source of water for people hiding out here, there were only the bees, and a buzzard circling and calling overhead. Very carefully, standing to the side of the entrance so as not to be an easy target, he pulled the foliage to one side and peeped in. Darkness. He knew that the cave started with about six feet of narrow passage and then turned to the right before opening up into a huge cavern. He listened again. Nothing. He breathed in, and summoned all his courage to face whatever might be waiting for him at the end of the passage. A troop of redcoats? No, soldiers would never be able to stay completely silent. The mangled bodies of his whole clan? Very slowly and silently he edged along the passage, and then peeped round the corner into the cavern.

Virtually the whole of the MacGregor clan were sitting there and started grinning at him as his face appeared. Angus was standing a few feet away, and made an elaborate bow as his brother came into view. Alex closed his eyes momentarily and let out the breath he hadn't realised he'd been holding.

"What the hell kind of welcome is this?" he said, not knowing whether to be angry or impressed by the utter silence greeting him.

"Look behind you," Angus said.

Alex looked behind him. Standing there in the passage he'd entered less than thirty seconds before were Dougal, Alasdair and

Kenneth, who was bent almost double in the low passage.

He jumped with shock and let out a girlish shriek that set the others laughing, thereby breaking the silence.

"I think we can say that all our work has been worthwhile," Angus said. A great cheer rose from the clan. "Welcome home, brother. We've a meal ready for ye and a fine bottle of claret, courtesy of the redcoat captain."

Alex leaned back against the wall of the cavern, his heart banging in his chest. How the hell had they managed to hide on the hill so close to the entrance without him seeing them?

"Where the hell did ye come from?" he asked the three grinning men, who now moved past him into the cavern, Kenneth straightening up with obvious relief.

"Do you want to eat first, or shall I show you?" Angus asked.

"Show me," Alex said, curiosity dispelling all other emotions.

Angus led him back out of the cave into the sunlight.

"Ye see over here," he said, pointing to the waterfall. "By the side of it there's a wee cave, hidden like this, by ivy and such."

"Aye, I ken that," Alex replied. "But it's barely deep enough for a bairn to hide in."

"It *was* barely deep enough for a bairn to hide in. Now it's deep enough for three men, four if one of them's no' Kenneth."

Angus led Alex over and pushed aside the foliage. Behind it was a freshly hollowed-out space, completely invisible once the foliage was back in place.

"In the past we've only ever needed this place for emergencies, for a few days at best. But while we were making the village look as though we'd no' been there for years, I was thinking that, wi' things as they are, we might need to be up here for a long time, and maybe even need tae defend it too. So when we'd moved everything and everyone up here, Dougal and I investigated to see if there were any other caves we could use. There isna, but when we looked closely at this one we realised that the stones and earth could be moved, if ye'd a useful giant to hand. And as we've a useful giant to hand, the stones were moved over to the other side of the mountain. Did ye see Lachlan?" Angus asked suddenly.

"No," Alex said, looking round. "Where is he?"

Angus grinned.

"And Jamie? And wee Simon?"

"No."

"Aye. Well, we kent it'd work for the redcoats, but we figured that if you didna see them, then it'd work for any other clans that come looking for us too, or if they ever find out who Sir Anthony is and come in force. If we're prepared, we could hold out a good while here. I ken your leg's paining ye a wee bit, but this is worth it. Come."

In spite of his best efforts, Alex was now limping a little. But he had walked twenty miles today, and thirty the day before.

Grinning hugely, Angus led his brother over the saucer and down the hill a short way, where he stopped, and bending, lifted a mat of heather up from the ground. Underneath it in a small hollowed-out space was Lachlan, smiling up at his chief.

"Come on out, laddie, ye've done well. He didna see ye."

Lachlan stood up, and Alex looked at him.

"When did ye ken I was coming?" he asked.

"Jamie tellt me," Lachlan said. "He's away down the hill a ways. I stayed here till ye'd passed, and then ran around the side of the mountain so ye wouldna see me, and tellt the others. And then I came back here, because Angus said he wanted to show ye what we've been doing while ye were away."

Alex looked at his brother with awe.

"I can retire as chief now then, and away tae my bed and die," he said. "Ye did a fine job wi' the village too."

"Ah, now, I canna claim the credit for that. That was Iain's idea. He said that when he was playing the deaf laddie, he stared around a lot like an idiot, and he noticed the way the villages looked when they'd been pillaged by the redcoats, and it gave him the idea to make it look like we'd already been burnt out. It was Graeme who said he'd seen abandoned villages in Cumberland and Northumberland, and why did we no' try to do that instead, for then the redcoats might think we'd been gone a while and just move on. And we can only do the hollowed spaces here for the wee ones to watch out because they can be in the same place every day while we're here. We chose places where they can see a good way, but no' be discovered unless they're actually stepped on."

"Ye've done well, better than I could have imagined," Alex said. He pulled his brother into a rough, but affectionate embrace. "Christ, I've missed ye. Ye canna imagine how I felt when I went to the cave and thought ye'd all gone, or been killed."

"Ah, I'm sorry, Alex. I didna think of that. I just kent that if ye didna see or hear anything, then no one would."

"No, ye were right to. It means we've a safe place, and God knows, from what I've heard, we might need it."

"What have ye heard?"

"Let's away back, and I'll tell ye all at the same time," Alex said.

They climbed back up to the cave together, Lachlan springing ahead of them, full of joy at not having been seen by his chief, who had passed only feet away from him.

"Did ye tell Morag about Robert?" Alex asked, as they toiled up the mountain.

"Aye, I did. We have no secrets from each other. I learned that from seeing what happened between you and Beth."

"What did she say?" Alex asked, choosing not to comment on his brother's observation. Angus was right. If he'd been honest with her about his intentions with Henri Monselle, and she'd been honest with him about Richard, they could have avoided the two arguments that had almost destroyed their relationship.

"She was sad, as we all were. But she said that Robert was lucky, too. When I asked her why, she said that he got to live two years longer than he would have done had Beth no' come upon them in the stables, for she thought he'd probably have forced himself on her if they hadna been interrupted."

"Aye, she's right in that, for I couldna have let that pass."

"I think she was meaning that *I'd* have killed him. And she was right. I wanted to anyway, at the time. And I doubt we'd have avoided a blood feud wi' the MacDonalds then. I didna mean tae kill the wee loon when I threw the rock at him, but I've made peace wi' myself about it now."

"Oh, this is good," Alex said blissfully ten minutes later, as he drained his first glass of wine. He stretched his bad leg out then looked round at the others, who were sitting outside now, gathered round him in a semicircle and enjoying the sun. "It does my heart good to see ye all alive and well, and to know that the redcoats rode on through the village without suspecting a thing. It's a fine idea ye had, Iain and Graeme, tae make it look abandoned.

"But now, I've a lot to tell ye."

"Before ye tell us anything," Angus broke in, "there's someone here wanting to ask ye a question." He nodded to the cave mouth behind his brother.

Alex looked round. Standing in the cave entrance was Allan MacDonald, face almost as white as his silver-blond hair, blue eyes wide with anxiety. He visibly gathered his courage together, and drawing his dirk, held it flat across the palms of both hands and came forward.

"I would be honoured," he said, voice trembling, "if ye would accept my allegiance, to yourself and to Clan Gregor, to fight and die for ye against all comers, and…"

Alex held up his hand, and Allan fell silent.

"Wait," he said. "Clan Gregor is proscribed. We *have* no lands, no rights, no name, in law. Ye ken that?"

"Aye," Allan replied. "I do."

"So why do ye want to join a clan that doesna exist in law? Ye can be killed just for being a MacGregor, wi' no comeback except what your sword can gain for ye. Why would you give up your own clan, wi' all the rights and protection that gives ye, to become an outlaw? No man in his right mind would do that."

"I did," Iain said softly.

"That was different, man. Your clan had forsworn ye. Has the MacIain forsworn ye, laddie?"

"No," Allan said. "But –"

Alex shook his head. "I canna accept your oath. I'm sorry."

Allan took in a great breath, and swallowed hard. He knew he should accept the decision without question, but could not.

"I'm here with MacIain's permission. He said that if ye'd take my oath, he'd accept it."

"Why?"

"I dinna ken why MacIain said –"

"No. Why do ye want to join Clan Gregor?"

Allan looked down, and thought for a minute. His flaxen hair blew across his face, and he pushed it impatiently out of the way. Alex closed his eyes for a second, then opened them again to find the young man looking straight at him. His hands, still holding the dirk, were trembling, but his eyes were steady, earnest. Beth's eyes.

"I want to continue the fight," he began, "as I ken you do. The

MacIain does not. The night ye left to prepare for the raid, Aunt Ealasaid spoke of you. She said that she hadna met a better man, nor one more fit to be chief, in a long time, and that any man would be proud to follow ye. She said that Beth had chosen the best man in Scotland to wed, and that she was honoured to call ye her kinsman. And then, when Robbie died…I could have tellt the MacIain of his death. Ye didna need to come too. Angus, maybe, because he'd done the deed. But ye came, because ye didna want your brother or me to deal with it alone. And ye didna hesitate, even though you had other things on your mind, because you're a man of honour. And I thought about what Aunt Ealasaid had said, and about the way ye planned the raid, and I kent that ye were a man I'd be proud to fight with. I've no interest to settle down and farm. I want to fight. So I spoke to MacIain, and he gave me permission to come here, if ye'd have me. Please, accept my oath. I'm a good fighter, and I'll no' disobey ye as Robbie did."

"Aye, I ken that," Alex said. "But ye've nae need to swear lifelong fealty to me just to join in a few raids."

"But ye've a blood oath, I heard, to kill two hundred redcoats. That'll take time. I want to join ye in it, for as long as it takes, for it burns my heart to see what the bastards are doing to the Highlands. And now Aunt Ealasaid is dead…well, we've always been different, ye ken. Some said we were changelings because we look so unlike the others of the clan. There are those will no' be sorry I've gone. Will ye take me?"

"Are ye sure ye ken what ye're doing? It's no' a light thing."

Allan nodded earnestly. "I'm sure."

"Angus, what do you say?"

Angus stood up, surprised to be asked.

"Ye'll be the chief when I'm no' here. Ye've done a good job in the last weeks. Are ye happy to accept this man to the clan?"

Angus nodded. "I am. He's a bonny fighter, and a brave one."

"Does anyone else object? Speak if ye do."

There was silence.

"So be it. I accept your oath, Allan MacDonald." He took the dirk from the young man's outstretched hands, made a small incision in the pad of the thumb of his right hand, and then gave it back. Allan made a similar cut in his hand, and then the two men clasped hands around the hilt of the dirk, mingling blood and iron.

"Welcome to Clan Gregor," Alex said solemnly. "Now, have we more of the wine we stole from the redcoats? It seems a fitting way to welcome our new member."

A great roar arose from the assembled clansfolk, and for the next hour, Alex's good and bad news was forgotten, in the celebration of a new fighter to the MacGregor fold.

"Now," Alex said an hour later, when several bottles of wine had been emptied and the sun was starting to sink in the sky, "as I was saying before I was so pleasantly interrupted, I have news, some good, some no' so good. So I'll start wi' the good. After I left Angus and Allan at Glencoe, I headed toward the Cameron lands hoping to hear something of Lochiel, and there I met some MacPhersons. They surrendered soon after Culloden, so their lands have no' been pillaged, no' overmuch anyway, and they're believed to have submitted completely to the Elector. So, what better place for Cluny MacPherson and Lochiel to hide out than on MacPherson land?"

Everyone started laughing.

"Lochiel is verra much alive, I'm pleased to say, and though lame and no' able to travel far on foot, he's healing well, although he's sore distressed by the price his clan has paid and is still paying, no' just the Cameron regiment, but the women and children too, and also by the fact that his brother, Father Alexander, has been taken prisoner. The MacPhersons are keeping an eye on the troop movements around Fort Augustus. Ye ken that Cumberland is away to London, and Lord Albemarle has taken his place, although word has it that he didna want the job. Anyway, two weeks ago, he left Fort Augustus and went tae Edinburgh, where he can conduct operations from a cosy house instead of a ruined fort.

"Now the good news for us is that most of the horse regiments have been put to grass, a lot of the troops that were at Culloden have gone south, presumably to go back to Flanders now they think we're beaten, and it seems that in future, instead of having hundreds o' redcoats terrorising the villages, there'll only be wee patrols going out. They'll be spending about a week or so living in wee bothies. And ye ken what that means."

"It means that they'll be sitting targets for us to attack

whenever we want to, because they don't know the land and they're not used to living in such conditions, so their morale will be low. And if they haven't got the likes of Hawley to terrorise them or Cumberland to keep discipline, they'll get careless," Graeme said.

Alex grinned.

"They will. But we canna attack close to home, so we'll need to go a wee distance away so they dinna ken who it is who's ambushing them. Which means we'll have to live in wee huts and bothies too, which will be awfu' inconvenient for us, as used tae feather beds and fine wines as we are." He raised his glass, and they all laughed and cheered him.

"So, tonight I'll tell ye the rest o' my news, then we can celebrate our new clan member some more, and then tomorrow we can start tae plan. Angus, Iain and I have a blood oath to fulfil. The rest of ye havena, and ye ken well that I've never been one to force people to fight. And dinna forget, we'll need some men to stay behind and defend the village if needed. Now as I've said before, it's my wish that all those men wi' wives and bairns should stay here. Of the rest, it's up to you as individuals. Just because ye came out for Charlie doesna mean ye should follow me in my oath of vengeance. There's no glory in this, and no crown at the end of it, and no knowing when it'll end. And those of you who do follow me will have to obey my orders without question. Ye can argue the rights and wrongs as we're planning and I'll listen to ye. But in the fighting ye obey me, instantly."

Several men started to get to their feet, but Alex held up his hand.

"I dinna want anyone to decide tonight. Tonight's for news and celebration. Tomorrow I'm going tae sleep late, for I'm weary and later I intend to be drunk too, and woe betide the man who wakes me at dawn tae tell me he wants to fight, for if he does, I'll give him a fight immediately."

The men laughed and sat down again, and everyone cheered their approval of the plan for the evening, and then they settled down to hear the rest of Alex's news.

"Now," he said, "Lochiel and Cluny are in a fine cave, wi' plenty of Cluny's clan to shelter them, and good hunting for food. I doubt the redcoats'll ever find them, and they've good intelligence about the army movements, but they didna ken what was going on wi' the prince, other than that he moved from Uist to Skye and then to somewhere on the mainland, and that was grieving Lochiel sorely, for he spent weeks sore wounded, in constant danger of being discovered, trying to arrange a rendezvous wi' Charles, to no avail. So, as I'm now healed, and no one's looking for me as they are for Lochiel and Cluny, I agreed to try to find out where he was and bring him to join them."

"Did ye find him?" Peigi asked.

"Aye, I did."

After he'd left Lochiel and Cluny in the cave on Ben Alder, Alex had headed over to Achnacarry, hoping to pick up some news of the whereabouts of the prince from the Camerons. There he was told that the prince was staying in a hut at Achnasaul, by Loch Arkaig, awaiting the return of some messengers he'd sent out.

The hut was completely derelict and empty, but it was clear that someone had been there recently. Alex had looked around for signs of which way they might have gone, but seeing nothing had decided to eat his meagre lunch at the hut and then retrace his steps through the wood, reasonably certain that the prince would remain on Cameron land hoping to make contact with Lochiel.

It was whilst he was eating the now somewhat stale bread and cheese provided by the MacPhersons two days before, that he saw someone coming down the hill towards him. He put his bread down on the grass, checked his pistol was primed and cocked, then laid it in his lap and continued eating, as though unaware of the presence of the man.

As he came closer, Alex could see that he was a Highlander; barefoot, he wore the kilt, a grubby shirt and a black coat. His reddish-coloured hair was loose and tangled on his shoulders and he sported a long red beard. Under his arm he carried a musket, but showed no signs of using it. Nevertheless, Alex gripped the pistol and stood, as the man was now too close for him to pretend he hadn't seen him.

The stranger stopped about ten paces away from Alex, the musket still carried loosely under his arm. A pistol and a dirk were thrust through his belt.

"Good day to ye, sir," Alex began politely.

The stranger smiled.

"Ah, Alexander MacGregor. You don't recognise me at all, and I think that's a good thing, in view of the circumstances I find myself in. No!" he finished urgently as Alex, now realising the identity of the stranger, had made to kneel. "We don't know who may be watching, and I think it better, as even you didn't recognise me, that we don't advertise my identity."

Alex deftly turned the obeisance to his prince into an apparent gesture to share his lunch, by bending to the ground and picking up his leather flask of water, then offering it to the other man, who politely declined.

"Ye're looking well, Your Highness," Alex said. "The country life suits you, I'm thinking." It was true. Although dirty and unshaven and completely unrecognisable as the man who had ridden proudly into Edinburgh at the head of his army the previous September, the prince looked in the peak of physical health, and his brown eyes were bright and sparkling with humour.

Prince Charles laughed.

"It does, although I would prefer to have more settled accommodation. I was told that you were looking for me and was so eager to see you I decided to come myself. Let us return to my lodgings. We shot a stag yesterday and can offer you a better meal than that." He gestured to the remains of the bread.

They walked together back through the wood, chatting, looking for all the world like two rural Highlanders who had met by chance, rather than two of the most wanted men in Britain. As they walked the prince told Alex a little about his exploits so far.

"There have been all manner of wild rumours going around," Alex said as they strolled along. "I even heard tell that ye'd dressed as a woman. Soon ye'll have been carried off by a selkie, I've nae doubt."

Charles grinned.

"Ah well, that particular rumour is not so wild. Let me introduce myself, sir," he said, performing a somewhat clumsy curtsey. "Miss Betty Burke, Irish serving woman to the delightful and courageous Miss Flora MacDonald."

Alex stopped and stared at the prince.

"Ye mean that was true? I ken ye're a master of disguise, Your Highness, but I canna imagine what manner of woman you'd make."

"Not a very good one by all accounts, but it served its purpose at the time, and got me to Skye. I would certainly have been captured else. Kingsburgh's wife apparently called me an 'odd muckle trollop'." He laughed. "In truth, I don't know how women walk about with all those skirts and petticoats weighing them down. I expected at every moment to trip over them and topple down the stairs or into the sea and drown. Miss MacDonald was taken prisoner a few days after I left her. I hope she is being treated well, although I know that many of my subjects are paying a heavy price for their support of me." The brown eyes lost their sparkle for a moment. "It grieves me," he said sadly.

"Aye, well, we were all aware of the possible consequences," Alex commented. That was not completely true. They had not been aware that the British Army would be allowed, encouraged even, to commit such atrocities against innocent people.

"I heard about your wife, Alex, and I'm very sorry for it. She was a remarkable woman."

"She was indeed, thank you," Alex replied, hoping that having uttered the conventional platitude, Charles would now change the subject.

"You know Lord Lovat is taken?" Charles asked.

"I do, Your Highness. I believe he was hiding in a tree at the time."

"You don't appear overly distressed by that news," the prince remarked.

"He was no' a man I could take to," Alex said tactfully. He wouldn't have trusted him as far as he could throw him, but there was no benefit to revealing that now.

"John shared your antipathy. You know he is taken too?"

"John…?" There were so many Johns, this could have been any one of a hundred.

"Murray."

"Broughton?" The prince carried on for a couple of steps before realising his friend had stopped. He turned back to find Alex's eyes wide with shock.

"I see you did not. Yes, Broughton is taken, some few weeks

ago, at his brother-in-law's house. I'm sorry. Had I realised you were close I would have told you more gently."

"No, it's no' that. But Broughton kens who I am, and that I was Sir Anthony," Alex said.

"You cannot believe he will talk, surely?" Charles said. "We had our differences, but he was always loyal to me. He has never wavered, not for an instant. I do not think you need to worry that he will betray you."

"I hope you're right, Your Highness," Alex said.

"I am sure of it."

Alex was not so sure, because he knew that torture could be a powerful incentive to betrayal, but there was nothing he could do right now. Once he had taken the prince to Lochiel though, he would head straight home.

"I find it hard to believe that any monarch, rightful or not, could treat his subjects as George and his son are now treating the poor Highlanders, many of whom did not even come out for me," Charles continued.

"They are trying to prevent us from ever rising again, by starving us out when they canna kill us," Alex said.

"Will they succeed, do you think?" the prince asked.

"I canna speak for all Scots, Your Highness. But for myself, no, they will not succeed. They have taken almost everything worth living for. My wife, my brother – they've already taken my name and my lands. All I have left now is to fight. And I will do that until I'm killed."

"You believe you will be killed?" Charles asked.

"Aye, before too long. For I'll no' be taken prisoner, and I've no reason to wish for a long life and to die in my bed at the end of it."

Charles was silent for a while, but whether it was because he was trying to assess his future chances of raising another Highland army, or whether because he was feeling guilty for having been instrumental in taking all meaning from the life of this loyal subject, he did not say.

"Well," he said finally, "I think you may be interested in meeting my current companions, when we reach my lodgings."

Alex was indeed interested when he met them. They were known as the seven men of Glenmoriston, although in fact there were eight of them, and they had all vowed to continue the fight against Cumberland and his army, in whatever way they could. For the past three weeks they had been doing that by sheltering the prince, disregarding the huge reward out for his capture as no fit price to pay for a man's honour.

They were currently sheltering in a cave at the foot of Loch Arkaig and waiting for word from Lochiel of his whereabouts so they could take the prince to him.

"I ken where he is," Alex said. "I'll gladly show ye the way. Lochiel would have come himself, but although he's healing, he's no' fit to make the journey yet."

They had discussed the importance of a good hiding place and the need to keep it secret and as well provisioned as possible, and the various tactics that could be employed to harass soldiers already depressed at being in this gloomy dark hell of a country.

And then, having nothing else to do for the evening, they had eaten a large meal, mainly consisting of venison, and had drunk an even larger amount of whisky, had sung Highland songs, of which the prince now knew a good number, and overall, in view of the circumstances, had been very merry indeed.

Alex smiled at the sea of faces around him, all raptly listening to his tale of meeting with the prince. It was growing dusk now and several people were waving their hands around their heads or slapping at their faces.

"It seems that Prince Charlie is one of us, now," Dougal said.

"Aye, he's happy here, in spite of the constant risk of discovery. Maybe because of it, for he's a man who seeks adventure and relishes danger."

"He must have MacGregor blood in him then," Janet said, and everyone laughed.

"Well, Clan Gregor's motto is 'Royal is my Race', is it no'?" Allan commented.

"Aye, that's true," agreed Alex. "We're said to be descended from the son of King Kenneth MacAlpin, as is he. And another way he's like us is that he's sore plagued by the midgies."

En masse they repaired to the midge-free safety of the cave, where they lit candles, having found a supply of them in the redcoats' baggage.

"Charles tellt me that one of the most miserable days he had was no' when it was raining, but when it was overcast and he had to spend the whole day and night in the heather, being feasted on by the wee bastards. He said he looked as though he had the measles by the end of the day, he was bitten so bad."

"What happened after your party, then?" Morag asked. She was snuggled next to Angus, who had his arm wrapped round her shoulder. Alex felt both happy to see the two of them clearly so much in love, and sad at the memories it roused. He would never hold a woman like that again.

He shook his head to clear it.

"The next day, while we were still all suffering, Dr Archie arrived and said Lochgarry was on the way too, to meet wi' the prince and guide him to Lochiel."

"Is that why ye didna take Charlie back yourself, then?" Kenneth asked.

"No, it isna. I was thinking to go wi' them, to make sure Charles arrived safe wi' Cluny and Lochiel. But then Dr Archie tellt me his news, and I left for home within the hour."

Everyone looked suddenly alarmed.

"What news?" Angus asked.

"He tellt me that Broughton has turned king's evidence."

The silence that followed this statement was almost as profound as that which had greeted him earlier in the day when he'd entered the cave, sword drawn. And then the questions came, all at once, so Alex could only make out the sense of a few. He raised his hand, and the noise died instantly.

"I dinna ken if the intelligence is good, because Sir Anthony is no' running the spy network frae London, being otherwise occupied, as ye ken well," he said, causing several people to laugh, and the tension to dissipate slightly. "I find it hard myself to believe Broughton would do such a thing, but on the other hand he was a secretary, no' a fighting man, and he's been ill for some time. I dinna ken what he'd do if threatened, or if his wife was threatened. In any case I canna take the chance that he willna betray me. Dr Archie has promised to send me news if he hears any more."

"Why did ye no' tell us this as soon as ye got back?" Kenneth asked.

"Because when I got back, I was thinking to do all the things that ye've already done here. Make the cave safe, try to find a way to defend it. Once I saw your fine work, I decided to enjoy my homecoming first, and tell ye the story in the proper order. And it's no' every day, in fact it's no' every year that a brave young warrior chooses to join the MacGregors. I didna wish to spoil that. And nor do I now. We have more celebrating to do. And then tomorrow we need to make this place more fitting for a longer stay, for we canna go back to the village yet awhile. If Broughton betrays me the redcoats will be up here within a week, because I'm damn sure that after the prince and Lochiel, yon wee German lairdie would rather see my head on a spike at the Tower than anyone's. And before I end up there, I've a good many more redcoats to send to hell before me.

"So, let's drink to that, to Allan, and to the children o' the mist. For we may have no name, and no lands, and no rights in law, but by God we've still got our swords, and our pride. *'S rioghal mo dhream*, and we'll be here when usurper Geordie's bones are dust, and his sons after him!"

The resultant cheer would probably have been heard across the loch, if anyone had been there to listen.

\* \* \*

## London, August 1746

It took Beth less than a week to adapt to her new surroundings. After she had beaten the bullying woman she had expected to be victimised by her protector, who the other women had identified as Meadows, a brute of a man who had a particular hatred of Scots. Well, Beth wasn't a Scot by birth, but she was by marriage and in her heart, although of course she couldn't reveal that. So she waited, determined that whatever Meadows did she would not break. While she waited for him to act, she spent her time getting to know the other women she shared the unspeakably filthy cell with, whilst giving away as little about herself as she could.

They were all rebel women. Some of them had been married to Jacobite soldiers and had been taken at some point after Culloden. Some of them had been caught sheltering men after the battle. Two of them had been prostitutes and had been reported by loyal citizens of Edinburgh and Inverness for giving their favours to rebels for free. And one had actually had nothing whatsoever to do with the Jacobites, but had picked up a white cockade in an Inverness street, thinking to unpick the ribbon to tie her hair back, and had been seen by a redcoat captain whilst holding it. Incensed by the treatment she'd been subjected to for that innocent, if foolhardy act, she now declared herself wholly for Prince Charlie, and to hell with Hanover and all its spawn of hell.

Some of them wore irons, not because they were more dangerous than the others, but because they could not afford the half-crown fee to have them removed. All of them, being on a diet of bread and water, and not enough of that, were malnourished. Nor could any of them afford 3s 6d a week for a bed, so they slept on the mildewed boards of the floor.

In the morning they emptied their chamber pots and then had breakfast, which consisted of a thin gruel and water, after which they were returned to their cells and left until mid afternoon, when the main meal of the day was served. To Beth's surprise, whilst the others who could not pay for good food had bread and water for six days a week and a cheap cut of meat on the seventh, she was served with a meal of meat and vegetables and a cup of beer, although she had not paid either.

When she got the same treatment on the second day, and then the third, she realised that the Duke of Cumberland had not given up on her as she had hoped, but was in fact just letting her have a taste of the difference between luxurious and common imprisonment. That was why she had not been fettered, but was in a common cell. And why she was receiving good food instead of starvation rations. And it was, presumably, also why Meadows, whoever he was, had not made an appearance after his whore had been removed for medical treatment.

She was still under the protection of the duke. Which meant she was probably being closely observed for signs that she was cracking under the strain of having to live without carpets and featherbeds, for signs that she was ready to betray Sir Anthony rather than live in a filthy stone room designed to accommodate five prisoners, with ten other women who were her social inferiors.

Thinking about this she smiled to herself, and raised an imaginary glass of champagne in a toast to the Elector's fat son. She was used to living in straitened circumstances. Unknowingly he had given her the one thing that she had been struggling to live without; sympathetic human company. The quiet courage of these women as they chewed their stale bread and settled down to shiver themselves to sleep reminded her of the MacGregors. And that gave her the will and determination to fight back.

On the third day Fiona, the woman who had had the misfortune to pick up a white cockade in front of a zealous soldier, complained of a headache. No one thought anything of it even when she refused to eat her meagre breakfast, saying that the sunlight coming through the small windows in the dining room was making her head hurt so badly she felt sick. It was no doubt a megrim; she would go and lie down in the cell and would feel better after a few hours.

The other women tried to be as quiet as possible to let her rest. But in the afternoon she started moaning and calling for Hamish, who presumably was her lover, and when Catriona shook Fiona to wake her, thinking she was having a nightmare, her skin was burning hot to the touch.

Word spread round the prison like wildfire: gaol fever. Feared even more than execution, an epidemic of gaol fever could decimate a prison's population, and was the major cause of death in jails. It was caused by putrid air, the surgeons said. And the air in this cell, in all the cells, was certainly putrid.

That evening Beth asked to see Mr Jones. He came to her a couple of hours later, but did not open the door as he normally would have done. Instead he addressed her through the grille. In the corner Fiona was alternately crying out with the pain in her head and her joints, and rambling about people she had known in happier times.

"How much would you give for my gown?" Beth asked without preamble the minute the grille was drawn back and the keeper's face appeared.

He looked at it.

"Fifteen shillings," he said.

Beth laughed.

"I'm sorry. I thought you were a businessman and knew the

value of things, but clearly I overestimated you. Good night to you, Mr Jones."

She turned her back on him and made to join the others, who had received sixpence from a well-wisher, and had spent it on a quart of brandy. They had given some to the sick woman in the hopes that it would ease her distress, and were now passing the rest around between them.

"Wait!" he said, once it became clear that this was not just a delaying tactic and that she really had dismissed him from her mind. Beth kept him waiting while she took a drink from the bottle, then turned back. "How much do you want for it?" he asked.

"Well, let me see. Brocaded satin of this quality costs eighteen shillings a yard," she said, thanking God that Sir Anthony Peters had been a man of fashion and had imparted this information to her, "and it takes around fifteen yards to make a gown like this. So the material alone would be over twelve guineas. Add to that the cost of making it up, the Brussels lace and silver embroidery on the bodice, *and* the fact that it had never been worn before the day I made your acquaintance, and you are looking at seventeen guineas of anybody's money."

The other women in the cell gasped. Seventeen guineas was a fortune! Who was this woman who could afford such costly gowns, who said she had no friends but was served meat every day, who spoke with a refined English accent, but had the Gaelic and drank from a shared bottle without hesitation?

"However," Beth continued, unaware that she was an enigma to everyone in the room, "I'm aware that you must have your profit, and after three days in here the dress will need cleaning. So you may have it for ten guineas."

Now it was Mr Jones's turn to laugh.

"Ten guineas? You do value yourself highly, don't you?" he said.

"You mistake me, sir. I am offering you my dress for ten guineas, not myself. I am not for sale, at any price."

"Everyone has a price," he said, nettled.

"Perhaps in your world they do," she replied. "But in my world, that is not the case. Ten guineas for the dress."

"Three," Mr Jones replied.

"Ten."

"Four."

"Ten."

"This is not how it works, madam," the keeper said, exasperated. "You must lower your price to meet me. Four and a half."

"Ten."

"Five."

"I see you do not want the dress. Very well. If you change your mind, come back to me with ten guineas."

She turned her back again and went to sit with the other women, and this time when he called her back, she ignored him.

Beth sat on a feather mattress in her petticoats and stays, warming her hands in front of the fire. Two candles cast a cosy glow around the room, which currently smelt strongly of the vinegar with which the whole room had been scrubbed, reducing the lice infestation in the cell considerably. At present the smell of the vinegar warred with the scent of lavender oil, which she had sprinkled on all the mattresses. It had worked in France for her and Alex; she hoped it would have some effect here. She had paid for four mattresses and blankets for a month, reasoning that the women could sleep in shifts. The rest of the money would pay for decent food for all the occupants of the cell, for a few weeks at least.

The room was no longer putrid-smelling, but it was too late to save Fiona. Beth had intended to spend part of her ten guineas on a doctor, but Mr Jones had told her in no uncertain terms that no doctor would visit Newgate Prison if there was gaol fever there, not for a hundred guineas. So the women took it in turns to bathe Fiona's forehead with rosewater, and to try to get her to eat a little soup and drink some wine, all bought at inflated prices by Beth.

She kept them all awake for three nights with her fevered ramblings, during which they learned that she had seven younger siblings and a grandmother who seemed to visit her in her delirium and with whom she would have long conversations. And then she developed a rash, which rapidly spread all over her body. And then she died.

The body was taken away, and her cellmates grieved for her.

But none of them contracted the fever, which was almost unheard of in such cramped quarters. As far as they were concerned this was all due to Beth, who had saved them by purifying the air and getting them good food which was building up their strength.

As a result of this Beth now had nine intensely loyal friends, none of them wearing irons any more, who respected her wish to keep her past private, and the atmosphere in the room, once they had said prayers for Fiona, was one of conviviality. It made Beth smile to know she had raised the morale of these women who had done nothing wrong except be loyal to their menfolk, have been caught helping strangers, or be in the wrong place at the wrong time. It had also raised her own spirits enormously. She had a clan of sorts again, temporarily at least, and was making the most of it to distract her from thoughts of the future.

This comfort they were all enjoying now and the high spirits that went with it, would not last. When the money ran out she had no means of getting any more, and then the warmth, the beds, the nourishment would all disappear. And the lice and vermin would return, and the smell. And with it the likelihood of disease.

On a personal level she could deal with malnourishment, with discomfort, even with death. Without Alex, and with no hope of release unless she betrayed him, life meant little to her. Defiance was all that she had now, and she was drawing her strength from that and from the camaraderie of the other prisoners. Dying of malnutrition or disease would be preferable to hanging or burning in front of a jeering mob, although if that was how she was to end, she would meet her death with as much courage as she could summon up.

What worried her, and what she now realised was very likely, was that if she remained here, in time she too would succumb to gaol fever. If the other women had been concerned or irritated by Fiona's ramblings, Beth was horrified; it was entirely possible that after withstanding every attempt by the authorities to get her to divulge the identity of her husband, she could nevertheless unknowingly betray Alex and God knew who else, simply by falling ill.

Every night Beth prayed for Alex, for the other MacGregors, and for Graeme and John, that they were safe and well. Nearly every night she dreamt of them; sometimes dark dreams that she woke from in the early hours, heart thumping and her cheeks wet with tears, and sometimes warm, loving dreams from which she would wake smiling and happy, only to be suffused by black despair as she took in her surroundings and realised that in all likelihood she would never hold Alex in reality again. She had lost count of the days again, but knew it was somewhere in the middle of August. She had said she would wait until October before she gave up hope of him contacting her, but every day that passed without any word killed a little bit of that hope in her, and she grew more and more certain that he must be dead, or a prisoner.

She thought about him constantly, and dreaded becoming ill and condemning him; but saw no way to be sure of preventing it once the money failed.

These were the thoughts of her dark hours, when she listened to the snores and moans of the other women and sleep would not come. In the daytime when she knew she might be observed by those who would report back, she was always in good spirits, laughing, telling stories, teaching the others card games she had learned as a child, and joining in with the singing that they all loved so much and that was part of their Highland culture.

It could be worse, and no doubt would be, in time. But for now life was good, given the circumstances, and she threw herself into that wholeheartedly, banishing the pessimistic thoughts to the back of her mind and the darkness of sleepless nights.

* * *

Beth had just started telling her version of Jack and the Beanstalk for Highlanders, when the door opened and Mr Jones came in.

"Miss Cunningham, there are two soldiers here for you," he said.

Beth closed her eyes, pulled all her resources together, then opened them again.

"Am I to be taken to trial?" she asked calmly.

"No, my lady. You are to be taken to Whitehall."

Cumberland then. Or Newcastle perhaps. If Jones was calling her 'my lady' then she was certainly not about to be tried for her life.

She stood and brushed down her petticoat. She had worn the same clothes for three weeks, with very primitive washing facilities.

Maybe the stench of her would make him feel sick. She smiled to herself.

"Very well," she said. "I am ready."

*But…on the other hand…*

"I trust," she added, scratching her head vigorously, "that suitable clothing has been brought from the Tower for me, and that you have provided the facilities for me to wash myself thoroughly."

Mr Jones looked at her as if she had just requested to bathe in the blood of a hundred virgins.

"I see by your expression that you have not. Very well. I am sure the duke will forgive me if I infest his office with lice and God knows what else. Of course he may wonder why I am being taken across London in a state of undress, but I am sure when I tell him of the prices you charge for commodities he will appreciate my situation. Take me to the soldiers, Mr Jones."

"No," Beth said, "I think that one will be more fitting for me to meet the prince." She pointed to a lemon-coloured brocaded satin gown. The colour would do nothing for her complexion, but the skirt and bodice were lavishly embroidered with gold thread. Maybe the dress would help to keep her in good health until she was executed. Kate smiled and carefully unfolded the dress, whilst Beth combed the tangles out of her freshly washed hair. On the table was a pot of tea especially for Kate, although Beth had not said that when ordering it.

Her apartments at the Tower had been kept ready for her return, she realised on entering them, after having been rushed there by the soldiers and told she had one hour to dress, as the prince expected her by ten. She would not prevaricate this time. This was not the time for small victories.

Kate sipped at the tea, but it was clear from the expression on her face that the chocolate had made a better impression.

"Next time, if there is a next time, I shall order chocolate for you again," Beth commented.

The maid was instantly flustered.

"Oh, no, my lady, I do not wish to seem ungrateful!" she exclaimed. She really did wear all her emotions on her face. She never would have been a good ally in deceit. Beth hoped Kate would never have to lie to save her life. Or tell a partial truth to end it.

"You are not ungrateful. I'm very grateful to have you to help me dress on such an important occasion. It's not every day that I get to meet the man who will, I am sure, change my whole life once he hears what I have to say."

"Of course. I hope all goes well for you, my lady," Kate said, blushing, which told Beth volumes. She put down her cup and moved behind Beth to help braid her hair.

"So," Beth said. "They are speculating in the servants' quarters as to whether I will become Prince William's mistress, are they?"

In the mirror, now restored to its place on the dressing table, Beth saw Kate flush scarlet.

"I'm sorry," Beth said. "I am not offended. Very little offends me. But let me give you some advice, in confidence. If anyone is running a bet, you might wish to put a little money down."

"Some of them are saying he will marry you, my lady," the maid stammered.

"But most of them are not. I do not think we will meet again, Kate, so here is my advice. Put your money on the option that I will become neither his wife nor his mistress. And when you win, will you promise me something?"

"Of course, my lady."

"Buy yourself some chocolate, and drink a toast to me."

Beth arrived at the Duke of Newcastle's office at ten on the dot. Her punctuality was noted by Prince William Augustus, who stood and came around the table to escort her politely to her seat. This time he did not kiss her hand, and he was wearing his military uniform which she had to admit suited him well, although the buttons of his waistcoat strained across his stomach.

*He is gaining more weight,* she thought. *It must be all those celebratory dinners.*

He was clearly not going to wear his heart on his sleeve for her to stab, as he had at their last meeting. She prepared herself for war. She had to achieve the outcome she desired, and this might be her only chance to do it.

"Good morning, Miss Cunningham," the prince said, once they were both seated.

"Good morning," she replied calmly.

"I have called for tea and cakes," he said. "I thought you might appreciate them, in view of your recent change of accommodation. Have you had time to think about your situation in the last weeks?"

This was it.

"I have indeed, had plenty of time to think," she said.

He nodded.

"I hope you have come to the right decision."

"I believe I have. I –"

She was interrupted by a knock on the door and turned her head to look, expecting a servant with a tray.

The door opened and John Murray of Broughton walked in. He was thinner than the last time she had seen him and had the pallor and shadowed eyes of someone who has suffered from a long illness, but nevertheless she recognised him instantly.

For a split second Beth knew that the horror of seeing him must have registered on her face, and she thanked God that she had turned away from Cumberland. Broughton's eyes passed over her with appreciation but no recognition, and then focussed on the duke.

Beth marshalled all the acting skills she had learned from her husband, and when she turned back to Cumberland she was once again calm.

"You called for me, Your Highness?" Murray asked.

"I did. I thought you might like to become reacquainted with the lovely Miss Cunningham."

Murray turned his attention back to Beth, and bowed.

"Your servant, madam," he said politely.

Beth nodded her head in acknowledgement of the courtesy.

"I regret to say that I am no' acquainted with this lady," Murray said coolly, "although if I were no' already happily married, I wouldna be averse to becoming so."

The duke scrutinised the two of them for a moment.

"Are you certain, sir? She would not have been dressed so grandly and would perhaps have been accompanied by a tall, well-built man, who would have been posing as her husband."

"I am sure that however she was dressed I would have recognised such a beautiful woman, had we met before,"

Broughton replied. For a moment he turned his back on the duke, and his expression changed. "Your hair is most remarkable, my lady," he said to her.

"Thank you, sir," she replied, to his facial expression rather than his compliment.

"This man who would have been with her," the duke persisted, "is the traitor known as Sir Anthony Peters. I would be most grateful to the person who could shed some light on his true appearance or his whereabouts. And there is a substantial reward on offer for his capture."

Murray nodded.

"As there is for the Pretender's son," he said. "But just as I have no notion of his whereabouts, I have no knowledge of this lady, nor of this Sir Anthony you speak of. I am sorry to disappoint you, Your Highness."

The duke *was* disappointed. It was evident in every line of his face as he dismissed the Scotsman and turned back to Beth. The tea arrived and they both waited until it was poured, after which the servant retired on the duke's nod.

"Mr Murray was secretary to the Pretender's son during the rebellion, but has now realised the error of his ways and has agreed to cooperate with us in all things. His information will most certainly assist us greatly in prosecuting the Fraser chief Lord Lovat, who is in custody at the moment, and he has also given us valuable information regarding the English Jacobites. You would do well to learn from his example. He will be treated most leniently by the authorities, in spite of his central role in the rebellion."

"For what is a man advantaged, if he gain the whole world, but lose himself or be cast away?" Beth said.

"I beg your pardon?"

"Luke, chapter nine, verse twenty-five," she explained.

"I know my bible, madam!" the duke said hotly. "What do you mean by it?"

"I would think that to be clear. I would rather die in prison than turn traitor, for no amount of money or leniency would ever salve my conscience. You are wasting your time. All I feel for this man is pity, for I believe, if he played such a central role as you suggest, he will regret this moment of weakness for the rest of his life."

She picked up her cup and coolly took a sip of her tea. It was strange, but now the moment was here she was calm and had no fear that the cup would rustle in the saucer. Alex had told her that sometimes, when both sides were lined up facing each other, ready for battle, there would come over everyone an eerie stillness, when all fear of death and injury fell away and in the silence you could hear the smallest sound, colours were brighter, and the world seemed exquisitely beautiful, life an intensely precious thing. And then the moment passed, the cannons roared, and the fight began.

So it was now, as she sipped the tea and tasted the bitterness of the leaves, the liquid warm on her tongue. She could hear her own heart beating strongly and slowly, and felt the blood pumping through her veins. Life was indeed intensely precious, and she knew without doubt that it was worth throwing hers away to protect so many others. And then the duke spoke, and the fight began.

"Elizabeth," he said, his voice kind and caring again. "Although many would not commend your stubbornness and loyalty to your mistaken cause, I do. There is something admirable in it. But you must now put these notions aside and be guided by those who wish to help you. There is no shame in recognising that you were misguided by rogues and traitors who care nothing for you. Women are by their very nature frail and easily led. No one will blame you for telling me what you know. They will understand that you had no choice but to bend to the will of your superiors. Please, Elizabeth, I beg you to reconsider. I cannot tell you what it cost me to commit you to the filth and degradation of Newgate, but I only did it to help you see the error of your ways." His expression was earnest, pleading even. He genuinely loved her, and genuinely wanted to help her.

Alex had told her, if this day ever came, that she should give him up. And she had given him her answer.

"Your Highness," she said, giving him the benefit of his title for the first, and last time, "my disgust at the filth and degradation of Newgate are nothing compared to the disgust I felt when I had to endure your tedious conversation and your clumsy attempts to seduce me, at the palace and the theatre. It was all I could do not to be sick when you laid your hand on my knee. You and your dullard of a father disgust me to my stomach, and the only reason I could tolerate the endless tedium of my time with your ridiculous family was because I knew that Sir Anthony and I were making fools of you all, and that one day you would come to know that. But it seems you still persist in your childish and repellent infatuation with me, so I will make myself very clear. I would rather lie with Satan himself than with you. The thought of spending more than a minute with you fills me with the utmost revulsion and always has. I will never, under any circumstances whatsoever, betray Sir Anthony or anyone else to you. Do you understand me now, or must I elaborate further on the emotions you aroused in me when you begged me to become your whore?"

At the start of her speech the duke had reddened, but by the end of it the colour had drained from his face, and Beth knew she had, irrevocably, burned her bridges.

What she wanted was death, and soon. She hoped she had done enough to get that. By the look on his face, she had. Wordlessly he rang the bell, and when the soldiers came, he told them to take her directly back to Newgate.

As she travelled back, firstly along the river then up St Andrew's street, she tried to absorb as much detail as she could; the warmth of the sun on her upturned face, the lapping of the water against the side of the boat, the bustle of the people thronging the streets, the soaring dome of St Paul's Cathedral.

And all the way she uttered one prayer, over and over.

*Let it have been enough to condemn me. And let me die soon, and well.*

When she arrived back at the prison she was returned to her cell, the duke having given no further instructions to her guards than to return her to jail. Her cellmates looked up as she entered, most of them wearing identical expressions of surprise. *So,* she thought, *it was not only the Tower servants who thought I would succumb to the charms of William Augustus.*

She looked around at them and smiled. Then she lifted her dress up at both sides as though preparing to curtsey, displaying the weight and beauty of the silk, the embroidery on it gleaming in the candlelight.

"Now," she said, "let us see how many comforts this will buy us. We must make the most of it, because I do not think the duke will be requesting the pleasure of my company again." She asked the turnkey, who was about to lock the door, to request the presence of Mr Jones at his earliest convenience, then sat down on one of the mattresses. The surprised expressions were now giving way to intense curiosity, and to forestall a barrage of questions she had no intention of answering, she spoke immediately.

"Now, where was I up to in my story before we were so rudely interrupted?"

"Wee Jack's mother had just found out the cow was diseased, and told him tae sell it to the redcoat captain," Annie, one of those who had sheltered wounded rebels, recalled.

"Ah, yes. So, on the way to the market, who should Jack come across but a crooked old man, who offered him five magic beans for the cow…"

The women took the hint, and settled down to hear the rest of the story.

# CHAPTER TEN

**Fort William, late August 1746**

Captain Richard Cunningham was ecstatic. When he had entered Colonel Hutchinson's office he had been somewhat apprehensive, especially when he saw the stern countenance of his superior officer. Richard suspected the colonel didn't like him, although he had never done anything to offend the man, as far as he knew. Following their previous interview, Richard had done his utmost to prove his loyalty to the crown and to distance himself from any taint of treason. His ferocity at Culloden and his ruthlessness in dealing with the Highland rabble since then had been legendary.

And finally, it seemed to have paid off. Far from taking him to task over the unfortunate deaths of three women last week who had later been found to be members of a loyal clan, Colonel Hutchinson had told Richard that he was to depart for London at the express command of the Duke of Cumberland, who had a particular task for him to perform.

When a stunned Richard had asked what the task was, the colonel had replied that that was for the Duke of Cumberland to inform him of. Which as far as Richard was concerned, was another way of saying 'I don't know'.

So, a particular task, and one that could not be entrusted to the colonel. Richard had no idea what it could be, but whatever it was, he would perform it to the utmost of his ability. This was a chance for him to shine, to prove his worth to those who could promote him to the stars if they chose!

He would not be sorry to see the back of Scotland, that was

certain. A darker, more barren shithole he had never encountered, although it did have its advantages, in that you could do whatever you wanted to any rebel men or women you came across, with no consequences whatsoever. He had done things with rebel women that no prostitute would let him do, not even the penny whores of St Giles, which was saying a lot. And if the woman died while he was taking his pleasure, no one gave a damn. Except perhaps their husbands, of course. But they were dead, or rotting in jail, or skulking in the hills starving, so they counted for nothing.

Yes, he would miss that aspect of Scotland. He had developed a fine taste for torture now, but he would have to rein that in once he was back in England, where even whores had *some* rights in law.

To celebrate his good fortune, on his last night in Fort William he picked up one of the beggars who were always loitering around the place, bought her a meal, made her wash herself thoroughly, and then had a pleasant few hours with her down by the side of the loch before rolling her body into the water. Usually he burnt the bodies of his victims in their ramshackle huts, but that was not an option here. She would no doubt be found and her injuries commented on, but she could not be linked to him, and no one would waste any time investigating the death of a beggar anyway.

His appointment with the duke was in ten days. For safety he rode to Carlisle with a group of other soldiers, all in very high spirits, heading home on leave. But once in England he travelled on alone, to the great relief of the others, whose spirits had been much dampened by the forbidding, taciturn captain.

Having sufficient time, he decided to travel via Manchester and spend a night in his house in Didsbury, which he hadn't visited for months but had left in the care of an elderly couple who had been instructed to keep it habitable at all times. That was one of the advantages of having married that dried-up frigid mouse Anne; he could now afford to pay to have fires burning in empty rooms. He only paid the couple a pittance, but they had free board and little to do when he was away. He would spend the night there, have a bath and a good meal, then get a decent rest so he would be at his best tomorrow. He had an important errand to perform in the town.

It was something of a shock therefore, when he rode up the drive to find that not only was there no one in residence, but the house was certainly not being looked after. Grass and weeds were growing up through the cobbles of the drive and the green paint on the door was flaking. For a moment he was transported back to that day four years ago when he had ridden up the drive to find the house in a similar condition. He looked around, half expecting to see his hoyden of a sister come racing across the grass astride a black mare, skirts round her knees and hair hanging in untidy straggles round her face.

He chided himself for his stupidity, and looked back at the house. His sister was gone, likely dead or hiding in France or some such place, and he was no longer a mere sergeant but a captain, and soon, hopefully, to be promoted again. He was the master here now and when the lazy bastards who were supposed to be caring for the house turned up, he'd flay them alive.

The door was locked and he had no key, so to his extreme irritation he had to resort to breaking into his own house by smashing one of the small window panes before lifting the sash and climbing in. Once in he realised that no one had lived in this house for weeks, maybe months; the rooms were cold, the air stale, and there was a layer of dust on everything. Grey cobwebs hung from the chandelier in the lounge, and when he made his way to his bedroom the bedding was damp and smelt of mould.

He could not stay here.

Raging mad and threatening all kinds of vengeance on the couple who had taken his money and given nothing in return, he headed into Manchester, where he spent an extortionate amount of money on an overcooked mutton chop and an indifferent room. It seemed reasonably clean when he went to bed, but turned out to have numerous unwelcome residents who, roused by the warmth of his body, had an all-night feast, with the result that the Captain Cunningham who arrived promptly at nine the following morning at the Deansgate office of Edward Cox, solicitor, was neither bathed, replete, nor rested.

"Good morning, Sergeant Cunningham," Mr Cox said, once recovered from the surprise of seeing his former client on his doorstep after an absence of nearly four years.

"Captain," Richard replied curtly.

"Really?" Mr Cox said, with a tone of astonishment that Richard would have found insulting had he not been fully occupied with trying to resist a whole body itch that made him want to tear his skin off. "Well, *Captain* Cunningham, how can I be of assistance to you?"

"May I impose on you for a few minutes?" Richard asked. "I have an important matter I wish to discuss with you."

He was shown into the solicitor's office, and coffee was sent for.

"Now Captain," said Mr Cox, sitting forward in his chair, "how can I help you with your important matter?"

"I am on my way to London, to an urgent meeting with the Duke of Cumberland," Richard said pompously, "but I thought it necessary to apprise you of the situation regarding my sister Elizabeth."

"Ah, yes, the delightful Lady Peters," Edward Cox exclaimed. "How is she? I have not seen her for…oh…nearly three years. Quite a memorable last meeting, as I recall."

"I hate to be the bearer of bad news," Richard said, "but I have to inform you that the man we all knew as Sir Anthony Peters was in fact a spy for the Jacobite cause, and has disappeared, along with Elizabeth. There is a large reward out for his capture. I had thought you would be aware of this."

Mr Cox blanched and sat back in his chair, his mouth open in shock. It was eminently clear that he had most definitely not been aware of this.

"Dear God," he gasped after a moment. "Has he harmed her? Have you heard anything of her whereabouts?"

"No, nothing," Richard replied impatiently. "But –"

"My dear sir, you must be distraught," Mr Cox interrupted, distracted. "How dreadful! Of course I will do anything in my power to help you find Elizabeth and restore her to her family. How can I help?"

Richard frowned. This was not going as he had intended.

"I assure you sir, that everything possible is being done to apprehend the traitor Anthony. And to find my sister," he added belatedly. "I have not come to ask for your help in finding her, although of course if you hear anything of the possible whereabouts of the man known as Sir Anthony, you will inform the authorities immediately."

"Of course," Mr Cox answered. "So, if you do not wish my help in finding your sister, why have you come to see me?"

"The real Sir Anthony Peters died of smallpox when he was a small child. This impostor married my sister under a false name, so their marriage was not a legal one. Therefore he had no right to the twenty thousand pounds which my father left as a dowry. As I am sure you are aware, the property of traitors is automatically forfeit to the Crown. I have therefore come to take possession of the money."

"I see," said the solicitor, in quite a different tone from that which he had used so far. "You think your sister to be a traitor as well. Is this the common view?"

Richard flushed.

"I do not know whether Elizabeth is a traitor or merely the dupe of this bast…this man, but regardless, he has no right to the dowry."

"No, indeed he does not. But if the marriage is invalid, as you say, then your sister is still single, is she not? And therefore any remaining monies would remain in trust until she attains the age of thirty. Or marries elsewhere."

"Or dies," Richard said bluntly.

"Indeed. In which case it would go to build a foundling hospital, under the provisions of your father's will. As I explained to you when you came to see me after your father's death."

"So you are saying that unless my sister is proved to be a traitor, I cannot claim the money my father left?" Richard said hotly.

"I am saying nothing of the sort," Mr Cox replied coldly. "In the event that your sister proves to be a traitor, her dowry will become the property of the Crown."

"In which case I will be entitled –"

"To nothing," Mr Cox finished. "Any money would become the property of the Crown, that is of the monarch. And as far as I am aware, Captain Cunningham, you are merely the cousin of a lord, and therefore unless the king sees fit to compensate you for your military service to him, you will receive nothing."

The solicitor sipped his coffee and watched in silence whilst a variety of expressions crossed the young soldier's face.

"I have an urgent appointment with the Duke of Cumberland

next Wednesday," Richard said finally. "I am sure that if I explain the situation to him, he will be sympathetic to me and will ask His Majesty for the necessary permissions."

"Do you know why His Royal Highness has summoned you?" Mr Cox asked.

"I…er…" Richard stuttered, cursing that he never had been able to lie readily.

"Ah. Then if he has summoned you for a *positive* reason, maybe you would be successful in your request. But in this matter at least, I am pleased to say I *can* be of assistance." He smiled.

Richard brightened.

"I can save you the effort of making such a request by informing you that your sister's dowry is no longer in my possession," Mr Cox finished.

"No," Richard said, deeply shocked. "It's not possible. Sir Anthony signed it all over to Beth. She *can't* have spent it all. She was never interested in material things. Has she deposited it elsewhere?"

"I have no idea where she has deposited it. That is not my concern. She came to me some considerable time ago and told me she wished to withdraw all of it. In guineas."

"And you let her have it?" Richard said.

"I tried to talk her out of it, but she was most adamant. I had no choice in the matter. She had all the relevant documents signed by Sir Anthony and duly witnessed."

"But…he's a traitor!" Richard cried.

"So you say. But I was hardly to know that at the time. I have done nothing wrong."

"You're telling me she took twenty thousand pounds in gold out of the bank and just walked away with it? No one could carry that much gold about their person. It would be impossible. I don't believe you."

"You may believe what you wish, Captain," Mr Cox said icily. "I assure you she made all the necessary arrangements to transport the gold. And I also assure you I have all the legal documentation regarding the transaction, all in order. If you want to take the matter further, then I wish you luck. Now I will wish you good day. I am sure you want to make an early start for your urgent appointment in London." He stood, forcing Richard to follow suit. "Your servant, sir," he said, opening the door. Richard walked past him, then stopped on the threshold. A muscle twitched in his cheek.

"You're enjoying this, aren't you?" he said, incensed. "You never did like me. Well, you've not heard the last of this, I promise you."

"Captain Cunningham," said Mr Cox, "It would give me the greatest pleasure to watch you fight a legal battle that would no doubt drag on for years, and which you could not possibly win. But I would suggest that you concede victory in this to your sister, who always did possess the superior intellect, and confine yourself to martial affairs at which I'm sure you excel. I will not take up any more of your time."

Richard stalked down the steps in a blind rage. One day he would find his bitch of a sister, and when he did he would tear her limb from limb. He mounted his horse and pulled so hard on the reins that the stallion reared up in pain, almost unseating him. He tore down the street at a gallop, heedless of the people who had to leap to safety.

Damn Beth, and Anthony, and Manchester, and that fucking horrible house that he'd never had a moment's happiness in since his mother had died. He would go back there now and burn the damn place to the ground. Then he would do everything in his power to find Beth and that simpering bastard she married, and when he did he would kill them himself. To hell with the reward. Nothing on earth would give him more pleasure than to watch them writhe in agony at his feet, begging for mercy.

By the time he got back to the house he had calmed down a little, and had decided not to burn it to the ground after all. That would be stupid. He could sell it, and the money from it could be put towards finding his sister and her so-called husband. In that he had not changed his mind. He turned from the house and rode to the Ring o' Bells, where he ate a very fine roast beef lunch and drank several glasses of rum punch.

He would set off for London this afternoon. But before he did that, he had a house call to make. He smiled. This would be fun, and might yield some useful information too.

\* \* \*

**Scotland**

As threatened, Alex did rise from his bed very late indeed on the morning after his return to the MacGregor fold. This was partly because it was pitch black in the cave, so the sun rising over the mountain failed to rouse him, partly because he had been completely exhausted and not a little drunk by the time he retired, and partly because his whole clan had crept silently out of the cave at daybreak so as to let him sleep on undisturbed.

By the time he finally staggered out of the cave, blinking in the sunlight, it was nearly midday, and most of the clan was sprawled around the saucer-shaped depression, relaxing. Some of the women had gone down to the loch to wash clothes accompanied by their husbands, who were keeping watch. Angus, Iain, Graeme, Allan, Dougal and his two brothers, among others, were busy sharpening their swords and dirks, and checking their pistols were serviceable. Which left him with no need to ask who intended to accompany him in his war of attrition. He nodded to them as he passed them on his way to the campfire, where some oatcakes were cooking on a hot stone. He liberated one and went to sit down, tossing it from hand to hand until it cooled enough for him to eat.

He was happy with those who had chosen to follow him. All of them except Allan had a personal reason to hate the redcoats as well as a political one. Iain because of Maggie's death, Angus because of his blood oath, Graeme because Beth had been as a daughter to him, and Dougal and his brothers because it was a redcoat's seduction of their sister Jeannie that had led indirectly to her death. Which left…

"Where's Kenneth?" Alex shouted across to Angus. "Is he joining us to fight?"

"He's away down the loch side. He said he had to have a wee blether wi' someone before he made his decision."

Alex's brow furrowed. Kenneth never consulted anyone before he made decisions, except his chieftain, but only then if it was a clan matter. Puzzled, he considered heading down to the loch, but then thought better of it and sitting back, bit into the oatcake. He had taken Kenneth's participation for granted, he realised, but if he chose not to fight they would manage without him. It would be a loss, though. Not only was he a formidable fighter, but he had the ability to scare people half to death just by looking at them. He would find out what was going on soon enough, no doubt.

The formidable fighter was currently looking down at the ground and feeling as nervous as a small child caught with his hand in the sweetie jar, as he stood on the banks of the loch some short distance from the women doing their laundry. Facing him was Janet, who stood with her hand on her hip and an expression of utter incredulity on her face.

"Have ye totally taken leave of your senses?" she asked him.

"*Isd!*" he said, glancing round to see if the others had heard. If they had, they were making a good pretence of disinterest. He turned his attention back to the subject of his proposal. "I...er...if ye need a wee while to think about it, I'll leave ye alone," he offered.

"I dinna need any time at all to think about it," she said. "The answer's no, of course."

"Janet, I'm no' a bad man," he said. "And I'm good wi' bairns, ye ken that. And –"

"Is this some sort of dare?" she asked suspiciously. "Has Angus put ye up to this?"

"No!" Kenneth protested.

"Because if he has, I'll skelp the wee gomerel, big as he is."

"Janet, it's no' a dare. Nobody kens that I've asked ye. It was my idea."

Janet looked up at him sceptically.

"So ye're telling me ye love me, are ye?" she said.

"No! I mean...aye, I love ye in a fashion, ye ken. But as I said, I'm good wi' bairns, though Jeannie and I never had any, and I ken what it's like to lose the one ye love, and I thought that if we were to marry we could be company for each other, and I could be a faither tae the wee ones."

He was serious. And, giant though he was, he was sensitive and shy, though normally he hid it better than he was doing right now. Janet's face softened.

"Come here, ye great dunderheid," she said, reaching out to him and wrapping her arms round his waist. She laid her head on his big chest and for a minute was soothed by the sound of his heart thumping against his ribs. He put one arm round her very tentatively, as though afraid of crushing her. She gave his waist a squeeze and then let him go and stepped back.

"Ye've a good heart, Kenneth, man," she said. "And I'd say aye to ye, but for two reasons."

He looked down at her expectantly.

"Firstly, there's a group of men up there sharpening their weapons for a fight, and waiting for you to join them. They'll be sore disappointed if ye stay here, and ye'll regret it forever if ye dinna go with them to avenge wee Jeannie's death."

He made to speak, but she stood on tiptoe, and reaching up put her hand gently over his mouth.

"I ken ye dinna speak of it, and I ken why," she said gently, "and she was wrong in what she did. But it wasna fighting fair tae seduce her into betraying us the way that soldier did. Jeannie was a bonny woman, but easily led, and he took advantage of that. Ye're right to want to avenge her, and Alex needs ye with him. So go."

He waited a moment.

"Ye said there were two reasons," he prompted finally.

"Aye," she said, "I'm already married. It's against the laws of God and man to have two husbands."

"Janet, *a ghraidh*, Simon's no' coming back," Kenneth said softly. "It's been over four months now."

"Ye didna see him fall at Culloden, did ye?" she said.

"No, but –"

"Well, then."

"I didna see Duncan fall, either, or Robbie Og, but I ken they're dead. Simon's –"

"No' dead," Janet interrupted. "He may be a prisoner, but he's no' dead. If he was, I'd ken it, in here." She hit her chest with her fist. "He's coming back to me, and I'll wait for him until he does. So thank ye for the kind offer, and it *was* kind, but no. Away and fight wi' the others."

"She's convinced that Simon's alive and coming back to her," Kenneth said a few minutes later after he'd climbed back up to the others and told them of his decision to fight. He was sitting with the other men a short distance from the rest of the clan, and had told them of his proposition to her. "She said that she'd ken in her heart if he was dead."

"Well, it is possible that he's been taken prisoner," Angus put in. "If so, he could be in jail for years or transported to the Colonies."

"Or hung," Graeme added.

"Whichever way, he's no' coming back," Alex said.

"He could. Remember those nine MacGregors that escaped from Dumbarton Castle in February? They dug their way out through the walls," Angus pointed out.

"Dumbarton Castle is a ruin. A good kick and the whole thing would fall down. Dinna be telling her that and raising her hopes," Alex said.

"I dinna think it'd make a difference. She's as sure that he's alive as if he were standing next to her," Kenneth said. "I'll away and get my sword and dirk. When are we off tae fight, then?"

"Give me another day or two to rest my leg," Alex said. He hated to admit that it pained him, but better that than it fail him in the middle of an ambush. "We can plan while we're waiting. And Lachlan and Jamie are away seeing what they can find out about Stirling. There are troops stationed there who are ranging out in small groups to raid the surrounding areas. That's far enough away from here for us no' to be suspected if we happen to come across a few of them out after dark." He grinned. "The laddies should be back in a couple of days. And if the redcoats think Scotland a hell on Earth now, they'll soon have cause to be sure of it."

While the others practised their fighting moves and Alex observed and gave sporadic advice, he mulled over what Kenneth had said about Janet. Was it possible to know whether someone was dead or not in your heart? He knew it was in those stupid novels that Charlotte and Clarissa read, and it would be a comfort to Janet to think so. But then in his heart he didn't feel that Beth was dead either, although he knew she was because Maggie had seen her shot in the head.

Maybe he should have told her that he'd seen Simon fall, even though he hadn't. At least then she'd have been able to grieve for him and move on.

Like he was doing? He smiled ruefully. Let her keep her illusions, poor woman. If they gave her hope, it was not such a bad thing. Not as bad as the endless sense of loss, anyway.

He ran his fingers through his hair and forced his mind back to the present. He would grieve for Beth for the rest of his life, but this was his version of moving on; and he intended to make a good job of it.

\* \* \*

## Didsbury

When the knock came on the door, Jane, who was passing through the hall on her way to the kitchen at the time, opened it. When she saw who the caller was she tried to close the door, but Richard put one booted foot in the doorway to stop her.

"Now, there's no need to be rude," he said jovially.

She contemplated opening the door wide then slamming it on his foot but his boot soles were thick, and she might well not only fail to shut the door, but also incite his anger.

"What do you want, Richard?" she asked loudly. Thomas had ears like a cat; if he was anywhere in the vicinity he would be alerted to the identity of the caller.

"Well now, can't a master call on his servants when he's passing through the town?" Richard said.

"We're not your servants any more, thank God," Jane replied. "And you are not welcome here. So if you will kindly remove your foot, I have work to do."

The foot stayed in place. She was very aware that if he chose to force his way in she could not stop him. She felt a frisson of fear run through her.

"Actually, I've come on a private matter, and would like a word with your husband or with Elliot, if he's at home."

"Open the door, Jane, and then step back," Thomas's voice came from behind her. She glanced back, then did as he'd bid her.

Richard looked at Thomas, who was standing a few feet behind his wife, a pistol, primed and cocked, levelled at Richard's head.

"You have nothing to say that I want to hear, Richard, so as you've been told you're not welcome, please leave," Thomas said, his green eyes cold and hard.

Richard smiled, apparently completely unperturbed by the gun pointing at him, although if Thomas chose to fire at that range he could not miss. He looked down the hall at the neat paintwork, the polished wood floors, the colourful welcoming rug on the floor.

"This is a nice place you have," he said conversationally. "It must have cost a fair sum. I assume it was paid for out of Elizabeth's dowry?"

"How this house was paid for is none of your business," Thomas said.

"Now that's where you're wrong," Richard replied. "It is very much my business if this house was paid for with money that belongs to me. I'm sure you've heard by now that my sister's lover was a Jacobite spy, and that they were never actually married. So neither of them had any right to the money that this house was bought with."

"That's as may be," Thomas said. "But you had no right to it either. The master gave me a copy of his will after he signed it, to keep safe. He told me exactly who he'd left his money to. And he told me why that wasn't you. Would you like to know?"

Richard's face darkened and his hand moved automatically to his sword.

"I wouldn't if I were you," Thomas warned him.

"You won't shoot me," Richard said arrogantly. "You'd hang if you did."

"You're wrong," Thomas answered. "I'd love to shoot you. You just need to give me a reason, that's all. I'll take my chances after that."

Reluctantly Richard let go of his sword hilt.

"Let's be reasonable," he said through gritted teeth. "I'm sure you know where the money is. If you take me to it, we can come to some mutually agreeable arrangement. Let me in and we can discuss it man-to-man. Or I can always come back another time, maybe bring a few friends with me. I'm sure you don't want that."

A brightly coloured ball came rolling down the hall and bounced off Richard's boot, which was still in the doorway. It was followed by a small child who ran past Thomas before he could stop her, her whole attention focussed on her toy. She dropped to her knees and picked it up, laughing and making guttural sounds of pleasure.

Richard's eyes widened and the colour drained from his face instantly, rendering his normally swarthy complexion a sickly yellow.

Having regained custody of her ball the child now became aware of her surroundings, and slowly looked up at the man standing in front of her, who was staring down at her, his face a mask of horror. She took in the black leather boots, the cream breeches, and then the scarlet coat. And then she started screaming, a high-pitched wail of pure mindless terror, and tried to scrabble backwards, her bare feet slipping on the polished floor.

Jane, heedless of everything but her adopted daughter's distress, ran forward and scooped her up, cradling the little girl's face against her shoulder so she couldn't see the soldier any more.

"Shhh Ann, sweetheart," she crooned to the screaming child, who clung to her neck with choking strength. Jane backed away, keeping her eye on Richard until she was behind Thomas, then she turned and walked into the kitchen, closing the door behind her. The child's wails became muted.

Thomas and Richard looked at each other.

"She recognises you," Thomas said to the ashen-faced soldier. "Thought you'd killed her as well as Martha, didn't you?"

"I…I don't know what you're talking about," Richard said shakily, all his arrogance evaporated. "Who's Martha?"

"Maybe you don't remember Martha," Thomas replied. "After all, it was four years ago, and I daresay you've killed a good many more innocent women since then. But it doesn't matter, because Ann remembers well enough for both of you. We haven't reported it to the authorities yet, because we didn't want to cause the child any more distress than she's already suffered. But we did take legal advice, and have written a deposition and lodged it with a solicitor just in case it's ever needed. It makes really interesting reading, particularly the statement from the man who found Ann lying in the road in the middle of the night next to her dead mother. I'm sure your commanding officer would find it fascinating. Of course, it's up to you whether he gets to read it or not. Now, if it's all the same to you, my arm's getting tired holding this thing, so either try to force your way in or leave."

Richard left.

Thomas waited until he heard the horse's hooves clattering down the road, then he closed and bolted the door before going into the kitchen. He put the pistol on the table and sank down onto the bench opposite Jane, who was still cradling the little girl. Her screams had turned to whimpers now, and her eyes were closing.

"She's tired herself out, poor mite," Jane said softly. She looked at Thomas, who rubbed his hands over his face. "He really did kill Martha, didn't he?" she said. "I know Beth told us he had, but I never truly believed it until now."

Thomas nodded.

"I've never seen him look so shocked," he said. "I told him that she remembered everything and that we've lodged a deposition with a solicitor, and that we'll show it to his commanding officer if he causes us any trouble."

Jane stared at him, shocked.

"But that's not true!" she said. "Ann can't even speak. And she screams at every red coat she sees!"

"I know that, and you know that, but Richard doesn't," Thomas replied. "And I know you don't hold with lying, but sometimes it's necessary. We all lied when we were questioned about Beth's disappearance."

Jane flushed.

"I wasn't comfortable with it, though," she admitted.

"No, but your loyalty to Beth came first, as it should. And I'd rather tell a lie than have to kill a man. Because if he'd returned, as I'm sure he would have done, with or without his friends, I would have had to shoot him. This was the lesser of two evils. I doubt he'll come back."

"What was he talking about when he said he was sure we knew where the dowry money was?" Jane asked. "Isn't it with Mr Cox in Manchester?"

"As far as I know, yes. But we know Sir Anthony signed it over to Beth, and she certainly did withdraw some of it. Richard was right about her buying the house for us. But no matter what, he can't claim the dowry and never could. His father made sure of that. He's just bitter and greedy, and always was."

"Do you really think he'll leave us alone now?" Jane asked.

"Yes, I think so, but me and Ben can take it in turns to stay up and keep watch for the next few nights. I'll teach him to use this, too. It's about time he learned how to defend himself. He's coming up for fourteen."

Jane looked at the pistol with a mixture of trepidation and disgust. Thomas smiled.

"I know you hate violence even more than lying, but we live in violent times, and Ben needs to learn to protect himself. He's a sensible lad, he won't do anything stupid. And he's brave too. Remember when that friend of Richard's tried to rape Mary, and Ben knocked him out with his own musket?"

In spite of herself, Jane laughed.

"He's very fond of Mary," she said.

"He is. And she's sweet on him too. I can see wedding bells for those two in the future, and I won't be sorry."

Jane smiled, clearly feeling the same way. Ann was asleep now, and Jane gently removed the child's arms from round her neck.

"She's getting heavy," she remarked, settling her on her knee.

"Do you want me to take her?" Thomas asked.

Jane shook her head.

"Do you think we'll ever find out what's happened to Beth?" she asked in a very small voice.

"I don't know. I hope so, and if we do I hope it's that she's alive and well, and that Sir Anthony fellow too. Because whoever he was, she loved him, and I think he loved her too. But we can't do anything about them except keep them in our prayers. I can, however, do something about teaching Ben to defend himself and us."

He stood up and stretched, picked up the gun, then impulsively he leaned across the table and kissed his wife.

"If Beth loved him half as much as I love you, we must hope that they're together, wherever they are. For I wouldn't want to live without you, and I'm sure she felt the same way for Sir Anthony."

With that he turned and left the room, closing the door quietly so as not to wake Ann, and leaving Jane open-mouthed. He was not one for endearments. Their love for each other was a given, and they both knew it. The fact that he'd voiced his love told her more than anything else could have how much Richard's visit had disturbed him, and how prepared he'd been to kill to defend his wife and child.

She adjusted the weight of the little girl on her lap, and then folded her hands and began to pray.

## Scotland

The ten men huddled in the tiny bothy listening to the rain battering against the door, shivering in spite of the fact that it was August. They had tried unsuccessfully to light a fire in the middle of the muddy floor, but as the wood was wet all they'd succeeded in doing was creating a large amount of smoke, which had left them all coughing and with sore eyes, and which swirled around the room for ages before finally making its way out of the hole in the roof.

On one side of the room a low stone platform ran the length of the wall, and all the soldiers were now sitting on it, aware that if they were going to get any sleep tonight it would be sitting up, because none of them were insane enough to lie on the rain-soaked floor. One of the men had managed to light a candle, which he had fixed on the little platform. It flickered wildly in the draught coming under the door, throwing huge shadows round the room. They passed a flask of brandy from hand to hand.

"I hate this bloody country," one man muttered. "How the hell do people manage to live in places like this? I wouldn't keep pigs in here."

There was a general murmur of assent to this remark.

"They don't know any better," one of his companions remarked. "They've always lived this way."

"Not any more. Now they're living out on the mountains, poor sods, which is the only thing I can think of worse than this. One thing about these places, the heather thatch burns well."

As one they all looked up at the roof, wondering if they could pull part of it down and light a fire with it. A bit of warmth would make a huge difference to their conditions and would allow them to cook the rabbits they'd shot and skinned earlier, which at the moment lay in a sad pink bundle in the corner.

"If you do, the rain'll pour in and the floor'll be like a bog in five minutes," another man, small and stocky with a shock of thick black hair tied back and clubbed, said.

"Yes, but if we pull some out from underneath the overhang outside, that'll be dry, and then we might be able to get a good fire going, and if we do even the wet wood'll burn."

The flask went round again, and then the man who'd made the suggestion, a tall, freckle-faced soldier, stood up and pulled his knife out of his belt.

"I'll go," he said. "If I crouch under the overhang on the side away from the wind, I won't get too wet."

He opened the door and letting in a shower of raindrops, he went out, closing it behind him.

The others waited for him to return. And then they waited some more. Finally one of them shouted out, "Jack, are you all right out there?"

Silence.

"I bet the daft bugger's gone off for a piss and got lost," the short stocky man said.

"Wouldn't he just piss against the wall?"

"You would, I would, but you know Jack's an idiot. It's pitch black out there. If you walked more than a few steps away you wouldn't know where you were." He stood up. "I'll go and see what's up with him." He went out.

"I can't wait to get back to barracks tomorrow," one man said. "At least it's dry there, and you can light a fire to cook with. I'm starving."

More time passed. The flask was emptied and another one started. Having eaten nothing, the soldiers were getting decidedly tipsy.

"Where the hell are they?" the man currently in possession of the flask said. He shouted out to the men outside, but there was no reply. All of them began to feel uneasy.

"Do you think they've been ambushed?" the youngest man, a private of eighteen asked fearfully.

At that very moment, from somewhere in the vicinity there came a loud mournful howl, which was answered a moment later by another, and then a third.

"Wolves!" cried one of the men.

"There aren't any wolves in Scotland, are there?" another asked the room in general. "They're dogs, that's all."

"Dogs stay with people, and there are no people round here

any more. We just spent a week driving them all away. And we killed most of the dogs," the corporal pointed out.

The howling continued.

"That's wolves, alright," one of the more experienced soldiers said. "There were wolves in Hanover when I was there, and the countryside's not as wild as here."

"Do you think –"

He shut up abruptly as a man's scream of pain rang through the night.

"Shit!" the corporal exclaimed, dropping the flask of brandy on the floor.

"Oh God, do you think they've got Jack and Harry?" asked the young private.

"Only one way to find out," said the corporal. "If we stick together we'll be safe. Wolves won't attack a group."

All eight men stood as one and unsheathed their swords. Their powder was wet, so the muskets were left stacked in the corner. They went to the door, opened it, and peered fearfully out. The rain battered against their faces, rendering them momentarily blind, and in that moment a huge hand reached out and grabbed the nearest soldier by the throat, crushing his windpipe and throwing him to the side as though he were a doll. He writhed on the ground for a few moments trying to drag air into his lungs, then he lay still.

Whilst Kenneth was doing that Alex and Angus had come at them from the other side, and had killed two more. The remaining five men, finally realising that there *were* people in the area after all, and very angry people at that, ran back into the bothy and shut the door, two of them leaning on it in an attempt to stop the attackers getting in. The other three ran for their muskets, fumbling to fix their bayonets in the pitch black.

Outside, Kenneth pushed his mass of dripping wet red hair back off his face, took a few paces backwards and then charged the door, knocking it off its hinges and driving both it and the two men behind it across the room.

The other men poured in behind him, making short work of the stunned and terrified redcoats. They hefted the bodies outside to bleed into the heather, then returned to the bothy and sat down where the soldiers had recently been. A puddle of water soon formed at the feet of each man as the rain dripped off their sodden kilts on to the floor. Iain picked the flask up, shook it, then took an experimental swig.

"Mmm!" he said. "Brandy. Pretty good quality too." He passed it to Angus, who was sitting to his right.

"That was a good idea about the wolves and the scream," Graeme commented. "It was a lot easier taking them from outside than if we'd have had to come through the door one at a time."

"Aye well, I was going tae wait till they slept, but they didna show any signs of doing so, so I had to think of something else," Alex said. "We'd have been here till dawn else, and we need to have them buried and be gone by then."

They all sat for a short time, resting. It had been a long day, what with tracking the soldiers, observing them to ascertain their experience as fighters, and then digging a big hole a few hundred yards away from the bothy. And then standing in the pouring rain outside for four hours listening to them chat and complain, waiting for them to go to sleep. The two men coming out had been a bonus; Kenneth had taken them as soon as they closed the door, breaking their necks and killing them instantly and silently.

"There are some coneys here, all skinned and gutted," Allan said. "Shall we make a fire and cook them before we go?"

Alex thought about it for a minute. He wanted the men out of there, the soldiers buried, and all signs of the brief fight obliterated before dawn. They would have to do a makeshift repair on the door Kenneth had smashed off its hinges. But the grave was already dug and it wouldn't take long to haul the men up there. Kenneth could carry two at a time.

"Aye, why not?" he said. There was a communal sigh of relief. Angus stood up.

"I'll away and get some dry heather from under the overhang, then," he said, grinning. "I'll try no' to get lost."

"Watch the wolves don't get you," Graeme said. "I'm damned if I'm coming to rescue you until my belly's full."

Angus returned, the fire was lit and soon the appetising smell of roasting meat filled the small room. Kenneth manhandled the door back into place to keep out the rain, and the cold dark place that was unfit for redcoats' pigs became a warm and homely shelter for nine Highlanders and an adopted Sasannach who still insisted on wearing breeches.

"If I can find a wee bit of wood, I can fix that hinge," Kenneth said. "It'll only take me a few minutes."

"Are we always going to be burying the bodies, Alex?" Dougal asked, as they sat companionably eating.

"No, we'll no' always be able to, but when we can we should, I'm thinking."

The men had objected when Alex had first told them his intentions for the bodies of their victims, back when they'd undertaken the cattle raid. But after he'd explained his reasoning, they'd happily taken on the extra work. It was worth it to keep the redcoats guessing.

\* \* \*

## Edinburgh

"Deserted? What, all of them?"

"I'm afraid so, my lord."

Willem Anne Keppel, Earl of Albemarle, currently and most reluctantly Commander-in-Chief of His Majesty's Army in Scotland, sat in his luxuriously appointed room in front of a blazing log fire, swirling a glass of fine cognac in one hand.

Colonel Hutchinson stood stiffly to one side, vainly hoping that the great man might invite him to sit down and partake of some refreshment. He had had a long, cold, wet ride to get here, and was heartily sick of being a messenger to great men.

"Are you sure?" the earl asked.

"Well, we cannot be absolutely sure, but from what we can ascertain, they obeyed their orders to clear out the villages to the north of Stirling and then they just disappeared, my lord."

"There is a difference between disappearing and deserting, Colonel," Albemarle said. "They were a small group of men. Are you sure they were not attacked by rebels?"

The colonel sighed inwardly.

"We have examined the hut where they were sleeping at night, my lord. There are signs of a recent fire, and of them having cooked and eaten there. But there were no signs of any disturbance; in the few instances of men being ambushed there have always been signs of a struggle."

*To say nothing of the bodies left lying around, which is the most obvious evidence of an attack*, he thought sarcastically.

"Have you discovered any more about the whereabouts of those men who went missing last month?"

"Last month?" the colonel said.

"Yes, the ones who were driving the cattle to Glasgow for that man, Grimley, was it?"

Light dawned.

"Ah, Grundy, my lord. No, they too seem to have disappeared. We can only assume that once they got to Glasgow, Mr Grundy and his friends carried on to England with the cattle and the men succumbed to temptation, being closer to England than to Fort William at that point."

"One of the men was a captain, was he not, with many years of devoted service?" Albemarle said, eyeing Colonel Hutchinson with suspicion, as though expecting him to dematerialise as it seemed the other officer had.

"He was. But there seems to be no other explanation than desertion. It is just possible that this latest disappearance was an attack, although that doesn't explain the lack of bodies or signs of a struggle. But it's not possible for forty men and two thousand cattle to just disappear without trace. The only explanation is that they deserted. Perhaps they killed the captain to do so, my lord," he added.

He would not be surprised if they had. The morale of the men had never been lower. In fact his own morale had never been lower. He had not become a soldier to make war on women and children. There was no glory in that. Many of the men felt the same as he did. Others were just sick of living in threadbare tents and damp draughty hovels, never knowing when they went out of barracks for an evening whether they'd be tolerated by the locals or dirked on their way home. When they were sent out hunting for rebels they had to endure the most appalling conditions and more often than not the men they were seeking melted away into the mountains before they arrived at their settlements, leaving them nothing to do but burn down the houses, trample or steal the meagre crops and drive off the cattle. The men were bored and miserable and all the more savage for that; all of them were desperate to go home, even the vicious ones who enjoyed brutalising others. No wonder they were seizing any chance to desert.

The earl sighed and took a deep drink of his brandy, while the colonel looked on with envy.

"Well, it cannot be tolerated. At this rate we will have no army at all! The men must be disciplined. This sort of thing did not happen when Prince William was in command, and I will not have it happen now. General Bland is besieged with letters from officers requesting leave on the most flimsy of pretexts. If the officers show such a bad example, how can we be surprised if the men follow them and take every opportunity to desert?" He leaned across to the table and picking up a bell, rang it briskly. A footman appeared, bowing.

"Tell Humphrey I have urgent letters to dictate," the earl said. "You may go to the kitchen, Colonel, and get some refreshments whilst I write letters, which you will then ensure are delivered to General Bland, Colonel Howard and Lord Ancrum."

The colonel escaped gleefully to the relaxed warmth of the kitchen, reflecting on the hypocrisy of a man who did nothing but complain to anyone who would listen about how unhappy he was with his position and how much he desired to go home. Perhaps he should look in a mirror if he wished to discover whose example the men were following. Cumberland had never openly demonstrated his antipathy to his position, even though Colonel Hutchinson knew he had been desperate to get back to London.

Whilst the earl waited for the arrival of his clerk with the writing paraphernalia, he finished his brandy and looked gloomily into the fire, heartily wishing he was in a position to desert his post. Unfortunately he was not. He had the good fortune to be the friend of Prince William, which had led to the bad fortune of him being left with the command of Scotland while the prince went off to London to be feted and adored.

He hated Scotland and all its people with a great passion. He had thought that by moving to a comfortable house in Edinburgh he would be able to endure his stay here, in spite of missing his family and friends greatly, whom he had not seen for a long time. But every day he received letters and messengers from all over the country; asking him for advice regarding pay for the men; what should be done about the dangerously overcrowded prisons; bringing him intelligence of the whereabouts of the Pretender's son, which always arrived too late for him to be apprehended (although the earl still had high hopes that he would be the one to deliver Charles in person to Cumberland); asking him for decisions regarding newly captured rebels of importance. And so on and so on.

He was kept busy from morning till night, and all with a much depleted force stretched very thin indeed, and yet he was expected to continue the pacification of a savage barbaric country seething with broken men and starving women and children.

And now, as if that wasn't enough, he was receiving almost daily reports of riotous, disobedient behaviour by the troops, no doubt inspired by the open dissatisfaction of their officers. It was not to be borne. He would write a series of scathing letters to the commanders, demanding that they bring their men back under control, and not to spare the whip. Severe discipline was needed. That was the only law the common soldier understood. If they were treated leniently they would take advantage, as they were clearly now doing, thinking they could just go home when they felt like it.

If he could not go home, why the hell should they?

He poured himself another brandy, sat back in his chair, and reflected morosely on how much longer he would have to stay here before his regular letters of complaint and pleading to be allowed to leave would be heeded, whereupon he would flee the country as fast as possible and, with luck, never have to set foot in the damn place again.

# CHAPTER ELEVEN

**London, August 1746**

It was evening, and after their meal of mutton and vegetables the women had retired to their cell. The light from the fire bathed the stone-walled room with a cosy glow, and the occupants passed a bottle of wine from hand to hand as they sat on their mattresses and were transported to Rome and the delights of a lightning tour of the city, conducted by the man all of them desired to meet more than any other living person, as told by Lady Elizabeth Peters, who was sitting amongst them currently attired in stays and a grubby quilted petticoat.

She estimated that the proceeds of the yellow dress would feed all of them and provide coal for another month, and prayed that by the end of that time she would have been brought to trial and executed, before the cold, damp, starvation and vermin returned, bringing with it the risk of fever and delirium, which she dreaded more than anything; more than hanging, more even than burning at the stake, which was the statutory punishment for female traitors.

She kept herself from these gloomy thoughts by entertaining her companions with tales of her time as the wife of Sir Anthony Peters. They all knew by now who she was, not because she had told them but because nothing remained secret for long in Newgate Prison. By the same token she knew that John Murray of Broughton had turned king's evidence and had informed on Lord Lovat, the Earl of Traquair, and the English and Welsh Jacobites.

And yet he had not told the authorities about Alex, or that he had met her before, many times. In fact from what she could ascertain, he had only given evidence against people who had betrayed the cause, or at least reneged on their promises. He had told them nothing useful at all about the whereabouts of Lochiel or Prince Charles, although he must have known something about what had happened to them after Culloden.

*He is having his revenge on those who failed to deliver, who he considers responsible for the failure of the rebellion,* she thought. *He is not really a traitor at all.* She doubted that the Jacobite leaders would see it that way though, and would not want to be him if he was ever released and sought to return home.

She also knew that three of the Manchester rebels had escaped from this very prison, and the rest had been hung, drawn and quartered, that Lord Balmerino and the Earl of Kilmarnock had been executed; and that Prince Charles was still, as far as anyone knew, in Scotland, and had not been captured. She knew that there were so many prisoners they could not all be brought to trial, and so they were being ordered to draw lots, with one in twenty going to trial and the others having to plead guilty to receive His Majesty's gracious mercy and either be transported, exiled or made to enlist in the British Army.

Although she knew it likely that John Betts was dead, she told herself it was not certain; and it was wonderful to have all the latest news after weeks of being locked in her gilded cage with no idea what was going on. She was part of the world again and was actually enjoying herself, as far as she could given the circumstances.

"Oh, it must have been so wonderful tae meet the prince," Catriona sighed dreamily. She had followed her husband to Culloden, and like Beth, had no idea what had happened to him. "Is he really as bonny as they say?"

"He is," Beth affirmed. "And although he's every inch a prince, he's interested in everyone, and has a God-given ability to speak to all kinds of people without patronising them. He'll make a wonderful king one day." She refrained from telling them about his temper and sulks when thwarted. Let them keep their dreams; they had little else. And in fairness the conditions the rebel army had met with and the squabbling among the council members would have driven a saint to distraction, let alone a prince accustomed to getting his own way.

"You still think it possible he could take the throne for James?" Màiri asked.

"While he lives, there is always a chance. He's determined to succeed and if he can only persuade King Louis to assist him, then he has an excellent chance," Beth said, praying that the wily Louis would actually commit himself, should Charles continue to evade capture and make it back to France. Surely all this sacrifice and bloodshed could not have been for nothing?

"Tell us again about the night at Versailles, when you and Sir Anthony danced in front of the king," Catriona suggested, to a chorus of agreement. They could not get enough of her real-life fairytales, of handsome princes and devious kings, and she was happy to oblige. Her reminiscences stopped short of the Henri Monselle affair though, and she would not speak a word about what had happened after she'd returned from her honeymoon. Apart, that was, from her rejection of the Duke of Cumberland in the box at the theatre, which had been witnessed by over a thousand people, although neither they nor the duke had known at the time how repulsed she had been by his overtures to her. She could only hope that the news would get back to Cumberland that Elizabeth Cunningham was openly bragging of how she had rejected the hero of Culloden, and that he would put an end to her tales and to her as quickly as possible.

"So then," Beth said, after taking a mouthful of wine, "I had no idea how to dance a menuet, having been brought up in the country, but Sir Anthony, who had always mixed with the best people, was an expert in all the social niceties." It did no harm to throw a few red herrings in. Hopefully the authorities would start trawling the aristocracy for him. "He made me dance from morning till night until I had nightmares that I was dancing in front of the king and when I looked down, I was naked!" Everyone laughed. "But when we finally did it, it was fine. I even enjoyed myself."

"Is it very different from the Scottish dances then?" Màiri asked.

Details. She must reveal nothing.

"I don't know much about the Scottish dances," Beth lied smoothly, "but if you want, I can teach you the menuet. If you all stand along the wall we should have just enough room to do the first few steps, at least. I will be Sir Anthony."

The sound of riotous laughter coming from the women's area drew the attention of the keeper, who had been asked to keep a watch on a particular prisoner to check for signs of her becoming dispirited and therefore more susceptible to persuasion. But when he drew back the grille and observed what was taking place in the cell, he shook his head in amazement. Beth was doing a very creditable impression of Sir Anthony Peters being overwhelmed by the beauty and impeccable dancing skills of one of the ragged inhabitants who had succeeded in mastering the first three steps of the dance. At that moment Beth was on her knees delivering a flowery speech of undying love to the fortunate woman, to the amusement of the onlookers.

The keeper shut the grille. In spite of himself, he had to admire the girl. She was tiny and looked as though a strong breeze would blow her away; but she had more courage and determination than most men he had met. In spite of the fact that she was undoubtedly an unrepentant traitor, he admired her spirit enormously. She was certainly not going to see sense and reveal the identity of her husband, not to anyone.

He found himself hoping she would be reprieved, to his own astonishment. He was not a man prone to sympathy. And yet there was something about this woman's unshakable loyalty to the man who, if not dead, appeared to have abandoned her to her fate, that caught at his heart. He prayed that she would, against all the odds, see sense and save herself. Because right now all he saw in her future was the gallows. Quietly he walked away and left the women to their amusement.

The women all now had a mattress of their own, so they no longer had to sleep in shifts, which had been very difficult in such a small space. Beth lay awake listening to the regular breathing of her companions, punctuated by the odd snore or muttering as one or other of them dreamt. It was strange that all the rebel prisoners were desperate to live, thanking God for every day that they got through without being brought to trial, whereas she was desperate to die, and doing everything she could to achieve that. Every time the cell door opened she prayed that they were coming for her, and every time she was disappointed.

She thought back to her time in Rome and Versailles, not with Charles or Louis or even with Sir Anthony, but with Alex, remembering again the beautiful slate-blue eyes, the ridiculously long eyelashes, the warmth of him against her back as she slept curled into him, one muscular arm wrapped around her. Four months with no word from him or anyone else that he was alive. The pain she felt at these times was physical, and she closed her eyes tightly in an attempt not to cry, releasing a small gasp of misery as she did.

"Are ye awake, Beth?" her neighbour whispered.

"Yes," Beth answered. "I'm sorry, Isobel. I didn't mean to disturb you."

"I wasna asleep. I wanted to talk with ye, in private."

Beth sat up and Isobel came to sit next to her, wrapped in her blanket.

"Do ye think the Duke of Cumberland will ask to see you again?" she asked in a low voice.

"I wouldn't think so, not after the things I said to him last time."

"Do ye no' think it foolish to anger him so?"

"No," Beth said. Was Isobel hoping that she'd intercede for her? "I'm never going to tell him what he wants to know, nor am I going to become his mistress. All I have left is my honour, and that I intend to take to the gallows with me."

"What about the bairn?"

What the hell was she talking about? Beth looked at Isobel's face, dimly visible in the light of the dying fire. She didn't look as though she was feverish; her eyes were lucid, her expression earnest as she looked at Beth.

"What bairn?" Beth asked.

Isobel's eyes widened.

"Holy Mother of God, do ye no' ken ye're with child, lassie?"

"What?!" Beth said loudly, then caught herself. "What are you talking about? I'm not pregnant!" she continued in a fierce whisper.

"Are ye sure? Because ye seem so to me, and in my trade I saw enough women who were. It's a risk of the job." She grinned.

"It's not possible!" Beth said. "I haven't…well…you know."

"When was the last time ye did?" Isobel asked.

The last time. The night before Culloden. The night before Angus's birthday. Cumberland's birthday. They had lain together on the edge of Drumossie Moor, inadequately shielded from the others by gorse bushes. The stars were rising in the evening sky, and she felt again the heavy warmth of his weight on her, his unbound hair soft on her cheek as he came to his climax…

No. Three years they had been married, and in all that time her womb hadn't quickened. It wasn't possible.

Of course it was possible.

"Four months," Beth whispered.

"Have ye bled since?" Isobel asked.

"I don't know about the first month, I was unconscious. But yes, once since then, but only a little. I thought it was the shock of the injury. After my father died I didn't bleed for three months."

Isobel considered this.

"Have ye felt sick? Have ye wee red veins on your breasts? Have your paps changed colour? Have ye put on weight?"

Beth's head reeled under the weight of questions.

"I haven't felt sick, no. I have a bit of a stomach now, but I haven't been able to move about much and I had wonderful food in the Tower, and even here it's quite good. I don't know about my breasts, I haven't been looking for anything."

"Tomorrow ye must look for it. And in a lot of the women I saw when I was in the whorehouse, they get a wee brown line down here." She ran her finger down her stomach.

Beth spent the rest of the night awake, praying that Isobel was wrong. Up until now her path had been simple. Alex was either dead or a prisoner, otherwise he would have found a way to get a message to her. If he was a prisoner he would never agree to plead guilty, so he would no doubt be executed. She would not betray him, and if he was either already dead or soon to be so she wished to join him. Therefore her whole aim was to be as insulting as possible to the people who had the power to order her execution. If she was pregnant everything would change.

She was not pregnant. God could not be so cruel as to deny her a child for three years when it would have been welcomed, and then give her one when it was not.

As soon as it was light enough to see she stood up, and walking to the tiny barred window, she pulled down her stays. Her breasts were pale and rounded, with no signs of red lines. But her nipples were definitely a brownish colour. Had they been pink before? For once in her life she cursed her lack of vanity. She had never been one to spend time looking at herself in the mirror. That had been Sir Anthony's job. She hauled her petticoats up round her waist, and with some difficulty peered round the bunched material.

And there it was; the slightly rounded stomach and running down it, a clear brown line.

"No," she breathed. "Dear God, no, not now."

She let go of the petticoats and turned round. Most of the women were still asleep, but a few of them were watching her. Isobel's expression formed the question she wanted to ask.

Beth looked at her and nodded. Then she burst into tears, waking up the women who had still been slumbering.

"I'm sorry," she mumbled five minutes later when the sobs had turned to hiccups and she was able to speak. She was sitting on one of the mattresses, Isobel's arm wrapped round her shoulder, the other women all crowding round her, their faces full of concern for their friend who until now had lifted all their spirits with her infectious optimism and unending courage and humour. They had expected her to be happy at the discovery that she was pregnant; a baby was always a blessing (unless you were a whore), but a pregnancy in jail was a double blessing, as it guaranteed a reprieve from the gallows.

"Here ye are greetin' over the news that ye're wi' child, and there's women all over Newgate allowing themselves to be swived by anyone who wants them, in the hopes of getting pregnant. Ye're safe now, lassie. They'll no' hang ye or burn ye once they ken. Is that no' good news?"

"No!" Beth cried. "I WANT them to hang me!"

The women exchanged looks of shock.

"Ye dinna mean that. I ken ye loved your man, but you're young. You've your whole life ahead of ye. And he might be alive yet," Catriona said consolingly.

There was no point in trying to explain. None of them had

husbands with huge rewards offered for their capture. None of them had husbands who had promised to come for them, and who had the courage and acting ability to do it, no matter the risks. She had said to herself that she would wait six months, but if he was alive he would have found a way to contact her by now.

"What happens, once they know?" she asked. "Do they let you go? Can you keep the child?"

"They'll no' let ye go, but ye'll no' be hung at least until after the baby's born, and often if you're found guilty, they'll transport ye instead. They may let ye take the bairn, or it may go to a foundling hospital," Màiri said.

That night, to her surprise, Beth actually fell asleep as soon as she lay down, probably due to the exhaustion of having had no sleep the previous night coupled with the emotional trauma of the day. She woke suddenly some time in the middle of the night from a deep sleep, and for a moment had no idea where she was.

Then it all came flooding back, and she stroked her stomach, both marvelling at and despairing of the tiny person growing inside her. This could be all she would ever have of Alex. Was there a way to save it? She ran through her options.

She could carry on as she had been, as though she wasn't pregnant, and if she succeeded, would kill both herself and the unborn baby.

She could tell the authorities and plead her belly, and hope they would let her keep the baby. In which case she would either bring her baby up in prison, with an almost zero chance of it surviving, or would be transported with or without the child, again, with an almost zero chance of it surviving the transport ship or the foundling hospital. If it survived being born. So many babies died at or just after birth, even those whose mothers had access to good food and conditions and medical attention. If she remained in prison she had almost no chance of her baby living for more than a few days or weeks at best.

Or she could strike a deal, and betray Alex on the condition that she received a full pardon and got to keep the child. She cradled her stomach in her hands and tried to imagine what the child would look like. There were many possibilities. Tall and strong with silver-blonde hair. Small and fragile, with chestnut waves. Or any number of variations between.

The child would be a constant reminder of that glorious final lovemaking, the skirl of the pipes, the laughter of the clansmen in the distance when they still believed they could win. So many of them now lay dead, in graves or rotting on the battlefield still, for all she knew.

The child would be a constant reminder that its life had been bought at the cost of its father's if he lived, and of his clansmen, who would be hunted down ruthlessly once the truth was known. Of the carefree reckless Angus, blue eyes brimming with mischief, of Duncan the peacemaker, fierce yet gentle, of Iain, who had loved Maggie so desperately, and must be grieving terribly. Of all of them, who had accepted her into their clan, made her one of them.

Alex would want her to betray him. He had wanted her to do that to save herself, even without having considered the possibility of a baby. If he were here now he would be ordering her to save herself and their child. He was her husband and chieftain. She should obey him.

She lay there and thought. And made her decision. And then, because Isobel had been the one to recognise she was pregnant, and because the next morning she asked Beth what she was going to do, she told her the truth, in confidence. And Isobel swore to keep that confidence, although she did not agree with Beth's decision.

Two days later they came for her again, telling her that the duke wished to interview her. This time they didn't let her choose the most expensive dress possible, but instead Kate arrived at the prison with a cotton gown, silk neckerchief, and a pair of soft leather shoes. All of which were very good quality, but which would not keep ten women in comfort for several weeks as the previous gowns had.

Beth dressed and apologised for not being able to order chocolate for Kate this time, then accompanied the guards to Whitehall once more. She was somewhat surprised that Cumberland still wanted to see her in view of her remarks to him the last time they'd met, but when the door opened and she was escorted in she was confronted not by the podgy prince, but by the Duke of Newcastle, who regarded her coldly from across his desk as she sat down on the chair opposite him without being invited to do so. She arranged her skirts and folded her hands in her lap as she had on their last meeting over a month ago. Then she turned her gaze on him, her expression neutral, giving nothing away.

Her wound was healing well, he noted, although she would be scarred for life. Otherwise she looked in the best of health. Newgate was hell on Earth, an odiferous verminous nightmare. People who had been incarcerated for any length of time were always changed for the worse. People of quality, as she was, unused to privation, were usually wrecks after a few days in the common cells. She had been there for four weeks.

He examined her carefully. She was perhaps slightly paler than previously, but other than that she was blooming, her hair lustrous, her skin clear, eyes bright. No sign of trembling or nerves.

"So, madam," he said, "have you had time to consider your position?"

"Indeed I have," she replied. "I have thought of nothing else for the past two days."

"And have you now come to a sensible decision?"

"I have come to the only possible decision, Your Grace," she said.

His hopes soared, partly because she had used the correct form of address, and partly because there was of course only one possible course of action for her to take. He smiled.

"I am glad to hear it. I will call my clerk to take your deposition."

She waited calmly while he sent for his clerk and instructed him to scribe her statement. The young man sat at a desk in the corner and prepared his writing materials.

"Now," said the duke once Benjamin was ready, quill poised above the paper, "tell me about the man known to us as Sir Anthony."

She thought for a moment and then began.

"Sir Anthony Peters is the most intelligent man I have ever met," she said. "He managed to fool everybody he met, including the Elector, yourself and me, into believing he was who he said he was." She paused, and waited considerately for the clerk to catch up.

Newcastle frowned at the use of the word Elector to describe the king, but decided to let that go for now. What a coup if he could be the man to reveal to the king the true identity of the most wanted spy in Britain!

"After I married him he taught me many things; he taught me duplicity, at which society in general is so adept and which I, being reared in the country, knew little about. But he also taught me about honour, loyalty and trust, and that without those life is worth nothing. So here is my deposition; I would rather die tomorrow with my head held high than live to be a hundred in shame and regret. I will never, under any circumstances, tell you anything about Sir Anthony Peters that you don't already know. You are wasting your time. That is all I have to say to you."

She sat back, eyeing the duke's shocked expression with obvious pleasure. Benjamin's pen scratched busily across the paper until Newcastle raised his hand, at which it stopped. Silence fell on the room. The duke glared at the young woman sitting opposite him.

"Madam," he said icily. "Let me warn you that this is your last chance to save yourself. If you think the Duke of Cumberland will continue to extend his protection to you should you refuse to give up this traitor, you are very much mistaken. He has told me that if you persist in your recalcitrance, he will wash his hands of you." This was not strictly true, but she did not need to know that.

"Thank God that something positive has come out of this interview, then," Beth replied. "At least I will no longer have to witness his pathetic infatuation for me. That alone was worth me coming here."

She said it as though she had decided of her own accord to pay him a visit. The woman was delusional! They had been too lenient with her. She needed a shock to bring her to her senses.

"Call the guard," he said, and Benjamin rose to do his bidding. The soldiers returned and Beth stood and moved to the door. The soldiers saluted, then, standing one each side of her, prepared to escort her back to Newgate.

"Sergeant," Newcastle said, just as they were about to close the door. "A word, if you please. You can wait outside." The other soldier led Beth out and closed the door. The sergeant waited, at attention. He was a florid-faced, beefy middle-aged man with the air of a career soldier. No doubt he would welcome the chance to gain the favour of a great man. Indeed, who would not?

"At ease, man," the duke said. The sergeant's shoulders dropped and he relaxed a little. "Now, I need to give the young lady a shock. She has some extremely valuable information about a man we very much wish to apprehend, but so far she is proving very stubborn."

"Do you want me to try to…persuade her, Your Grace?" the sergeant asked. He looked as though he would relish the task, but the methods he would likely use would not do at all.

"I am sure you would be capable of doing so, Sergeant, but I must tell you that she is not to be brutalised in any way. Nothing that will leave any lasting marks or scars. Can you think of such a punishment that may bring her to her senses?"

"We could starve her, Your Grace. A week or two without food in solitary confinement should bring her round."

The duke considered this.

"No," he said. "We have wasted far too much time already. Unless we can get the information soon, it will be worthless." *Indeed*, he thought, *it could already be so*. "I want quick results, Sergeant."

The sergeant thought for a minute.

"Well, Your Grace. When I was in Inverness, there was a vault in the bridge where people were put, where they could neither sit nor lie, but had to stand all the time. It became very painful very quickly, and their legs swelled something terrible at the time, but I don't think it was lasting."

"Excellent! Well, I am sure that you can improvise something to make sure that she does not lie or sit down. Keep her on her own, and a guard with her at all times for when she decides to cooperate. I am sure it will not take long. She is a gently reared young woman, unused to suffering of any kind."

"Of course, Your Grace. Is she to be fed?"

"No. But give her water. On no account must she die of thirst. Report to me daily, Sergeant. I am entrusting this task to you and will be most grateful if you succeed in bringing her to a confession."

The sergeant smiled.

"You can rely on me, Your Grace."

After the sergeant had left, Benjamin returned to clear away his writing materials.

"Er…do you wish to keep the lady's deposition, my lord?" he asked.

"What?" said the duke, deep in thought. "No. It's worthless. Throw it on the fire."

Damn Cumberland! They had wasted far too much time. This Anthony had no doubt gone to ground, and could be anywhere by now. If Newcastle had had his way, he would have flogged her the moment she regained consciousness instead of spending months treating her with kid gloves. The prince was making this very difficult, saying that Miss Cunningham must remain unblemished apart from the scar she had already sustained. How could he still entertain the notion that she was an innocent dupe of Sir Anthony's? It was true that the man had been a master of disguise and extremely charismatic and deceitful, but this woman, fragile and beautiful as she was, was no victim. Newcastle was sure of it.

However, the young prince was infatuated and, in spite of all she had said, still entertained the notion that she would come to her senses in time, still could not believe that any woman could resist him, based on the fact that no other woman he had set his heart on to date *had* refused him.

Well, while the sergeant was working on the prisoner, he would see if he couldn't find another more willing beauty to tempt the prince with. Once he had another outlet for his passion, he would forget about Miss Cunningham, the duke was sure of it.

\* \* \*

On return to Newgate Beth was not reunited with her cellmates, but instead was led into a small, windowless cold room in the bowels of the prison, lit by tallow candles whose rancid fat smell warred with the odours of damp and effluent and which cast enough light to show that the walls were glistening with damp. Once there she was told that she was to stand, and was forbidden to sit or lie down. Then she was left with a young soldier to guard her, who was told not to touch or interact in any way with the prisoner.

She stood for perhaps an hour and then she sat down, leaning against the wall.

"You can't sit down," the soldier said to her.

"Yes I can, as you can plainly see," she said.

"You have to stand up. You're not allowed to sit."

"Well here I am, sitting, and to hell with what I'm allowed," she replied. She stretched her legs out in front of her.

He came to her, and putting his hands under her arms lifted her up. As soon as he let her go and returned to the corner of the room, she sat down again.

He had been told not to interact with her in any way. He had already touched her, which strictly speaking was against orders. She could almost see his mind working, wondering what to do.

After a couple of minutes he banged on the door, then waited. In due course the sergeant appeared. He eyed the prisoner, who looked to be very comfortable leaning against the wet stone wall.

"You were told to keep her standing, Private," the sergeant said.

"Yes, but she won't stand up, and you said I'm not allowed to touch her," the soldier pointed out.

The sergeant walked over to her.

"Get up," he ordered.

She ignored him.

He bent down and grabbing a fistful of her hair, dragged her to her feet. To his astonishment, although her face contorted with the pain, she made no sound.

"Now you will do as you're told, and bloody well stand!" he roared in her face. The private flinched. The sergeant let her go and walked to the door.

Beth sat down. The sergeant turned back to her.

"Let us both save some time," Beth said conversationally. "I am not going to stand up because you tell me to. I am not going to stand up unless I wish to. I am not going to tell the Dukes of Newcastle or Cumberland anything at all, as I have made quite clear to them. So you can drag me up and down all day, if it makes you happy. I really don't care."

His fist clenched and he took a step towards her. Inwardly she braced herself, waiting for the blow. Then to her surprise he beckoned to the private and they both left the room.

She sat, shivering and feeling the damp from the walls soak through her cotton dress. She looked at the door, saw the grille was shut, and then put her hand gently on her stomach.

"I am so, so, sorry," she whispered to the tiny life growing inside her, "but I cannot save you without condemning your father, and others, and I can't do that. Better we die together while you're too small to suffer, than let you be born and die in a place like this or in an orphanage. Please forgive me."

She swallowed back the tears that threatened to fall. She must not show weakness now. No matter what. She remembered the girl who had been accused of theft, who she had watched hang, remembered her stamping her feet and standing so proudly on the scaffold, cursing her accuser.

*I can do this,* she thought. *They will not break me.*

Some time passed and then the sergeant returned, carrying some rope. He handed the rope to the private, who had followed him in, and then hauled Beth unceremoniously to her feet.

"Tie her arms," he ordered the young soldier. "Tightly, but not too tight. No, wait." He drew his knife and cut a piece from the bottom of her quilted petticoat. "Put this between the rope and her wrists so it won't take the skin off. She mustn't be marked."

Her arms were pulled behind her and tied at the wrists. The sergeant let her go, and then threw the other end of the rope over a beam that ran across the middle of the room just below the ceiling. It had been set there for this express purpose, although normally people would be hung by the neck, their feet just touching the ground, or by the ankles, and then would be beaten until they divulged whatever information they had.

But this woman could not be marked. And when he had looked her in the eyes, he had seen not only defiance, but despair. If he tied her by the neck as he'd intended, he would not put it past her refusing to stand anyway, and hanging herself. He could not have that. He pulled on the rope until her tied wrists were raised enough that, although her torso was bent over, she had to remain standing or cause herself excruciating pain, then he tied the end of the rope to a hook in the wall.

Now she wasn't going anywhere. He walked over to her, and gripping her by the hair, he pulled her head back so she had to look at him. He smiled.

"Now sit down, you bitch," he sneered.

She looked at him for a moment, and then she spat with perfect accuracy straight into his left eye. His hand shot out automatically and grabbed her by the throat.

"No marks," she reminded him, her tone mocking.

He let her go, and trailed one finger down her neck, over her throat and then along the edge of the fashionably low-cut bodice of her dress. Then he plunged his hand inside and pulled, liberating one plump, perfectly-formed breast. He weighed it in his hand and then, bending down, he sucked greedily at the nipple, circling it with his wet tongue. His prick swelled in his breeches. He lifted his gaze to hers, to see her looking at him with the utmost contempt, as though he were something nasty she'd just stepped in. He released the nipple and stood up, leaving her breast hanging out. Her expression didn't change.

"One day," he said, "they'll get sick of your games. And when they do, I'll be waiting." He turned away. "Let me know when she decides to talk," he told the other man. "Until then enjoy her dugs, but don't fuck her or mark her."

He walked out and shut the door. The soldier waited until he heard the sergeant's boots retreat down the corridor, then he walked over to Beth.

"I'm sorry, Miss," he said, blushing furiously. Very gently he lifted her exposed breast and tucked it back inside the bodice of her dress. Then he stepped away, his eyes lowered.

She raised her head and stared at him, astonished.

"What's your name?" she asked softly.

"Ned, Miss. Ned Miller."

"Thank you, Ned Miller. You're a gentleman."

He looked up then, clearly expecting her to be looking at him with the same derision she'd just bestowed on his sergeant. But her beautiful eyes were warm, and a tear trembled on her lashes. She blinked it away impatiently.

"He oughtn't have done that, Miss. T'aint right, treating a lady like that."

She smiled at him and he wanted to release her on the spot,

but he didn't dare do that. So he did the only thing he could.

"Would you like some water, Miss?" he said. "Or some ale? The water in here ain't fit for a dog to drink."

"Will you get into trouble if you give me something to drink?" she asked.

"No," he said. "I can give you water, or ale, but that's all. And if you want to…well…" he pointed at the bucket in the corner, his face crimson with embarrassment, "I'm supposed to hold it up, while you…er…but that ain't right neither, so if you don't tell, I'll unhook the rope and turn away while you relieve yourself, Miss."

She smiled at him.

"You're very kind, Ned. Of course I won't tell. I would love some ale. Thank you."

He fetched his flask of ale, and held it to her lips while she drank.

"Now, I know you've been told not to talk to me, and I don't want your sergeant to be angry, so in case they decide to listen maybe you should keep quiet now. Just one thing, though."

"Yes?" he said.

"My name is Beth. You're a good man, Ned. Don't let the army turn you into an animal."

"I won't, Miss…Beth. I promise."

He moved back to his place, and she marshalled every ounce of her determination. This was not going to be pleasant. But people had suffered worse, much worse, she was sure. They would not break her. The more they tried, the more determined she was that they would not. Trust and loyalty. Well, she had both, and that would see her through. That and the knowledge that in death she would be reunited with Alex, forever.

# CHAPTER TWELVE

**London**

The night Richard had found out that the dowry had disappeared, the child Ann who he'd thought was dead had reappeared, and that everything seemed to be going wrong for him, he'd returned to the Ring O' Bells and had got thoroughly drunk, after which he'd picked a fight with some random oaf, had been prevented from killing him by the landlord and three of his cronies and had been thrown in the roundhouse for the night to cool down and sober up. The next day he had appeared before the magistrate, who had released him immediately on discovering that his drunken ramblings of the night before about meeting the Duke of Cumberland were actually backed up by a missive to that effect.

Then he had gone back to the Ring O' Bells, with numerous bells and hammers ringing inside his own head as the alcohol wore off and the hangover kicked in, to be told by the disgruntled landlord that he owed a goodly sum for the overnight stabling of his horse and the replacement of two chairs and a table which had been demolished in the brawl.

Normally he would have balked at the ridiculous sum the landlord asked for, but he was very aware that if he did, he might end up either in the roundhouse again, or in a ditch somewhere, bleeding, and time was now of the essence if he was to arrive in London in time for his interview. So grudgingly he paid up, silently vowing vengeance at a later date.

All this meant that he arrived in London with not even enough time to go home and bathe before his appointment. He had to make do with changing his travel-stained breeches and stockings in the back room of an inn, where he also brushed the worst of the mud off his coat and gave his boots a quick polish.

This was all very unsatisfactory, and as a result the Richard Cunningham who was now sitting on a chair outside the Duke of Newcastle's offices, awaiting the great man's pleasure, was almost paralysed with anxiety, which was not helped by the long carpeted corridor he had had to walk down before reaching the double doors outside which he was now waiting, flanked on both sides by forbidding statues of Roman Emperors. He stared at them now, trying to compose himself. He wiped his sweating palms on his breeches and took a deep steadying breath.

Although he knew these were Newcastle's offices, he assumed that the Duke of Cumberland was using them due to the fact that St James's Palace, where he normally resided, was permanently besieged with people wishing to congratulate the hero of Culloden on saving them from papist tyranny.

So when he was finally shown in and saw not Prince William Augustus, but Thomas Pelham-Holles, Duke of Newcastle waiting for him, his first reaction was one of acute disappointment. However he managed to cover it up well, and stood smartly to attention until invited to sit down, which he did, removing his hat and placing it on the floor at his side.

The duke called for refreshments and then turned to the young man sitting opposite him.

"Firstly, Captain Cunningham, I must convey Prince William's apologies. He had intended to see you himself today, but as you will appreciate he is a very busy man, so has asked me to take his place. I hope you are not too disappointed?"

Oh, God. Perhaps he hadn't covered it up well after all.

"No, of course not. I am deeply honoured that you would condescend to notice me at all, Your Grace," he gushed. Was that too much?

"Quite. So I will come straight to the matter at hand. You will of course be aware that your brother-in-law, Sir Anthony Peters, has turned out to be a traitor of the most perfidious kind."

Richard reddened.

"Yes, I am aware of that. Although I believe that means that the marriage between him and Be…Elizabeth was invalid, and so he is not actually related to me in any way, Your Grace."

The duke had been perusing a paper on his desk, but at these words he looked up.

"You are correct, Captain. I have taken the time to read over your file. It seems that in the past four years you have advanced considerably, rising from Sergeant to Captain. Quite remarkable."

"Thank you, Your Grace. I have worked –"

"However," the duke interrupted, "I also note that your promotions were all financed by the spy known as Sir Anthony Peters. I am sure you will understand that this casts an interesting light over your career so far, which may preclude any future promotions."

Richard felt beads of sweat break out on his forehead, although the room was not overly warm. If anyone else had said this to him, he would have called them out for the insinuation that he was a party to Sir Anthony's treachery.

But this was the Duke of Newcastle.

You did not challenge the Duke of Newcastle to a duel, no matter how he impugned your character.

"Your Grace, I assure you that when I accepted his help I had absolutely no idea what manner of man he was. Nobody did. Even the king himself had no idea –"

The duke raised his hand imperiously, and Richard fell silent.

"I am not saying that *I* believe you to have been in collusion with this traitor, Captain. I acknowledge that your dedication to duty in pacifying the Highlands has been most…impressive. Your colonel has remarked upon it to me himself."

Richard brightened a little.

"Nevertheless, I'm sure you can see how this might look to others. If you wish to be promoted to Major in the future, with all the trust and responsibility that entails, your reputation must be impeccable in every way. Do you agree, Captain?"

"Of course, Your Grace." What was the duke up to? One minute he was suggesting that he would never rise any higher, and the next he was talking about promotion to Major. Richard was thoroughly confused. The refreshments arrived and Richard accepted a cup of coffee and a honey pastry. He took a bite of the pastry.

"Good," the duke continued, once the servant had vacated the room. "Now, you are almost certainly not aware that your sister was taken prisoner at Culloden and is at the moment in Newgate Gaol."

Richard had been about to take a sip of his coffee, but on hearing this totally unexpected news he froze in shock and the cup tilted, spilling the hot liquid onto his lap. It took all of his presence of mind not to swear and leap up. He put the cup down on the table and drew out his handkerchief, mopping at the spreading brown stain ineffectually while the duke regarded him impassively.

"I see that has come as something of a surprise to you, Captain," Newcastle said with spectacular understatement once Richard had given up on the stain and replaced his handkerchief in his pocket.

"It has," he agreed, his mind racing. Culloden? What the hell was she doing at Culloden? He knew she was a hellion, but not even in his worst nightmares could he imagine her charging over the moor, broadsword in hand. "Um…Culloden, Your Grace?"

"You were also at Culloden, were you not?"

"Yes," Richard said, "but I had no idea…I didn't see her there. Why was she there?"

"We can only surmise. She refuses to tell us anything. We must assume that she was accompanying this Anthony fellow. She was hiding in a hut with some other rebel women and when the soldiers discovered them, she stabbed one of them, killing him."

Richard tried to imagine Sir Anthony mincing across the battlefield dressed in silk and lace, and failed. Then he tried to imagine his sister stabbing a soldier, and succeeded. He closed his eyes for a moment. When he opened them again the duke was staring intently at him.

"We have no time to lose, Captain. She was wounded at Culloden and rescued by the Duke of Cumberland himself. It was nearly a month before she was out of danger. Since then she has been treated exceptionally well, due to the duke's…former friendship with her. But she has repaid us with insolence and a blank refusal to divulge anything whatsoever about the real identity of Sir Anthony. She is now being held in more insalubrious conditions, but still persists in her ridiculous loyalty to the traitor. She is bringing your whole family into disrepute by her attitude, sir. And that is why the duke and myself saw fit to call you to London. You are her closest family member and therefore stand to lose or gain the most by her cooperation, or lack of it."

"I…er…we are not really close, Your Grace. I left home while she was still a child, and we did not see each other again until after father died."

"But then you were reconciled, clearly. That *is* the reason Sir Anthony volunteered to pay for your commission, is it not? Or is there another reason I should know about?"

Richard coloured. *Shit*. He could not tell the duke the real reason why Sir Anthony had paid for his commission. To do so he would have to betray that he had suspected Beth to be a papist. And that she had threatened to stab the king and declare for the Pretender, which unstable behaviour had led to him intensifying the search for a suitable match. No. That would incriminate him beyond redemption.

"No, there is no other reason," he said hurriedly. "I would be only too pleased to help you in any way I can. What do you wish me to do, Your Grace?"

"I was hoping that you might be able to persuade her to see sense, Captain. You probably know her better than anyone, having shared a childhood, or part of one, and will no doubt be able to draw on family memories and obligations perhaps, to bring her round. And of course you will be aware that there is a large reward for information leading to the arrest and conviction of the traitor. But I am sure, having married into wealth, you will not be concerned with this. If you succeed however, you will have the gratitude of both myself and Prince William. Do you think you are up to the task?"

The gratitude of the hero of Culloden? Was he up to the task? He would happily beat her till she begged for mercy for the sheer pleasure of it, but to gain the favour of Prince William, he would do anything, anything at all.

"Yes, Your Grace. She has always been stubborn, but I'm sure a word from me will have the desired effect."

The duke had been perusing Richard's records, but now looked up again.

"A word. Yes, let us call it that."

"Do you want me to go to her immediately, Your Grace?"

Newcastle looked Richard up and down and he squirmed uncomfortably, aware of how bedraggled he looked.

"No. She is in somewhat uncomfortable circumstances at the moment, and I can see you have had an arduous journey. Another night and she may be a little more receptive to your fraternal entreaties. Go home and see your wife. I'm sure she has missed you, and you her. And get some rest. You can visit your sister tomorrow. Shall we say eleven o'clock?"

Richard smiled. This had been the most confusing interview he had ever had. But in the end it would all turn out well. He couldn't wait to see her face when he walked in the room. And he would not walk out until she had told him exactly what he wanted to know. He stood, and bowed to the duke.

"Thank you, Your Grace," he said. "I won't let you down, I promise."

"I am glad to hear it," replied the duke. Richard turned to leave. "Oh, just one thing, Captain, while you are having this talk."

Richard turned back.

"She is scarred from the gunshot wound, but the prince has specifically ordered that under no circumstances is she to acquire any more scars or be permanently disfigured. I have examined your file in depth, Captain. You may be forceful in your conversation, but discreet, if you understand me."

He did. He understood perfectly. Cumberland was still hoping to swive her, and didn't want damaged merchandise. This was going to be fun.

After Cunningham had left, the duke closed his file and put it to one side. Then he sat for a while, brow furrowed, deep in thought.

He had not got where he was by taking people at face value. It was apparent to him that the captain was hiding something regarding his relationship with his sister, although he had clearly been thunderstruck when he'd been told she was at Culloden. He thought it unlikely that Cunningham had known about his sister and brother-in-law's Jacobitism. He was obviously a dedicated soldier through and through.

His colonel had stated in the report the duke had asked for that Captain Cunningham undertook his duties in Scotland with extreme zeal, and that there had been a number of complaints from the citizens of Inverness among others regarding his conduct during the pacification raids, but that no independent witnesses had ever been found who would testify against him, therefore no charges had ever been brought against the man.

So, for extreme zeal, read brutality, and for no one to testify, read intimidation of witnesses. The captain was quite clearly in the mould of Fergusson and Scott.

*Which,* the duke thought, *will serve my purpose well.*

Personally he found it ridiculous that such an important potential informant should be treated so leniently because of an infatuation. Prince William was renowned for his realism and practicality – except where beautiful women were concerned. And it was true that this one was exceptionally beautiful.

Even so…

The duke smiled. He could not lose. *If Cunningham succeeds in extracting the information about Sir Anthony from his sister without marking her, I can take the credit. And if he gets it by torturing her, as is more likely, I can state, with complete honesty, that I told the man not to mark his sister, and that he acted in flagrant disregard of my instructions.*

But he would still have the information. And if Cunningham tortured her and still failed to get the information, then he could put all the blame onto the hapless soldier and come out of it smelling of roses.

He thought that unlikely, though. Cunningham was probably the only male alive who would be indifferent to her extraordinary loveliness, being her brother, whilst she was surely accustomed to wielding the power great beauty brings, and no doubt believed that being made to stand for a couple of nights would be the full extent of her suffering.

*Unless I am very mistaken in my assessment of Richard Cunningham,* thought the duke, *she is about to be disabused of that notion.*

\* \* \*

When the footman opened the front door and saw who was standing on the step, the supercilious expression on his face was momentarily transformed to one of complete horror, before he regained control of his facial features and adopted a neutral aspect. He bowed deeply.

"Good afternoon, sir," he began. "What an unexpected pleasure –"

"I'm sure," Richard interrupted impatiently, pushing rudely past the man and striding down the hall in the direction of the drawing room. He had no time for insincere platitudes. All Anne's, or rather Lord Redburn's servants detested him, as he well knew. Now he was home for a time, he would dismiss the lot of them and employ more malleable staff.

Before the footman could catch up and offer to announce him Richard had thrown open the doors and walked in, to be confronted by a complete stranger attired in silk and lace, who was currently lying at full-length on the chaise longue, languidly helping himself to raspberries from a crystal bowl by his side. As the door opened, the young man tilted his head backwards to see who had entered in such a rush.

"Good afternoon, sir!" he said brightly, without getting up. "Would you care for a raspberry? They really are succulent. Aunt grows them herself, you know. Well, she's not *actually* my aunt. I suppose she's my aunt-in-law, if there is such a thing."

"Who the hell are you?" Richard asked rudely.

The languid man popped another raspberry in his mouth, licked the juice off his fingers, then stood up and proffered a soft lily-white hand, which Richard regarded with the utmost contempt.

"Oliver," he said. "Delighted to meet you sir, whoever you are. I must say, what a fine job you brave soldiers are doing, saving us from papery and all that."

"Popery," Richard growled.

"Popery, quite," Oliver acknowledged.

"So, Oliver, what the hell are –"

He was interrupted by the sound of footsteps running down the hall, and then his wife appeared in the doorway, breathing heavily as though she had run a great distance, although she had in fact merely run down one flight of stairs, the rest of her breathlessness and her alarming pallor resulting from being told who had just appeared at the door.

"Richard!" she cried. "I did not expect you."

"Clearly," Richard said, gesturing to the young man, who had sat back down again. "I can see I have not come home a moment too soon, if this ignorant fop is the sort of company you keep when I am away!"

"You have me to a T, sir!" Oliver said pleasantly, completely unfazed by the insult to his appearance and intelligence. "Anne, should we call for wine, perhaps? Toast the great victory over the unwashed rabble and all that?"

Both Richard and Anne ignored him completely. She was still standing in the doorway trying to recover her composure.

"I…er…I…" she stammered.

He took one step toward her, then stopped, staring over her right shoulder and down the hall in amazement. She turned to see what he was looking at and then stood aside with obvious relief to let the wizened old woman who was the cause of Richard's amazement, and her younger companion into the room.

The old woman strode straight up to Richard and looked up at him, an expression of utter contempt on her face.

"Hell are you doing here?" she barked. "Bloody nerve!"

Richard was stunned. What was going on? It seemed as though his house had been taken over by lunatics; a limp-wristed idiot, a wrinkled old crone dressed as a man, and standing in the doorway a young woman as tall and almost as broad as himself, who was smiling at him, clearly highly amused by his discomfiture.

With an effort he pulled himself together and attempted to gain control of the situation.

"This is my house, madam," he announced disdainfully. "I am Captain –"

"I know who you are, man!" she interrupted. "Didn't ask who you were, did I? Bloody cowardly son of a bitch enjoys raping women and murdering babies!"

"Trying to," the large-boned woman supplemented dryly.

"Right. Trying to. Don't look like you can get it up." The old woman looked down at Richard's crotch with disgust.

"No, Aunt. Trying to murder babies. Didn't succeed. Probably gets stiff on rape, though," the woman corrected.

Richard's face flushed even more scarlet than his coat. Did everyone in the country know about Martha and her brat?

"Saved us from pap…popery, though," Oliver supplied from the sofa.

"Popery my arse," the crone replied. "Don't need to butcher

women and children to save us from that. Like bloody Hawley, aren't you?" she said accusingly.

Richard felt the rage rise up in him. He didn't give a damn what this old witch thought she knew. No one spoke to him like that. He would throw her and her foul mouth and obnoxious relatives out on the street, right now! And then he would have a word with his wife.

He raised himself to his full height and opened his mouth to order her out.

"Seems Billy thinks that's the sort of bastard needed to do the job. Must have a word with him about it," the old lady continued, unaware that she was about to be bodily ejected from the premises. "When are we due at St James's next?"

"Tuesday week," Oliver said.

"Right. Give him a piece of my mind then. And George. Anne!" she shouted.

Anne, who had been trying to melt into the wall, jumped violently. She came forward, trembling.

"Yes, I'm sorry, how remiss of me. Richard, this is Lady Harriet, and –"

"Marchioness of Hereford," the young woman interrupted. She came forward. "Lady Philippa Ashleigh, and this," she waved a hand at Oliver, "is my husband Oliver, Earl of Drayton. Oliver, get up! Captain Cunningham is about to order us to leave."

The young man, once more supine on the chaise longue, unfolded himself and stood.

"Oh," he said sadly. "How dashed inconvenient. I was looking forward to dinner. Ragout of veal you know, my favourite."

Philippa looked at Richard expectantly.

"Well?" she said when he failed to issue the order.

"No, of course I wasn't going to order you to leave," he managed, backtracking rapidly. "I was just a little…er…surprised. I didn't expect my wife to have guests, that's all."

"Why not? Husband like you, needs friends, don't she?" Harriet barked. She moved over to the fireplace and tapped her pipe out on the hearth. Philippa grinned and Richard's fingers itched to wrap themselves round her throat. He didn't dare order a marchioness and an earl out of his house, particularly one who was on familiar enough terms with the royal family to call the

Duke of Cumberland 'Billy' and the king merely 'George'. It would be social suicide for him to do that.

*And you know it, you bitch*, he thought, glaring at Philippa, who smiled sweetly back.

The following four hours were the longest and most excruciating Richard had ever spent in his life. He was not comforted by the fact that Anne clearly felt the same way, though for different reasons. She hardly spoke a word the whole evening, which left him, no conversationalist at the best of times, having to make opening gambit after opening gambit, to have all of them disdainfully rejected by Lady Harriet, who clearly despised him, and presumably due to her elevated status, or perhaps just because she was barking mad, felt no need to observe the social niceties. Oliver seemed to live in his own little world, oblivious to the hostile atmosphere that permeated the room, while Philippa observed his humiliation with amused hazel eyes.

He hadn't even been able to change out of his dusty, coffee-stained uniform, his tentative suggestion that he do so being shot down by Lady Harriet, who announced that she wasn't about to eat cold veal because he wanted to prance about trying to make himself look respectable, an impossible task in any case. Instead he sat there in utter mortification until, after what seemed like a century the crone announced that she was off to bed, and he managed to make his excuses and flee the company.

Anne had told the servants to prepare his room for him, and waited around downstairs for a while after he'd gone up, no doubt hoping he'd be asleep by the time she retired.

Once in his room, he took off his coat, changed his breeches and combed out his hair, then waited until he heard her door close. Then he waited for another ten minutes before he tiptoed barefooted down the corridor and opening her door, marched in.

She was sitting at her dressing table brushing her lank brown hair, and gave a little shriek of shock when he entered. He closed the door quietly, then walked straight over to her and grabbed her by the hair, lifting her off the stool and pulling her round to face him.

"You enjoyed watching me be humiliated tonight, didn't you?" he snarled.

Her eyes opened wide, her pupils dilating in terror.

"No! I swear I –" she began.

"Shut up," he said, and she quietened immediately. "Listen to me, you mealy-mouthed bitch. You're lucky that I'm tired tonight, and I need my sleep because I've got an important job to do for the Duke of Cumberland tomorrow. But after that I'm coming home, and when I arrive I expect your friends to be gone. Do you understand me?"

She stared at him white-faced, paralysed with terror. He gripped her hair tighter, pulling her head backwards until she cried out in pain.

"Do you understand me?" he said again, softly this time.

"Yes!" she cried. She was trembling like a leaf.

"Good. I expect to be here for some time. We can discuss our domestic arrangements when I get back from my appointment. And where the false accusations that old witch threw at me tonight came from."

He let her go, and very gently ran his finger down her cheek. She flinched as though he'd hit her, and he smiled.

"I look forward to resuming our marital relations," he said. "It's about time you fulfilled your duty and got me an heir. Until tomorrow."

He left the room, leaving her ashen-faced and weeping.

This had been a horrible evening. He had never been good at making small talk, even when the company was congenial. But tomorrow he was going to do what he was really good at. It promised to be enormous fun. And to enjoy it to the full, he needed a good night's rest.

He walked back to his room with a spring in his step, the unpleasant evening already fading as he thought of the joys tomorrow would bring.

\* \* \*

She had been standing for two full days now, and this was the third. She knew that because the two soldiers who had been ordered to watch her did twelve-hour shifts, and the nice one, Ned, was about to come on duty again.

The other one, whose name she had not discovered, did not speak to her at all. He might have been dumb for all she knew. If she asked for a drink he gave it to her; if she asked to relieve herself he lifted her skirts and held the bucket provided so that she could urinate, and then he took it away. Otherwise he stood or sat in the corner, biting his nails or playing solitaire with a pack of grubby cards. His silence had been unnerving at first, but Beth had got used to it now. At least he left her alone, which was a small mercy.

She tried to wait until Ned was back to use the bucket, because he, as he'd promised, would untie the rope from the hook, help her to straighten up, and turn his back, which at least afforded her some measure of dignity, and more importantly the opportunity to sit for a few seconds, rest her legs and try to move her arms a little. She didn't take advantage of Ned's good nature by trying to sit for longer, partly because she knew that he would probably be flogged if it was discovered that he was releasing her, even for a minute, and partly because they would then remove him, and his replacement could be a man of the sergeant's ilk.

Periodically she would move one leg or the other, and at first that had brought her some measure of relief, although she risked overbalancing and causing damage to her shoulders. But now her legs, her arms and her back were just a throbbing mass, and any movement at all caused her agonising pain. She no longer tried to lift her head, because her neck hurt too much for her to do so. So she stayed, legs straight, body bent at the waist, arms behind her, looking at the floor and wondering how long it would be before her legs gave way.

She was hungry too. She had not eaten anything since she had been brought here, and had stomach cramps from time to time. The hunger she could stand; but she was also starting to feel faint at times, little silver lights dancing at the edge of her vision. If she lost consciousness, would they leave her hanging there until she came round? She reasoned that she would find out in time, because she was not about to tell them anything and they showed no signs of releasing her.

How long did it take to die of starvation? She had no idea, but thought it must be weeks. Could she stay like this for weeks? *The men walked all night to attack Cumberland's camp then walked back and fought a battle, with only a biscuit to eat in two days,* she told herself. *I can stand here for as long as they make me. To hell with them.*

The door opened and the welcome sound of Ned entering greeted her. The nail-biting soldier stood, the two men saluted each other, and then the door closed and she was alone with the kind young man.

"Good morning, Ned," Beth said, trying to sound cheerful. "It *is* morning, isn't it?"

"It is. Would you like a drink, Miss?" he asked.

She smiled and nodded, then closed her eyes for a moment as even that movement sent a spasm of pain down her neck to her shoulders, which were pulled back in an unnatural position.

He picked up the flask, but instead of coming directly across to her as he usually did, he looked at the door and then approached her from the side, so that anyone looking in at the grille would see his broad back which concealed her from view.

"I was thinking last night," he said in a soft voice, "if you'll allow me the liberty to touch you?"

Without waiting for an answer, he wrapped his left arm round her waist, and as he held the flask to her lips with his right, he lifted her off the floor. The pressure on her shoulders eased immediately and she gave an involuntary moan of relief.

"No one can see what I'm doing," he whispered in her ear, "I can give you as much drink as you want. If I take a minute or two each time, it might help you a little? If anyone opens the grille I can let you down and move back, and they'll not know a thing."

She flexed and pointed her feet, closing her eyes tightly against the pain it caused, trying to ease the stiffness in the muscles.

"You're a good man, Ned," she said. "Thank God for you." Tears sprang to her eyes and she blinked them back, not wanting to embarrass him, not wanting to show weakness even to this gentle man, knowing that once she allowed a crack to appear in her defences the whole structure would collapse. She had to stay strong.

"'Tis barbarous to treat you like this. I was going to ask to be relieved of duty yesterday, because I can't bear to see you suffer, but –"

"No!" she interrupted. "Please don't do that. You're helping me more than you know. It would be a lot worse without you."

"That's what I thought. So I didn't ask. But it pains me to see you hurting so."

"Many people are treated a lot worse, Ned. I'm a traitor, as they see it."

"Why don't you tell them what you know? I'm sure they'd let you go if you did."

"If you were me, Ned, would you betray the people you loved more than anything, knowing they'd be killed if you did?"

He let her down again, very gently, and she took a deep breath, bracing for the pain, which came as soon as her legs took her weight again.

"No," he said, standing back. "I wouldn't. But others are turning evidence, and they're men, and made to stand pain. No one would blame you, I'm sure."

"I would blame myself, and that's what matters to me."

"You're very brave, Beth, traitor or no."

He went over to the hook where the rope was secured and untied it. Then he played out a few inches of the rope, releasing a little of the pressure on her arms and allowing her to bend her legs slightly.

"Thank you," she said.

"I'm sorry I can't do more. If the sergeant comes in and says anything, I can tell him the rope must have stretched and I hadn't noticed. But if I loosen it any more…"

"You'll be flogged and I'll be in a much worse position, and neither of us wants that," she finished for him. "I understand. Don't feel guilty, Ned."

He sighed, corked the flask, moved to the corner, and the long day began.

Beth was endeavouring to take her mind off the pain she was in by reciting poetry to herself. Currently she was trying to remember a poem by Dryden, which she had learned at her father's knee, but which now was all too appropriate:

> *Feed a flame within, which so torments me*
> *That it both pains my heart, and yet contains me:*
> *'Tis such a pleasing smart, and I so love it,*
> *That I had rather die than once remove it.*

*Yet he, for whom I grieve, shall never know it;*
*My tongue does not betray, nor my eyes show it.*
*Not a sigh, nor a tear, my pain discloses,*
*But they fall silently, like rain on roses.*

No, that wasn't quite right… what was it? She frowned, trying to remember.

*But they fall silently, like dew on roses.* That was it! She smiled to herself.

The door opened, and Richard walked in.

Ned instantly shot to attention, and saluted. Richard didn't even favour him with a glance; instead he looked at his sister and laughed, a sound of pure delight. Beth could not remember the last time she had heard Richard laugh, and would have given a great deal never to hear him again. A wave of despair washed over her; and then she summoned every ounce of strength she possessed, lifted her head and looked him straight in the eye.

"Good morning, Elizabeth," he said brightly. "Prison life doesn't suit you, it seems. You have let yourself go."

"Whereas the military life clearly does suit you, Richard," she replied coolly. "You have put on weight. If you are not careful you will soon have jowls, like Edward."

It was not true. He looked in the prime of health and fitness, but the barb hit home and he frowned. He turned and looked at Ned, who was still standing to attention.

"Out," he said curtly, gesturing to the open door with his head.

"I have been ordered to stand watch, sir, until six of the clock. I cannot desert my post," Ned replied stiffly.

Richard looked at him and the young man flinched, but didn't move.

"And who ordered you?" he said.

"My sergeant, sir,"

"Well, Private…"

"Miller, sir," Ned supplied.

"Well, Private Miller, the Duke of Newcastle has ordered *me* to have a chat with my sister. And *I* am ordering you to get out. Is that clear? If your sergeant has anything to say about that, he can come to me."

Ned blushed, clearly aware that this man was a captain, but

also aware that if he *was* her brother, as he said, he didn't seem to have a congenial relationship with her.

"I…" he began.

"I will be alright, Private Miller," Beth said. "Do as my brother says."

Ned glanced from her to Richard, undecided.

Richard had had enough. He grabbed the young soldier by the shoulder, turned him toward the door and propelled him out of it with such force that Ned hit the wall on the other side of the corridor. Then he slammed the door closed and turned back to his sister.

"So, Newcastle has sent you, has he?" she said. "Well, you can save yourself some time. Tell him I have nothing to say, either to him or to you."

Richard smiled again, and walked over to stand in front of her.

"I don't have anything else to do with the rest of my morning," he said pleasantly. "And I've been looking forward to our chat all night. It would be a shame to cut it short. His Grace has sent me to try to make you see sense. He seems to think a little brotherly persuasion might make you change your mind. What do you say?"

"And did you tell His Grace what your idea of brotherly persuasion is?" she asked.

Richard gritted his teeth.

"You mean to hold that one mistake against me for the rest of my life," he snarled.

"Not at all," she replied calmly. "I am sure you've done far worse than that." Just in time she stopped herself from mentioning Martha and Ann. It was a small thing, revealing that she knew about them, but it was small things that betrayed people. "You enjoy brutalising people, don't you? Particularly when they can't hit back."

His expression told her she'd hit home and she braced herself, preparing for his reaction, but to her surprise, instead of hitting her he glanced at the door and then leaned in to her until his face was close to her ear.

"Where is it?" he said urgently in a low voice.

"Where is what?" she asked, genuinely puzzled.

"The money," he said. "I went to see Cox, and he told me you'd withdrawn it all. Tell me where it is and I'll get it, put it somewhere safe. Then you can tell Cumberland any old rot about Sir Anthony. He's soft on you, you know that. He'll believe you and no doubt he'll let you go. There's a five thousand pound reward for information. You could live reasonably for years on that. We'll both be rich."

She stared at him in shock. Had he forgotten that he was already rich? His marriage to Anne Redburn had left him immensely wealthy. She had expected him to try to beat her to obtain information, not to attempt to talk her into it.

"We can even split the dowry, if you like," he added, misunderstanding her silence. "What do you say? You must see that it makes sense. Anthony never gave a damn about you, you know. He only married you to cover up the fact that he prefers boys. He's probably in France now, where they don't give a damn if you fuck boys or not."

To his surprise, she laughed, a genuine laugh of true amusement.

"You must be mad if you think I'd trust you for one second with that money," she said.

"It belongs to me by right," he said sullenly. "You know father would have changed his will if he'd had time."

"You're right, he would," she agreed.

"Well then, you must see –"

"He would have changed it to make sure that when he died he didn't put me in the position of being dependent on you in any way at all. If he'd known that his will would make me have to choose between marrying someone I despised or being swived by my own brother, he'd turn in his grave."

His hand shot out and closed round her throat, squeezing.

"You fucking bitch," he spat. "You tell me where the money is, and where that traitorous bastard's hiding, or I'll cut you in pieces."

She made a rasping sound in her throat, and he eased the pressure a little.

"If you're so desperate to know where the money is, I'll tell you," she croaked. She tried to speak again, but coughed instead.

Richard went to the corner and picking up the flask, took the stopper out and held it to her lips. She drank and swallowed, then cleared her throat.

"Where is it?" he asked eagerly.

"Some of it's in the bellies of the army," she said. "Some of it's probably rusting away on Drumossie Moor. And some of it was used to skewer redcoats like you. And some of it will probably be hidden, though I don't know where, waiting for the next rising."

"What?" he said, unable to believe what she was telling him.

"It's gone, Richard. But don't worry, every penny was well spent."

"I don't believe you," he said, his colour rising.

"That's up to you. But it's true. Father might not have approved of the cause, but I'm sure he'd rather I spent the money on that than let you have it. You were always a great disappointment to him, Richard. He just hoped you'd grow up one day. But you never have, have you? You'll always be that spoilt brat crying for his mummy."

She was goading him, looking for the muscle ticking in his cheek which would tell her he was losing control. She needed him to lose control, because when he did he would kill her, which was what she wanted.

Even so she was unprepared for the blow when it came. She saw his fingers curl and expected him to hit her in the face, but instead he drove his fist into her stomach with such force that he lifted her off the ground. Her legs collapsed under her as her body automatically tried to double over against the pain, and all her weight was taken on her shoulders, which rotated backwards, tearing the tendons in the process.

The pain was more excruciating than anything she had ever known, or imagined possible. She tried to scream, but the blow had driven all the air from her lungs and all that came out was a guttural moan.

He stepped back, watching with satisfaction as she fought for breath, her face contorted with agony, tears streaming down her cheeks. Finally she managed to drag in a sip of air, then another. And then by a superhuman effort she got her feet under her and stood again.

"Tell me who he is," Richard said. He had believed her about the money, then. "What does he look like? You must have seen him without the paint. You must know his name. Who is he?"

Chest heaving, she glared at him.

"When you go back to Newcastle," she said, her voice hoarse as she fought the pain, "please thank him for his consideration in sending you here. It has fortified me more than anything else could have done. If I was in any danger of forgetting how much I hated the murdering redcoat bastards Cumberland has the nerve to call an army, you have reminded me. Tell the duke he will rot in hell before I ever say anything he will want to hear."

He moved forward and kicked her in the shin, smiling as her legs gave way and her whole body weight was taken by her arms. This time she did scream, and he laughed.

"Who is he?" he said again.

She stood again and looked at him, her blue eyes dark with hatred and pain.

"Burn in hell, Richard," she said.

"I probably will," he agreed pleasantly. "But between now and then, I intend to enjoy myself." He looked at the rope binding her arms and then up at the beam. Then he walked over to the hook in the wall and untied the rope. The release of pressure was so sudden and unexpected that she almost fell forward on her face, but managed to drop to her knees and save herself.

"You know, they're not doing this right," he said conversationally, wrapping the end of the rope around his fist. "It's called the strappado. You should know about it, it was a favourite of the Inquisition. They were Catholics too, like you. Here, let me show you."

He pulled hard on the rope, lifting her until her feet were completely off the ground. Her shoulders rotated and she felt one of them pop as it dislocated, and she screamed, a long, ear-rending cry of pure agony, not caring whether he was getting pleasure from it or not. No one could bear this level of pain silently.

He secured the rope again and then walked back to stand in front of her, watching as her screams died to moans. Her face and neck were rigid with pain, her eyes closed tight. He reached up and gripped her chin hard.

"Look at me," he commanded.

She opened her eyes and looked at him. His expression was flat and hard, but his eyes were dancing with arousal. She glanced down and saw the unmistakable bulge in his breeches, and felt the bile rise in her throat. As brutal as he'd been the night he'd tried to rape her, he had still attempted to restrain himself at first, and had been remorseful later.

But the man standing in front of her now no longer had the capacity for remorse, or for any decent human emotions at all. He probably would kill her, given time, if Newcastle had told him he could; but he was no longer the brother she had known, who could be goaded into losing control and killing her quickly. In spite of herself a shiver of fear ran through her, and recognising it, he smiled.

"Good. We're getting somewhere," he said. "Because this is only the first stage. There are two more variations of the strappado that I'd be delighted to show you, and then I'm sure I can think of a few more. I don't think it'll come to that, though, do you?"

He paused, obviously expecting her to plead with him to stop. She remained silent.

"Tell me his name, his real name," he said, "and I'll let you down and call the surgeon to you."

She opened her mouth to speak, but her throat had been strained with the screaming, and she whispered something he couldn't hear. She closed her mouth again and convulsed. He stepped in closer, his face right under hers now, looking up at her.

"What did you say?" he asked.

Her mouth twisted in the rictus of a grin, and then she opened it and released a stream of foul-smelling yellow bile, which hit him in the face and splashed onto his immaculate uniform.

He jumped back, cursing, and she laughed derisively. Then he punched her in the stomach again, twice. The first blow was agonising, and her legs jerked upwards automatically. But when he hit her the second time she felt the impact, but strangely no pain. She knew he was shouting something at her, yet his voice seemed to be coming from a very long way away, and it was joined a moment later by another voice.

Ned.

She tried to speak, to tell him that she was alright, that this was what she wanted, to die, and that he should stay outside, but then the blackness took her, and she sank willingly into it.

\*\*\*

## Whitehall

The Duke of Newcastle was sitting in his office trying to deal with some of the mass of paperwork he had to face every day. He had thought that after the rebellion was over he would have less to do; but dealing with countless hundreds of prisoners, trying to discover who might turn evidence, arranging for witnesses to be brought from the far corners of the country to testify against those going to trial, and arranging transportation to the Colonies for those who were not was a time-consuming business.

He sat back, rubbed the bridge of his nose with two fingers and sighed. It was going to be a long day.

A tentative knock came on the door, and then it opened and Benjamin's head popped through.

"You have a visitor, Your Grace," Benjamin said.

Newcastle frowned.

"Does he have an appointment?" he asked.

"No, Your Grace, but it's the keeper of Newgate and he says he has information about a prisoner you will want to hear."

Newcastle would have given a great deal never to hear about any prisoner again, ever, but there was a slim chance it might be important.

"Show him in. Five minutes only," he said.

The keeper came in and stood by the door, nervously turning his hat round and round in his hands.

"Well, Mr Jones, what information have you got that you think worth disturbing me for?" Newcastle said, his head still bent over a paper, using a tone that rendered the keeper even more nervous, if that were possible.

"I…it's about Miss Cunningham, Your Grace," Mr Jones stammered.

Newcastle stopped reading and looked up.

"What about Miss Cunningham?"

"Well, Your Grace, one of the women sharing her cell, Isobel Henderson, she comes to me this morning, and she says that she feels really bad, but that she thinks I ought to know something important about –"

"For God's sake, man, out with it!"

"Miss Cunningham's pregnant, Your Grace," the keeper said.

"What? Has she had relations with another prisoner?"

"No, Your Grace. It seems she must have been with child since before she was captured. She didn't know the signs to look for, so she didn't know herself, it seems. When Isobel told her that she was sure, Miss Cunningham checked for herself, and then she got very upset and told her not to say anything about it and that it didn't make any difference."

Of course it made a difference! If it was true.

"Is this Isobel woman sure about this?" Newcastle asked.

"Yes, very sure. She feels bad about breaking her promise, but said she's worried about Miss Cunningham, especially when she didn't come back to the cell. She said she can't have the death of a baby on her hands if Miss Cunningham's hung, Your Grace, and thought telling me was the only thing she could do."

Newcastle looked at the clock. Eleven fifteen. The captain would have just arrived in her cell, and would no doubt spend some time talking to her before he began his more physical persuasion. It would take the keeper about twenty minutes to return. He would be back before any real damage had been done.

If this was true, it could change everything. He tapped his quill on the desk thoughtfully for a moment, then came to a decision.

"Go back to the prison, Mr Jones. Tell the sergeant to allow Miss Cunningham to sit down. Feed her but keep her on her own for now with a guard. And then bring this Henderson woman to me. I want to speak to her myself. Go, man! Quickly!"

Mr Jones jumped, sketched a clumsy bow and then fled.

Newcastle put the quill down on the table. It was extremely clear that however badly this Anthony traitor had treated Miss Cunningham, she still believed herself in love with him. Surely then, once she had come to terms with her pregnancy she would do anything to keep his child? If she could be brought to believe her lover was almost certainly dead, she would undoubtedly realise that it was foolish to conceal the identity of a dead man and sacrifice her unborn baby in order to do so. He would offer her a complete pardon and a small income for her and the child, if she told what she knew. Women were notoriously protective of their babies – it was their natural instinct to be so.

He would speak to this Henderson woman, and then he would have Miss Cunningham examined to make sure she was not merely trying to cheat the gallows with a false claim. If the child had been conceived in April, then it would surely be easy to determine if it was a true pregnancy or not.

He smiled. This was the best news he had heard all week. And the very best chance to get her to reveal what she knew about Sir Anthony.

\* \* \*

When she came round, she was lying on the stone floor. Ned had taken off his jacket and had folded it up to form a makeshift pillow, and was sitting next to her, his young face deeply troubled. She tried to lift her head to see if Richard was still there, but the resulting pain made her cry out.

Ned was instantly alert.

"Don't try to move, Miss. You're hurt."

She didn't need him to tell her that. She couldn't remember ever being in this much pain before.

"Richard…" she mumbled.

"The captain's gone. He won't be coming back while I'm here, I promise you, even if I'm court-martialled for it. It ain't right to treat anyone like what he did you, no matter what."

"I heard you come in, before I fainted. I'm sorry," she said. "I didn't want you to get into trouble."

"After he threw me out, I was so angry I went outside for a bit to calm down," he said. "I wish I hadn't. I should have stayed right outside the door. If I'd know what he was going to do, I never would have left you at all."

"I'm glad you did leave. Richard's a bad enemy to have."

"When I came back I opened the grille very carefully, just to see if you was all right, and when I saw…" He stopped and ran his hand over his face, "…I came straight in and told him to stop. He told me to f…a bad word, and that the duke had authorised him to interrogate you, and I said that I couldn't believe he meant for him to kill you. I thought you was dead, Miss, I did. And he laughed at me and said you was just pretending! He ain't no human. He's a devil."

"He's not the only one, Ned. If you stay in the army, no doubt you'll meet others like him. And others like you, too. Nathan…" She stopped, aware that her tongue was running away with her. Ned was older than Nathan had been. Fifteen and mortally wounded, but he'd tried to protect her from the wild Highlanders when he'd seen them approaching her. But Alex and Duncan had been no danger to the young redcoat. Richard was most definitely a danger to Ned.

"Did you make him leave?" she asked. If he had, his life would not be worth living.

"No, Miss. I was going to, but then the sergeant came in and said the duke had ordered you to be allowed to rest. The sergeant's a harsh man, but even he was horrified when he saw you hanging there like that. It was him what told the captain to leave. He didn't want to, though. Said he's…never mind."

*Said he's coming back.* She knew Richard. He'd believed her when she told him she'd given her dowry to Prince Charles. He would never forgive her for that. He didn't need the money any more; it was the principle of the thing. He wanted the dowry as revenge for their father rejecting him. That was why she'd baited him, hoping he'd be infuriated enough to kill her. She'd underestimated how much he'd changed. But then he'd underestimated her too, underestimated her hatred of him, hadn't believed her capable of lying to him, or of withstanding such pain. She had told him one truth, though; Newcastle could rot in hell before she'd tell him anything. And so could her brother.

"Why are they letting me rest, Ned?" she asked.

"I don't know. The sergeant said you can eat, too. He's sent for some soup for you. Your legs is all swelled up, but I think they might be alright if you can rest for a bit. But the keeper's trying to see if he can get a surgeon to come, because your shoulder is out and it needs to be put back."

The door opened and Mr Jones entered, bearing a bowl of hot soup and some bread.

"Are you alright, Miss Cunningham?" he asked worriedly.

What the hell was going on? Why were they all suddenly so worried about her?

"Private Miller tells me my shoulder is out," she said. "You said the surgeon won't come here, didn't you?"

"He might if the Duke of Newcastle's ordered it," the keeper said. He put the bowl down on the floor.

"Has the Duke of Newcastle ordered it?" she asked. If he had, then that meant they were not just letting her rest to give her a false sense of security before starting again, but that something important had happened. Something concerning Alex. It had to be. Why else would they stop?

"No, he hasn't," the keeper said, to her immense relief. "But I think he would if he knew the state you're in. So I've taken it on myself to fetch him."

"That's kind of you, Mr Jones."

"Not at all," he said, as though she'd insulted him. "You can pay me back the next time you get to wear a fancy dress."

"I think that may be a long time coming," she replied.

He stood up.

"I'll take my chance," he said. "I'll go for him now." He left the room, closing the door behind him.

The soup smelt wonderful. Her stomach rumbled and then contracted painfully, making her gasp. Ned picked up the bowl.

"I'll have to feed you, Miss," he said.

"I can't eat lying down," Beth said. "Help me to sit up."

He looked at her doubtfully.

"That's going to hurt a lot. Your arm's all twisted."

"I haven't eaten for three days," she said practically. "My stomach's hurting more than my arm at the moment. I need food. Let's go slowly." Another cramp hit her and she moaned, then took a couple of deep breaths.

"Now," she said, and very gently he lifted her upper body off the floor, propping her against the wall. The pain was excruciating, but she managed by a sheer effort of will not to faint. Her arms hung uselessly, one by her side, her hand resting in her lap, the other one twisted behind her. She tried to move the fingers of the hand resting in her lap, and failed.

"I think you will have to help me, after all," she said.

He knelt in front of her and fed her, slowly and with great tenderness.

"When you've finished, I'm going to see if I can get you a blanket," he said, noticing that she was shivering.

"I'm not cold," she said. Her teeth chattered and they both laughed. She realised that she must be cold, although she really didn't feel it. She did feel light-headed though, but that would be normal, with the pain and lack of food.

It was while she was swallowing the last mouthful of bread that she suddenly felt her bladder void itself, soaking her dress at the back.

"Oh God, I'm sorry," she said, mortified. The dancing lights were back, swimming at the edge of her vision.

"What's wrong?" Ned asked.

"I think I've just pissed myself," she said bluntly, and then started to slide sideways down the wall.

Ned caught her, eased her back down to a lying position, then looked at her, suddenly alarmed. All the colour had drained from her face; even her lips were white. Gently he tapped her cheek, but got no response. She'd fainted again. He decided to take the opportunity to move her into a more comfortable position, while she was unlikely to feel the pain. In fact he would take her out of the cell altogether. In the corridor there was a bench that the soldiers and turnkeys sat on, and a brazier to take the chill from the air. He would take her there and if anyone told him off for it, they could go to hell.

He opened the door, then went back and lifted her up carefully. She weighed almost nothing. Her dress at the back was sodden. He could feel the urine soaking into his shirt, and grimaced. He walked down the corridor and very gently laid her down on the bench. Now he would light the brazier, and at least he wouldn't have to leave her to get a blanket. She would soon warm up.

He took his hands from under her, settling his folded coat back under her head. Then he looked at his soaked shirt sleeve and hand, which were bright red.

"Oh fucking hell," he breathed, and forgetting he wasn't supposed to leave her, he stood up and tore down the corridor, shouting for the sergeant as he ran.

* * *

Richard was not happy. How dare that puppy charge in and tell him to stop, just when he was getting started? He'd waited years for this moment, and had been enjoying himself immensely. If the sergeant hadn't come in and told him that Newcastle himself had ordered him to stop, he'd have beaten the young private to a pulp for his insubordination to a superior officer.

And it had been a learning experience too. He'd heard about the strappado, of course; he had an interest in such things, but he'd never actually tried it out on anyone. It would have been really interesting to progress to the next stage, of jerking her up and down on the rope. Judging by the agony she'd been in, he doubted she'd have survived that without giving in and begging him to stop.

Although she was incredibly stubborn. But if she'd held out after that, he could have tried the third stage. He didn't have a weight to tie to her feet, but pulling on her legs would have had the same effect. In truth, in view of the fact that the bitch had vomited on him, he'd intended to try that even if she *had* given in.

And he'd kept to Newcastle's instructions not to mark her. True, her shoulder had been pulled out of joint, but putting it back in place, very slowly, would have just added to the pleasure.

What the hell was Newcastle up to, stopping him like that? He was absolutely sure that before the day was out he would have known everything there was to know about Sir Anthony Peters. It was infuriating.

Now he would have to start again, and the element of surprise would be lost. But on the other hand, now she knew how agonising the strappado was, the mere anticipation of it might drive her to divulge the information he wanted.

And then he would continue anyway, just to watch the traitorous bitch scream.

God, he needed a woman. He was as hard as a rock. Even riding at a slow walk was uncomfortable. He would visit a whore house on his way home.

No. Why pay when you could get it for free? His wife would be alone when he got in. He had no doubt that she would have got rid of those titled lunatics by now. She wouldn't disobey him. He could have the whole evening alone with her, doing whatever he wanted.

True, Anne would be a poor substitute for Beth. She would disintegrate before he even touched her. But it was better than nothing. And whatever he did, short of murder, he'd be safe from the law. A man could not be prosecuted for raping his wife. And she wouldn't dare to make a complaint, anyway.

When he got home, he ran up the steps and hammered on the door. It was opened by the same footman as yesterday, except this time he did not have a supercilious expression on his face, nor a horrified one. This time he looked positively radiant on seeing the young captain at the door. He bowed, and Richard walked past him into the hall.

"Tell my wife I wish to see her immediately in the library," Richard said brusquely.

The footman smiled.

"I am afraid Lady Redburn is not at home, sir."

Richard halted his progress up the corridor.

"Mrs Cunningham, you fool," he snarled. "Where is she?"

"Gone, sir. As I intend to be, this very minute. My resignation is on the drawing-room table with the others."

"What others?"

"The other servants, sir. They have all left. I merely waited to admit you to the house, as I knew you did not have a key, and there is no one else here."

"How considerate," Richard said sarcastically. "Where has my wife gone?"

"I believe she has left you a note, sir. On the table. With the others."

This was unbelievable! Was it some sort of joke?

"Are you insane?" Richard said. "If you leave now, I will ensure that neither you nor any of the other servants ever work again."

The footman nodded.

"I am sure you would if you could, sir. But we have all found employment elsewhere, this very day. Good day to you, Captain Cunningham."

The footman walked out of the door, closing it gently behind him, leaving Richard standing in the hall, alone.

# CHAPTER THIRTEEN

**Loch Lomond, October 1746**

It was a dry day, the first one for over a week, and possibly one of the last there would be for some time. Although it was sunny, the air was crisp and there had been a heavy frost that morning. It would not be long now before the snow came. Because the weather was dry a small fire burned outside the well-hidden cave entrance in the mountainside. Over it was suspended an iron pot from which came the appetising smell of rabbit stew.

Around the fire ten men were sitting on a variety of stones placed there for that purpose. All but one were wearing the great kilt or *feileadh mhor*, in various muted shades of brown, green and purple tartan, in direct flagrance of the Dress Act passed by Lord Chancellor Hardwicke some two months previously, which banned the wearing not only of the kilt, but of any tartan material at all. Although if any of them were to be caught, the wearing of the kilt would be the least of their transgressions against His Majesty King George's government.

At present the formidable group of muscular, heavily-armed warriors were in fact in the process of planning their latest illegal activity, and to this end one of them was drawing a map on the ground with a stick while the others looked on, engrossed.

"So I was thinking," commented the cartographer, indicating a wavy line which represented the river, "that if we cross here in the dead of night we'll catch them by surprise, because they dinna think that anyone can ford the river except by the bridge, so they're no' guarding it."

"Can we ford it?" the sole observer of the Dress Act, if of no other law, asked.

"Aye, it's nobbut a wee stream, no more than three feet deep," Angus replied.

"In the summer. It's October now," Alex pointed out.

"Maybe four feet, then," Angus amended. "A bath'll wash the dust of marching off, and prepare us for the fun."

"And on the way back a bath'll wash the blood off, and prepare us for the stroll home," Kenneth added, to cheers.

Graeme looked doubtfully at the wavy line. In the last months he'd battled his way up and down many a 'wee hummock' and had been nearly drowned in the raging torrent of several 'wee streams'.

"I'll carry ye, laddie, if ye're feart to get your fine troosers wet," Kenneth offered, casting an eye over Graeme's tattered breeches and torn hose. Everyone laughed.

"Piss off," Graeme said good-naturedly. "So, when we've waded across the 'wee stream', how many redcoats will we be facing?"

"I counted twenty," Angus said. "They post two sentries, here and here," he indicated two spots on the map. "If we take them out quietly, the rest of them will still be asleep. They'll be supping in hell before they ken we're there." He sat back, and everyone looked to Alex to make the decision. He continued to look at the map as he worked out the logistics of the proposed attack.

There was a short silence, during which Allan stirred the stew and added a few sticks to the fire.

"Aye," Alex said at length. "It sounds feasible, providing we can cross the river. Let's get there first. If it's four feet like ye say, we can wade across in the night and attack directly. If the water's higher than we're expecting, we can always cross a wee bit further up, and take a rest to get our breath back first."

Eight men cheered and one groaned.

"If I drown, I'm going to come back and haunt you for eternity," Graeme threatened Angus, who laughed before looking over the older man's shoulder to the brow of the hill, over which a young woman had appeared and was making her way towards them. Angus waved her over and patted the stone next to him.

"Sit down, *a graidh*," he said. "Are ye wanting some stew? It's nearly ready."

Morag ignored his offer and remained standing.

"I'm wanting a word with ye, Angus MacGregor," she said.

Angus smiled. "Have some food first," he suggested. "We've been planning the next raid. We'll be heading off tomorrow, and –"

"Now," she interrupted.

Angus's smile faded, and the other men all looked at each other warily.

"What's amiss?" he asked.

"Ye dinna ken?" she said, glaring at him. His expression clearly said that he didn't. "I promised to wait for you till I was sixteen, and you promised to marry me before ye were twenty-two." Angus opened his mouth to protest, and she held her hand up. "I ken well why ye didna marry me then, but it's over six months since Culloden and I've waited long enough. I want ye to set a date, and soon."

As one, nine of the formidable warriors, recognising a foe that was beyond any of them, stood and found other things to do in the clearing. Angus, left to it, tried a conciliatory smile, which failed to penetrate Morag's set expression. He sighed.

"Sit down," he said, patting the stone next to him. She did as he asked, but took a seat opposite him, out of arm's reach. She knew him well, and was not going to allow him to persuade her out of her viewpoint by means of an embrace.

"Morag, ye canna possibly want to marry me now, with things the way they are," he said. "Ye've been awfu' patient, but we need to wait a while longer, till things settle down."

She snorted derisively.

"Settle down?" she said. "Things will never settle down for the MacGregors. We've been outlaws for over a hundred years."

"Well, aye," Angus responded, acknowledging the truth of this. "But this is different. I've sworn a blood oath tae Maggie, and I canna go back on that."

"I'm no' asking ye to break your promise to Maggie," she countered. "I'm asking ye to keep your promise to me. Or do I mean less to you than she did?"

"Of course not!" Angus exclaimed.

"Well, then."

"But a blood oath's different, as ye ken, *mo chridhe*. I canna marry you until I've fulfilled the oath. I've tae kill –"

"Two hundred redcoats. I remember. How many is it up to now?"

"Fifteen," he answered, "myself, but we've killt near a hundred between us all."

She nodded.

"So, at this rate I'll have tae wait another five years at least for ye to fulfil your oath. I've already waited two. If ye think I'm waiting seven years for ye, Angus, ye've another think coming. We're getting married and there's an end of it. Being wed'll no' stop ye killing the redcoats."

Angus leaned forward in an attempt to get hold of her and pull her onto his knee, but she scuttled back out of reach. He dropped his arms and looked at her pleadingly instead.

"I canna marry ye yet," he said. "What sort of man would I be to marry ye now, when I could be killed at any time? I'll no' leave ye a widow."

"I'd rather be a widow than a spinster for the rest of my life," she said. "I'll no' wait forever for ye, even if ye are the chieftain's brother."

"I'm no' asking ye to," Angus replied, his colour rising. In the distance he could see the other men, all with their backs studiously turned to him. Their stance told him that the acoustics of the saucer-shaped depression they were in ensured that they could hear every word that was being said.

Morag stared at him, her blue eyes wide with shock.

"Are ye telling me ye dinna love me any more? That ye want me to look for another man?" she asked.

"Of course I'm no' wanting ye to look for another man!" he shouted, making her jump. The mere thought that she might made his heart burn with jealousy. He ignored the message his emotions were telling him, and lowering his voice, sought to make her see reason.

"Morag, I love you, of course I do. But I canna just abandon my vow and come down to live in the village with you. Ye need to be patient a while longer, that's all."

"That's fine. Ye dinna need to live in the village. I'm quite happy to move up to the cave. At least the roof doesna leak like Pa's does."

Angus stared at her incredulously.

"Are ye havering, woman? Ye canna come and live here, wi' ten men! It isna fitting!"

"I'll be safer up here than in the village, if the redcoats come," she reasoned. "And I can take care of you all, wash your clothes and suchlike."

"If the redcoats come ye'll all be up here. That's different to ye being alone wi' ten men."

"I've known most of those men since I was a wee bairn," she replied scornfully. "There's no' a one of them that'd harm a hair of me. Or are ye saying yon Sasannach Graeme's a ravisher of women?"

"No, of course he isna. I trust him with my life."

"Well, then," she said simply.

Angus scrubbed his hand through his hair in exact imitation of his brother. He couldn't marry her. In battle as in everything else, he was a risk taker. It was who he was. Although he thought about her constantly when he was at home, he could put her from his mind when he was out raiding. If they were married he would be responsible for her in every way and any risks he took would impact on her. And they would share a bed, and he knew he would want to be with her every minute of the day. She would be a distraction, even when he was away. And ambushing redcoats was not like reiving your neighbours' cattle; it was far more dangerous. They all knew that. It was why Alex had insisted the married men with families stay at home.

If he got married he would have to stay at home, Alex would insist on it, and if he did then he would not be able to fulfil his oath, and he would no longer be a man. He couldn't tell the young woman sitting opposite him, face eager, waiting for his answer, that he needed to be able to put her from his mind. He searched for another delaying tactic.

"We canna be married yet awhile anyway," he said finally. "There are no priests left to marry us. They're all in hiding."

"We can handfast," she shot back immediately. "The Church willna hold it against us, given the circumstances."

"No. We've to be married properly, or no' at all," he said primly. To the best of his knowledge there were no priests to be had for a hundred miles. They were all in prison, or escaped to France, or so deep in hiding that no one knew where they were.

"Is that your final word?" she asked.

"It is," he said firmly, clinging to his moral point like a drowning man clinging to a straw.

She sat for a minute looking down, as though perusing the map he'd drawn earlier. He was just about to start explaining it to her when she stood.

"Ye swear ye're not trying to put me off because ye dinna love me any more?" she asked, looking down at him.

"Morag, I swear to ye, I love ye more than anyone," he said fiercely, his slate-blue eyes meeting hers. "I've loved ye since we were bairns, and I always will. I'll marry ye, as soon as I can."

She stared at him for a long moment, then seemed to come to a decision.

"Well, there's no more to be said, then," she announced, and ignoring his outstretched arms she turned away and started to walk back down to the village.

"Oh, I almost forgot what I came to tell ye," she called back from the edge of the dip. "Will ye all be back from your raid by a week Friday?"

"Aye, we should be," Angus said. The other men, finding their voices again now the danger was past, agreed. Ten days was more than enough time.

"Good. Peigi's found out she's having another bairn, and we thought to have a wee party. Celebrate that and your successful raid before the snows come and we canna dance outside."

"The raid hasna been successful yet," Dougal pointed out. "We dinna leave till tomorrow."

"Ye'd better make sure it is, then," Morag said. "For we're needing a wee dance to lift our spirits. It's been a hard year."

Angus watched her until she was out of sight, and then he watched some more, a variety of expressions crossing his face. The other men came back and started sharing the stew out into bowls.

"Thank ye kindly for supporting me in my time of need," Angus said sarcastically, accepting a bowl from Allan. "You could have forbidden us to marry, *mo bhràthair*. You're the chieftain."

Alex held his hands up.

"I make a point of never fighting a battle I ken I canna win," he said. "Anyway, I gave ye the same support ye gave me when I tried to get Beth to leave me after she found out I wasna Sir Anthony."

"That was different," Angus retorted, then looked across and caught the look of raw anguish on his brother's face. Alex had spoken lightly, but was clearly now remembering what her refusal to leave had cost her. Had cost both of them. Both brothers fell silent.

"Ye were a wee bit hard on the lassie, though," Kenneth said, clearly trying to divert them from their thoughts. "It's clear she loves ye, though I canna for the life of me think why. And the Church acknowledges handfasting, even in peacetime."

"Aye, I ken that. But what else could I do? I canna offer her any kind of life while I'm away most of the time killing redcoats. And what if I get her wi' child, and then I'm killt? Ye heard her, she wouldna take no for an answer."

"She's awfu' thrawn, always has been," Hamish commented.

"It's one of the things ye love about her though," Alex said, rousing himself with an effort from his dark thoughts.

"It is," Angus acknowledged sadly. "But she'll be better off without me."

The others weren't so sure that was the case, but it wasn't for them to argue. It was his life, and he was old enough to make his own decisions.

And so was Morag.

\* \* \*

Four days later nine of the ten men returned in great high spirits. The ambush had gone exactly as planned. The river, to Graeme's relief, had indeed only been three feet deep when they crossed it, the two sentries had been dispatched silently by Dougal and his brother Hamish, and the remaining soldiers had, in the main, been killed before they had time to do more than register that there was something amiss outside their tents. It was one of the easiest attacks they'd made, and Angus was praised highly, as it had been his idea.

Alex had stood back and let his brother take command, and was happy with the result. It was now certain that John Murray of Broughton had turned king's evidence and that the information he had given about the Fraser chief would certainly condemn him, although in fairness even without Broughton's testimony there was no doubt that Lord Lovat would be executed. But he'd also named several of the English and Welsh Jacobite leaders, and was universally hated by every Jacobite from Prince Charles to the poorest clansman.

Alex knew it was only a matter of time before he would have to leave the country and let it be publicly known that he had, and then his clanspeople would have to take to the heather for a time if they were to have any chance of surviving the vengeance that would certainly be visited upon them. And in that case they would need a new chieftain, and Alex had decided that new chieftain would be Angus.

Duncan's death had changed them both, but Angus had loved Beth and Maggie fiercely, and his experience at the bothy, coupled with the fear that his older brother would also die, had forced him to take on an almost unbearable burden for which he had not been prepared. That he had done it, and done it well, was a credit to him. If he did have to take on the chieftainship full time, he would be able to cope.

Nevertheless Alex, who had so often worried about Angus's recklessness and carefree attitude in the past, now found himself missing that aspect of his brother, and hoped that one day circumstances would allow the old Angus to resurface.

As the raid had gone so well, and had taken less time than the men expected, Alex had decided to visit Ben Alder in the hopes of seeing the prince, Lochiel, and Cluny Macpherson and getting the latest news. He returned the day before the party and called an impromptu meeting of the clan to relay his news, which was important.

"Charles has finally sailed for France, and Lochiel with him," he said without preamble, once the clan was assembled. It was cold and raining, so they had retired into the cave to stay dry. Someone had lit a fire, and the light showed the shocked expressions of the MacGregors on hearing the news.

"That's good news, then?" Janet asked. Some of them had hoped Charles would winter in the Highlands, and lead a new campaign in the spring.

"No' for the Camerons," said Kenneth. "Who'll lead them now?"

"Lochiel couldna lead them anyway," Alex said. "They were in more danger of further reprisals while he was in Scotland than they'll be now it's known that he's gone. He kens that. He'd no' have left otherwise. It must have fair broke his heart to do so. So aye, it's good news. Charles will be safe from capture once he's in France, and hopefully he'll be able to persuade Louis to raise an army and invade again, maybe next spring."

"Ye dinna sound so sure of that," Iain said.

"Aye, well I hope I'm wrong, but Louis makes Lovat look positively honest and transparent. Charles will have his work cut out to persuade him that putting a Stuart back on the throne is in France's or more importantly, Louis' best interest."

"But while he's free there's always a chance of a restoration. And he's shown he can lead an army now. And we've shown that we'll rise for him," Angus said, to general approval.

"That's true. But the English in the main have shown they willna."

"It would still be in France's interest to have a Stuart king on the throne of Scotland and to break the union though," Kenneth pointed out.

"Christ, you mean that I'm going to have to move here permanently if I want to be ruled by James?" Graeme said gloomily.

"Aye, we'll pass a law that says ye have to wear the kilt to live here, just for you," Kenneth quipped.

"I'm not sure I wouldn't rather have German Geordie on the throne, in that case," Graeme said insincerely. "There are limits to what any man should have to endure, even for King James."

There was laughter and someone threw their bonnet at Graeme, which he caught deftly and placed on his head at a jaunty angle. Alex smiled and waited for the noise to die down before continuing.

"Cluny has said that he'll keep me informed by letter when he hears that the prince and Lochiel have arrived safely. He's got a big clan and they have ears everywhere, so his information's good. He's still living in his cave, and intends to stay there in readiness for the next rising. He's also promised to contact me urgently if he hears anything more about Broughton."

A brief silence greeted this final sentence, then Kenneth spat on the floor of the cave in disgust.

"The bastard," he said. "I dinna ken how he sleeps at night."

"I doubt he does," said Angus. "I canna understand why he turned on us, and him Charlie's secretary an' all, and a Jacobite to his bones."

"I'll break every one of his bones, an I ever see him again," Kenneth said.

"He was sick, and his wife's about to have a bairn," Alex pointed out. "We dinna ken what they threatened him with. And he didna surrender – he was taken."

"How can ye defend him, after what he's done?" Iain asked incredulously.

"I'm no' defending him. But the man's no' a soldier, remember. He's no' used to pain. And he loves his wife dearly. But no, he's still a traitor. What I canna understand is, they've had him for over three months now, and he kens that I was Sir Anthony, and yet he doesna appear to have tellt a soul." Following the news of Broughton's betrayal, the clan had lived in the cave for a few weeks, and then, with no sign of the expected redcoats, had posted guards and moved back down to the village.

"No' yet," Iain said. "But he may."

"Aye, he may," Alex agreed. "But hopefully no' till after the morrow, at least. Peigi, is the party for ye still going ahead?"

Peigi grinned, along with all the other women.

"Aye, it is, now ye're back. We were going to wait for you. Now all we need to do is pray the rain stops. We canna use the barn, for it's full of cattle."

"And if it doesna stop raining, we'll have the party in here," Morag said. "Angus said ye brought back more candles from the raid. We can light the place up like day if we have to."

"Would we no' be better to wait a day or so, if it's raining tomorrow?" Angus suggested.

"No," Janet put in firmly. "We've waited a long time for this party. It's happening, no matter the weather."

"Ten days isna a long –" Dougal began.

"It's happening," Peigi interrupted, to a chorus of agreement from the other women.

The men surrendered. It appeared the party was happening, and it would certainly be wiser to go along with it and dance in the rain than suffer the consequences of displeasing the womenfolk.

\* \* \*

To everyone's relief, although it rained all the following morning, in the afternoon the clouds blew over to reveal a blue sky and a somewhat watery sun. It seemed that they would not have to dance in the rain after all, although it promised to be somewhat soggy underfoot.

Food was prepared and set out in the chieftain's house, it being the largest dwelling in the village, with whisky and ale to drink. The fiddlers assembled in the clearing in the middle of the houses, and the party began.

A couple of hours into it, Alex had to admit that the womenfolk had had the right idea in suggesting it. The last months had been tense for all of them, with them never knowing when they'd have to flee their houses and take to the hills. It was true that they were used to danger, but the brutality of the so-called 'pacification' of the Highlands had surpassed anything they'd ever known.

He'd heard rumours that Inversnaid barracks, completely destroyed by the MacGregors last year, was about to be reactivated. If that was true the redcoats would have a base only a day's march away from them, and they would then be open to the same sort of treatment that had been meted out to the Camerons, Frasers and other clans loyal to the Stuarts.

He would not mention that until rumour became certainty though. Let them enjoy their party. He intended to try to enjoy it himself, and dismiss the memories of the last big party the MacGregors had had, which had been to celebrate his wedding. And the best way to do that was to get thoroughly drunk, he decided, reaching for the whisky.

He, along with most of the other men, but oddly none of the women, had made good headway in achieving inebriation when Morag walked into the clearing with a stranger in tow, a middle-aged man dressed in a dark *feileadh mhor*, but who appeared to carry no weapons. This was an unusual enough occurrence to cause those of the men still coherent to stop what they were doing and look at the newcomer, although the women seemed completely unperturbed, which Alex would have found strange had he not been concentrating all his attention on attempting to appear sober in order to greet the man as the chieftain should. He stood up somewhat unsteadily as Morag and her companion made their way towards him, but to his surprise she led the man straight past him and over to Angus.

"Angus, I want ye to meet a kinsman of Allan's, Fergus MacDonald," she said.

Angus, along with half the MacGregors, looked at Allan who, clearly recognising his kinsman, blushed furiously and suddenly found something of great interest in the patch of grass at his feet. Angus, forced to take on the role of the chieftain by Morag's disrespect of the proprieties, held his hand out to the stranger.

"Pleased to meet ye, Mr MacDonald," he said. "But really it's my brother ye should –"

"Mr MacDonald," Morag interrupted rudely, "more commonly goes by the title 'Father'. So if ye've no more objections, Angus Malcolm Socrates MacGregor, we can get straight on with the wedding."

There was a moment's silence while the women, who were clearly in on the conspiracy, grinned and Angus sat down suddenly as though he'd been hit on the head. Then Kenneth let out a great whoop of laughter.

"She's got ye, laddie," he called. "I'd marry her and quick if I were you, for if ye dinna, I'll take her to wife myself!" Several others laughed at that.

Angus looked helplessly at Alex, who held his hands up in a gesture of defeat.

"Morag," he said, "I canna marry ye now. I've a blood-"

"…oath to fulfil. Aye, I ken. Ye've tellt me often enough. Alex," she said, turning to face the chieftain, "when we marry, if I've nae objection, will ye allow your brother to carry on raiding wi' ye till he's had his fill of killing redcoats?"

"Aye, I will," Alex replied, recognising a lost cause when he saw one, "as long as you're aware of the danger that ye could end up a young widow wi' a bairn to look after."

"We're all aware of that danger," Peigi called out. "We're MacGregors. We take care of each other."

There was a cheer from everyone which Alex ignored, keeping his eyes fixed on Morag's, whose expression had now become serious, although her eyes were still sparkling. She walked over to her chieftain and took his large hand in her small, work-reddened one.

"I'm aware o' the danger," she said softly to him. "I'm no' the wee lassie I was two years ago when I nearly let Robbie have his way wi' me in the barn. I saw the way you and Beth were together, and I love your brother the same way she did you, and I believe he feels the same for me."

"Aye," Alex said, equally softly. "I believe ye've the right of it. But –"

"And I ken you're grieving something fierce, and that ye'll never be the same again. But at least ye had that time together. Married or no, I'll mourn him dreadful if it comes to it, but if we marry now, at least I'll have the memories to comfort me."

"They're no' always a comfort, lassie," he told her.

She nodded.

"Even so, better to have them than live the rest of your life regretting that ye didna grab the happiness when it was there for the taking." She looked up at him, her heart in her eyes, and he took her in his arms.

"I'll be proud to call ye my sister-in-law," he said. He gave her a quick, fierce hug, then let her go and smiled at her, although tears sparkled in his eyes.

"Well, then," he said, in a voice that carried round the clearing, "It seems we've a wedding to attend! Are ye wanting to go and dress in your finery?" he asked his white-faced brother, who had now managed to stand up again.

"No," Morag answered before he could open his mouth. "I've waited long enough already. I'd as soon get on with it, if it's all the same to you."

Father MacDonald looked from the glowing bride to the stunned groom.

"Before I conduct the ceremony," he said, "I have to ask if you are both willing and happy to be joined in matrimony this evening."

"I am," Morag answered immediately. She glanced across at Angus, who was staring at her, took in his pallor, and for the first time a shadow of anxiety clouded her face. He licked his lips nervously. Father MacDonald waited calmly for the young man's response. A profound silence settled on the clearing.

Angus closed his eyes, and breathed in deeply through his nose.

"Aye," he said. "I'm willing and happy to be joined in matrimony this evening. But dinna think ye can get your way in everything, lassie, for there'll be a reckoning later for what ye've done here today."

"I hope so," she shot back. "Ye'd better stay sober enough for the 'reckoning' tonight, for I've been waiting over two years for it, and I'll no' wait any longer!"

A great roar of laughter rose from the impromptu congregation, and Morag's father moved forward, all smiles, to hand responsibility for his daughter over to her husband-to-be, who was now regaining his colour and his general good humour with it, and had clearly accepted his fate.

After which everyone, male and female, got happily and spectacularly drunk, including, unfortunately, the bride herself who, by the time her new husband carried her over the threshold into her new home, was incapable of doing anything but sleep, with the result that the long-awaited 'reckoning' had to be delayed until the following morning.

\* \* \*

## London, November 1746

Sarah was concerned. For the last two hours a man had been loitering outside her shop. She couldn't see him well enough through the opaque green glass of her window panes to tell if he was someone she knew; all she could ascertain was that he was dressed in rags, was very thin and had dark hair. He might have been there for longer than two hours, but she had first noticed him at around two o'clock. At first she had taken him for a beggar, but he didn't appear to be accosting people as they passed by or as they came into her shop, which was odd.

She had also dismissed the possibility that he might be a robber of some sort; no one intending to commit theft would hang around outside one building so conspicuously for such a long time.

She got on with her work and tried to forget him, but as the clock struck four and she could still see him standing outside, she decided to confront him before it got dark and passers-by became scarce. If he seemed a decent sort, she'd give him a few coppers and send him on his way. She went to her counter and took out a few pennies, and her pistol, which she hid in her skirts, in case he *didn't* seem to be a decent sort. Better to be safe than sorry.

When she stepped out of the shop he had walked a few paces up the street and had his back to her. She observed him for a moment. He was indeed dressed in rags, but even in the dim light of the evening she could see that he had made an attempt to look respectable; although hatless, his brown hair was clean and tied neatly back with a scrap of ribbon, and while he wore no hose and his shoes were very worn, his breeches had been carefully patched, as had his tattered coat.

Then he turned and saw her, and jumped violently. She decided to take the initiative.

"Why have you been waiting outside my premises for over two hours?" she asked. "Are you begging?"

"No!" he exclaimed. "No, I works for my living, Miss. I'm a link man."

"A link man," she echoed. His face was in shadow, but there was something familiar about his voice. She didn't know any link men. "Wouldn't you be better waiting outside the theatre then? You won't get any custom here. And where's your torch?"

He looked at his empty hands as though expecting a torch to materialise there, and then at her.

"I'm…I'm not working tonight, Miss," he said.

Deeply suspicious now, she gripped the pistol, still concealed in her skirt.

"Well, I suggest you find something more entertaining to do with your free time than loitering outside my shop," she said firmly.

He took a step toward her, and she moved backwards into her doorway. She would run back into the shop and lock the door if he made a move on her. If he attempted to stop her she would show him she was armed. That should be enough to frighten him away.

He stopped and held his hand up in a conciliatory gesture.

"Miss Browne, you won't remember me, but I know you and

I need to tell you something awful bad, Miss. I've got to tell someone and I don't know no one else who was close to her. I don't mean you no harm, Miss, I swear it."

"Let me see your face," Sarah said, frowning. There was a candle burning in her window to show that she was open for business. Obligingly he turned his face towards it, and she saw his profile; young, snub nose, firm mouth. She gasped.

"I know who you are," she said. "You're Lord Edward's coachman."

"Not no more, Miss," he replied, and took another step forward.

"You keep away from me," she said, her voice rising. "You're the bastard who helped Lord Daniel when he kidnapped Beth. Tom, isn't it? You've got a cheek, coming here! If you think I'll feel sorry for you just because you're out of work, you're wrong. You deserve to rot in hell!"

"I didn't know Miss Elizabeth was so against him, Miss! Lord Daniel, he told me that she didn't want to marry Sir Anthony and that I was helping him rescue her. I haven't come here to beg off you, Miss. I – I owes Miss Elizabeth my life, I does. She made them let me go. I'd have hung, else."

"You should have done, for what you did!"

"I think of it every day, Miss. I told her I'd never forget what she done for me, and I haven't. That's why I'm here. I needs to speak to you about her, Miss, most desperate."

He looked at her, and now he was a little closer she could see that he was shaking, but whether from the cold or emotion, Sarah couldn't tell.

"What do you need to say?" she said. If he asked her to let him come in the shop now, she'd show him her pistol, call for the watch and have him arrested. She wasn't falling for that one.

He didn't. He glanced up and down the street to make sure no one was in earshot, and then he took one more step toward her so he was close enough that she could hear him if he spoke quietly, and started talking earnestly.

"Miss Elizabeth, she's in Newgate Prison, Miss, or she was a couple of months ago. And she…she was…she…" He choked, and swallowed hard.

"She was what?" Sarah asked.

"She was tortured, Miss, most terrible," he said, then burst into tears.

Sarah stood frozen with shock. No. It wasn't possible. How could Beth be in Newgate, and nobody know? Edwin and Caroline would have known…Anne would have known. Something like that could never be kept from London society. And if society knew, she, who heard everything, would know.

She looked at him as he cried, great racking sobs. No man cried like that. He was insane. The few people still out and about were crossing the road to avoid him. She should get herself behind a locked door, now.

"I don't believe you," she said bluntly instead. "I'd know if Beth had been arrested."

"It's true, Miss, honest it is," he replied desperately. He took a great sobbing breath, trying to get control of himself. "Ned said it's been kept close, Miss, because she knows who Sir Anthony is, but she wouldn't tell, and then they…sent her brother to talk to her, to see if she'd tell him."

"Richard," Sarah breathed.

"Richard. Yes, that's him," he said.

"Who's Ned?"

He flushed.

"I shouldn't have said his name, Miss. I told him I wouldn't. He's scared, Miss, of the captain, says he'll kill him if it gets out that he told me."

"Well you *have* said his name. So you might as well tell me who he is. I'll tell you this much; I hate Richard Cunningham. If you're telling me the truth about Beth, then I'm not going to say anything that will get this Ned in trouble with him."

Tom hesitated for a minute, then came to a decision. "Ned's my brother. He's in the army, and he was set to guard Miss Elizabeth. We're very close; he tells me everything, and when he came home on leave he said he had this secret and he had to tell someone, and it was when he said her name was Beth and she had this lovely silver hair that I knew it was her, because I never saw no one else with hair like that. But you mustn't tell no one, because the captain, Miss, he's crazy and he mustn't know that –"

For the second time in as many months, Sarah followed her instincts and allowed a stranger to come into her premises when she was alone. But this one she kept in the shop and made him sit on a stool at first, while she sat on the other side of the room, her hand still on the pistol. Just in case.

He made no move towards her. Instead he sat and told her what his brother had told him; that he'd been ordered to guard an important prisoner who had crucial information, that she wasn't allowed to sit down but had anyway, what the sergeant had done to make her stand, and how he'd tried to help her, and that she'd been concerned that he'd get into trouble for it.

And then Sarah knew Tom was telling the truth for certain, because that was Beth all over, so she went into her living room, checked on Mary, and came back with a mug of warmed ale for him. When she came back he was still sitting in the exact spot she'd left him, so she took him into her home and let him get warm by the fire while he told her the rest of the story.

"…and then when Ned saw all the blood, Miss, he ran to fetch the keeper, and met him coming back with the surgeon, who was coming to put her shoulder back in, and then they both ran to see her and the keeper, Mr Jones, he told Ned to forget everything that had happened, forget there was ever a prisoner, or it'd go very badly for him."

"Dear God," Sarah said.

"But he said he couldn't forget, and so he told me because he was having bad dreams about it, and he thought telling someone he trusted might stop them."

Sarah closed her eyes. She had to ask the question, but wasn't sure if she could bear the answer. She summoned all her resources.

"Was she dead?" she asked, and in her fear her voice sounded cold and impersonal. Tom looked at her oddly, but answered.

"I don't know, Miss. Ned wanted to find out, but he was posted away the next day so he couldn't ask anyone. But he said she wasn't dead when he left her to fetch the keeper, no."

"How long ago was this?" she asked.

"August, Miss."

*August?* Three months ago! Anything could have happened since then.

"Why did you wait all this time to come and tell me?" she asked.

"I didn't, Miss! I came as soon as Ned told me. He came home on leave three days ago, but he only told me yesterday."

She thought, quickly.

"I want to speak to your brother," she said. "Not that I don't believe you, because I do. What you've said about Beth, and Richard, that's just what they'd do. But he might remember more. Take me to him."

"I can't, Miss. He left this morning. He's bound for Flanders. I told him I was wanting to come and see you because I owed Miss Elizabeth a big debt, and I didn't know anyone else who was so close to her who'd even look at me. And he agreed, because he knows the captain's in Scotland and can't do anything to him from there, and because he said he'd feel better if I could find someone to help her. If she's alive."

If she was alive. Damn, damn, damn. Sarah sat and thought furiously. Tom sat opposite, drinking his ale, eyeing her nervously over the rim of the tankard.

"It's worth a try, I suppose," she said to herself.

"What is?" Tom asked.

"Are you really a link man?" she asked.

"Yes. I couldn't get another job as a coachman, couldn't get any job at all, after…" His voice trailed off.

"Go and get your torch," she said. "Can you be back here in half an hour?"

"Yes," he said. "What are you going to do?"

"I'm going to Newgate," she said.

Tom was back in twenty minutes, by which time Sarah had dressed in her finest clothes, had checked that Mary was fast asleep, and had put several shillings and a golden guinea in her pocket. She tucked the pistol in the back of her skirt just in case anyone should try to rob her, and then putting on her cloak, scrutinised herself in the mirror.

She couldn't pass for a lady, she knew that. Her clothes were of excellent quality, but her accent would betray her. Although she had worked hard to improve her vocabulary and soften her flat northern vowels, she did not have the cut-glass accent of an aristocrat. Nor did she have the natural arrogance that seemed to come with a title. But she would pass for a wealthy businesswoman, or at least the wife of a wealthy businessman, and that would have to do.

On the way, she practised walking with her head high as though she owned the street, and tried to ignore the butterflies that were having a party in her stomach. She had no idea how she would secure Beth's release if she was still in Newgate. If she was still alive. She would worry about that later. First things first.

When she arrived at the keeper's lodge, which was on the opposite side of the road from the actual prison, she stopped for a minute to gather her wits, coughing as the greasy smoke from Tom's torch blew in her face. Then she stepped forward and hammered loudly on the door.

A few moments passed and then a small hatch slid back and a face appeared. The owner of the face looked his visitor up and down and then the hatch closed, and the sound of bolts being drawn back told her that she clearly looked respectable enough for the keeper to consider her worth speaking to. The door opened.

"Can I help you, madam?" the man asked politely.

"Mr Jones?" The man nodded. "I am here to visit a prisoner," Sarah said.

"It's too late for visitors now, madam. If you come back tomorrow…" His voice trailed off as Sarah moved forward slightly and the coins in her pocket jingled merrily.

"I understand it's a little late," she said, reaching inside her pocket and drawing out a shilling, which she handed to him, "but I have been in the country for some months and have only just discovered that my dear friend is here."

He assessed her with expert eyes, and she knew that it was going to cost her everything in her purse to see Beth tonight. But it would be worth it and more to know she was alive.

"It's most inconvenient to admit anyone to the cells at this time," he said. "The prisoners will all be settled down for the night."

This was an obvious ploy to extort money from her; it was highly unlikely the prisoners would all be asleep at eight o'clock in the evening. Now was not the time to argue though. If she was going to discover Beth's whereabouts she would have to play along.

"Oh, I'm sure we can come to some agreement," she said. "Come a little closer, boy, so I can see what I'm doing," she demanded imperiously of Tom, who obligingly moved forward, lighting up both the coins in her hand and the keeper's face. She placed another shilling in Mr Jones' palm.

"Maybe we can. And who would this dear friend be?" he asked, smiling.

"Her name is Elizabeth Cunningham," said Sarah.

The smile vanished and Mr Jones' face closed down immediately.

"We don't have anyone of that name here," he said. "You've wasted your time."

"You might know her as Beth," Sarah persisted. "Small, with long –"

"I told you, there's no one of that name, of any of those names here."

"Oh, how disappointing. Perhaps she has now been moved elsewhere?" Sarah said.

"I wouldn't know. I've never had anyone here by that name, or that looked like that."

"But I haven't told you what she looks –"

"Goodnight to you," he interrupted and stepping back, rudely shut the door in her face.

She stood for a moment in the street, and then turning, started to walk back the way she had come.

"I'm sorry, Miss," Tom said after a moment. "I was sure Ned said that it was Mr Jones who was the keeper, but maybe he got it wrong. He was very upset."

"Ned didn't get it wrong," Sarah said. "Didn't you see his face? That's why I told you to come closer. I don't need to see a coin to know what it is. I wanted to see his reaction when I mentioned Beth's name. He was frightened. And for the keeper of Newgate Gaol to be frightened, he must have been given his orders by someone important."

"Like who, Miss?"

"I don't know." She stopped again, and came to another decision. "But I'm going to find out. Are you in the mood for a walk, Tom? I'll pay you for lighting my way."

"I'll walk wherever you want, Miss. I don't want no pay for this."

"Very well, then. Come on. I'll get Mary first. I can't leave her alone for long. Damn. I should have done this in the first place. I've warned him now. That was stupid. I just hope she's home."

Tom looked at her, clearly at a loss as to what she was talking about.

Having made her decision she set off at a brisk pace, Tom following, trailing a cloud of greasy smoke from the rush light behind him.

# CHAPTER FOURTEEN

Caroline was sitting in her cosy cream and blue decorated parlour with her feet up on a footstool, reading a book and sipping a glass of wine. She had just returned from a tiring but pleasant two weeks at Summer Hill, where she had overseen the final touches being put to the ballroom and three of the bedrooms and had had a long discussion with William Kent about the design of the gardens. She'd returned a day earlier than expected and was relishing an evening alone. Edwin was at his club and would stay overnight, having a long session in parliament tomorrow. She couldn't wait to tell him about the gardens. She had a copy of the plans all ready to show him. Maybe they could go there together soon. Spend Christmas there, just the three of them. She smiled to herself and moved the cushion supporting her back a little to the left. She would finish this chapter and then have an early night.

There came a soft tap on the parlour door. She waited a moment, and when no one came in she knew who was standing outside.

"Come in, Toby," she shouted, knowing he wouldn't hear her otherwise. The elderly manservant was becoming increasingly deaf, which was useful if you wanted to chat with friends about something confidential while he was tottering about the room serving tea, but not very useful when you had to startle said friends by bellowing at him to fetch some cakes from the kitchen.

The door opened, Toby walked in and bowed deeply.

"I'm sorry to disturb you, my lady," he began, "but Miss Browne is here to see you."

Caroline glanced at the clock on the mantelpiece. Toby, who might have been deaf but could still see a fly on the wall at fifty paces, correctly interpreted the gesture.

"She said it is most urgent, my lady."

"It must be for her to call at this late hour. Very well, Toby, send her in."

There was a pause, in which Caroline placed her bookmark at the page she'd been reading, closed the book and placed it on the table, while Toby continued to stand in the doorway. She sighed.

"Send her in!" she yelled.

He must have heard her now, but instead of doing as she bid, he took another step into the room. *Really,* she thought, *we have to pension the poor man off. This is ridiculous.* She took a deep breath, readying herself for another attempt.

"She has a…personage with her, my lady," he said.

Caroline looked at him. His face wore an expression of the utmost disgust. She turned in her chair so he would see her face, and hopefully be able to read her lips.

"What kind of personage?" she shouted.

"A link man, my lady."

"Very sensible of her," Caroline commented. "Show Miss Browne in and allow the link man to warm himself in the kitchen. Keep an eye on him," she added.

"Er…Miss Browne insists you will wish to speak to this…creature, my lady."

Caroline was intrigued. Sarah's visits could be interesting, for want of a better word, and this one had potential.

"Well then, send them both in. Now," she added when Toby, clearly horrified, was about to object. He shuffled off, returning a couple of minutes later with Sarah, who was cradling her sleeping baby in her arms and who looked very worried, and the 'personage' who looked absolutely terrified.

"I'm sorry to bother you at this time of night, Caroline," Sarah said, "but I didn't know who else to come to. This is Tom. He used to be Lord Edward's coachman."

Caroline looked at Tom. "Toby told me you were a link man," she said. To her surprise the ragged young man blushed to the roots of his hair.

"I am, milady," he said, addressing the floor.

"I'm sorry, Tom, but I'll have to tell her so she'll believe that what you told me about Beth is the truth," Sarah said to him.

Caroline's face changed. Her gaze moved to Sarah then to Toby, still hovering at the door, clearly unwilling to leave his beloved mistress alone with a ruffian.

"That will be all, Toby!" Caroline bellowed. Sarah flinched, accustomed to Toby's deafness but Tom jumped a foot in the air and looked round in panic, clearly intending to flee. Sarah laid a placating hand on his arm.

"I'm sorry," Caroline said as the door closed behind the reluctant Toby, "I should have warned you Toby is deaf. I didn't mean to frighten you. Sit down, both of you. You have news of Beth?"

Tom looked wildly at the couch, then at Sarah, who gripped his arm more tightly.

"Caroline is a friend of mine, Tom. And she was a friend of Beth's too. You can trust her." She cast a pleading look Caroline's way.

"That's right," Caroline said. "I was a friend of Beth's, and if you have news of her, then I would like to hear it. I can see that you are a little down on your luck at the moment, but you clearly take pains with your appearance."

"I does, milady," Tom said to the rug. "I looks after my clothes as best I can, and I washes every day. And I ain't got no vermin, neither," he added with some pride.

Caroline repressed a smile.

"Sit down," she repeated gently. "And tell me what you know about Beth. Sarah seems to think it very important."

They sat down, and with occasional prompting from Sarah, Tom told his story, and then Sarah added her account of her visit to Newgate and the reception she'd received.

"I realise that I shouldn't have gone," Sarah finished, "because I've warned him now. I should have come to you first, but I didn't want to involve you."

Caroline sat back in her chair and closed her eyes for a minute, while the other two waited anxiously. Then she opened them again, and looked at Tom.

"You used to be Lord Edward's coachman, you say. Are you good with horses, then?" she asked.

"Yes, milady," Tom said hesitantly, clearly having expected Caroline to comment on the situation with Beth, not on his prowess with animals. "I was a stable boy for four years, before I started learning to drive. I love horses, milady, I've been around them all my life, until…" His voice trailed off, and he looked down at his hands.

"Well then," Caroline said briskly. "I have a country house, Summer Hill, at Twickenham, and I am in need of reliable, trustworthy staff. Are you interested?"

Tom abandoned the scrutiny of his hands and instead stared at Caroline as though she'd just grown another head.

"I…I…" He stopped, swallowed, and tried again. "I am, milady, but I haven't got no character. Lord Edward, he said –"

"Never mind what Lord Edward said," Caroline interrupted. "I've seen enough of your character this evening to know that you are both loyal and courageous. If you are hard-working as well, I will give you a chance. Go home and gather your belongings. In the morning, call back here and I will give you a letter recommending that you be taken on as a stable man. We will see how things go from there. It will be up to you to prove yourself. What do you say?"

"I…but…"

"We all make mistakes, Tom. I have made many myself, and I am sure I will make more." *Probably this very night.* "But the important thing is to learn from them." She waited.

"Say yes, Tom," Sarah prompted.

"Yes," Tom said obediently. "Milady. Thank you," he added hurriedly.

"Excellent," Caroline said, standing. "You need not wait for Sarah. I suspect we will be some time." She bent and lifted the bell from the table, and then sighed and replaced it. "I will see you out myself," she said. "My throat is already strained."

She returned a few minutes later.

"That was a kind thing you did," Sarah commented.

"Nonsense," Caroline replied. "If he lives up to his promise, I will be the winner. Edward is a pompous idiot with no sense when it comes to hiring servants. A character from him would be a deterrent to me rather than a recommendation. Now," she continued, "I've called for tea and a cold collation, and for the bed to be made up in the green room for you and Mary. Let us formulate a plan. There's no point in my going to Newgate and demanding to see Beth, because as you said, the keeper is forewarned."

"I'm sorry," said Sarah.

"No, it could work to our advantage," Caroline said, "because if he refused good money and denied Beth had ever been there, then it's likely he'd have said the same to me, but more politely. His instructions have probably come from someone in high office. It's strange that Beth would be in Newgate, though. Important or titled prisoners are usually lodged in the Tower."

"Do you think she might be in the Tower, then?" Sarah asked hopefully.

"It's worth asking, certainly. It's possible that she was in the Tower, refused to say anything and then was moved to Newgate to be questioned, but…I still can't understand it. Prisoners of importance, male or female, if not lodged in the Tower, are kept in messengers' houses."

"Messengers?" Sarah asked.

"Yes. Messengers are paid handsomely to securely lodge prisoners in their own houses. Some of them treat their charges well, others not so well. But I never heard of a high-born lady being put in Newgate. I'll start at the Tower tomorrow, see what I can find out. I must send a message to Anne, too."

"I haven't seen her in months. Is she still at your Aunt Harriet's?" Sarah asked.

"Yes, she is. She'll be very relieved to know Richard's in Scotland. She hasn't heard from him since…no, it's not possible," Caroline said. "No, I can't believe William would allow such a thing."

"William?" Sarah asked, puzzled.

"The last time Anne saw Richard, he told her he had an important job to do for the Duke of Cumberland. But I can't believe William would order Richard to torture any woman like that, let alone Beth. He was very infatuated with her."

"I could believe it," Sarah said. "They're calling him the Butcher, you know."

"Yes, I've heard that, and there have been criticisms of the way the rebellion was put down in Scotland," Caroline said. "But you have to remember that for many of the rebels, this is not an isolated act of treason. The same clans came out in 1715, and no doubt would rise again if they got the chance. It's William's and the king's belief that this rebellion only took place because the rebels were treated too leniently after the '15. His methods may seem brutal, but none of us want to see the country plunged into another civil war, like it was a hundred years ago. It's necessary, Sarah."

"It's not just in Scotland, though," Sarah said. "The Manchester men were treated terribly too."

"Ah, you mean the executions we saw. Yes, that was harsh. But I think they were made an example of to stop the English from rising too. This confines the unrest to Scotland, and –"

"It's not the executions. It's the way the prisoners are being treated, starving and chained like dogs, and left to lie in their own filth. Some of them are children, babies even. John said –" Sarah stopped abruptly and reddened.

"I don't want to know about the man who came to the execution with you, Sarah. We'll call him your brother. But you must be careful. I know how close you were to Beth, and I know what she did for you. But she would be the first to tell you not to put your life at risk for her or anyone else."

"But you are going to help Beth, aren't you?" Sarah said fervently.

"I'm going to find out what's going on if I can, yes," Caroline said. "And if she's alive and I find her, I will do what I can to help her. But I won't put my life or anyone else's at risk for her. She's a traitor, Sarah, her and Anthony both. You must remember that. And you must think of your niece too, now. She depends on you."

Sarah nodded.

"I do remember that, and Mary is dearer to me than my life," she said. "I don't know much about politics like you do. I don't care who's sitting on the throne, and I wouldn't raise a finger to fight for or against any king, because they don't give a damn about me or people like me. But Beth did give a damn about me - she was the first person who ever showed me any kindness. Everything I have today is because of her. I'd most likely be dead by now if she hadn't helped me. When Mary grows up I'm going to tell her about Beth, and I won't be able to hold my head up if I've left her to rot and die in a cell somewhere when I could have done something about it. So if she needs more help than you can give her, you tell me."

\* \* \*

## Tower of London

"No, I haven't heard of an Elizabeth Cunningham, my lady," the young yeoman warder said. "She's certainly not lodged with us now, hasn't been since I've been here."

"This seems like an excellent position for a smart young man like yourself," Caroline said, smiling at the freckle-faced youth. "How long have you been here?"

"Since September, my lady," he replied, beaming.

"Well, I wish you the very best. Thank you for your time. I did not wish to inconvenience Thomas with my little query, busy as he is, but I think I shall have to." She pressed a coin into his hand and started to turn away. The warder looked at the coin and his eyes widened.

"Thomas, my lady?" the enterprising young man asked, clearly wondering if he could inconvenience this Thomas fellow on her behalf and earn himself another sovereign for his pains.

"Yes. Ah…of course you won't know him by his Christian name…the Duke of Newcastle. I'm sure he will know where my dear misguided acquaintance is. Although of course I would be most grateful if I didn't have to bother him with such a trivial matter. But there it is. Good day to you."

She made three steps before he called to her.

"It is possible that she was held in Mr Carlton's house, across the green. He sometimes takes care of particular prisoners, although he has none lodging with him at present. Would you like me to enquire for you?"

She turned back.

"How very helpful! I would be most obliged if you would accompany me to Mr Carlton's, yes," she said, smiling.

They crossed the green together and knocked at the door, which was opened by a maidservant, who curtseyed, and on hearing that Lady Caroline Harlow wished to ask a question of her master hurried off, returning moments later with a portly middle-aged man, who bowed obsequiously.

"What a pleasant surprise, Lady Caroline," he gushed. "May I offer my congratulations to Sir Edwin on his recent knighthood?"

"Why, thank you, Mr Carlton. How kind," Caroline replied.

"Would you care for some refreshment? Girl," he said to the hovering maid, "go and fetch tea and –"

"No, no, please do not trouble yourself," Caroline said. "I merely wished to enquire after the health of a somewhat misguided acquaintance of mine, who I believe may have been in your care for a time. You would perhaps know her as Lady Elizabeth Peters, or possibly Elizabeth or Beth Cunningham. A petite young lady with silver-blonde hair."

She watched with interest as a variety of expressions crossed his face.

"I'm sorry, Lady Caroline," he said after a pause. "I cannot help you, I'm afraid. I know nothing of such a person."

"Ah, I see," Caroline replied. She took another coin from her reticule, making sure that its denomination was visible to all, then turned back to the young warder, who was still standing on the step, having not been invited in. "Thank you," she said, handing it to him. "You have been most helpful. It is such a pleasant day for the time of year, I think I will take a turn around the green and take the air before I return to my carriage. If there are no objections?" Her tone implied that the warder would be unwise to answer in the negative.

"No, of course not, my lady," said Mr Carlton, bowing again and eyeing the lost sovereign with avarice. Not enough avarice to tempt him to amend his story, though.

She closed her reticule with a snap and walked out onto the green.

She had been walking for some fifteen minutes in the crisp air, and was starting to wonder whether she should just go back to her carriage now and revise her plan, when the green-painted door she'd been keeping an eye on opened and the maid stepped out. Caroline immediately cut her circuit of the green short and strode down the path until she was out of view of the house. Then she stopped and waited for the maid to catch her up.

"You have some information for me?" Caroline said without preamble. "If you have you may rely on my discretion, and you will be rewarded appropriately, of course."

The maid curtseyed and looked distinctly nervous. She glanced around to make sure no one was in earshot and then spoke, softly and urgently.

"There was a young lady here, my lady," she said after a moment. "But she's not here now."

"When was she here?" Caroline asked.

"A few months ago, June time. In July she was taken to see Prince William, two days after he came back to London, and she didn't come back here then."

*Damn.*

"Ah. Well, thank you." Caroline made to open her reticule.

"She was taken to Newgate Prison, my lady. The soldiers brought her back once, to dress for another interview, but then the next time they sent me to Newgate with some clothes for her, and I helped her to dress. I haven't seen her since then or heard anything about her."

"And when was this, that you went to Newgate?"

"August, my lady."

"How did she seem?"

"Very cheerful the first time, when they brought her here. I think she sold the first dress she had to buy food and suchlike, because she was wearing stays and petticoats. She was very friendly, told me…never mind, my lady."

"What did she tell you? It's alright, I won't tell anyone."

The maid hesitated.

"She told me that if the servants were betting as to whether she'd become Prince William's wife or…er…mistress, that I should bet she would become neither."

In spite of the seriousness of the situation, Caroline laughed. That was Beth all over.

"Did you? Place a bet?" she asked.

"No, my lady! I didn't think it was right. I tried to find out about her, after, but everyone was told to keep quiet and not say anything about her."

"But you're telling me. Why?" Caroline asked.

"She was good to me. She asked my name and ordered chocolate for me the first time, and then tea the second time when she was brought back here to dress. And she talked to me as though I was her equal, even though she was a lady. And at Newgate she apologised for not being able to get chocolate for me. She thought of me, even though she seemed upset about something. She hadn't seemed upset before. I hope you find her, my lady."

"So do I," Caroline said. "So do I."

\* \* \*

"From there I went straight to Newgate Prison. Well, no, I stopped and bought some provisions on the way, and I pulled at my hair a bit, so I looked a little eccentric."

"Eccentric?" Edwin said. When he'd returned home an hour before, he'd been overjoyed to see his wife, who he had missed greatly, and had looked forward to hearing news of Summer Hill. The expression he now wore conveyed another emotion entirely, but he had agreed not to verbally express his opinion until she'd finished her story.

"Yes. You know, the way those bored society women with no common sense look. The ones who have a great fervour to help the needy, but have no idea what the hell they're doing?"

Edwin laughed. Caroline had just described half the women he had to deal with on a regular basis.

"Anyway," she continued. "I knew there was no point in asking for Beth, so I ignored the keeper's lodge and went straight to the prison, said I'd come to ease the affliction of the poor misguided rebel women, who had paid the ultimate price for following their men into folly and treason. The turnkey offered to take the basket of food off me and said he'd ensure that it got to the unfortunate women, but I insisted on seeing them myself. I flashed him a half crown and said I'd been up most of the night preparing an inspiring lecture that would make them see the error of their ways."

"And did you make them see the error of their ways?" Edwin asked, still grinning.

"No. He told me that there were no rebel women prisoners in Newgate at the moment. I told him that my friend had visited them in August and there were certainly a number then. And he said there had been, but they'd all been transferred elsewhere a while ago, possibly to the transport ships. I think he was telling the truth."

"Please tell me you gave him the provisions for the use of the other prisoners, and left," Edwin said.

"I gave him the provisions for the use of the other prisoners, and the half crown, and left," Caroline repeated.

"Thank God for that," Edwin said.

"And then I went to Tilbury," Caroline continued. Edwin sighed, and dropped his head into his hands.

"They do boat trips, Edwin," she said, leaning forward. "Boat trips, so that genteel people can sail past the ships where hundreds of people are being kept in unspeakable conditions, so they can shudder delicately with excited horror at having been so close to an actual Jacobite, and then go home and tell themselves and others that this is a fair and just punishment for people who dared to rebel against His Most Wise and Gracious Majesty."

Edwin lifted his head.

"What's the difference between people doing that and going to see the lunatics in Bedlam?" he asked.

Caroline coloured.

"None, I suppose. But when I did that I was young and stupid, and I hadn't met you. And I suppose if I'd actually known someone in the asylum I would have felt differently. I feel differently now, anyway. I wanted to tell them that these were human beings, including women and innocent children that they were mocking, and that it was shameful behaviour."

"You didn't actually say that, did you?"

"No, of course I didn't!" Caroline said. "They wouldn't have heard me if I had, anyway. Most of them were too busy vomiting over the edge of the boat," she added with obvious schadenfreude.

"Was the river choppy, then?"

"No. They were being sick because they couldn't stand the smell coming from the ships, even from a distance. I have never smelt anything so putrid in my life, not even in Bedlam. There are people, men, women, children, being kept in absolute hell. This is not a just punishment. This is savagery. I was not the only one who thought that way, either, by the end of the trip."

"The prisons are overcrowded, and they have to be kept somewhere until we can bring them to trial," Edwin said, still with his politician's head on. "There are so many of them. The system of lotting is going well, though, and the situation should ease soon, once sufficient numbers have been transported, and –"

"I know that," Caroline interrupted. "And I know that our

prisons were not designed for such a huge influx of people. But they could be allowed up on deck for air, Edwin. They could be fed properly and allowed to wash themselves, instead of being left to lie in their own piss and shit and starve to death!"

"Caro!" Edwin said, shocked by her language.

"You didn't see it. You *should* see it," she continued fiercely. "This is what the government you're part of are sanctioning. They wouldn't let me on board, said it was too dangerous. They told me that even the hardened sailors are struggling to keep their food down because of the smell from below decks, but that soon it won't be such a problem, because they're dying like flies down there. And yet every day I'm hearing about how savage and barbaric the North Britons are, and how Cumberland is right to be severe on them. If we can treat helpless prisoners like this in London, I can't begin to imagine what's going on in Scotland, with bastards like Scott and Hawley allowed free rein. And Richard," she added.

"It's true there are complaints about the situation in Scotland, and they are being looked into," Edwin said defensively. "But with Charles back in France and being feted all over Paris as a hero, there's a real chance that King Louis might actually decide to finance another expedition in the spring. We have to make sure the rebels can't rise again and the only way we can do that is by brutal means. These people don't acknowledge the law. They're born and bred to be warriors. For them the only law is what their chieftain tells them to do. If he tells them to fight for the Stuarts, then that's what they do. And the only way to bring them into line is to destroy the power of the chiefs, to crush the clan system, once and for all."

"I said something similar to Sarah last night when she told me that they're calling William 'Butcher Cumberland'. And I understand that you have to take harsh measures to show we mean business. I said that to you when we went to see the Manchester men executed, if you remember. You were shocked by how they suffered," Caroline said.

"I was very upset, I admit. But I was more shocked at the enjoyment people got from seeing them suffer. I don't think that traitors and criminals should be glorified. But I do believe that if we are to have peace in this country, then the Jacobites must be crushed, once and for all."

"I agree. But you must also take into account that public opinion is easily swayed. In April William was the hero of Culloden; less than five months later he's the Butcher of Culloden. You said yourself that if the Jacobites had carried on to London instead of turning back, the mob may well have welcomed Charles, because he knows how to act as people expect royalty to.

"It's also becoming known that Charles treated the prisoners he took with respect, and released many of them on parole. And that the barbarian savages didn't rape and pillage as they invaded, but for the most part treated the citizens of the towns they occupied with respect. In the meantime everyone's heard about the 'pacification' of the Highlands, that our soldiers are raping women, murdering children, burning their houses, and leaving the old and weak to starve to death. This does not give a good impression of the Hanoverians, Edwin, either at home or abroad."

Edwin sighed.

"That's true. But remember, in his treatment of the prisoners and the people he met, Charles was trying to win them over to his cause by showing them how just and merciful he was."

"And King George is trying to show that he's the better choice of king by being unjust and barbaric," Caroline countered. "I think Charles had the right idea. And we both know that if he gains enough support from the French to make this an equal fight, and succeeds in taking the throne, Britain will be at the mercy of the whim of an autocratic hereditary monarch. And that is why we support Hanover, because we want the king's rule to be tempered by an elected government. But that government has to show it can govern better than Charles would."

"But Charles wouldn't *be* king," Edwin pointed out.

"I think he would, if James had any sense. But that's not my point. My point is that you can only go so far in brutalising the losers before public opinion turns in favour of the underdog. I've seen it time and time again at executions. And we are rapidly going that way. The main reason the common people don't want the Stuarts back is not because they fear autocracy; they have no more say in electing the government than they do in choosing a king. Right now they believe the Pretender, once king, will force them to become Roman Catholics. If the Stuarts can convince the mob that they will practice religious toleration, they could gain the upper hand. Because Charles has already proved he can lead, and lead mercifully. And Cumberland is proving the opposite."

Edwin, deeply uncomfortable, could not argue, because he was hearing similar stories in parliament. Every day new reports of atrocities committed in the name of keeping the peace were drifting down from Scotland. And he *had* heard rumours about prison conditions, but he was aware of his sensitivity and tried to curb it when in parliament. This was an exceptional situation. It would ease, and hopefully soon.

"Did you find anything out about Beth?" he asked.

"No. It seems that she has simply disappeared."

"I am sorry," Edwin said, and was. "She may well be dead, you know."

"I know. It seems likely, from what Tom said. But I would like to know for certain."

"Well, you have done everything you can," Edwin said reassuringly. He looked at his wife; she did not look reassured. "I can make enquiries if you like, see if I can find anything out," he offered. "I would like to know what has happened to her as well. But I will have to be very careful."

"No," Caroline said. "It's too risky. You have just been knighted for your loyal service to the king. If you start asking about the welfare of a known rebel, you'll be putting your career at risk."

"I will be very discreet," he said.

"There is something strange going on here," she continued thoughtfully, as though she hadn't heard him. "How is it that nobody knew Beth had been arrested, that she was being kept in the Tower, and in Newgate? It's virtually impossible to keep anything a secret, but even you didn't know. Clearly no one wants you, or anyone to know. So you mustn't ask, mustn't tell anyone at all that you know anything. Leave it to me."

"What are you going to do?"

"I'm not sure," she said. "But if you're not involved in it, if word gets out that I'm trying to find Beth, you can be deeply shocked at the behaviour of your wayward wife, and discipline her accordingly."

Edwin tried to imagine disciplining his wayward wife, and failed. It would take a far braver man than he was to attempt it. He had not married her for her docility. He had married her because she was strong, courageous, and loyal to the death to those she cared for. And she cared for Beth, in spite of everything. And so did he. So he wasted no breath asking her not to pursue this, because he knew she could not do otherwise. It was one of the things he loved about her.

"Be careful, please," he said instead. "If you find out she's alive and where she is held, we can make sure that she is as comfortable as possible. But we cannot interfere with the legal process."

"I won't do anything reckless, I promise," she said.

And with that she steered the conversation into calmer waters, and they spent the rest of the evening poring over the plans for the landscaping of Summer Hill.

\* \* \*

The following morning after Edwin had gone out, Caroline lingered at the breakfast table, drinking chocolate and weighing up her options.

Her first thought had been to approach her family. Not those who had alienated her after her marriage to Edwin; although they were now coming round since Edwin's star was rising, they were nowhere near agreeing to help her locate a prominent rebel. And in any case, she didn't want to be beholden to any of them.

There was Aunt Harriet, of course. She knew everyone and was more capable of putting the fear of God into people than anyone Caroline knew, in spite of her age and eccentric manners. But if Beth had been held and tortured, then it must be because she'd refused to divulge anything about the identity or whereabouts of Anthony. Harriet was a renowned man-hater; she would most likely say the idiot deserved everything she got and should betray the scoundrel immediately. And Harriet had never met Beth, so would have no idea what a special person she was.

No. Caroline had to find someone who was influential enough to countermand orders from Newcastle, possibly from Cumberland himself, and who had known Beth personally and had liked her.

She poured herself more chocolate and sat for a while staring unseeingly out of the window. Then she called for her carriage to be made ready. It was a long shot, but in fact the only possible one to attempt.

Having flouted all the rules of society by arriving at Leicester House unannounced, Caroline was kept waiting for only a minute before being shown by a footman into the library, where a small, swarthy-skinned man was sitting reading a book by the window. He rose as she entered and she curtseyed deeply to him.

"Caroline!" he exclaimed with obvious pleasure. "How wonderful to see you! It's been a long time. I have missed you. Sit down." He beckoned to a chair on the other side of the window.

"I'm sorry, Your Highness," Caroline said, deciding to favour honesty rather than a specious excuse for not having visited in over a year. "I did not want anything to stand in the way of Edwin's career. It's so important to him, and also, I think he is a voice of moderation in parliament, which is sorely needed at present."

Prince Frederick laughed and clapped his hands.

"And that is why I have missed you. You are one of the few people I know who speaks the truth to me. I believe my father has recently knighted your husband. Is he then secure enough in his position that you can resume your visits to the black sheep of the family?"

"I hope so. Your parties are rarely boring. And I do miss seeing Great-Uncle Francis being publicly humiliated on a regular basis. But I am here today on a mission of mercy, completely independent of my husband, and I believe you are the only person who can, and maybe will, help me."

"You have intrigued me. Please elaborate."

"Do you remember Lady Elizabeth Peters, Your Highness? Small, very beautiful, silver –"

"How could I forget Lady Elizabeth?" the prince interrupted. "It is not every day that beautiful young ladies fight impromptu duels with pompous young men in my salon. It cost me a fortune to get Daniel's blood out of the carpet. And worth every penny," he added, his eyes sparkling. "But she disappeared, did she not, with Sir Anthony, when their treachery was discovered?"

"She did. But yesterday I discovered that it seems she has been arrested, and has been kept prisoner."

"Has she? Is she then at the Tower, or with a messenger? You wish me to help you secure permission to visit her?"

His face expressed concern rather than disgust or pleasure at the news of Beth's arrest. This was promising. Caroline sat forward in the chair.

"Your Highness, it is somewhat more complicated than that. I will tell you everything I know, and if you feel you cannot help me I will of course understand completely."

She explained everything, from Sarah and Tom's visit to her experience at the transports in Tilbury, and then he sat for a little while thinking, his fingers steepled under his chin.

"So," he said finally, "the last place we know she was held for certain was Newgate Prison. In which case that seems the logical place to commence our search for her."

"You are going to help, then?" Caroline said.

"Of course I am! *Noblesse oblige* and all that. I believe it is compulsory for handsome princes to rescue damsels in distress," the prince said flippantly. Then his expression changed, and he looked at the young woman sitting opposite, whose face had lit up at his agreement to help. "You are aware that she might be dead, Caroline? You are prepared for that?"

"Yes, I am," Caroline answered. "And I'm also prepared for the fact that we might not be successful in locating her."

"Oh, we will be successful in locating her, I assure you, although it may take a little time. After all, my position does confer certain privileges. And I am about to exercise one of them." He looked down at his drab woollen breeches. "I will send for refreshments for you whilst I dress appropriately. I shan't be long."

Caroline had just finished her second cup of tea and was considering another slice of lemon cake, when the prince returned.

"Are you ready, my lady?" he asked.

She stood and turned to him, and then smiling, accepted his arm and they left the room.

"Please take this as a compliment, Your Highness," she said, once they were in the royal carriage and clattering down the street in the direction of Newgate, "but your outfit would have sent Sir

Anthony into raptures." It would indeed. He wore an expertly tailored outfit of dark green silk, beautifully embroidered in gold thread. In the centre of each golden coat button sparkled a diamond, matched by the gold and diamond encrusted buckles on his soft leather shoes.

"As long as you're not referring to my choice of colour, I am flattered indeed. Sir Anthony had exquisite taste in tailoring and fashion. Just a little overstated. I miss his wit greatly, although not his treachery," Frederick said, almost wistfully.

"I feel as though we are about to go on a state visit," she said by way of changing the subject, aware that she had made a faux pas in mentioning Anthony's name. Frederick was so informal in his manners and speech that it was sometimes easy to forget he was the Prince of Wales and heir to the throne.

"Not quite. I did think wearing the ermine and crown would be overdoing it a little," he replied, eyes sparkling with humour. "But I take your point. I much prefer to dress in more practical and comfortable clothing, as you know. But not today. Ah, here we are."

They descended from the coach assisted by two footmen, one of whom then proceeded to hammer on the keeper's door. The hatch opened and a face scrutinised the visitors, and then it closed again, the door opened immediately, and Mr Jones appeared and knelt down in the street before his visitor.

"Your Royal Highness!" he cried.

Prince Frederick, all trace of informality vanished, observed the keeper of Newgate Prison with great hauteur and kept him kneeling for a good thirty seconds before bidding him rise. No one watching him now would forget he was the Prince of Wales and heir to the throne.

"Mr Jones, is it not?" he said.

"Indeed, Your Royal Highness, at your service. I cannot tell you how honoured I am that you have graced –"

"Quite," the prince interrupted. "I am here to visit a lady who is currently lodged in your establishment."

"Of course, Your Highness. But I cannot imagine –"

"You have no need to imagine, sir, merely to lead the way. Take me to Miss Elizabeth Cunningham, immediately."

The keeper's face drained of all colour instantly. For a second it seemed he would actually faint at the prince's feet. Then he swallowed, and with an effort pulled himself together.

"I…we…there is no one of that name in –"

"You may know her as Lady Elizabeth Peters, or Beth Cunningham, or any permutation of those names. You will take me to her. Now."

"Your Royal Highness, I regret to say that I'm not familiar with anybody of that name," the keeper replied uncomfortably.

"I think you may be aware that my father the king has been on the throne for over twenty years, and we all hope that he may reign for many more," Prince Frederick said conversationally, eyeing the keeper with disdain. "But one day, sir, I will take his place, and on that sad day I intend to clear the kingdom of people who have dared to lie to me and waste my time. But let us not look into the distant future, sir. Let us look instead at the next five minutes. I ask you, do you wish to still be the keeper of Newgate Prison at the end of that time?"

Mr Jones looked so distressed that Caroline almost felt sorry for the man. His orders had definitely come from someone with great authority. Had they not, he would certainly not have hesitated at this point, as he was doing. Beads of sweat broke out on his forehead, although it was a cold day.

"Come sir, I grow impatient," the prince said.

Mr Jones wiped his forehead, swallowed and came to a decision.

"If you would care to step inside my humble lodgings, Your Highness, I will fetch Miss Cunningham to you," he said.

Caroline forced her expression to remain neutral, but she wanted to drop to the ground and kiss the prince's feet. Beth was alive, and here! It had been that easy!

"No," Frederick replied. "I do not wish to wait. You will conduct us to her cell."

Mr Jones' complexion turned a sickly green.

"Immediately."

Without further comment, the utterly defeated keeper took out his bunch of keys and opening the prison door, led his exalted visitors into the prison.

"Dear God," Frederick said when they were a few feet inside. "What is that dreadful smell?"

"You don't notice it after a time, Your Highness," Mr Jones said.

"You mean the place *always* smells like this?"

Mr Jones stopped.

"I…er…I can arrange for someone to fetch a nosegay for you, Your Highness. That helps to get rid of the smell. Or if you would care to go outside, I can fetch Miss –"

"No. Just take me to her," the prince replied, breathing through his mouth.

They made their way down a series of stone corridors, poorly lit by rushlights set into wall sconces, coming finally to a locked wooden door, outside which the keeper stopped.

"Are you sure you wouldn't rather –"

"Open the door," Frederick ordered.

The door was opened, there was a skittering noise in the room as the vermin ran for shelter, and then Mr Jones walked in, holding the candle he was carrying high so it cast a gloomy yellow light around the small room, illuminating the damp glistening on the rough stone walls and a pile of rags in one corner. The room was bitterly cold, and the smell of stale air, excrement and sickness was intense. The prince retched once, and then with an effort, recovered himself.

"I thought you said that Miss –" he began, then stopped as the pile of rags moved slightly.

"Beth!" Caroline cried, and forgetting all the proprieties, pushed past the prince and the keeper and fell to her knees at the side of the occupant.

"Dear God in heaven, what have they done to you?" she said, although it was so dim that Caroline could only see that the young woman's face was whiter than her hair, which was matted, and that the rags were the remnants of clothes which appeared to have rotted on her body. Her eyes were closed, and she seemed to be unconscious of their presence.

The prince took the candle from the unresisting keeper's hand, and moving forward, came to stand next to Caroline. He bent slightly so that the light fell on the prisoner's face. Then he inhaled sharply, straightened, and turned to the keeper.

"Who has done this?" he said icily.

"I…I…I was ordered not to –"

"Never mind. I will deal with you later. Take this please." He handed the candle to Caroline, then in one fluid movement he bent, lifted the unconscious woman up and turned to the door.

Mr Jones stood inadvertently blocking the exit, horror-stricken.

"What are you doing?" he gasped.

"I am taking this young woman out of here," Frederick said.

"But she's a prisoner! My orders have come from the highest –"

"Higher than myself, sir?" Frederick asked. "Are you telling me that the king my father has personally ordered you to torture and then starve this young woman to death?"

"I…no…but…"

"Then get out of my way."

Mr Jones wisely got out of the way, and the prince strode down the corridor, out of the prison gate and straight into the waiting carriage, where he carefully laid his burden down on the bench seat before looking back to see Caroline following him. She climbed into the carriage and sat down next to the prince, her eyes brimming with tears of horror and rage. He leaned over and held his hand above Beth's nose and mouth. An unbearable smell filled the carriage, a smell of dirt, of urine, and of something rotten which Caroline dared not think about right now or she would fall apart.

"She's breathing," he said. "We must get her home, now. And then call for the surgeon." He lifted his hand to bang on the roof of the coach to tell the driver to leave.

"Wait," Caroline said, thinking hard. She had expected at the best to find Beth, talk to her, make arrangements with the keeper for her to have the best accommodation and food available. She had not expected to be sitting in the Prince of Wales' coach opposite a woman on the brink of death. She looked at the prince, sitting there in his now badly soiled outfit; the expression on his face told her that he had acted impulsively in removing her from the prison in flagrant disregard for the law, but that now it was done he would not go back. "You cannot take her to Leicester House, Your Highness," she said.

"Why not?" he asked, still overcome by rage and indignation.

"There are already rumours that you are a Jacobite sympathiser," Caroline replied.

"What? Is there nothing I am not accused of? Why on earth would I sympathise with the man who is trying to usurp me?"

"It is said that you intervened to save the life of Lord Cromartie, and that you stopped Oxford University being censured."

"The king granted the reprieve to Lord Cromartie, not I, because his pregnant wife fainted at his feet, and many others supported the motion for his reprieve. And as for Oxford, I merely intervened to stop the loyal majority of the student body being tainted by the actions of the Jacobite few. That hardly makes me a Jacobite sympathiser! No more than rescuing a misguided young woman from the utmost barbarity does," he added, glancing across at the skeletal form of the unconscious figure lying opposite him.

"I know, and I am not saying you *are*, I am merely saying that your action today, when it is known how she's suffered, will certainly enhance your reputation as a just and kind prince. But if you take her into your home for however long it takes for her to recover, your enemies will have time to invent a malicious story about your loyalties. It could damage your reputation far more than mine. I have little to lose anyway. I don't care a fig for society, and I'm not the heir to the throne."

"No, but your husband is a highly favoured Whig politician."

"My husband knows nothing of what we have done today. This is all my doing, and I would have that reported widely. He will be incensed when he finds out, and I would have that reported widely too," Caroline said, hoping that Edwin would not in reality be *too* angry at what she was about to do. She turned to the prince, and the tears spilled over her lashes. "I believe that one day you will make a wonderful king, and I would not have my regard for this woman, and your kindness in helping me to find her, jeopardise that. And neither would Edwin. Please, take her to my house. I will take care of her. But I will accept the offer of your surgeon, Your Highness."

The prince took Caroline's hands in his.

"You are a most extraordinary woman, Caroline," he said. "I will not forget this day, or your loyalty to your friends, of whom I hope I can count myself as one."

"Indeed you can, Your Highness," she replied. "And I am honoured to say so."

The prince leaned out of the coach window, instructed one of the footmen to make all haste to the surgeon, and then ordered the coachman to drive to Caroline's, but slowly, so as not to risk the extremely fragile cargo they carried.

\* \* \*

## Whitehall

"Mr Jones here to see you, my lord," Benjamin announced, adding when it was obvious that his master had no idea who Mr Jones was, "The keeper of Newgate Prison."

"Ah. Did he say it was important?" the Duke of Newcastle asked.

"No. But I think it is. He looks somewhat discomposed, my lord."

"Very well. Show him in."

Once Mr Jones had been admitted, the duke could see that 'somewhat discomposed' was something of an understatement. The man was sweating and trembling as though he had the ague.

"Are you ill, man?" the duke asked, alarmed. If the man had gaol fever, he should not be coming here, infecting his staff and himself.

"No, I am quite well, my lord," he said, sketching a bow. "You told me that you wished to be notified immediately if any man came to the prison enquiring about Miss Cunningham." He took out a handkerchief and wiped his brow.

"Excellent! Give me all the details. What manner of man was he?"

The keeper mumbled something at the floor, of which only one word reached Newcastle's ears.

"What? The man said his name was Prince?" he said. "Speak up, man!"

"No, my lord. It was the prince," Mr Jones said despairingly.

"The prince? You mean Prince William Augustus? What did you tell him? Did he see her? What is her condition?" the duke barked, thinking rapidly. He had thought the prince to be too preoccupied with his new lover to think about Miss Cunningham.

"Not Prince William, my lord, Prince Frederick."

"Prince *Frederick?!* You mean *the* Prince Frederick?" Newcastle asked, astounded.

Mr Jones was clearly confused, having had no idea that there might be more than one prince called Frederick.

"Yes, my lord," he replied uncertainly.

"And did you tell him that you had no one of that name in the prison, as we agreed?"

"I did, my lord."

"Ah, good."

"But he didn't believe me, my lord. And he demanded to see her. I had no choice," Mr Jones said.

*Oh, no.*

"What condition is the prisoner in? Is she in good health?"

"Well, no, she's in a bad way."

"What? You mean she was not being kept in a manner befitting her station as the cousin of a lord?"

The keeper's eyes widened, and his mouth dropped open in shock.

"No, my lord. You expressly said that she was to be kept in solitary confinement and given minimum rations and no privileges or medical treatment whatsoever. I followed your orders to the letter."

"Don't be ridiculous, man," the duke scoffed. "I would hardly order such treatment for a member of the aristocracy, even a traitor. You must have misunderstood me. Transfer her to the Tower immediately. Ensure she gets the very best of everything. I will speak with Prince Frederick and clear this misunderstanding up."

The keeper muttered something at the floor again. Sweat dripped off his chin and landed on his shoe. The duke eyed him with distaste.

"What did you say?"

"He took her, my lord. The prince took her away. I couldn't stop him. I don't know where she is."

After he'd had the man thrown out, the Duke of Newcastle sat with his head in his hands, thinking rapidly. This was terrible. How the hell had Prince Fred found out the Cunningham girl was in Newgate Prison? And why was he taking such an interest in her? Where was she? And, more importantly, what was the prince going to do? Go to his father? His brother? Was Cumberland still soft on the woman? Even if he wasn't, he would never countenance a woman of her status being tortured and then slowly starved to death.

*Thank God I didn't put my orders to Jones in writing*, Newcastle thought. No one else knew. He would deny everything, let the keeper take the blame if there was any comeback from this. He had already covered his tracks regarding the disastrous situation with Captain Cunningham. He could do it again. As for Elizabeth Cunningham, it was clear she was never going to reveal anything about Sir Anthony. Jones had said she was in a bad way. With luck she would die, and then it would all blow over in no time. If she lived it would be most inconvenient, especially as he could hardly arrange for an accident to befall her now she had come to the notice of Frederick.

Cumberland was extremely busy and would be out of the country fighting soon, and she had rejected his romantic proposal quite brutally; he was unlikely to spend precious time making enquiries regarding her ill-treatment. Hopefully.

But Frederick was another matter; his ongoing estrangement from his father, and the king's unwillingness to allow his heir to undertake any royal duties left the young prince with nothing to do but interfere in matters that were none of his concern. As he just had.

The duke realised that with Miss Cunningham out of his control, there was nothing he could do to try to cover this up without calling attention to himself. What he *could* do was distance himself from the whole situation, to absolve himself from blame as best he could.

And absolving himself from blame was something the Duke of Newcastle was very adept at.

\* \* \*

By the time Edwin returned home that evening Beth had been very carefully undressed, washed, and gently laid between warmed and scented sheets in the main guest room. The surgeon had visited and had spent the whole afternoon and evening with his patient, telling Caroline that in truth he did not think he could save her, but he would do his utmost. Throughout all of this Beth had remained insensible, her breathing shallow, her pulse barely discernible, while Caroline had prayed with a fervour she had not shown since she was a small child, and had prepared herself for her husband's reaction.

"I thought you said you would not do anything reckless!" Edwin said when Caroline told him what had transpired.

"I didn't expect Fred to take her from the prison!" Caroline replied. "I don't think he did, either, to be honest. It was an impulse. But I'm glad he did."

"Did you have to bring her here, though? She's the wife of the most wanted man in Britain! What happens if she escapes?"

"Come and see her. Then you'll know how likely she is to escape," Caroline said.

Edwin shook his head.

"I can't be involved in this, Caro. It will be political suicide if it becomes known that I'm sheltering her. You've broken the law, too. You can't just spring someone from prison!"

"No, I can't. And I didn't. Fred did that, and he'll take the responsibility for it. And I brought her here for two reasons; firstly because Fred and I will make it widely known that we acted without either your knowledge or permission. But now it's done you can hardly go directly against the express wish of the Prince of Wales. No one would expect you to do that, so your career is not in jeopardy. By taking responsibility for her now, I am earning you the good favour of the future King of Great Britain, and hopefully assuring your future career too."

Edwin stared at his wife.

"You have really thought this through," he said in wonder.

"No. I acted on the spur of the moment. I didn't have time to think it through."

"Even so…you said there was a second reason for bringing her here?"

"Yes. My first instinct was to take her to Summer Hill, where it's not only quieter but more discreet, but I don't think she would have survived the journey. And if you see her, Edwin, you'll understand why Fred did what he did. I'm sure you would have done the same, in fact."

"Is she really that ill?" Edwin asked.

She took his hand. "Come and see," she said.

When they entered the room, the royal surgeon was just packing away his things. He stood, and bowed slightly to them.

"I have done everything I can for now," he said. "She has taken a little sustenance, thank God, but…"

"Is she conscious, then?" Caroline asked.

"No, but when we spooned a little warm milk into her mouth, she swallowed automatically. I do not wish to raise your hopes, however. I do not know if we can bring her back from this." He snapped his bag closed. "If she recovers consciousness, try to get her to drink a very little warm, thin broth. Only a little, though. Her stomach will not be able to cope with more than a few spoonsful. I will return first thing in the morning, but if there is any change between now and then send for me immediately." He was shown out by a footman.

Caroline went straight over to the bed, and sat down on a chair at the side of it. Edwin stood hesitantly in the doorway. Caroline held out her hand and he moved forward reluctantly, his eyes on the still figure lying in the bed.

"Oh, dear God," he gasped when he was close enough to see her clearly. He turned his head away for a moment, then looked back at the remains of the beautiful, vibrant woman he had once called his friend. Tears spilled unheeded down his cheeks and he sank to his knees at the side of the bed.

She was wearing a nightdress of Caroline's and the bedding covered most of her body, which hardly made any impression in the bed. All that was visible of her was her head, neck and one arm, which was resting on top of the bedclothes, the wrist and hand heavily bandaged, but that was enough for all Edwin's reservations about taking care of her to be completely obliterated.

She was a skeleton. The skin of her face, paper-thin and yellow, followed the contours of her skull perfectly. Her cheekbones looked about to break through the fragile covering, and her closed eyes were sunk deep into the sockets, the pale lashes showing starkly against the surrounding shadowed skin. Below the cheekbones her face was sunken; so little flesh remained that Edwin could see the hinge of her jaw bone. Her neck was a stick, her windpipe visible, and the double bones of the lower arm could be clearly distinguished, her elbow appearing huge by comparison. Her once glorious hair was now lifeless, strawlike and matted.

"Who has done this?" he asked, his voice hoarse with emotion.

"I don't know. At the moment, we have to put all our effort into bringing her back. If we *can* bring her back," Caroline said. "The surgeon couldn't believe that she'd actually managed to survive this long. She's literally skin and bone. She has wounds on her wrists that have partially healed, but then become infected, and have not been treated. And she has rat bites on her legs. Sit down properly, Edwin, you look about to faint," she added, seeing the ominous grey pallor overtake his face.

Instead he sat on the floor and put his head between his knees, breathing deeply for a few minutes until he recovered enough to speak.

"I'm sorry," he said.

She was about to say that he had no need to apologise for being dizzy, but before she could speak, he continued.

"You were right. Of course she must stay here. No one deserves this, least of all someone as kind, as spirited as she is…was. We must find out who is responsible. This is not punishment. This is barbarity. God, I thought the executions were bad, but this…this defies everything."

"I think those who have been executed have been the lucky ones," Caroline said softly. "She is not the only one being treated this way, I believe. I told you about the transports yesterday. The only difference between Beth and those poor souls is that she is highborn, and they, as far as we know are not."

"We must make arrangements," Edwin said. "Get a nurse for her, several nurses. She must have someone with her at all times. And we must…" He stopped, arrested by Caroline's hand on his arm.

"I will stay with her tonight," she said. "If she makes it through the night, then we can engage a nurse for her. Frederick said he will arrange for us to become official messengers, so that we can have legal responsibility for her. He thinks a guard may have to be stationed outside the door, in view of her importance as the only person who knows Anthony's identity."

Edwin snorted in disgust.

"Important enough for a guard, but not important enough to feed," he said.

"I think she has refused to compromise in any way at all," Caroline said. "She told the maid at the Tower to place a bet that she would neither marry nor become William's mistress. I suspect she may have told him the same thing, in no uncertain terms. You know how direct she always was."

He smiled, remembering, then looked at the figure in the bed, and his mouth twisted with grief. He looked up at his wife, whose eyes were also shimmering with tears.

"To hell with everything," he said. "If we can bring her back from this, we must. Whatever she has done, she's our friend."

"'*Not a day goes by that I do not think of you and wish that I still had your friendship, but I understand this can never be,*'" Caroline murmured.

"You remember the exact words of her letter?" Edwin said.

"I do. I read it several times before I burned it," Caroline replied, then her eyes widened. "Oh God, I forgot to let Sarah know we'd found her! I must send a message, straight away!" She rang the bell and gave the order. Edwin waited until the servant had left the room before he spoke again.

"She was wrong," Edwin said. "She does still have our friendship. Highbury was wrong too when he said Anthony had not compromised anyone. This poor girl *has* been compromised by him. And I will never forgive him for that."

"Go and get some rest, Edwin," Caroline said. "You've had a long day. I will sit with her tonight, and then we can discuss the details of her care tomorrow."

He stood, kissed his wife, and prepared to leave. At the door he turned back.

"You will wake me, if…" His voice trailed away.

"Of course," she replied.

"And tomorrow," he added, as he opened the door, "I will go and visit the transports."

He closed the door quietly behind him, and Caroline settled herself for her all-night vigil.

# CHAPTER FIFTEEN

**Paris, January 1747**

"Your Royal Highness, I beg ye to reconsider," Donald Cameron of Lochiel said fervently to his prince, who was currently slouching in a chair by the fire, a cold damp cloth across his forehead. Last night had been a long one and had involved, as usual, a ridiculous amount of drink and a number of whores. Charles was clearly not in the mood for a lecture. But it was rare nowadays for Lochiel to find him alone without that corrupting bastard Kelly by his side, and he could not waste the opportunity.

"Donald, have I not been good to you? Are you not one of my closest advisers? Have I not applied for a regimental command for you?"

"You have, Your Highness, and I'm verra grateful of course. But –"

"So why do you persist in troubling me when I am unwell?"

*You're no' unwell, you're hungover, ye drunken sot,* Lochiel thought, then hastily chided himself. This was the man for whom he had sacrificed everything, his prince, the only hope the Stuarts now had of a restoration to the British throne; he deserved respect. But Charles also needed to know that the course he was heading on now could lead only to a further estrangement between himself and King Louis, which neither he nor the Jacobite cause in general could afford.

"Because this canna wait, Your Highness. Please, if you will give me a few minutes of your time."

Wearily Charles indicated with a wave of his hand for the Cameron chief to take a chair on the other side of the fire. Lochiel sat down.

"Your Highness, I beg you to abandon this plan to leave Paris and go to Avignon. It will be a direct affront to His Majesty to do so."

"Good. That is what I intend it to be. How does he expect me to live in a style appropriate to my status on a mere twelve thousand livres a month? It is an insult. As is his refusal to allow me a royal residence to live in, as he promised me when we met at Fontainebleau. How can I command the respect of my followers if I allow the French king to treat me thus?"

Lochiel forbore from pointing out that surrounding yourself with drunken debauchers and spending a fortune on liquor and whores, to say nothing of insulting the only person who could finance another rising, was far more likely to alienate your followers than allowing King Louis to prevaricate, as he did with everyone.

"You have the respect of all of us," he said instead. "We all ken well that it's the nature of the king to dither a wee bit, but –"

"Dither a wee bit!" Charles exclaimed, then moaned and put his hand to his head. "The king has done nothing. Had he acceded to my request for twenty thousand troops to accompany me to England, I could be mounting a winter expedition right now and taking the throne for my father. If England falls to me there will be no need of a campaign in Scotland. We need to strike hard and fast, drive the Elector off the throne before he knows what has hit him. Once the throne is secure, the rest will follow, I am convinced of it."

"But Louis will not agree to commit such a force to England, Your Highness," Lochiel pointed out. "Whereas he is far more amenable to granting us troops for another invasion of Scotland."

"Scotland has been crushed by Cumberland's troops, though," Charles said, a note of sadness entering his tone. "Those loyal to me have been disarmed and driven from their homes. They could not rise now if they would. And I have no reason to believe those who did not come out for me last year feel any differently now."

"I *do* have reason to believe it," Lochiel said, reaching into his coat pocket and producing a letter. "I received a letter yesterday from Cluny Macpherson, and another today from Alex MacGregor. As ye ken, Cluny has clan members everywhere wi' their car to the ground, and Alex is a master of intelligence gathering. They both give me great hope, for they tell me that the brutality of Cumberland's men is having the opposite effect to that they intended. The clansmen are incensed wi' the treatment they've received, and no' just the clans loyal to you, Your Highness. The redcoats have no' discriminated overmuch in their plundering between those who rose and those who didna. The Macleans are for rising, Ardshiel and others are still hiding out near Appin, and Keppoch's, my own Camerons, the MacGregors, Grants, Frasers…there are many who are waiting for ye to come back. It's my belief that ye'll raise more than twice the number ye did last year, and more maybe. Wi' the addition of a small French force, ye could take Scotland back for the Stuarts, easily."

Charles took the towel off his forehead and looked at his most loyal follower, not without sympathy.

"Donald, I understand you, and I value your loyalty and that of Cluny and Alex, and others. But if I lead another rising in Scotland, the same thing will happen. I may take Scotland for my father, yes. But without England that means nothing."

"How can that mean nothing?" Lochiel said, aghast. "The Stuarts reigned in Scotland alone for hundreds of years, until Queen Elizabeth died barren. Ye could do it again, break the union, and Scotland could hold her head up once more as an independent country. Your Highness, you owe it to the people who have fought and died for you, and those who are now suffering for it, to abandon this scheme for an English invasion, which the king will never agree to, and settle for a Scottish expedition, which he *will* agree to."

"My father is the rightful king of all Great Britain, not just Scotland," Charles said belligerently.

Lochiel swallowed down his frustration, forcing his tone to remain calm. He was desperate to get back to his country, to his people, who were suffering while he sat here in relative luxury, trying to make the prince see reason. They had to mount another campaign in Scotland. If they didn't the Highland way of life would be obliterated. However, he had known the prince for long enough to know that shouting at him was not the way to go.

"Would ye no' rather have Scotland than nothing at all?" he asked gently instead.

"That will not happen," Charles said confidently. "If I cannot get Louis' approval, I will seek elsewhere."

"Elsewhere?" Lochiel asked. Charles coloured.

"In the future," he added hastily. "But in the meantime I will go to Avignon and seek to set up court there. It is after all a papal state, and I think that Pope Benedict will look favourably on me."

"Your Highness, an ye leave French territory now, and insult the king by doing so, you will give Louis the chance to make peace with Britain, as some are urging him to do."

"I have made up my mind," Charles persisted stubbornly. "I am giving my brother plenipotentiary powers while I'm away. I'm sure he will come up with some plausible reasons for my absence that will satisfy the king. Now, I am ill, and I wish to be alone. Please leave us."

Lochiel had no option but to leave. He had tried his best, he told himself; he could not have done more. But that would not help those who were starving and dying at home, and were waiting desperately for news of a French landing in Scotland.

He could of course drive his sword through the heart of George Kelly, the adviser who was encouraging Charles to take this ridiculous stand against the French king, which he could not win. But then he would have to kill all the other sycophants who had the prince under their sway too. And even if he did that, Charles would still go his own way.

All he could do was remain loyal and wait, hoping that the prince would see sense and take advice from those who genuinely sought a Stuart restoration rather than those who sought to line their pockets.

\* \* \*

## London.

Very slowly, hour by hour and day by day, under the expert treatment of one of the best surgeons in the country and the expert nursing of one of the most belligerent and determined women in the country, with the aid of her equally formidable assistant and the intermittent presence of Edwin when not on parliamentary duty, Beth started to recover.

When Sarah had received the message that Beth had been found, she had gone immediately to Caroline's, and apart from a brief trip home to collect clothing and other necessaries, had stayed there ever since. Caroline had insisted on paying her, because she was earning nothing while she was looking after Beth, and when Sarah had balked at being paid for taking care of someone she loved, Caroline had pointed out that she would have had to pay a nurse anyway, but would far prefer someone who had a personal interest in the recovery of the patient.

After a few days the surgeon informed the Harlows and Sarah that he believed Beth to be out of danger of imminent death, although it was impossible to tell how much damage her vital organs had sustained due to the prolonged starvation. He confessed himself to be astounded. He had never seen anyone come so close to death's door and not cross the threshold. It was a miracle, and a testament to the immense will to live that this tiny, fragile body harboured.

Neither Caroline nor Sarah thought it to be a miracle; they knew that Beth was one of the most stubborn, determined people they'd ever met, with a great zest for life. They were not surprised that her survival instinct caused her to automatically swallow the food and medicines she was given, even though she was still unconscious for much of the time, and when conscious showed no awareness of her surroundings or her situation.

After ten days of constant care and incrementally larger meals, Beth finally recovered both consciousness and awareness, to the relief and joy of the three people whose lives currently revolved around her.

And then the real work started. Because once awake, far from being happy to be alive and grateful to those who had made it so, she was distraught. Her treacherous body might want to accept nourishment and survive at all costs, but the owner of it most certainly did not. With every fibre of her being she wanted to die and join her husband, who she was now certain must not have survived Culloden.

The first time that Caroline tried to feed the fully conscious Beth, still too weak to move, a bowl of soup, she closed her mouth and turned her head away like a small child refusing its greens.

"Come on, Beth," said Caroline, misunderstanding the gesture. "I know it's embarrassing to be fed like a baby, but soon you'll be able to lift a spoon yourself. Mr Platt says you're making a remarkable recovery."

To Caroline's astonishment, on hearing these words Beth's face crumpled, and she gave a huge sob. Tears welled in her eyes, spilled over, and trickled down the sunken cheeks. Caroline abandoned the soup, and leaning over, very carefully took the emaciated woman in her arms.

"I don't want to," Beth murmured into Caroline's chest. "I'm so close. Please let me die."

"It's all right," Caroline said. "You don't need to be afraid. We won't let you go back to Newgate."

"No, you don't understand," Beth said, but Caroline was already reaching for the soup again, and too exhausted by her brief emotional outburst to protest, she dutifully swallowed the soup before falling into a deep sleep.

Upon awakening the following morning, however, she made a further attempt to make her wishes known.

"I want to die," she told a startled Caroline who, thinking her patient to be deeply asleep, was sitting by the side of the bed engrossed in a novel. She closed it with a snap and put it on the bedside table.

"You're very weak," Caroline began, "Mr Platt, he's the surgeon, said you would be low in spirits for a time. And as I told you yesterday, we won't let you go back to Newgate. At the moment Edwin has permission for you to stay here until you are completely well. And Prince Frederick is determined that if you are to remain a prisoner, it will either be here with us, or in luxury in the Tower. But I really think we might be able to secure your release before too long. Once you're a little stronger, you'll feel differently."

"No I won't," Beth replied. "I've been trying to die for months. Why won't you let me?"

"You don't mean that," Caroline said, shocked.

"I do," Beth persisted. "I tried to get them to execute me, because I was scared of getting gaol fever, but they wouldn't. And then after Richard, when they told me about the baby, and then they left me alone, really alone, I knew they'd given up, and then I didn't mind if I got it because they wouldn't hear me, but I didn't. And then they stopped bringing food and I was happy because I knew we'd be together soon. And now it's all spoilt."

She was delirious. She had to be. Nothing she was saying made any sense.

"Well you'll just have to stop trying to die," Caroline said briskly. "Because we love you and we're not letting you die, and there's an end of it."

A few evenings later Caroline and Edwin were in the cosy parlour chatting about the affairs of the day, when there came a tentative knock on the door.

"Come in!" Edwin shouted at the top of his voice, expecting Toby.

The door opened and Sarah poked her head round it.

"Can I have a word?" she asked. "Beth's asleep," she added by way of explaining her dereliction of duty.

She came in and sat down, a worried expression on her face.

"She's much stronger today," she said. "She said she was only eating because she feels bad about all the trouble she's causing us. We had a long chat."

"Right now I don't care why she's eating, as long as she is," Caroline replied. "Her mood will lift when she's stronger."

"That's why I want to talk to you," Sarah said. "I'm not sure it will."

"What was the long chat about?" Edwin asked.

"She told me that she was interviewed by the Duke of Cumberland and the Duke of Newcastle, and that she wouldn't tell them anything, which was why they sent her to Newgate. One of her cellmates died of gaol fever, but before she died she rambled in her fever and told the others all sorts of things about her life. After that Beth was terrified of getting sick and revealing everything about Sir Anthony. So she deliberately provoked the duke, hoping he'd order her execution."

"Except he didn't. He ordered her to be tortured instead," Caroline stated.

"Yes. But she told me something else. She was pregnant," Sarah said.

"What?" Edwin asked. "Did she know this when she saw the duke?"

"Yes."

"And he *still* ordered her torture?" he said, aghast.

"Which duke?" Caroline asked, her expression showing that whichever one it was, he was going to regret it.

"Newcastle," Sarah said. "But he didn't know. She didn't tell him, because she knew that he wouldn't have her killed if he knew she was pregnant."

"I don't understand," Edwin said.

"She didn't want him to use her own child to try to make her betray Sir Anthony. And she knew that if she didn't the baby would have almost no chance of surviving anyway, in prison or a foundling hospital."

"You mean she thinks so much of that traitor that she was willing to kill herself *and* her baby rather than give him up?" Edwin said, astounded. "What's wrong with her? He's abandoned her, for God's sake! Can't she see that? I wish *I* knew who he really was. I'd give him up to Newcastle with the greatest pleasure."

This uncharacteristic display of anger silenced both women for a moment. Sarah opened her mouth, then closed it again, unsure of what to say.

"He might not have abandoned her, Edwin. He might be dead," Caroline pointed out.

"That's what she thinks," Sarah added. "She said that he told her he'd come for her, and if he was alive he certainly would have done by now. So he must be dead, and she wants to join him. She lost the baby after Richard…" She stopped for a minute, her face twisting with hatred, "…after he tortured her."

"This is ridiculous," Edwin said, still incensed. "Whether he's dead or alive, he doesn't deserve this loyalty. He knew what he was when he married her. He had no right to put her in that danger, to talk an innocent, gullible girl into following him into treason and then letting her go on campaign with him–"

"Are we still talking about Beth?" Caroline interrupted.

"Of course we are!" Edwin said, puzzled. "Who else would we be talking about?"

"I don't know," Caroline retorted. "But the only way that Beth was innocent before Anthony married her was in understanding how manipulative and two-faced society is. And she was *never* gullible. She was already a Jacobite, Edwin. Surely that's obvious? Anthony recognised that, and married her to get her away from her obnoxious family before she gave herself away anyway. I don't know what happened after that, but as for *letting* her do something, can you imagine anyone trying to stop Beth doing something she really wants to do?"

"He was her husband," Edwin said. "A husband should be able to control…" He looked at his wife, and his voice trailed away. "Anyway," he continued a moment later, "if she thinks he's dead, why doesn't she tell Newcastle what he wants to know? It can't do Anthony any harm, but we could almost certainly get her a pardon if she does."

"She said that if she betrays him, she'll betray some other people too, people that she cares for," Sarah said, her colour rising a little. "She won't do that. I admire her for it."

"So do I," Caroline agreed.

Edwin wiped his hand across his face in exasperation.

"I give in," he said. "You must both have been reading those stupid romantic novels that women swoon over. We're talking about traitors here. Men who are trying to overthrow the king; dangerous, ruthless men."

"Unlike the kind and compassionate men who are not trying to overthrow the king, but who are happy to order the torture and starvation of a young woman because she won't give up the man she loves?" Caroline said coldly.

Sarah looked from one to the other in shock. She had never heard them exchange so much as a cross word before. Now they looked about to embark on a full-blown argument. Her guilt at being the unwitting cause of this marital disharmony emboldened her to intervene.

"Arguing with each other about whether she should give him up or not is pointless, because she won't do it. Instead we should be trying to work out how to be the first people to stop Beth doing something she wants to do," she said. "Because right now all she wants to do is die."

"I'm sorry," Edwin said, his naturally placid, kind-hearted nature prevailing over his outburst of anger. "Neither of you are the sort of idiotic woman who swoons over dreadful romantic novels. I shouldn't have said that."

"I'm sorry, too," Caroline replied. "We're all overwrought. Let's see what we can come up with to persuade her that she has good reason to live."

\* \* \*

After trying a multitude of tactics, from talking about the bright future she could have, that she was too young and lovely to die, that lots of people loved her, even (from Sarah) that when released she could continue her fight to restore the Stuarts, they finally hit upon the two things that made her agree to try to get well.

The first was to tell her of the huge amount of effort, time and money that had been put into rescuing her. The soldier Ned risked the wrath of Richard if it became known that he had spoken about her ordeal; Prince Frederick risked further alienation from his father by freeing her from jail; Edwin had put his political career on the line by agreeing to keep her in his house; and Sarah was losing a lot of custom and goodwill by spending all her time nursing Beth. She owed it to them if not to herself to stop being so selfish and repay their efforts on her behalf.

And the second was to tell her that Richard would be overjoyed if he knew that she had utterly lost the will to live and had committed suicide because of his attack on her.

She spent the next two weeks valiantly forcing down food, gritting her teeth at the resulting stomach cramps, trying not to feel embarrassed when she lost control of her bladder which happened frequently at first, enduring the cramps and frustration once she tried to start performing herculean tasks such as feeding herself and sitting up unaided; and all of it done with a sullen and resentful attitude towards those who were resorting to emotional blackmail to stop her killing herself.

It was only when she was finally capable of sitting, and was able to be lifted out of the bed by Edwin and seated in a chair by the window for a short period of time, and could look out at the people passing by in the street to relieve the boredom of convalescence, that she saw the spire of a nearby church. And suddenly the third reason, and the most important one, the only one that really mattered, hit her.

If she had died in the prison cell, that would have been fine. But to deliberately refuse aid and choose to starve to death, was suicide. In the Roman Catholic faith, the faith to which both she and Alex belonged, suicide was a mortal sin. If she died by her own hand, she would go to hell. And if she went to hell she would never be reunited with Alex, because if he was dead, as she believed he must be, he had died fighting for what he believed in and for the right to worship freely, and would therefore be certain of a place in heaven.

She had to live, and go on living, until God decided it was time for her to die and join the only man she had ever loved, the only man she ever *would* love. And if she was going to live, then she might as well do it wholeheartedly, as she had always done everything.

That afternoon, to Edwin's surprise, when he returned to carry her back to bed Beth bestowed a smile on him which actually reached her eyes, and asked him if he thought she might be able to attempt to stand by herself soon.

"I'll call for the surgeon and ask his advice," Edwin said. "I don't want to say yes and then risk you breaking your leg."

When Sarah came in later with some mashed potatoes and carefully de-boned fish, Beth had pushed back the bedcovers and was attempting to raise and lower her legs, her face contorted with the effort. Eyeing the stick-thin shins on display, Sarah forced down the tears and pasted a smile on her face.

"Dinner!" she said brightly. "And there's a syllabub for dessert, too."

Beth looked at her, grimaced at the bland food which was all her stomach could tolerate at the moment, and pulled the sheet back over herself.

"Edwin said that he's worried I might break my legs if I try to walk right now," Beth said, "so I thought I'd build a little muscle without putting any weight on them at first. When I was in the Tower," she continued, lifting a forkful of potato to her lips and blowing on it to cool it a little, "I used to run on the spot, and hold a book at arm's length for ages to stop my muscles wasting away. When I think of all the walking I did, when we were…never mind. I took my health for granted."

"You'll get it back," Sarah replied.

Beth smiled at her.

"Yes," she said. "I will. Thank you. All of you. I'm sorry I've been so ungrateful. I've been feeling very low, but I'm much better today."

"She's turned the corner," Sarah said later in the parlour. "I don't know what's happened, but she's suddenly got the will to live, really got it. She's not just eating and moving to please us any more."

"Thank God for that," Caroline breathed. "I've missed the old Beth, more than I expected to. And maybe we can all start living a more normal life now if one of us doesn't have to sit with her every night for fear she'll find a way to kill herself."

"I can't imagine feeling so desperately unhappy with life that all you want to do is end it," Edwin said. "It must be terrible."

"It is," Sarah replied without thinking, then blushed as Edwin and Caroline both looked at her. "But if you don't give in to it, then time goes by and things change, and one day you're really glad that you kept going, because life is a wonderful gift, and you come out stronger for having survived the bad times."

"Maybe she'll be able to have visitors now," Caroline said. "It'll do her good to have some different conversation. I know Tom wants to see her if she wants him to, and Prince Frederick does, too. I didn't want to take the chance on letting them see her in case she was rude to them."

"I don't think she will be now she's not angry with everyone who saved her life," Sarah said. "Can I ask a favour of you both?"

"Of course!" Caroline replied. "I don't know how we'd have managed without your help."

"Don't mention Mary to her. At all."

They had agreed not to mention that Sarah was looking after her niece while Beth was very weak, in case it reminded her of the baby she'd lost.

"But surely once she's a little stronger, she'll be able to deal with it? You can't keep Mary from her forever," Edwin pointed out.

"Maybe not. But will you let me be the one to decide when to tell her? However long that might be? Please?" she added, with desperation in her voice.

"Of course, if that's what you want," Edwin said. Caroline nodded agreement. They wore matching puzzled expressions.

"It is. Thank you," Sarah replied, with enormous and obvious relief.

\* \* \*

Although not willing to talk about Mary, now that Beth was more receptive Sarah told her the details of John's escape from prison, and their attendance at the execution of the other rebels.

"I know he knew things about Sir Anthony, but the authorities didn't know that so they didn't question him, and he wasn't going to volunteer anything," Sarah added. "I wouldn't let him tell me anything either. I've been interviewed by the Duke of Newcastle once, and I don't want to know anything that could hurt them…him," she amended hurriedly.

Beth leaned forward in the chair she was sitting in and grasped her former maid's hands.

"I really appreciate that," she said.

"John's very fond of you," Sarah said, her eyes on the thin hands linked in hers.

"He is, but I mean I really appreciate you not saying anything to Newcastle."

"I didn't have anything to say," Sarah replied. "I never saw Sir Anthony without his makeup."

"No, but you could have given him descriptions of Jim and Murdo at the very least."

"I didn't see what good it would do to give descriptions of servants, when it was Sir Anthony they were interested in. Anyway, I only saw them a few times," Sarah persisted, her colour rising a little.

Beth released her hands.

"Did Caroline read you the message I sent for you, when I wrote to her?" she asked.

Sarah blushed scarlet.

"I read it myself," she said. "I've learnt how to read, now. I'm slow, though. I can write, too! I wanted to ask you if I can write to Thomas and Jane, tell them that you're alive. They'll be so happy to know you're well."

"I'll be able to write to them myself soon," Beth said. "I'm getting the strength back in my hands now. You might like to know that the person who dictated the postscript was still alive on the morning of the battle. He gave me a message for you."

Sarah's eyes widened. She stood up, looking frantic.

"I don't know….do I want to hear it?" she said.

"I think you should, but it's up to you."

Sarah breathed in and out slowly a couple of times, and then came to a decision.

"Tell me," she said.

"He said that he loves you, and that if things had been different he'd have married you, if you'd have him," Beth told her. "But he said that if…you know…that there are other good men out there and that you mustn't keep your promise, but look for happiness. And to remember the spider."

Sarah sat down suddenly on the edge of the bed. Her chin trembled and tears welled up in her eyes and spilled down her cheeks. She wiped them away impatiently.

"He hasn't written to me," she said. "Do you think…?" She didn't finish the sentence, but Beth knew what she was asking.

"I don't know," she said. "I'm not going to give you false hope, because you deserve more than that. But it could be that because we lost, he thinks it's kinder to let you forget him and move on with your life."

"I can't forget him," Sarah said. "I'll never forget him. How can I? And I would marry him, if he still wanted to. I don't care about his stupid king, and who won or lost. And I don't want anyone else. Is there…no, of course not."

"Is there what?" Beth asked.

"I was going to ask if there was a way of contacting him."

"No," Beth said. "There's no way I know of. If we tried, we'd betray him, and others."

"Better not to know, then," Sarah said, blowing her nose furiously. "Better never to know than risk that. If you can live with it, I'm damn sure I can."

"I can live with it," Beth replied. *But I don't know how.*

Once the Christmas season was over and Beth was able to stand and walk a few steps before her growing, but still very weak muscles started to shake, a trickle of visitors was allowed in to see her. The first one was Tom, who had been desperate to see her and apologise to her in person for months. She reassured him that she'd forgiven him long ago for his part in her abduction, and far from apologising to her he must accept her gratitude, and must also convey that gratitude to Ned, because without his intervention she would have died.

The next visitor was Prince Frederick, who waved away Beth's attempts to thank him for rescuing her, saying it was only what anyone would have done, that he owed her that and more for giving him a story to dine out on for years when she'd impaled Lord Daniel with her knife.

And then, at the start of February, when Beth was able to walk properly, when she had regained most of the weight she'd lost and a good deal of her strength, and was sitting in the library downstairs reading a book, the Earl of Highbury was announced, and upon her saying that she was certainly well enough to receive him, he was admitted.

She rose and curtseyed, and said how honoured she was to have such a distinguished visitor. He in his turn took a seat and commented on how well she was looking. She ordered refreshments, and the polite conversation flowed freely while they awaited the sandwiches and coffee they'd ordered.

"Edwin told me that you were at death's door," Highbury said. "But you seem radiant. And may I say that your hairstyle is very fetching, if a little unusual."

Having endured two days of Sarah's attempts to comb out the mat that had once been so admired by society, Beth had told her to just cut it all off and have done with it. It was starting to grow back a little now, the silver waves reaching to chin level.

"It's a lot easier to look after," Beth said, with her customary lack of vanity. "I'm sorry if the scar is unsightly, although you don't seem the sort of person to be perturbed by that."

The earl smiled.

"Very little perturbs me," he said. "And the wound has healed well. The surgeon made an excellent job of stitching it. In time it will be hardly noticeable, I think."

"Oh!" Beth replied, clearly disappointed. "I was hoping it would disfigure me."

"Whyever would you want that?" he asked with genuine puzzlement.

"Because if I am ever released from prison, I don't want to excite the interest of any men. Ever," she added with finality.

"Ah, you mean like Daniel," he said.

"No, I mean like anybody. I wish to remain single."

"I think you may have a good chance of that, being both a traitor and without any dowry at all," he said, his eyes sparkling as he looked at her. "I believe it all went to Ch –"

He stopped abruptly as the door opened and a servant entered, bearing a tray of refreshments. They resumed their small talk, commenting on the weather, the likelihood of snow, and the contents of the indifferent novel she was reading. And then the servant finished bustling about, the door was closed and they were alone. After a minute or so Beth stood up, and walking to the library door, opened it with a flourish. The hallway beyond was empty. She closed it again and came to sit down.

"Have you heard from him?" She asked the question she'd been burning to ask from the moment he'd been announced.

"No," Highbury said. Beth paled, and he hurried on. "But that doesn't mean anything, my dear. We had an agreement that if he was betrayed, he was on his own. He is a man of honour, as we both know. He would not compromise me by trying to make contact."

She looked down at her hands, which were resting in her lap.

"He said he would come for me, if he lived," she said sadly. "I waited for him, thinking he might have been injured, that he had been delayed…but now…it has been ten months. If he was alive he would have tried to reach me, I know he would."

"No one knew you had been arrested," Highbury pointed out. "It was a remarkably well-kept secret, you know."

Beth looked at the older man sitting opposite. His eyes were warm, understanding.

"Do you think Alex would have been put off by that? He would have found me. If anyone could, he would. We both know that."

"He could have been taken prisoner," the earl said. "That is possible."

She stared at him.

"You have made enquiries!" she said, and it was not a question. He smiled.

"I have made some discreet enquiries, yes, although I admit I should not have. There is no one of the name of Alexander MacGregor on the available lists of prisoners. But he may have used another name, especially being a MacGregor."

She thought for a moment, then shook her head.

"No, he was too well known as the chieftain, and as a member of the council," she said. "Somebody would have revealed his real name."

"Although Broughton has not," the earl said softly.

"You know about that?"

"Yes. Although Broughton does not know me, or anything about me."

"They brought him to see me when I was being interviewed by Cumberland," Beth said. "William was very disappointed when Murray said he had never seen me before."

"He did that? Interesting," Highbury said. "Maybe he is not the complete traitor most of the Jacobites think him to be. He could profit greatly from revealing the identity of Sir Anthony."

"I know. I am very grateful to him, anyway."

"You are alone in that, I think. Even his wife has disowned him."

"Oh, that saddens me. He loves Margaret very much. I thought she at least would stand by him."

"Would you stand by Alex if he was captured and turned king's evidence?" Highbury asked.

Beth thought for a minute.

"He wouldn't do it," she said finally. "Under any circumstances. But Murray is different. He was never a soldier. He wasn't accustomed to pain."

"Neither are you, Beth. But you have endured the most terrible pain, and yet you have told nothing. Which is why I am here. I wanted to thank you for revealing nothing about me, and to tell you that I admire you enormously. And I am not alone in that. If, or rather when you are released from prison, you will not be without friends in London."

"I thank you for that, my lord –"

"William, please."

"I thank you for that, William. But if I am ever released from prison, I will leave this godforsaken city and never return. I hate the place. It holds no happy memories for me. And I have no wish ever to return to society again."

"Where will you go?"

"I will go home," she said simply. And he did not ask her where that was, because he already knew.

\* \* \*

## Scotland, February 1747

Captain Richard Cunningham examined his new quarters minutely. The newly rebuilt room was small, but comfortable. The interior walls had been whitewashed, the wooden bed was plain but functional, and had been made up to military standards. His spare uniform had been brushed and pressed, and hung on a hook behind the door. There was a small chest in which, neatly folded, his spare shirts and stockings had been placed. A fire was burning in the small grate, and a pile of logs was stacked at the side of it. There was not a speck of dust in the room, and absolutely nothing that he could find fault with.

He scowled blackly, and pulling off his boots, moved to the small window and stood looking moodily out at the snow-covered mountains that hemmed the barracks in. It had been hell getting here. Even he, who was afraid of nothing, had found himself trembling as they'd crossed the mountains, dreading at every moment that his horse would put her foot through the snow into fresh air rather than solid ground and catapult him over the side of the ridge to certain death.

But his bay mare had been sure-footed, and now he was here, in a foul mood, as he had been almost continuously for the last six months, ever since the Duke of Newcastle had stabbed him so comprehensively and effectively in the back.

Of course he hadn't intended for Richard to torture his sister, especially as she was in a delicate condition! That had been the very reason why he had asked him to have a word with her, hoping that filial attachment would prevail where other methods had failed. It was hardly the duke's fault if the captain had assumed that by 'a word' he meant commit acts of unspeakable brutality! In fact by his vicious and inept attempt to extract information from his sister, which had resulted in the miscarriage of her baby, he had deprived the duke of his best chance of finding out the true identity of Sir Anthony Peters.

Yes, he had most certainly mentioned that the young lady was *enceinte*. He remembered quite clearly mentioning it. It was hardly his fault if the captain had not heard him, and had misinterpreted his clear and precise instructions not to physically assault the prisoner.

In fact, the duke had finished, in view of the appalling fiasco he had made of what should have been a gently persuasive interrogation of his sister, it was better he depart the capital immediately and return to Scotland. Perhaps given time, a considerable amount of time, he might redeem himself by an assiduous attention to duty.

The lying, two-faced fucking aristocratic bastard! Richard turned from the window, and moving across to the fireplace grabbed the poker and stabbed it into the hearth so viciously that a shower of sparks flew out onto the small brightly coloured hearthrug, the only homely touch in the otherwise Spartan room, threatening to set it alight. He stamped out the smouldering embers with his stockinged feet and sat on the chair, staring into the flames with deep malevolence.

One day he would get his revenge. Not on Newcastle; as much as he would love to disembowel the scheming piece of shit and watch him die writhing in agony on his exorbitantly expensive Aubusson carpet, Richard knew that would only ever be a happy daydream. He was not stupid enough to attempt to assassinate the brother of the Prime Minister.

But one day, hopefully, he would meet his sister again. And that would be a glorious day indeed. In fact, it would be a glorious several days. At least having a free rein in this savage dungheap of a country had given him the opportunity to hone his skills, and he was now confident that he would be able to keep her alive for days in excruciating agony.

If she was still alive. Having been packed off almost immediately after the humiliating interview with Newcastle to Scotland, he had been unable to find out whether or not his ministrations had resulted in Beth's demise. But he could wait. In the meantime, as soon as the snows melted enough for him to take his men out on raids he would make the most of this opportunity to show how effective he was at bringing the rebels to heel.

The barracks had only recently been rebuilt sufficiently to house a regiment, which meant there were plenty of Highlanders in the vicinity who no doubt thought they had got away with their treachery unscathed. He was about to disabuse them of that notion. In the meantime, while waiting for the weather to improve he intended to bring his men up to scratch so that they would obey him without question when he commanded them to do things they might otherwise balk at.

He threw another log on the fire, and sat back. Yes. Even if he couldn't make the duke's life hell, or, at present, his sister's, he was certainly distressing his wife, and he could also make his mark here.

His career had suffered a setback, that was true. But here was his chance to redeem it, to prove himself the equal of Scott, and of Hawley, who he admired greatly. And he intended to make the most of that.

\* \* \*

"Really, it's quite ridiculous!" Edwin fumed on his return from Whitehall, where the Prime Minister had informed him that now Miss Cunningham was ambulatory, certain precautions would have to be taken to ensure that she did not try to escape.

"I can understand it, Edwin," his wife said reasonably. "After all, she's a very valuable prisoner." Caroline was engaged in throwing a ball gently to her son, in the vain hope that he would catch it. He certainly held his hands out, laughing, to receive it, but had not quite grasped the fact that he had to bring them together to actually catch the ball, with the result that it hit him repeatedly in the chest and then fell to the ground. But he was happy enough picking it up from there and giving it to her to throw at him again. And it was a very soft ball, so the repeated collisions with his sturdy little chest would do him no damage.

"They didn't think her that valuable last November, when they were happy to let her die!" Edwin said.

"No, but we must think of Beth's welfare now. She's happy, or as happy as she can be, living here with us. Until she is pardoned, we must do everything we can to keep her with us. And if that means having a constant guard outside her quarters and bars on the window, so be it. I'm sure she'll agree to it. She'll still be able to receive visitors. And she'll still be with people who care for her."

"You're right," Edwin said. "But it feels like an insult, somehow. Other messengers don't have soldiers posted in their houses."

"No, they don't. But then you and I both know that unlike other messengers we are not indifferent to our charge, and are not accommodating her for financial gain. And Henry knows that too. I don't believe he's trying to insult you. If anything he's trying to protect you. If she *does* escape, you cannot be blamed if you've agreed to abide by all the precautions."

"You don't think she'll try to escape, do you?" Edwin said, suddenly alarmed.

"No, I don't. She has given her word that she won't, and I believe her. Now, let us look on the bright side. Freddie will be very excited to have real live soldiers in the house. I hope they like children, that's all," she said.

When Caroline went up to explain about the results of Edwin's interview with Henry Pelham, Beth was sitting by the fire re-hemming some sheets. Next to her was a basket full of assorted items of clothing, all of which were in need of some minor repair. She took the news that the windows were to be barred and a soldier posted in the hall in her stride, as Caroline had expected.

"You know, you really don't have to do that," Caroline said, sitting down opposite her.

"I don't mind at all," Beth replied. "It keeps me occupied, and it takes some of the burden off the maids."

Caroline sat for a minute watching Beth's nimble fingers as the needle flashed in and out of the cotton automatically. The seam was perfect, the stitches tiny, and yet Beth was hardly paying any attention to what she was doing. It was mesmerising.

"Anne would like to pay you a visit, if you're not averse to it," she inserted into the silence. The fingers faltered for a second, and then carried on.

"Why would I be averse to it?" Beth said. "It's not Anne's fault that Richard's an animal. I pity her. Is she still living with your aunt?"

"Yes," Caroline said. "I told her Richard's in Scotland at the moment, but I think she feels safer living in Hertfordshire. She hasn't recovered from his last unexpected appearance at the house."

"Tell her she's welcome to visit," Beth said. "It'll be nice to see a new face."

Anne turned up two days later. Afraid the presence of a child might upset Beth, she had left little George with Philippa and Oliver, but had brought with her presents, including flowers, and a tonic wine she had made herself.

"It is delicious," she said, pouring a glass for Beth, "and contains powdered gentian root, which will help to stimulate the appetite, prevents swooning, and comforts the heart." She looked at her subject doubtfully. "Although I admit you are looking very well, far better than I had expected."

Beth dutifully drank the potion, and had to admit that it was indeed delicious, and knowing Anne's comprehensive knowledge of medicinal herbs, it would probably be effective too.

"I've been here for four months now," Beth reminded her. "I looked very different when I arrived. I'm completely well now. That's why there's a soldier outside the room, in case I attempt to overpower Edwin and Caroline and flee."

Anne's subsequent look of alarm at this prospect reminded Beth that, although kind and caring, and more confident now she was under the beneficial influence of Caroline's eccentric relatives, her sense of humour remained non-existent.

"How are you, Anne?" Beth asked, hoping to put her at ease. "And George? He must be a fine boy by now."

"He is very well," Anne said happily. "He's talking now and knows his numbers to a hundred, and all the colours, and he looks more like Stanley every day. I had hoped to have his miniature painted, but he will not sit still for long enough. Oh! I'm sorry!" she finished inexplicably.

"Why are you sorry?" Beth asked.

"I thought perhaps you…I had not intended to speak about George, in case…" She wrung her hands in her lap, and blushed.

"Anne," Beth said gently. "You are very kind. But you know I cannot avoid children, nor do I wish to. Freddie comes in to see me most days, and we play little games together. If anything I should be apologising to you for not warning you what a bast…brute my brother was before you married him."

To Beth's amazement and relief, Anne neither defended Richard nor came out with some platitude about owing him her loyalty as his wife.

"I do not think I would have listened to you if you had," she said sadly instead. "I was very lonely after Stanley died, and he…he seemed to care for me. I was very foolish."

"I don't think Richard has ever cared for anyone but himself," Beth said. "Do you intend to stay at Harriet's on a permanent basis? I know Richard is in Scotland now, but he will probably return in time, and it is imperative that…"

To her surprise, Anne immediately burst into tears.

"I'm sorry," Beth said. "I should not have mentioned him. I meant only to advise you…but I have distressed you."

"Oh, God!" Anne cried. "I am so afraid!"

"He cannot hurt you from Scotland," Beth said gently.

"But he is," she wailed. "He is seeking to take George from me!"

"What?! But he is not George's father! How can he do that?"

Anne didn't reply, but instead made a valiant attempt to bring her emotions under control, and after a few minutes of gulping and hiccupping while Beth put her arm round her sister-in-law's shoulder and offered her a handkerchief, she succeeded in regaining control of herself.

"I am so sorry," she sniffed. "I came here to cheer you, not to distress you."

"I am not distressed," Beth said. "Tell me what's going on."

"He has written to me and told me that as I have deserted him without reasonable cause, he wishes to take charge of George immediately."

"But you're his mother! And he is Stanley's son. Surely Richard has no rights at all?"

"He does," she said sadly. "When I married him, everything I had became his."

"All your money, yes," Beth said, "and your property. But not your child!"

"It would have been different of course, had Stanley known. He was so meticulous with legal matters," Anne said. "I am sure that he would have named me in his will as legal guardian if anything happened to him. But of course he didn't know I was with child when he died."

"You mean that just because Stanley didn't name George's own mother as his legal guardian before he died, that means my bastard of a brother can take him?!" Beth cried. "That cannot be right. You must fight this, Anne."

"That's what Harriet said. She said…she said some bad things. But yes, she said that she will fight it through the courts if she has to."

"Well, then," Beth said soothingly. "I am sure everything will be fine."

"What Aunt Harriet actually said was that if she lost the case, she'd cut the bastard's balls off herself and choke him with them," Caroline elucidated when Beth broached the subject after dinner that evening. The three of them had retired to the parlour to enjoy a bottle of orange wine which Anne had brought for them, and which was absolutely delicious.

Edwin winced.

"I am only repeating the words of my dear aunt," Caroline said coolly. "Although I'd like to watch when she fulfils her promise."

"How can she not win?" Beth said. "Anne's George's *mother*! And Richard's insane!"

"Even so, it's distinctly possible that she *will* lose, in spite of her influence," Edwin explained. "Because in law Richard has done nothing to justify Anne leaving him, and in view of that he can automatically claim custody of George. The courts won't grant Anne custody unless there are extremely powerful reasons to do so, because if they do it will set a precedent."

"But there *are* extremely powerful reasons to do so!" Beth fumed.

"We know that, but Richard has not been charged with raping Sarah, nor has he been charged with murdering your servant and attempting to murder her child," Edwin pointed out. "As far as the law is concerned, he's a respectable captain in His Majesty's forces."

"And if he wins, then Anne will either have to surrender George to him, or return to live with him as his wife," Caroline said.

"Of course she might be allowed to keep George temporarily, because Richard is on active service and a Scottish barracks is no place to keep a child. Although he may engage a nanny, and take him anyway."

"Anne will never allow that," Caroline said. "George is her life. She will go back to him."

"She cannot go back to him," Beth said frantically. "If she does George will die, and soon, and she will follow, and it will look like an accident. Richard has changed. I have not told you this, but when he came to see me in prison, I taunted him. The Richard I knew would have lost his temper and beaten me to death, which is what I wanted then, as you know. But he is different now. He's colder, and controlled. If Ned hadn't come in when he did, Richard could have tortured me for hours, maybe days without killing me."

"But he did nearly kill you," Caroline pointed out.

"Only because he didn't know I was pregnant," Beth replied. "He didn't hit me hard enough to kill me. It was the miscarriage and the loss of blood that nearly did that. He is much more dangerous now than he used to be."

The three of them sat and thought about it.

"Perhaps we could have a word with his colonel, Hutchinson, isn't it? Maybe he can persuade Richard to abandon this custody idea," Edwin said doubtfully.

"Could the colonel demote him if he refused?" Beth asked.

"No. He would have to commit a serious breach of military law for that."

"Then he wouldn't agree. Richard's only weakness is his ambition. He wants to be a general one day," Beth said. "You said there would have to be powerful reasons for the court to grant Anne custody. What sort of reasons?"

"Well, the chancellor has *parens patriae* jurisdiction. So if for instance it was feared that a father was going to put his child into prostitution for example, or indoctrinate it in the ways of the Roman Catholic Church, or otherwise corrupt it morally. That sort of thing."

"I wouldn't underestimate Harriet, though," Caroline said reassuringly. "She is not enamoured of Richard, and would do a good deal to thwart him. And she really does know *everyone*. We must wait and see what happens. We can't do any more for now."

The next day Beth discussed the situation with Sarah, who shared her outrage and her fear for what would happen to Anne and George if Richard won the case.

"It's terrible. I don't know why *any* woman with independent means chooses to get married at all," Beth said.

"You married Sir Anthony, though," Sarah said.

"I didn't have independent means. I wouldn't have looked twice at him if I had," Beth said. "Anyway, I wasn't really married to him, as Cumberland and Newcastle delighted in pointing out. I was his whore."

"Do you ever wish you hadn't?" Sarah asked. "Married him, I mean, real or not?"

"No," Beth replied without hesitation. "I love him. I will always love him. *'I am yours until I die, I will love you, and only you, and will take no other',"* she finished softly, almost to herself. She remembered his voice as he'd spoken the words, the gentle strength of his hands as he'd cupped her face, the scent of the suede gloves he'd worn, the blue intensity of his gaze.

"Who said that?" Sarah asked.

"Sir Anthony. When we were on our honeymoon in Italy. Anyway," Beth said, pulling herself with obvious reluctance from the past, "Anne *did* marry Richard, and now she and everything she owns including George belongs to him, it seems."

"Let's hope he comes to see me when he comes back to London, then," Sarah said.

Beth cast a puzzled look her way.

"After last time," Sarah explained, "I bought a pistol, and Caroline taught me how to shoot it in case Richard ever came back. I'm a decent shot now. I keep it under my shop counter all the time. In fact I threatened John with it before I knew who he was. I always thought that if Richard came back I'd threaten him with it too, to make him go away, but in view of what you've told me about how he's changed, I think I'd just shoot him the moment he came through the door."

Beth looked at Sarah in amazement. She was serious.

"You can't do that!" she said.

"Why not?"

"Because if you did, you'd hang!"

"Not if I said he'd tried to rob me, and rape me."

"Sarah, he's a soldier, a captain, not a beggar. You couldn't just kill him and get away with it."

"I'll take my chances then," Sarah said. "Because I'll be damned if I'll let that bastard get anywhere near me or…near me again. He'd kill me anyway if he did. At least if I hang I'll have the satisfaction of knowing he's already burning in hell."

\* \* \*

"Good morning!" Beth said brightly to the redcoat guard stationed outside her room as she opened her door the following morning. "Have you breakfasted already?"

The soldier almost smiled at her and then stood to attention and attempted a frown, reminding himself, as he had to several times a day under the onslaught of her persistent friendliness to him, that she was a traitor and his job was to ensure she didn't escape, not to become her friend.

"I am not hungry," he replied formally. His stomach grumbled, giving the lie to his words.

"Hmm. Are Sir Edwin and Lady Caroline at home?" she asked conversationally.

"I believe they are," he said.

"Excellent. Then I will join them. I should be with them for at least half an hour, so if you want to go to the kitchen and get something to eat, I promise not to run away."

He didn't reply, but followed her down the stairs and stationed himself outside the breakfast room door. From inside came the clattering of cutlery and the soft murmur of conversation. His stomach rumbled once more. A moment later the door opened again and Beth reappeared, carrying a plate with two warm spiced rolls.

"I suspected you were too conscientious to abandon your post. There you are," she said, handing him the plate. "Now you can do your duty without going hungry."

This time he did smile at her. She really was kind. Such a shame she was a rebel.

Beth returned to the breakfast table, and sitting opposite Caroline and Edwin, spread butter on a roll and took a bite. She sighed blissfully. She was going to miss these rolls. She was going to miss a lot of things. She swallowed.

"I have made a decision," she announced. Edwin looked up from his newspaper and Caroline, drinking tea, eyed Beth over the rim of the cup.

"I have imposed upon your kindness for long enough. No, please hear me out," she said when both of them instantly made to speak. "I know you're going to say that I can stay here for as long as I like, but I can't stay here forever, and because of who I am I don't think I'll ever get a pardon if I won't reveal the true identity of Sir Anthony. I'm completely well now, so I've decided it's time that I faced up to reality. I'm ready to go back to prison, and I want you to send a message to the Duke of Newcastle and tell him that I want to talk to him."

The reaction from the two people listening to this could not have been more different. Edwin grinned from ear to ear, while Caroline looked at Beth in utter shock and disbelief.

"That's the best news I've heard in a long time," he said. "I mean, you're welcome, you know that, to stay as long as you want, and after you've spoken to Newcastle we can arrange for you to come back here until your release. I'm sure that once you've told what you know, that will be soon."

"I'm not sure about that," Beth said, "but I've decided to tell what I know anyway."

"It's the only sensible thing to do," Edwin agreed. "After all, if he *is* dead, as you think, then revealing his identity can't hurt him, and if he isn't…well, he's abandoned you, and he really doesn't deserve your loyalty."

Caroline, who had remained frozen until now, suddenly put her cup down on the saucer with a clatter.

"I can't believe this," she said incredulously. "After everything they've put you through to make you talk, why now, when you're safe and Newcastle's obviously given up on you telling him anything, do you suddenly want to give evidence against the man you say you love?"

"I need to talk to Newcastle because a lot of people have already been hurt by my silence," she said. "I need to do what I can to make things right and to stop anyone else suffering. And I'm the only one who can. I know what I'm doing. And I think Anthony would approve."

"You're doing the right thing," Edwin said. "I'll send a message straight away."

Beth stood up.

"Thank you," she said. "And thank you for everything you've

done for me. I don't think I can ever repay you."

"You don't need to repay –" Edwin began.

"Who is he?" Caroline interrupted.

"Who is who?" Beth asked.

"Anthony. Who is he, really?"

Beth coloured slightly, but remained calm.

"I think the Duke of Newcastle should be the first to know," she said.

"Why? We won't tell anyone. And after all, we deserve to know. He masqueraded as our friend for over three years."

"He didn't masquerade…no," Beth replied. "What I have to say is only for the duke to hear. I'm sorry."

She turned away, and walked to the door.

"What are you up to, Beth?" Caroline asked suspiciously as Beth opened the door.

"Nothing," she said without turning back. Then she went out, and closed the door gently behind her.

\* \* \*

The Duke of Newcastle, as expected, was ecstatic to hear that the stubborn Miss Cunningham had finally come to her senses, and revised his whole schedule for the following day so that he could see her.

Her appointment was for one o'clock, and she was in her room trying to decide between two suitable outfits when there was a knock at her door. She opened it to reveal a maid in a state of nervous excitement.

"You have a visitor, my lady," she said, bobbing a curtsey.

"You don't have to call me my lady," Beth replied. "Who is it?"

"It is I," came a voice from down the hall. "I hope you don't mind. I have brought someone who particularly wanted to see you."

The soldier immediately shot to attention, and the maid curtseyed so deeply she almost fell over.

Beth stepped out of the room and curtseyed expertly.

"Your Royal Highness," she said. "What an unexpected pleasure! Of course I don't mind. I'll come downstairs directly. Would you care for refreshments?"

The prince waved his hand dismissively in a gesture reminiscent of Sir Anthony.

"Oh no, let us not be formal. If it does not disturb you, your apartment would be fine. Your reputation will be quite safe. We have a chaperone." He smiled and stepped to the side, revealing Prince Edward, who, slight as he was, had been concealed behind his father.

She invited the royal pair in, and soon they were comfortably seated in her tiny living room, Prince Frederick opposite her, and Prince Edward, after a perfunctory 'good morning' by the window, where he gazed absently out onto the street.

"You have grown considerably since we last met, Your Highness," Beth said to the boy, who did not appear to hear her and continued to look out of the window.

"He celebrated his eighth birthday last week," Prince Frederick said proudly.

"Happy birthday, Your Highness," Beth said. "I am sorry I am a little late."

No response. The proud father sighed.

"Eddie did say that he particularly wished to see you," he said. "I of course also wished to see you. I have grown fond of you in the last months, and am so happy that you are about to put your future happiness first. I am sure it is what your husband would have wished."

He was a kind man, still referring to Anthony as her husband, even though his brother and Newcastle had both made a point of telling her she was his whore and therefore ruined.

"It is what Anthony would have wished, yes," she said. "He told me I should betray him if I was ever arrested."

"It is to your credit that you have held out for so long," the prince replied. "Although they are my enemies, I admire the loyalty that both Anthony and Charles inspire in their friends and followers. There was a considerable reward out for the capture of both, but no one has ever claimed it."

Beth looked at this scion of Hanover, who had damaged his reputation to save her life.

"Your Highness," she said impulsively. "I have made no secret of the fact that I am a Jacobite, and have spent the last years actively working to remove your family from the throne. I will always believe that the Stuarts are the rightful monarchs of Great Britain, and if they are restored to their place, I will rejoice. I do not mean to insult you. I am just stating my opinion. But I have to say, with the exception of King James and his son, that you are the most fitted to succeed to the throne, and if I have to accept a Hanoverian monarchy, then you are the only member of that family under whom I would be happy to serve."

The prince smiled.

"I am not insulted, Elizabeth. I am honoured that someone as committed as yourself to the Stuart cause considers me a worthy alternative to my cousin. No," he continued as she made to speak, "I am not being sarcastic. I know what a compliment you are paying me, and I accept it as such. I hope one day to be a worthy king, and when I am I also hope that my eldest son, indeed all my children, will enjoy a cordial relationship with me, as I unfortunately do not with my father, as everyone knows."

"I am sure they will. Your devotion to your family is well known, Your Highness," Beth said.

"I want you to know that once your interview is over, I will try to obtain a pardon for you," he said.

"No," Beth answered, to his surprise. "You have done more than I ever would have expected. After today I want you to forget about me. I want no more help, from you or anyone else. I will accept my fate, whatever that is to be."

"You feel guilt for what you are about to do. But you do not need to. I know of no other woman who would have endured what you have and refused to give up her husband. If he is alive, I am sure Anthony will understand what you are doing."

"Anthony is dead," she replied flatly. "I have resisted accepting that for so long. But now I know it to be true."

"He thinks of you," Prince Edward said suddenly, making both adults jump. He had been so silent they'd forgotten he was there. He turned from his perusal of the street and directed his gaze at the fireplace. "All the time."

"Who does?" his father asked, puzzled.

"He doesn't know, you see, that's why," he said absently.

"Eddie, please don't speak in riddles. What do you mean?" Frederick asked his son. But Edward seemed to have lost interest, and had already turned back to the window. "I am sorry," the prince said. "He can be a little…er…odd at times. He doesn't mean anything by it."

"He's fine," Beth said, looking at the boy strangely. "He warned me that Lord Daniel was going to hurt me when we were playing cricket, just before he threw the ball at me."

The prince laughed.

"When in fact it was the other way round, as I remember. It took him a long time to heal from the wound. His reputation has never recovered! But now I think we have taken up enough of your time. I'm sure you wish to prepare yourself for your interview."

"I do need to," Beth said, pulling herself back to the moment. "In fact I would appreciate your opinion on my choice of outfits. I am undecided at the moment."

He advised the navy blue and white striped silk as being the most appropriate, and wished her the very best of luck, stating that he would honour her wish not to help, if that was what she really wanted, but he would most certainly never forget her, and would be delighted to hear from her when she wished to renew their friendship.

And then he left, taking his son with him, and Beth turned her attention to dressing and calming her nerves in readiness for the forthcoming interview, which she knew was not going to be easy and in which she would have to employ all the skills Sir Anthony Peters had so painstakingly taught her.

# CHAPTER SIXTEEN

**Whitehall, London**

"Good morning, Miss Cunningham," the Duke of Newcastle said, by way of greeting the young woman who had just entered his chambers. He was hopeful that this interview would be more productive than the previous one had been.

"Good morning," Beth said coolly, and without curtseying or being invited she walked across the room and took a seat opposite the duke, who was seated, as was his custom, behind his imposing walnut desk.

"I take it you do not object to my clerk, Benjamin's presence? He will record the details of our interview," Newcastle said. Beth turned to the corner of the room, where a young man was sitting behind a smaller, sloped desk, quill and paper at the ready. She smiled at him, a smile of warmth and friendliness, and he inhaled sharply, felled by her outstanding beauty, outlined perfectly by the shaft of early April sunshine falling onto her face, which highlighted the glossy silver-blonde cap of hair, the perfect skin, and the cerulean blue of her eyes.

"I trust that this time Benjamin will be gainfully employed?" the duke's voice cut in. Benjamin blushed and bent his head immediately to his task. Beth turned to face her interrogator.

"Indeed he will. I have information for you which I am sure you will wish to act upon immediately," she reassured him.

"Excellent!" he said, relaxing a little. "I am glad to see you looking so well."

"I confess that I am surprised to hear that," Beth answered. "After all, you did your very best to achieve my death. I expected you to be somewhat disappointed rather than happy by my current state of health."

"I assure you, Miss Cunningham, that your brother acted completely contrary to my orders. I asked him to have a word with you in the hopes that familial advice would make you see sense, when it seemed nothing else could. I was both shocked and dismayed when I heard of your injuries. Captain Cunningham was severely disciplined for his behaviour."

Beth smiled.

"I am sure he was. Did you believe then that my injuries would best be treated by my being incarcerated in a damp, cold cell and slowly starved to death?"

"Mr Jones –"

"-has been severely disciplined. I am sure," Beth interrupted, to the duke's astonishment. No one ever dared to interrupt him. "Your Grace, I am not a fool; please do not treat me as one," she continued. "Mr Jones was ordered by someone in very high authority, not only to starve me to death, but to hide the knowledge of my whereabouts from anyone who asked about me. Otherwise he would not have dared to attempt to lie to Prince Frederick himself. My brother is a brute, and has good reason to wish me dead. I know that you did not know that when you sent him to me. But there is only one thing Richard cares about, and that is military advancement. He tortured me because he believed that he had permission to do so from someone who could positively influence his career."

"I do assure you that I gave him no such permission," the duke said, frantically indicating to Benjamin to stop transcribing the interview.

"Very well, then. If I am to believe you, the only other people who have such influence and who knew I was a prisoner, are the Duke of Cumberland or the Elector. Are you telling me that one of them ordered that I be tortured and then starved to death?"

"I am telling you nothing of the sort. Indeed, madam, it is supposed to be *you* who are telling *me* something today," Newcastle replied hotly.

Beth sat back in her chair and folded her hands demurely in her lap.

"You are right. Benjamin, you can start writing again. I am sure

His Grace will want what I am about to say to be recorded."

To the duke's irritation Benjamin immediately picked up his quill in response to her command, only belatedly realising that he should have waited for the duke to give the order. Newcastle nodded curtly to him, and the clerk bent his head over the paper.

"When you ordered my brother to have 'a word' with me, you made him very happy. As soon as he entered my cell I knew he would try to kill me, because it would probably be the only opportunity he would ever have of stopping me from telling you what I know. Unfortunately for him I survived, and after what he did to me I no longer see any reason to protect him. My brother is a traitor, Your Grace."

The duke looked at her disbelievingly.

"You wish me to believe that your brother, who is known for his devotion to the army and his zeal in pursuing rebels, is a Jacobite?"

"No. Richard is not a Jacobite," Beth responded. "But he knew I was, and has known it since he came home after our father died. He also knew Sir Anthony was a Jacobite, and that he was a spy, although he does not know his true identity." She looked across at Benjamin, who was writing fiercely, and waited a moment for him to catch up.

"When my father died, he left very little money. But, as is widely known, he did leave twenty thousand pounds in trust for me as a dowry, which could only be accessed either when I married or when I reached the age of thirty. If I died before either of those things happened, the money would go to building a foundling hospital. Richard was desperate to purchase a commission, and was willing to overlook the fact that I was both a Roman Catholic and had great sympathy for the Stuarts, because he believed that I could make a good marriage to someone who could help him advance in the army. As you can imagine, I was averse to this, but as he displayed so well in Newgate last August, he could be very persuasive.

"When Sir Anthony showed an interest in me, Richard was ecstatic. Anthony was well known for his generosity and his stupidity. When my brother discovered he was a Jacobite spy, Anthony offered to pay for his promotion if he would keep quiet. And Richard agreed, because he knew it was his only chance of getting preferment, as he had no money of his own. Anthony subsequently paid for another promotion, for the same reason.

"When Lord Daniel discovered that Anthony was a spy, it was Richard who warned us we were about to be denounced. He was terrified that if we were caught we might betray him. He gave us the chance to get away, and I was very grateful for that. Until our last meeting. After that I have no reason to be grateful to him ever again."

Newcastle sat in silence for a moment, digesting this unexpected information.

"How do I know that you are not inventing this out of pure malice against your brother?" he asked. "After all, if nobody else knew that Sir Anthony was a spy, how did Captain Cunningham find out?"

"He came into the library at Lord Edward's one evening and found me with a rosary. He took it from me and threw it into the fire. Sir Anthony disturbed us in the middle of our argument, and we left. But a little later I went back to see if there was anything left of the rosary. It held great sentimental value for me. Sir Anthony was still there, and we spoke together. Unknown to us, Richard was listening outside the door. He threatened to denounce us then, but Anthony agreed to pay for his commission if he would keep quiet. We already intended to marry, but thought it better to do it quickly, as it would seem more natural for a man to pay for his brother-in-law's commission, and of course, once married we had access to the dowry, which helped to fund not only Richard's commissions, but also the uprising."

"Do you have any proof of this?" the duke asked.

Beth considered for a minute.

"No written evidence, no. But it is a matter of record that Anthony paid for both of Richard's commissions, and that he funded his lifestyle until he married Anne Redburn and became wealthy in his own right. Also, if you interview Richard and ask him about the library and the rosary, you will be able to see for yourself if he is lying. His colour alone will tell you that, but even as a small child he always gave himself away in an untruth. There is a muscle in his cheek which twitches whenever he's lying. He's quite unaware of it, but Father always knew whether he was guilty of some misdemeanour or not by that."

The Duke of Newcastle pursed his lips.

"Benjamin, will you step outside for a moment?" he said.

The clerk looked somewhat surprised at this unexpected command, but obeyed immediately. Once the door was closed, Newcastle sat forward and leaned his elbows on the desk.

"As you know, when I asked your brother to speak to you, I did not know you were with child," he said softly. "I discovered that later, and once I knew I ordered that the interrogation be stopped. I was sorry that you miscarried."

"I'm sure you were," Beth replied. "You hoped to use the baby to blackmail me into betraying its father."

The duke ignored that comment.

"Afterwards the captain told me that he had not intended to injure you badly, merely to force you to tell him the identity of Sir Anthony. He said he did not know you were pregnant."

Beth laughed.

"Of course he told you that. He would hardly reveal that I told him myself I was pregnant and begged him not to hurt the child. Nor would he tell you that he was not interested in knowing about Sir Anthony. He knows Sir Anthony could incriminate him if he was captured. Why do you think he threw the guard out of my cell? All he wanted to know before he murdered me was the location of my dowry. He had been to visit our solicitor in Manchester, who told him I had withdrawn it all. I'm sure Mr Cox will corroborate that. Once Richard knew that the money had been spent, all that remained was for him to kill me, making it look as though he had just been a little over-zealous in his interrogation."

"Very well, then," said the duke. "Let us assume that you are telling me the truth for once."

"I have always told you the truth," Beth replied.

"The best way you could prove that the information you are giving me about your brother is true, and not merely malicious," Newcastle continued, "would be to cooperate with me fully by now revealing the identity of Sir Anthony."

"As I said, Your Grace," Beth replied, "I have always told you the truth, and I will continue to do so now. Richard and I have never been close and I will not deny that I despise my brother for what he did to me. Richard cares about only two things; money and power.

He has now obtained the first by marrying Anne Redburn, although he still wanted my dowry to spite our father, who left him nothing. The second he is obtaining by rising higher in the military. If you wish to disregard what I have told you today, and are happy to have a man who is willing to compromise his loyalty to the Hanoverians in the pursuit of power, then so be it. It has certainly worked to the advantage of the Stuarts so far, and may do so again in the future. As for my husband, I thought I had already made it very clear that I would never betray him, under any circumstances. If you think there is anything whatsoever that you can do to change my mind on that, you are very much mistaken. I have told you everything I am ever going to tell you. It is up to you to act on it or not, as you choose. And now I have spoken my last words to you."

She sat back calmly, folded her hands once again in her lap, bestowed her cool blue gaze on him and remained silent while he urged her to reconsider, advised her that she would neither be pardoned nor returned to the care of Sir Edwin Harlow, and finally, called in the guards and told them to take her to the Tower for the present. Then she stood and silently left the room.

When she had gone the duke sat for a while, pondering his options. Not regarding Captain Cunningham; he knew what he would do there. He would write an urgent letter to Colonel Hutchinson telling him what Miss Cunningham had said and ordering him to interview the captain immediately, and that if he had any suspicions at all, to send him under guard to London for further questioning. No, that was an easy decision. Hutchinson was an intelligent man of integrity; if Cunningham was hiding something he would certainly find out.

The issue that concerned the duke now was the sister. She posed far more danger to him personally. If that idiot keeper Jones had not brought a surgeon to her directly after the interview with Cunningham, she would certainly have died and saved him a good deal of trouble. But as it was she had survived and here she was, a constant thorn in his side.

If it came to it, no one would believe the word of the keeper if he said the duke had ordered her to be kept in solitary confinement and deprived of food. Indeed he had *not* ordered it; he had merely suggested it.

But Elizabeth Cunningham was another matter. She had friends in high places; Sir Edwin Harlow, a rising star in the Whig government; his wife Caroline, whose family, if somewhat odd, were influential and indisputably loyal to the Hanoverians. And the heir to the throne had actually rescued her, and sent his surgeon to ensure her recovery! They would certainly listen to her if she told them that he had ordered her torture and starvation, even though he had covered his tracks as far as possible.

It was true that she was a confirmed traitor and that her word was unreliable; but she was also beautiful. There was an increasing outcry against the brutality of the treatment being meted out to the defeated Jacobites in general; imagine the damage a beautiful, intelligent, high-born woman could do to his popularity, were she allowed to. She could not destroy him, but she could certainly cause a lot of damage.

The duke weighed up his options.

He could not return her to Newgate hoping she would die there, not now it was known that she was a prisoner. She had already cheated death twice. And she was of noble birth. He could not keep her in the Tower either, where she could and would be visited, and able to spread her poison against him.

Neither could he bring her to trial and execution. If he did that, not only would she have the opportunity to use her beauty and apparent fragility to the very best advantage in the court, but the publicity of such a trial would undoubtedly bring her back to the attention of Prince William, who was currently involved with an actress of some sort and had all but forgotten her. Newcastle had no wish for the prince's infatuation with Elizabeth Cunningham to be reignited. Even the thought of it made him shudder.

None of the female Jacobite rebels had been executed anyway, and, nearly a year after Culloden, it was unlikely that any of them now would be.

*Damn*, he thought, *there must be something, some way to keep her from talking to those who would listen and take notice.*

He sat some more.

And then it came to him. Of course. It was obvious. Why hadn't he thought of it immediately? He rang his bell, and Benjamin was summoned. Once he was seated at his desk again and ready, the duke spoke.

"I will dictate two letters. One to Colonel Mark Hutchinson and the other to Mr Samuel Smith," he said. "Both are to be delivered with the utmost urgency."

For every problem, there was a solution. The duke relaxed back in his chair, smiled, and began dictating the content of the letters.

\* \* \*

## Scotland, May 1747

It was a beautiful spring day. The sun was shining and was warm enough to evaporate the heavy dew off the grass and heather, the snow had finally melted from everywhere except the mountain peaks, and nature was bursting into life. Unfortunately that also meant that the redcoats, bored and restless after a long and brutal winter of enforced incarceration in their barracks, had also burst into life, and were back on the rampage.

Alex and his men were lying at the top of the hill, looking down on the scene of wanton destruction being inflicted on the village below with a mixture of rage and frustration. Rage because they were aching to make use of the weapons they'd spent the winter honing to razor-sharp perfection; and frustration because there were just too many redcoats below for them to have any reasonable chance of surviving an attack in broad daylight.

Alex had one all-important rule when deciding the viability of an attack; there had to be a good chance that all of his precious few men would come out of it alive, with few, if any injuries. The military side of his reasoning was that the longer he and his men survived, the more redcoats they would kill; and recklessly throwing themselves into situations where the odds were stacked against them was not the way to achieve that.

A good methodology. But unfortunately sometimes it led to situations like this, where they were forced to watch as men were killed, women and sometimes children were raped, and the survivors driven away from their homes and possessions, which were then stolen or burnt. Alex was confident that none of the men would act without his direct order to do so; they could argue and debate all they wished when planning a raid or ambush, and did, but once in the field he demanded, and got, unquestioned obedience to his orders.

It did not do morale any good, however, to watch wholesale destruction going on when you were helpless to do anything about it. When, from inside one of the huts below, a woman started to scream, first in fear and then in obvious agony, Alex decided enough was enough.

"Come on, let's away," he said softly. "We canna do anything here. Dougal and Allan, you follow the redcoats at a distance later. I'll send Lachlan over. If they dinna go straight back tae Inversnaid, but set up camp somewhere, send him back wi' a message, and we'll see if we canna take a few of the bastards tonight."

The men sighed, and reluctantly began to back away over the ridge.

"Wait," said Angus, who had remained in place and was still peering down at the village, which was slowly becoming shrouded in smoke from the burning thatch of the houses. "Something's happening."

Alex moved back up next to his brother. Something *was* happening. The men had clearly finished their work and were standing about, waiting. The cattle had been too weak to walk after a harsh winter of little fodder and their blood being taken and mixed with oatmeal to feed their starving owners, so the soldiers had shot them. The bodies of several Highlanders who had attempted to resist were also strewn around the grass, and a pitiful line of ragged women and children were making their way out of their settlement away from the burning remains of their homes. Only one hut remained intact; the one that contained the screaming woman.

All of the soldiers were looking at the hut expectantly. Alex got to Angus's side just in time to see one of the soldiers disappear inside it and then reappear almost immediately, retching and then doubling over and vomiting at the side of the door.

"What the hell's going on in there?" Alex said, half to himself.

The redcoat straightened up, approached the group of soldiers, half-hidden now by smoke, and said something, gesticulating back at the hut from which he'd just emerged before marching off to a group of six horses tethered at the edge of the village, mounting one and then turning back to the group.

"Are you coming, or not?" he shouted angrily, loud enough for the ten Highlanders, now all back in place and observing, to hear. There was a low-voiced discussion from the group of redcoats, and then fully three-quarters of them followed the horseman, three of them mounting their own horses, the others following on foot as he rode out of the village along the glen. The remainder stayed in place, looking uncertainly at the undamaged hut, from which frantic but muted screams could still be heard.

"I canna believe it," Kenneth said in awe.

Neither could Alex. It appeared that upwards of fifty redcoats were heading out of the valley, leaving only...

"Twelve o' the bastards left," Iain said, smiling.

...only twelve soldiers, plus whoever was in the hut. It was too good to be true.

"Are we going to attack, then?" Allan asked eagerly.

"Wait," Alex said. It was a trap. It had to be a trap. In the last nine months of watching similar scenes of destruction, he had never seen such a thing. However large or small a group of soldiers, they *always* entered a settlement together, and left it together at the end. It made no sense to split up in the way they just seemed to have done.

"Dougal, Allan, you're fast," Alex said. "Go round the side of the hill and watch to see if the redcoats double back. I'm thinking maybe they're suspecting an ambush and are hoping to draw us out, then come back and slaughter us."

Allan and Dougal shot off like arrows, and the rest of the men settled to wait. Down below the remaining soldiers seemed to have settled to wait too. They certainly didn't appear uneasy or apprehensive as you'd expect men who thought to be ambushed would look. In fact they were all sitting down, and one or two of them were sprawled at full length, as though hoping to have a nap.

"How can they sleep, with that noise?" Graeme said, referring to the screams which showed no signs of abating.

"If we attack, I'm taking whoever's in that wee hut," Kenneth said, his face set.

After a short time Allan and Dougal reappeared, red-faced and breathing hard, but faces aglow with excitement.

"They're really leaving," Allan said when he had breath enough to speak. "We followed them as far as the road, and they turned straight for the barracks."

Kenneth took out his dirk and raised his eyes heavenward.

"Thank you, Jesus," he said, then kissed the blade. "Can we take them? I canna wait to get my hands on the bastard in that hut."

"Aye," said Alex, "we can take them. But no' by charging straight down the hill, just in case they've got scouts we havena seen. We dinna want to give them time to get to the others. Hamish, you drive the horses away so they canna ride off and raise the alarm. The rest of us get as close as we can to them without them seeing us. If one o' them does, we all charge. I'm thinking if we're quiet and slow, we'll get within about twenty feet or so, especially wi' the smoke to help us. Let's go."

They went, edging first of all round the side of the hill and then crawling slowly and silently downhill on their stomachs, their illegal green and brown plaids blending perfectly with the hillside. Then, when they could go no further in that manner, they stood and charged as one into the village, drawing their swords and roaring in Gaelic, succeeding in frightening the recumbent redcoats half to death before they were among them.

The ones who managed to actually draw their swords before being cut down made a fight of it, and for a minute or two the fighting was fierce. Out of the corner of his eye Alex saw Kenneth making for the hut and a man emerge from it, sword drawn.

And then he forgot the man he was supposed to be killing, kicked him out of the way, and was running towards the hut screaming at the top of his voice as Kenneth brought his sword back in a huge arc with the obvious intention of decapitating the man on the spot.

Later Kenneth would say that he had no idea how he managed to obey his chieftain's order. It was too late to stop his sword hitting the target, but by a herculean effort he managed to turn the blade and rein in the power of the strike so that instead of taking the redcoat's head off, the flat of the blade hit him in the side of the face, breaking his cheekbone and knocking him flat on the ground.

The soldier lay for a minute, stunned, the side of his face numb, the coppery taste of blood filling his mouth. Through his ingrained will to survive he managed to remain conscious, aware that he had to defend himself. He shook his head to clear his vision, automatically reaching for his sword, which lay on the ground beside him where he'd dropped it. He managed to touch the basket hilt before his hand was pinned to the ground, his wrist cracking loudly as it snapped, and he looked up into the face of one of the largest men he had ever seen in his life. In his fist the giant held the bloodied sword that had hit him in the face, and his foot was grinding the soldier's hand into the dirt.

And then he relaxed and closed his eyes, because he knew he was a dead man, and he waited for the killing blow to fall.

The killing blow did not fall.

Instead, after a moment he felt his sword being pulled from his throbbing fingers, and then the pressure on his hand eased. He opened his eyes again. The giant had moved away and was standing a few feet away with a group of fellow savages, a puzzled expression on his face.

Another man, not quite as tall but equally as fierce-looking was gazing down at him with cold blue eyes. His red-brown hair was long and hung loose on his shoulders, and his muscular legs were muddy and bare. He wore one of those ridiculous short skirts that the Highlanders loved, and a dirty shirt, now stained, as was the sword he held, with the blood of the men he had just killed. His men.

The redcoat lifted his head, ignoring the pain that knifed down the side of his face, and looked around the clearing, taking in the lifeless scarlet-coated bodies. He inhaled sharply and turned to look back up at the man standing over him.

"If you're waiting for me to beg for mercy," he said, "you'll be standing there forever."

The Highlander smiled, and then to the redcoat's utter disbelief, he spoke, not in the apelike gibberish they called a language, nor in the barbarous accent the Scots used when massacring the English tongue, but in a voice that made the young soldier's blood run cold.

"I am waiting for nothing of the sort, dear boy," the savage said. "I confess I am somewhat distraught that you have forgotten me. After all, we were once so well acquainted, were we not? But it matters not, for I recognise you and that, after all, is the important thing."

The hand holding the sword, which had hung limply and somewhat effeminately at the Highlander's side during this astonishing speech, now straightened, and the unmistakable long-lashed slate-blue eyes of Sir Anthony Peters regarded him for a moment with pure joy.

"Hello, Richard," he said pleasantly, and then, aiming very carefully, he drove his sword home.

* * *

Nine men and one woman were sitting in the saucer-shaped hollow on the hill overlooking Loch Lomond. Down below in the settlement the rest of the clan, who had restored and spent the winter in their lochside houses were preparing to move up to the large cave for an indefinite period, as the redcoats from the hastily rebuilt barracks at Inversnaid were now starting to 'pacify' the clans who resided around the loch, the MacGregors being a prime target.

The nine fighting men and one woman had already moved their belongings, and were now eyeing the small cave with a mixture of expressions ranging from anxiety to distaste. Initially hollowed out to accommodate four men with a squeeze, over the winter it had been excavated some more, and would now hold six with ease.

At the moment, however, it held only two, and the people sitting outside were discussing the situation in low voices.

"It isna right," Dougal said. "It's no' fighting fair."

"You could argue that nothing of what we do is fighting fair," his brother Hamish pointed out. "The redcoats'd no' say it's fair for us to ambush them in the middle of the night when they're all asleep in their tents. Or to pick stragglers off from the back of the line at dusk."

"Or to pretend to be wolves," Angus said, to laughter. Morag was sitting next to him, one hand on his knee, the other on her belly, which was swelling nicely with their first child. His arm was wrapped round her shoulder.

"Aye, I ken that," Dougal conceded, "but this is different. When we fight, we kill. We dinna deliberately stab a man in the gut, twist the blade and then bring him back here to let him die in agony. We canna call the redcoats savages if we behave the same way they do."

"He's no' behaving the way the redcoats do," Angus said. "If we came upon a load of redcoats' families, we wouldna rape and butcher them."

"That's true," said Allan, speaking for the first time. "He's no' behaving the way the redcoats do. And he's our chieftain, so we have to accept that he's got a reason for what he's doing." His words were belied by his facial expression, which stated clearly to everyone present that he was starting to wonder what he'd let himself in for by accepting this man as his chief.

"He clearly kens the redcoat," Hamish said. "He called him by name, did he no', before he stabbed him? Has he a grievance wi' the man?"

Angus, Graeme and Iain shared a meaningful glance, and then Angus sighed and came to a decision.

"Aye," he said, "Alex has a grievance wi' the man, although I dinna ken the whole of it. His name's Richard Cunningham, and he's Beth's brother."

"Brother?" Allan said, shocked. "If he's Beth's brother, then he's –"

"No relation to you," Angus interrupted. "He's rightly Beth's half-brother. They had the same father, different mothers. Beth and Richard hated each other. She told me a wee bit about him and I met him a few times myself. I couldna take to the man. She married Sir Anthony even though she couldna stand him, to get away from Richard."

"Aye, well, that worked out in the end," Dougal pointed out.

"It did. But there was something else. Do ye mind at Manchester, when we were moving north, Alex and Beth had the stramash and he didna speak to her for a while?"

"Christ, aye," said Dougal. "He was a bastard. I've never seen him so miserable. And angry wi' everyone."

"Beth tellt Duncan what happened to cause that. I dinna ken rightly what it was, because she tellt him in confidence, but it was to do wi' Richard."

"Richard is an evil, vicious piece of shite," Graeme cut in suddenly. "I've known him since he was a child, and there's always been something wrong with him. He used to torture animals then, and later he moved on to people. He whipped John for the fun of it, and beat Beth's maid Sarah badly when she was in Manchester.

He hurt Beth too. And he probably raped and murdered another maid, Martha, and tried to kill her baby as well. I'm glad that bastard's finally dying. I'm not so happy with the way of it, but more because it doesn't seem the sort of thing Alex would do."

"So do ye think it's because of Beth that –" Dougal began.

"I dinna give a damn what it's about," Kenneth interrupted, speaking for the first time. "Alex has the right of it, and if he needs a rest, I'll sit and watch the bastard writhe in agony mysel', and wi' the greatest pleasure. I'm only thankful that Alex stopped me killing him quick and clean, as I was about to."

The whole group looked at him in shock, not just at his words, but at the viciousness of his tone. Giant he was, fearsome in battle he definitely was, but he was not a vindictive or vengeful man. Unusually for the Highlanders, he was not one to bear a grudge for any length of time and was by nature gentle and caring.

"You went in the hut," Iain said softly after a minute.

"Aye, Alex and I were the only ones to go in," Kenneth said, "and I wish to God I hadna."

"What did you see?" Angus asked.

Kenneth looked around the group, his eyes settling finally on Morag.

"No," he said.

Angus took his arm from round his wife's shoulder.

"Morag, *a graidh*, will ye gie us a wee minute?" he said.

Morag looked at Kenneth, took in the hard, tight line of his mouth, and without any argument stood up and walked away. Angus waited until she was out of earshot before he spoke again.

"Kenneth," he said. "I ken ye dinna want to talk about it, but if some of us are sitting here wondering what's possessed Alex and doubting the right of what he's doing, then we can be sure the whole clan are thinking the same. I dinna ken how long the man's going to take in his dying, but I canna allow this to undermine our trust in Alex's leadership."

"We'll follow him anyway," Dougal said. "He's our chieftain."

"Aye, we will," Angus agreed. "But until now we've done that because we've complete confidence that when he makes a decision, it's based on reason, and is just. If ye ken something that will make what he's doing now reasonable and just in the eyes o' the clan, Kenneth, ye need to tell me at least, as Alex's brother, and as the chieftain when he's no' here. Then I can choose whether to tell the others or no'."

They all watched as Kenneth sat in silence for a while looking down at the ground. His enormous forearms rested on his knees, his strong, long-fingered hands clenched into fists. Then he nodded to himself and looked up, speaking directly to Angus.

"Alex glanced in the hut after he saw I'd knocked the redcoat down. He saw the woman, but he thought she was dead. I went in after wi' the thought to bury her," he said. "When I got close to her I saw she was alive, but the only kind thing I could do was to kill her, quickly. She was tied to the roof beam, her hands above her head. And her arms…Christ!" He stopped for a moment, and, taking a great shuddering breath, fought to bring his emotions under control. "He was flaying her," he continued, his voice harsh with suppressed rage and hatred. "He'd cut the skin at her wrists, and had peeled it back, very carefully so she wouldna bleed to death, both arms, right back to the oxters, like he was skinning a rabbit. And he'd started to cut down her sides too. She was alive and she was conscious, and I've never seen anything like it, and never want to again. No one could do that, no' without a good deal of practice first." He looked around the group of silent, white-faced men. "I hope the bastard takes weeks to die, and then I hope he burns in hell for eternity. And that'll still no' be long enough."

The silence after Kenneth had finished was profound and prolonged. After what seemed to all of them like a very long time, Angus stood.

"Are we all in agreement that Alex has the right of it?" he asked quietly.

Wordlessly the men nodded.

"I'll away and tell him, then," he said. "It'll comfort him to ken that we're all in accord wi' him."

\* \* \*

Alex sat on a flat-topped stone in the cave, carefully whittling away at a piece of wood with his *sgian dubh*. After a while he stopped, and observing his handiwork, smiled.

"Aye, it'll do. I havena got the skill of my brother, but even so it's a bonny way to pass the time," he said pleasantly to the man sprawled on the ground a little further back in the cave.

Richard's back was propped up against the stone wall so he was half-sitting, his legs stretched out in front of him. The left side of his face was puffy and black with bruising, the eye on that side almost closed. His right arm, the wrist badly swollen, rested uselessly in his lap. There was some sort of protuberance in the cave wall behind him, which was pressing into his spine. Bracing his left arm on the dirt floor, he attempted to shift position a little, halting abruptly as the pain knifed through his gut. White lights danced across his vision and he clenched his teeth, determined neither to faint nor cry out. He couldn't stop the shivering, or hide the icy sweat which soaked his hair and shirt, but he was damned if he'd give voice to his agony. He could not last much longer now, surely? He must have lost a lot of blood; the constant pins and needles in his arms were intensely painful, his heart was racing, and his breathing was fast and shallow.

"Ye'll no' bleed to death," Alex said conversationally, as if reading his mind, "no' if my aim was true. And I think it was, because it's been over a day now. No, ye've a wee while to go yet."

Had it been a day? He had no idea how long it had taken them to carry him to where he was now, because when they'd lifted him he *had* fainted from the pain. But he knew it had been dark when he'd woken for the first time in the cave, and now it was daylight; the sun filtering through the foliage hiding the cave entrance told him that.

He was very thirsty. He ran his tongue around his lips, which were dry and cracked. Alex, seeing the gesture and interpreting it correctly, put down the little carving and the knife, and reaching for a flask at his side, moved across to Richard, holding it to his lips then tilting it. The cool water poured into his mouth, and he swallowed, thinking in that moment he had never tasted anything as delicious as this.

And then the water hit his stomach and he convulsed with the pain, and this time in spite of all his efforts, he did cry out, tears of agony and rage spilling down his cheeks. Alex waited patiently until the spasm had passed, and then offered the flask again.

"No," Richard managed, fighting back nausea. Going down it had been agony; he could not begin to imagine what it would feel like to vomit it back up again. Sweat poured down his face, dripping off his chin.

Alex observed him coolly.

"Aye," he said. "Maybe ye've no' got as long as I'd hoped." He sat back down and picked up the carving and knife again. "I'd offer to fetch ye a priest," he continued calmly, "but ye're no' of the faith, an' it'd take a lot longer than ye've got left to make your confession, I'm thinking." He settled back to his carving, the wisps of wood drifting to the floor in front of him.

The nausea successfully suppressed, Richard observed his torturer, taking in the long fingers wielding the knife expertly, if not artistically. A scar snaked across the back of the man's right hand; a battle wound, most likely. His sleeves were rolled up, exposing strong brown forearms, dusted with reddish hair. No doubt his upper arms and torso were equally heavily muscled; certainly his long legs, visible from the knee downwards due to the kilt he wore, were perfectly defined. He had the body of an athlete, every inch of him betraying him for what he was; a seasoned warrior in the prime of life.

It was unbelievable that the man sitting in front of him now was the same perfumed and powdered limp-wristed molly who had pranced around the drawing rooms of London society, dressed in eye-wateringly hideous shades of silk and velvet. Everything about him was different; the voice, the mannerisms, everything.

Except the eyes. Now he came to think of it, Sir Anthony Peters had bestowed the same icy blue stare on him on more than one occasion in London. When they'd rescued his bitch of a sister from Lord Daniel at the Fleet Prison, for one. Now that he thought about it, he realised that he should have suspected something was amiss with the man then. No one as feeble as Sir Anthony seemed to be would have behaved as he had that night when the whore Sarah had come bursting into Lord Edward's drawing room with the news. Even so, the man was a master of disguise, Richard had to give him that.

"Even if I was a papist, I'd have nothing to confess," Richard inserted into the silence, trying to move his mouth as little as possible because of the pain it caused him. "I'm a soldier. I do my duty. I've nothing to repent of."

"I dinna ken the whole of what you've done, but if I was as close to meeting my maker as you are, I'd be at least repenting what ye did to that woman yesterday, murdering Martha and trying to kill her bairn, and attempting to rape your own sister," Alex replied coldly.

"Is that what Beth told you?" Richard said. He smiled, and then wished he hadn't as the skin stretched over his ruined cheek, making him gasp with the pain. "She didn't tell you that she begged me for it then, that she came to my room every night until I gave in to her?"

"Ah, no, *mo bhràthair-cèile*," Alex replied softly. "Ye'll no' rouse me to finish ye off wi' your lies. I ken the truth of it. Ye can answer to Beth yourself in…" He lifted the candle that was standing in a stub of wax at his feet, so that it shone full onto Richard's face, "…maybe a couple of hours or so."

Richard's mind was slowing. He knew this because it took him a few minutes to absorb the words and realise the import of them. When he did, he laughed involuntarily, and then cried out in pain. A new wave of sweat oozed through his pores, drenching his shirt under the scarlet coat and running into his eyes. He waited a moment until he was sure he could speak without crying out, and then he looked up at his brother-in-law.

"You think she's dead?" he asked.

"I ken well she is," Alex replied. Another wisp of wood joined its comrades on the dirt floor.

"She isn't dead, you fool," Richard replied contemptuously. "I saw her myself, just a few months ago. She's in Newgate Prison."

Alex stopped whittling for a moment and met Richard's gaze, slate-blue meeting bloodshot brown.

"I'm no' sure what your motive is for lying," Alex said after a minute, "but she killed a redcoat and was shot on the day of Culloden." He looked away and observed his handiwork again.

"You didn't see it though, did you?" Richard persisted.

"I didna need to. My brother tellt me himself, and if ye're addled enough to think I'd believe you over him, ye're closer to dying than I thought."

He *was* close to dying now; the numbness had spread to the top of his arms, and he only knew his legs were still there because he could see them, stretched out uselessly in front of him.

"She stabbed a soldier; the Duke of Newcastle told me that. She *was* shot in the head though, here," Richard said, automatically trying to lift his hand to the left side of his face, then giving up. "She was shot in the left side of the head," he continued, "and she'll be scarred for life. But she didn't die. Cumberland sent her to London to be treated, hoping she'd talk. You'll be pleased to know she didn't betray any of you worthless scum. But she paid for it." He had Alex's full attention now and smiled again, ignoring the resulting pain.

"Ye're lying," Alex said, but there was doubt in his voice now.

"I wish I was," Richard said viciously. "I wish the fucking bitch had died. It's because of her that I was sent back to this shithole. She wouldn't tell me anything when they let me see her either, and Newcastle –" He stopped abruptly. *Shit*. He hadn't meant to say that. He hadn't meant to say anything that would give this savage bastard pleasure.

But then he looked at the savage bastard and thought he saw a momentary expression of pain cross his face; he believed now that Beth hadn't died at Culloden. Now he'd be roused to anger, or grief, or something, and with luck the fucker would put him out of his misery.

"When did they hang her then?" the fucker asked indifferently, "or did they burn her at the stake?"

"I've no idea. I doubt they have, though. I don't think they've killed any of the rebel bitches yet. And even though she's a traitor, she *is* beautiful. Newcastle hates her guts, though. I doubt there'll be much left to hang by the time the warders and turnkeys have finished with her." He eyed Alex intently, hoping to see a sign that the expression he'd seen before *had* been pain, but all he saw was utter indifference.

Christ, the man was made of stone! The pained expression must have been a trick of the light. He had stopped carving his stupid bit of wood though, and instead was turning the knife over and over in his hand, obviously pondering something.

A short time passed, during which Richard's mind wandered. He had always thought to die in battle, or since he had married Anne and money was no longer an issue, perhaps to become a general and live to a fat old age, stumping around the battlefield giving orders and making the soldiers' lives hell. At least as a captain he'd managed to make a few men's lives hell, had toughened them up a bit, if not for as long as he'd expected. If only he'd been able to take this bastard with him, that would have been something to be proud of, even if no one ever knew about it. But although Richard had many faults, he was realistic; he no longer felt any pain, his heart was slowing, and he could feel the extreme lethargy of blood loss and infection threatening to pull him into unconsciousness, and then death. He could not kill this man, this arch-traitor who was sitting so coolly watching him die; but he might yet cause him pain. It was worth a try.

With every ounce of his remaining will, he held death at bay and spoke, his tongue thick and heavy in his mouth, his voice slurring.

"Did she get a chance to tell you she was pregnant, before you left her at Culloden?" Now the big Highlander stopped twirling the knife and looked directly at him, and Richard saw the distress clearly in his face. "No, I see she didn't," he continued. "She probably didn't know herself then. She tried to use it to avoid being...questioned, but Newcastle let me have some nice family time alone with her anyway." His eyes started to close, and he forced them open with an effort. He wanted to see this bastard suffer. "At least I got that," he said, almost to himself. "I got to make that bitch pay for everything. God, that was fun, hearing her scream."

The Highlander was staring at him now, his body rigid, the hand holding the knife so tightly that his knuckles were white. *If I wasn't about to die anyway,* Richard thought, *I'd actually be afraid of this bastard.*

"Don't worry though, I did you one favour, at least. I made sure there are no bastards of yours running around London. She lost the brat just after I left her in her cell, screaming for mercy. Of course one of the turnkeys or guards might have put another one in her belly by now, who knows?"

Alex lunged suddenly, gripping him by the throat and half-lifting him off the floor.

"You're lying," he said, his voice harsh with pain and rage.

Vaguely, Richard realised that he no longer felt any pain at all; even the hand squeezing his throat like a vice he registered only as a sense of pressure. *This is it, then,* he thought calmly.

With an immense effort he smiled, for the last time.

"Why would I bother lying now, when the truth is so much

better?" he said. And then he heard the Highlander's roar of agony and dimly registered the first blow to his already ruined cheek, before, finally, death took him.

The MacGregors had in the main now abandoned their settlement, had moved their belongings up to the main cave and were lounging around on the saucer-shaped depression outside it, taking in the last of the afternoon sun. When they heard their chieftain's roar of anguish, as one they all moved instinctively towards the small cave, the men's hands gripping the hilts of their swords. Then they stopped uncertainly. When Alex had carried the redcoat into the cave, he had told his clansfolk not to disturb him. They all looked to Angus, who thought for a moment then came to a decision.

"I'll go," he said.

He was about ten feet from the cave entrance when the foliage covering it parted and his brother emerged, stopping him dead in his tracks. Alex's face was white and drawn, and he seemed to have aged ten years. His right hand was covered to the wrist with gore. He stood for a moment, squinting as his eyes adjusted to the bright sunlight, and then he moved forward.

"He's dead," he said as he reached Angus. "Take the body back to the hut. Leave it there, so it can be found."

Angus nodded, and then to his surprise Alex continued past him and strode towards the edge of the depression.

"Where are you going?" Angus called.

Alex turned back to face his clan. "Beth's alive," he said to them, his voice husky with emotion. "I tellt her to be strong and that I'd come for her. She's kept her promise. Now I'm going to keep mine."

Then he turned, and started to make his way down the hill.

# HISTORICAL NOTE

As is now my habit, and because some readers have told me they find it interesting, I'm enclosing a note about the historical background to some of the events featured in the book.

In the prologue I mention that a signed letter was found on one of the dead rebels to the effect that Prince Charles had issued orders to the Jacobites that no quarter was to be given to the enemy at Culloden. This was certainly given as a justification for the brutal behaviour of the British troops towards the rebels in the days following Culloden. The day after the battle Cumberland gave orders to his men to search the area around the battlefield for rebels, and in them he stated: 'the public orders of the rebels yesterday was to give us no quarters'. This was taken by the men as an order to kill all rebels they met, which they subsequently did.

The Jacobite leaders categorically denied that any such orders were given by Charles, and it does seem odd that he would do so, when until then he had been renowned for his mercy to what he considered to be misguided subjects of his father. There are surviving orders written by Lord George Murray, none of which mention that no quarter was to be given, and yet the press were told that such an order had been found, and this was widely printed in the newspapers at the time as justification for the brutality meted out to the rebels both at Culloden and later.

In Chapter Three I detail the attempt by the rebels to continue the fight. This happened pretty well as I've described it in the chapter. Lord Lovat did, after prevaricating all the way through the rebellion and sending the Frasers out under his son, the

Master of Lovat, finally commit wholeheartedly to another rising. He was cordially hated by John Murray of Broughton, and distrusted by many others.

The aim of Cumberland appears to have been to wipe out the Camerons in a pincer movement, but the northern arm of the pincer movement under Lord Loudoun got bogged down in the dreadful conditions, made worse by the frequent heavy rainfall, and failed to arrive in time to stop Lochiel and his men escaping along Loch Arkaig. Lochiel did watch helplessly as the whole of his clan lands went up in flames, which must have been extremely distressing for him.

It does seem that Cumberland offered Lochiel favourable terms if he agreed to surrender – Lochiel mentions this himself in his later account, *Mémoire d'un Ecossais*, and Glencarnaig was also told that if he would surrender, the proscription of the MacGregors would be lifted. His reply to the offer was as I've written.

Eighty-one Grants surrendered on the advice of their chief, who had taken no part in the rebellion himself. They expected, once they had laid down their arms, to be allowed to return home, but instead they were imprisoned on transports at Inverness, some being sent to Barbados, and some to English prisons. Three years later, only eighteen were still alive.

I also mention in Chapter Three the Highland hut constructed for the Duke of Cumberland by his loyal Highland regiments. This is true, and to his credit he did live in it, to the delight of his men, although he must have found it extremely primitive and uncomfortable.

In Chapter Five I talk about the cattle auctions at Fort Augustus. These really did take place, and cattle dealers came from all over the lowlands of Scotland and England to take advantage of the ridiculously low prices they were being sold for. This was a deliberate attempt to starve the Highlanders by depriving them of their only means of sustenance through notoriously harsh winters, which had considerable success. The starving women and children did beg at the gates, and ask to be allowed to lick up the blood of the slaughtered animals. The men were forbidden to give them any food or money at all.

Chapter Six deals in part with the escape of John Betts, John (Jack) Holker and Peter Moss. As I wrote in the historical note to *The Storm Breaks*, they were real people. Nothing more is known of John Betts than that he was an Ensign in the Manchester Regiment, was captured at Carlisle, imprisoned in Newgate Gaol along with the rest of his regiment, and subsequently escaped, along with John Holker and Peter Moss. I've appropriated him and given him a history as Beth's stable boy, and a future, although he disappears from history after his escape. John Holker, however (who also features in Books One and Four) was apparently sheltered for six weeks by a stallholder before making his way to France and becoming a lieutenant in the Irish Brigade. He went on to have a very distinguished career in France.

In Chapter Eight, John and Sarah attend the execution of the Manchester Rebels. Again, I've drawn this directly from history, even down to the weather and the unease of the crowd at the men having no Christian priest to minister to them on the scaffold. Thomas Deacon did throw his hat to the crowd, and it would be nice to think that it was returned to his father, Bishop Deacon. Thomas's head was placed on a spike on the Market Cross in Manchester, and his father was later fined for raising his hat to his son's head as he passed by and saw it.

The Duke of Cumberland was indeed feted all over the country as the hero of Culloden, and when he returned to London in July, St James's Palace was besieged by people hoping to catch sight of him, and the city erupted in celebration.

However, as early as May questions were being raised as to why none of the prisoners taken at Culloden were listed as wounded, and if it was true that no quarter had been given, even to the injured. Numerous stories started to circulate that all the wounded rebels had been summarily slaughtered, and reports coming back to London from Scotland of continued acts of brutality following the battle, led to a newspaper reporting at the end of May that when the duke returned to London he was to be made a Freeman of the Guild of Butchers. The name stuck, and the Duke of Cumberland has gone down in history as Butcher Cumberland. Historians have disputed whether he deserved the nickname or not. I have examined the evidence on both sides and come to my own personal conclusion that his treatment of the Highlanders did warrant the appellation.

In Chapters Eight, Nine and Eleven I discuss Newgate Prison. Daniel Defoe, who had briefly been incarcerated there, described it in his novel *Moll Flanders* as, 'That horrid place…an emblem of hell itself', which aptly summed up the eighteenth century view of it. Even by the standards of the day, Newgate was a dreadful place.

The first reference to Newgate being used as a prison was in 1188, but the prison Beth is in had been rebuilt after the great fire of London in 1666. It was said to be one of the most expensive places to lodge in London, as the warders extorted every penny they possibly could from their prisoners. Some of the charges have been documented, but they would vary according to the wealth of the inmate. They were charged 2s6d on entry to the prison if they wished to be removed from the reception cell (a dungeon through which an open sewer ran), a further 2s6d to have manacles removed, and then a variable fee for everything else from reasonable food to coal, candles, receiving visitors etc. Prisoners who were unable to pay were treated abominably. They were also charged a fee to leave the prison – even if they'd been found not guilty of the crime they'd been arrested for. If they couldn't pay the fee they remained in prison.

The keepers paid good money for the position, as they stood to make a fortune from the extortion. There is an interesting document in the National Archives in London, in which the rebel prisoners lodged an official complaint against the warder (Richard Jones) in September 1747, regarding the conditions they were kept in and the extortionate amount of money he demanded even to allow a surgeon or apothecary to visit. Mr Jones of course strenuously denied the allegations.

After Culloden the prisons really were full to overflowing, which led to even worse conditions than normal, not only at Newgate and other land-based prisons, but also on the transport hulks, ships which were docked at Tilbury and other ports for the purpose of receiving the overflow of prisoners. These were widely condemned as hell-holes, with prisoners being kept in the most unbelievable conditions and dying like flies (as Caroline mentions in Chapter Fourteen - they really did run pleasure cruises out to the hulks).

In an attempt to reduce the overcrowding, a lotting system of rebel prisoners was brought in, in which the common prisoners would draw lots in groups of twenty. One man would draw the short straw and be tried for his life, the others, if they agreed to plead guilty would receive 'His Majesty's Pleasure', most of them being transported as indentured servants to plantations in America or the Caribbean; others were forced to enlist in the army, or remained in prison until they either died or were eventually released.

Gaol fever (typhus) was justly feared by everyone. It was carried by fleas and lice, and spread like wildfire amongst the prisoners, due to the insanitary conditions. It was largely ignored by officials until 1750, when forty-three officials at the nearby Old Bailey died of it, including the Lord Mayor. It was thought to be spread by foetid air, and a windmill was installed on the roof to provide ventilation. Seven of the eleven workers died of typhus while installing it.

In Chapter Nine I give a description of Prince Charles as he comes down the hill to see Alex. This is lifted in its entirety from a description of him when he was on the run in Scotland, from April until September 1746. He certainly seems to have thrived on the excitement and danger of being hunted and passed from one loyal clansman to the next, many of whom risked their lives to keep him safe.

However, anyone who has been to Scotland on holiday and experienced the dreaded midge will be amused to know that they drove Charles insane as well, biting him very badly as he lurked in the heather on overcast days. Some things never change!

I won't go into detail about his adventures with Flora MacDonald, when he was disguised as her maidservant 'Betty Burke', as this story is widely known. It is however true that Kingsburgh's wife, upon seeing him pacing up and down the hallway of her home in his long dress, described him as 'an odd muckle trollop' and was somewhat afraid of the appearance of this strange woman.

Charles was indeed sheltered for several days in July 1746 by the Seven Men of Glenmoriston (in fact eight men), a group of freedom fighters or terrorists, depending on your point of view, who vowed to continue the fight, and had some remarkable adventures worthy of a novel in their own right.

John Murray of Broughton was arrested, and later did turn king's evidence, giving information against Lord Lovat and naming a number of the English Jacobite leaders as well as the Welsh leader, Sir Watkin Williams Wynne. He was universally hated and vilified for this, by Prince Charles and others, and understandably so, but in his defence, he was sick and exhausted, very worried for his wife who was heavily pregnant, and disillusioned with many of the chiefs, who had let him down badly when he was desperately trying to rally them to continue the fight after Culloden by means of guerrilla warfare. He did remain devoted to the Stuart cause to his death, in spite of being ostracised by the Jacobites and deserted by his wife. And he certainly did not tell everything he knew – he did not reveal the whereabouts of Lochiel, or of Prince Charles, and it is feasible that he would not have betrayed Beth or Alex either. He seems to have mainly given information about chiefs and leaders who promised support for the Stuart restoration but failed to deliver on those promises.

In Chapter Thirteen I point out that Earl Albemarle ordered Inversnaid barracks to be reoccupied with the express intention of keeping the Loch Lomond MacGregors in check. This did happen, but I admit to having taken liberties with the date this was done in order to allow Alex and his clan to spend some time unmolested at home, and to carry out various raids once the redcoats started to relax their vigilance. In the book it is reoccupied over the winter of 1746/7, but this in fact happened sometime in the summer of 1746.

I also realise that many of you will not know what a link man was. Link men (or more often boys), were frequently to be found hanging around theatres and other places of entertainment. They would carry a lighted torch and offer to lead people home at night, when there was little if any street illumination. They were very poor, usually dressed in rags, and not always honest – sometimes instead of taking a customer home, the link boy would conduct him down an ill-lit alley to be robbed by a gang of thieves, for a share in the proceedings.

# About the Author

Julia has been a voracious reader since childhood, using books to escape the miseries of a turbulent adolescence. After leaving university with a degree in English Language and Literature, she spent her twenties trying to be a sensible and responsible person, even going so far as to work for the Civil Service for six years.

Then she gave up trying to conform, resigned her well-paid but boring job and resolved to spend the rest of her life living as she wanted to, not as others would like her to. She has since had a variety of jobs, including, telesales, Post Office clerk, primary school teacher, and painter and gilder.

In her spare time and between jobs, she is still a voracious reader, and enjoys keeping fit, exploring the beautiful Welsh countryside around her home, and travelling the world. Life hasn't always been good, but it has rarely been boring.

A few years ago she decided that rather than just escape into other people's books, she would quite like to create some of her own and so combined her passion for history and literature to write the Jacobite Chronicles.

People seem to enjoy reading them as much as she enjoys writing them, so now, apart from a tiny amount of transcribing and editing work, she is a full-time writer. She has recently plunged into the contemporary genre too, but her first love will always be historical fiction.

## Follow her on:

**Website:**
www.juliabrannan.com

**Facebook:**
www.facebook.com/pages/Julia-Brannan/727743920650760

**Twitter:**
https://twitter.com/BrannanJulia

**Pinterest:**
http://www.pinterest.com/juliabrannan

Printed in Great Britain
by Amazon